PAGE-TURNER

By
Nick Rossi

For MM, duh.

Chapter 1

"But your place is here, in Grimolonia," the Prince said, his voice slowly rising as his hand softly caressed her exposed shoulder. There was no denying his eternal love for her. His longing gaze upon her alabaster skin was bursting with adoration. The gaze itself was as intense as it had been that day years ago when he had laid his eyes upon her for the very first time. For her, it seemed just like yesterday they had met and immediately fallen in love. She wished she had known at that first moment that their love would be full of strife and heartbreak. Regrets – she'd had a few.

His soft touch upon her skin made her shudder and a chill reverberated from her bruised toes to her flushed cheeks. She looked at him longingly, feeling lost in his liquid blue eyes, which caused her to momentarily forget the painful decision she was about to make.

"Oh, Elijah, the choice has already been made for me. You know I must go," Carissa whispered, her lips barely moving but her

1

heart beating madly. She threw herself forcefully into his arms, feeling the safety and strength of his imposing stature. She quickly felt him wrap his muscular arms around her tiny waist, tightening his grasp around her as she began to pull away. She knew she couldn't stay within his secure hold any longer, despite that being exactly all she wanted to do.

She ripped herself from his solid embrace, the force of the sudden movement nearly causing her to stumble upon the jagged rocks that lay at her feet. She pensively looked outwards at the dense valley full of trees and rivers that surrounded them, full of the lives of those she must leave behind because of what her fortune foretold. The idea of departing her loved ones made her inwardly cringe with the strength of the most powerful lions.

Elijah tried to reach for her but Carissa has already begun to run towards the safe refuge of the impressive ring of nearby trees, narrowly faltering upon the long, billowing tresses of silk and linens that comprised her gown. A gown she had put on just hours ago to attend her own wedding.

She flung herself abruptly into the impenetrable underbrush, the low-hanging branches of the fir and pine trees gently caressing her exposed shoulders and arms. There was a slight tug on her gowns' tail, but she didn't know if it was Elijah grasping for her one last time, or if the world was pulling her away into a lost land devoid of love, joy and happiness.

"Darcyyyyyyy," an omnipresent voice bellowed, echoing from all around her. She did not know who the voice belonged to, or how it could at once be both an echo and a scream. The words sliced through her stomach like a sharp knife, forcing her to the rocky and sharp ground. She wondered if she might be going delirious with all of the intensity and unpleasantness of the hours that had just elapsed in her life.

She looked all around her, watching as the valley began to fade away, changing colors from its lush midnight green to a rich, navy blue. The foreground of the horizon began to merge with the opulent, overhead sky, immediately causing her to feel sick to her stomach. She thought perhaps she would faint from the sudden changes of emotions and environments she found herself in.

"Darcy, your break is over," the voice said again, now harder and more urgent, causing the expansive sky all around her to abruptly change into an extra-terrestrial-like flat, cold, and barren surface. The light of the muted heavens above her soon turned into a fluorescent beacon prism of yellows and reds.

She felt at once both confused and scared. She then turned around hoping to find Elijah still in pursuit of her and of their forbidden love, but her eyes saw nothing but a blinding white. Her shoulder was then softly touched from an unseen body. The touch itself was both manly but gentle, and not at all unsettling.

"Seriously, Darcy, you're going to be late," the voice continued, now cold and callous in its tone. It was clearer now, too; stern and foreign to Carissa's gentle ears. It caused a chasm of pain to resound through her already sore, battered body. She didn't know which direction to turn or how she was going to survive her current predicament.

"Who is Darcy?" she whispered silently to herself, no words actually escaping her cherry-colored lips. The mossy, moist ground once more suddenly gave way, causing her to fall deeply and swiftly into a seemingly endless white oblivion to which there seemed to be no beginning and no end.

* * *

"Oh no!" Darcy screamed, fluttering her eyes open, her arms frantically grasping for anything to break the frightening fall. Her outstretched arms grabbed nothing but air. She rapidly realized that there was nothing that was going to help break her fall because she actually *wasn't* falling at all. In reality, she was already firmly

3

ensconced in her desk chair.

She sat up from her apparent daydream and looked around hastily. A momentary confusion enveloped her as to where she was and where Elijah had disappeared to so quickly. Instead of finding her betrothed lover before her, her eyes instead immediately took in a gray, sterile, monochromatic desk directly in front of her field of vision, as well as a flashing computer screen, a red light gleaming on the mammoth phone on her desk, and endless piles of paper that, at first glance, seemed to have been written in a foreign language (she was not exactly that well-organized, a self-proclaimed character trait).

I'm at work, she thought to herself once she realized where she was, instantly feeling embarrassed. *Obviously.*

She glanced around to see a female co-worker standing closely behind her, the woman's hand on her shoulder with a grasp that was both at once reproachable and maternal. Darcy turned her chair around instantly to face the woman. Sylvia. The one co-worker she could tolerate and not have to stifle the fantasy of stabbing in the eye every time she saw her. She felt the redness of her embarrassment slowly begin to creep upon her face, and it imminently took over any clear area of skin with its ferocious tenacity.

"Oh, wow, I must have fallen asleep," she said, her voice small and meek.

She felt her voice becoming smaller and meeker as the monotonous and unexciting days of her life passed by. Her heartbeat began to slow and the sudden redness in her cheeks thankfully began to fade. She remembered in earnest at what had just happened, the memories reassuring her that was she not indeed going insane (though still a little silently crazy, much like everyone else she knew though they never admitted it).

She had missed her afternoon break due to a pressing deadline she was working on, which at that moment she couldn't for the life of her remember what it was regarding. She had decided to zone out, as she often did on her coffee breaks, by continuing to read the newest installment in her favorite book series, 'Bright Nightfall'. She apprehended that she must have indeed fallen asleep. Her insatiable lust and fervor for reading age-inappropriate books often caused her to stay up late into the night, much to the chagrin of her dog (and her stomach) the next morning.

The latest book of the series was titled 'Bright Nightfall: Dusk', and found its heroine, the brave but incredibly naïve Carissa Powers, the last descendant of the Powers Dynasty, a clan which governed the land of Grimolonia, declare her love for Elijah, the requisite and complicated rebel. The result of their illicit relationship was rather unsurprisingly catastrophic for the residents of Grimolonia. The clearly taboo love affair amongst two star-crossed lovers of different social classes and governing powers was strictly forbidden. For all of her might, Carissa just could no longer refute her blossoming love for the chiseled Eijah, her clandestine true love. Sure, it wasn't exactly groundbreaking literary fiction, nor would it ever win the Nobel Prize, but she loved it nonetheless and appreciated a good teen fiction novel. Scratch that – her love for teen fiction was beyond an appreciation. It was more akin to an obsession.

She was not a teenager anymore, nor had she been for a long, long time (a fact that she was thankful for a million times over), but as she aged, she found herself drawn to the sordid tales of angst-y and rebellious teens, forbidden loves and ultimately happy endings. She called it her 'bad habit' but she was secretly proud to keep her finger perpetually on the pulse of what Entertainment Weekly was griping about (or harping praise upon) in that week's teen star gossip-fueled issue.

She straightened up and patted down her plain beige blouse, replete with its hounds tooth buttons done all the way to the top as she didn't want her nosy workmate Carl to begin eying her boobs (that was an ordeal she didn't want to endure again). She ran her small hands down the black slacks she always seemed to be wearing to work these days. The repeated outfits did not at all mean that she was disinterested in buying 'adult clothes' for work (as she referred to them), it was just that she'd always been the type of person who invested in multiples of pieces that she knew fit well and went with that (and bought in bulk, Costco styles).

Her co-worker (and begrudgingly part-time confidante) Sylvia looked down at her with an expression on her remarkably line-free face that was on par with the grasp that she held upon Darcy's slight shoulder a moment ago: equal parts disgust and pity, with a dash of kindness. The middle-aged woman had taken Darcy under her wing when Darcy had started at the firm. She then began quickly attempting to fix Darcy up with her sons, and when that didn't work out, with her son's friends and cousins. Sylvia had finally relented playing matchmaker when Darcy would consistently come up with endless excuses to not go out with them. Her favorite excuse of all time was unquestionably when she said she couldn't meet yet another prospective date because she was enhancing the size of her breasts. Sylvia's face had been all kinds of priceless on that April day, especially since Darcy delivered the lie with a straight face and calm voice. Some of her finest work, she had silently admitted.

"You know, Darcy..." Sylvia began, her voice motherly and disciplinary. The condescension was literally dripping from her every word, forming a small puddle on the semi-dirty carpeted floor at their feet. The hand that was just on Darcy's shoulder now joined its immaculately manicured partner in a pray-esque hold.

Oh God, she thought, *I know where this is going. I had better prepare myself for another fascinating episode of Sylvia Knows Best. Now commercial-free AND in high definition. Barf.*

"... you did fall asleep again," her work buddy continued, releasing her prayer hands and gingerly made a seat for herself on Darcy's desk's grey and shiny surface, instantly forcing the files that Darcy had earlier laid out to bend and twist and one to actually rip. Under the firmness of Sylvia's rear all sound was muted, but she could have sworn she thought she heard the pages scream out *"Help me! I'm being suffocated and mistreated by a huge bum"* in tiny, frightened voices.

"Those books are written for teenage girls, not thirty-something year old women," Sylvia went on, moving her perch from atop the desk (*Hallelujah*, the papers screamed, *We can breathe again!*) and sat in Carl's currently empty chair which sat adjacent to Darcy's own. She was one of the fortunate few in the office who didn't have to frequently share her Antarctica-sized monochromatic monster of a workstation with another co-worker as Carl was on 'long-term disability'. It was those little things that sometimes kept her sane in the gross monotony of her workdays. That and her endless access to state-of-the-art office supplies. Nothing made the bitter Monday morning pill easier to swallow than a bright red stapler, colorful paperclips, and some tri-colored Post-It's.

"You should be reading books that are more intellectually stimulating for your young brain, like Danielle Steel or Nora Roberts," Sylvia rattled on, picking up 'Bright Nightfall' then instantly dropping it as though it were on fire. "Those fine authors really know how to get into the mind of a character and talk about things that women should be thinking about".

Darcy looked at Sylvia and shrugged, knowing full well that if she remained quiet, Sylvia was bound to finally walk away and leave her in peace. It was a conversation they'd had many, many times before. Darcy loved to read, a passion she felt both proud and shy about. Ever since she was knee high to a grasshopper and hanging off her mother's angular hip, she relished in the joy of being able to open a book and become wholly absorbed in fictional worlds where logic was often suspended and true love always conquered all.

Her mother had always made a point to ensure all members of the Platt clan read books of various genres and styles to enhance their knowledge and awareness of how the world operated. This maternal requirement had often angered Darcy as a young girl because she often had preferred to re-read Sweet Valley High for the 10th time rather than Moby Dick during the summer vacation of sixth grade. Sure, in retrospect she certainly was thankful for this early exposure to the literary geniuses of the world, but she vividly remembered having difficulty explaining to her childhood friends why she was reading Death of a Salesman when everyone else was reading Judy Blume.

As she grew older and escaped the literal hold of her mother's reading choices, she found herself reading more and more of a particular style of book: teen fiction. Naturally, she had begun reading these books when she was a teenager herself. She had boarded the Judy Blume train after all (albeit late), and then quickly traveled through The Babysitters Club, the Fear Street series, and finally made her way to the bubblegum world of Sweet Valley High. She peppered in some popular books of the moment, but she always found herself back within the comfort hold of the teen fiction world.

There was something inexplicably charming and innocent about the characters depicted in the stories she avidly read. The portrayed characters were often depicted as growing up and facing problems that had a firm resolution by the novel's end, much unlike real life which had heart breaks and pain that seemed to go on indefinitely. The books acted as a proverbial security blanket for her as she had experienced first-hand the heartache and ferociousness of being a teenager. While her friends lounged by the community pool during the never-ending summer breaks of elementary and high school, she could always be found reading some teen book in her treasured hammock in the backyard, immersed into the words that provided not only escapism to her actionless life, but giving her an intense joy in vicariously living the lives of assorted teen heroes and heroines who were, in some bizarre, crazy, unrealistic way, like her.

As she headed to university life and became an adult (whatever that label meant; she still tried to define that role every single day of her existence) she continued to find herself reading only teen fiction novels almost exclusively. She wasn't all that picky or particular about which ones would take up her undivided attention. The only real requirements, if she had to choose some, were:

1. She had to be able to find the books in the bookstore easily and quickly;
2. The book itself had a somewhat interesting cover depicting teen issues, and;

3. Access Issues: She had to be able to enter and exit said bookstore easily and speedily without drawing any public attention to her 'bad habit*

* Note: – These were the days before the advent of Amazon and online ordering. In-person purchases were the only option for satiating her 'bad habit'. In current day, she had no qualms on surfing the 'net and the numerous competing retailers who could feed her habit without any remote possibility of being embarrassed or shy about her purchases.

Much to her dismay, she had noticed her sacrilegious genre had changed its overarching plot formulas and typical character profiles fairly severely in recent years. Authors seemed to now opt to create elaborate and sometimes overly confusing metaphors and mythologies comprised of characters that weren't human, or if they were, had characteristics that were indeed other-worldly and slightly supernatural. She still loved to read these books though, but was definitely less brazen (if that was even possible) with pulling these books off the dusty shelves they rested upon to read while relaxing in a coffee shop or on the subway. Often times, while commuting to and from work, she found herself ashamed and awkward to take whatever teen novel she was reading at that moment out of her bag as she often noticed (or thought she did) teen girls look at the book and then at her with looks of confusion and wonder - and unequivocal disdain. She had always found it fascinating how those expressions transcended cultures and ethnicities.

It wasn't necessarily that she didn't like to read Danielle Steel or

Sandra Brown or any other popular authors; it was just that reading teen fiction and its associated spin-offs, sub-genres and influences, really and truly made her happy and content. And happiness, as she knew all too well, was hard to come by, especially so as she grew older. In fact, the more she thought about it, the surer she became that it just did not exist.

It was at that specific moment that Arin Moore, office manager and resident sleaze-ball, decided to meander over determinedly to where Sylvia and Darcy casually sat. Arin relied on his boyish good looks and perpetual smile of a thousand shiny ivory teeth to get the staff to like him (mostly the semi-sad middle aged single ladies and a few of the naïve and emotionally unstable gentlemen), but he wasn't fooling Darcy, the self-proclaimed cynic. She absolutely knew that his seemingly disingenuous intentions were not to create a cohesive synergy at the office, but rather to get closer to running the entire place and taking full charge. Either way, Arin was aware that she saw through his disguise, and the two never really minced words. It wasn't an uncomfortable dynamic per se, but it certainly wasn't a healthy one.

She had secretly pined to have a boss that would foster and mentor her and motivate her to escape the current career lull she was in, but Arin was certainly not going to provide that. The most she would get out of him was a half-hearted 'Thank you," which, in all fairness, was as rare as snow in July.

Upon Arin's hasty approach towards them, Darcy and Sylvia looked hurriedly at one another, feeling like literal deer in the headlights. They speedily attempted to grab for anything that sat atop the workstation to give the false but convincing illusion that they were chatting about something work-related. Both of their hands fell on some of Darcy's prized office supplies, in this case a rather suggestive looking wrist rest and a fluorescent Post-It dispenser. They both soon realized that they weren't going to fool anyone with their random grabs, but were secretly pleased nonetheless at their effort made at pretending.

"Well, well, what do have we here?" Arin said, his voice just a tad too high for the assertive role he was aiming to play. His white shirt was just also just a tad too big, and his shoes a bit too shiny, somewhat undermining his attempted portrayal as a literal Mr. Know-It-All. It was almost as though he heard those specific thoughts as they entered Darcy's head, causing his smile to turn into a deep frown.

He began to slowly shift his faze from Darcy to Sylvia, and then back again. His characteristic wide smile (which was once said to have caused an employee's small child to go temporarily blind at the annual Christmas Party) was now a small and tiny slit across his face. Even the dimple in his left cheek seemed to disappear into the expanse of the cleanly shaven skin.

She noticed his gaze shift amongst the two women a good three or so times before his upper lip began to quiver, which was what it always seemed to do when he interacted with her. Sylvia believed the lip quiver happened because Arin was secretly and madly in love with Darcy, which disgusted her completely. It wasn't that Arin was repulsive because of his looks, in fact, she found him somewhat decently attractive. It was actually his unattractive 'holier than thou/I'm a Kardashian' elitist attitude and evident lack of filter that made everything about him seem ugly, shiny shoes included.

"We were just looking at the memo you emailed to us," Sylvia lied, hoping Arin didn't notice the obvious waver in her voice.

On the computer screen that was turned off? Darcy thought. *Or the lack of any paper with the title "Memo" on it remotely near them?.* She didn't even attempt come up with an excuse. The two colleagues had been on an approved coffee break, pure and simple. They had nothing to hide or be ashamed of.

"Were you now?" Arin said, looking slowly from Sylvia to Darcy's darkened computer monitor. "On a computer screen that's turned off?"

Busted, Darcy thought. *Now the fun's going to begin.*

"I don't appreciate being lied to, and I certainly don't appreciate a lack of productivity from my employees on a Friday afternoon with a major deadline that is looming for Monday," Arin continued, lip quiver and too-big shirt in full effect.

Darcy reached over to the CPU that was adorned in dust bunnies and turned on the monitor. The wide screen then quickly illuminated to the Wikipedia page for Powers family tree. She had been doing some refresher research before beginning 'Bright Nightfall' and her afternoon break. Her cheeks once again immediately began to redden and a cold shiver ran down her back.

Sylvia and Arin both gradually took in the slowly illuminating screen set to its obscure Wikipedia page but clearly didn't understand what the browser window was trying to explain. Darcy manically reached over to grab the mouse that lay atop her desk but couldn't minimize the window fast enough, her cheeks now a fire-blazing red. Once the browser window was safely minimized, she promptly doubled clicked and opened the spreadsheet she was *supposed* to be working on. Once the spreadsheet was upon the screen, she dazedly noticed all the assorted numbers and colors that in unison were creating a cacophony of nonsense that gave her a slight twinge of a headache upon her temples.

"And please don't misuse the office resources," Arin said, his voice deeper so as to denote some sense of authority. He turned around from his vantage point of his two staff members and began to quickly walk back to his office, leaving a trail of cheap cologne and a tinge of sweat in his wake.

Sylvia sighed heavily and faced Darcy, her eyes soft. No one appreciated getting scolded, even if the scolder had no grounding or credence to do said scolding.

"Back to work," she whispered and walked away to her own desk which was in the same general direction as Arin's office. Darcy, still completely embarrassed, returned to her meaningless-processing job. She soon found her mind swimming with thoughts about her future and general current state of relative unhappiness, as her mind always seemed to do at some point during her workday. She never denied the fact that she was completely unchallenged in her job, but she also didn't do much to change her current situation. She had had grandiose aspirations upon graduating from college, as did all of her friends, but as time gradually went on, the aspirations seemed to become farther and farther away, and, as a result, harder and harder to achieve. When she had finally got this job a few years ago, she thought she would stay at it until she found something better, something more motivating. But she always found herself still there. Always just still there.

***

Sure, she was making a bit more money, but the lack of joy in the actual work she was doing was tangible. Ever present. Almost heavy in its existence. Ditto went for her sense of motivation and hope, but she had tried earnestly and quite hard at times to not entertain the latter emotion. Nothing good or positive ever came of that.

Being in her 30's was not easy. Actually, being in her 20's had not been easy either, but that she attributed to growing pains and 'life experiences'. She felt that at her current age   there was always a quantifiable repercussion to her actions, as miniscule as they may have seemed to be. On paper, she figured she seemed decent. She had a little apartment close to downtown, a dog that she adored with all of her heart, and she sometimes even went on the random (non-Sylvia-organized) dates. She had been at her job at the firm for close to five years and knew she was underutilized, but when that paycheck was deposited every other Thursday into her bank account, she would conveniently forget about that part of things.

As she aged, she had found herself with less and less friends, but her core group remained the same, a fact to which she was grateful. Well, her core group was comprised of a friend, singular, but she couldn't have foreseen the fact that most of her college friends would be married with kids and inhabit the foreign lands of suburbia that were only accessible by motorboat or RV.

Her family was interspersed all over the city and its associated suburbs, and she found it difficult to visit them. Difficult may have been a misleading term. Painful was more apropos. It wasn't that it was difficult to travel and physically *see* them, heck, it took more time to get to work sometimes than it did to visit her childhood home. No, it was the prescient and constant passive-aggressive conversations that were always had, leaving her to feel inadequate and immature and overfed. Every time she vowed that she was going to see her family only on Christmas and the odd momentous birthday, she would find herself sucked into emotion-laden family drama from time to time. When she would deliberately not entertain and immerse herself in the illogical and unnecessary events that were unfolding with her family, in particular her older and cranky sisters, she would cement her reputation as the black sheep of the family who did not care about anyone but herself. If that was the reputation she had and if it successfully worked in keeping her out of the melodramatic familial operettas, then it was a reputation she welcomed with open arms.

In fact, she accepted the reported stigma of being the black sheep of the Platt family wholeheartedly. If being the black sheep of her dysfunctional Platt clan intrinsically meant maintaining her sanity, she prayed for the label wholly and truly.

Her family had always referred to her as the 'different' one, which was not really a compliment or insult. The one who backpacked through Europe instead of working full time at the family bakery once she graduated from college, and the one who was just oh-so-overly sensitive and took everything to heart.

She was single, that was true, but that omission was not

something that really caused her much chagrin or heartache. She had had boyfriends, in fact, she had broken up with Harold just a few months ago, but she found herself infinitely happier as a single woman. She didn't have the worry of living up to any grandiose expectations of a needy partner, or making sure her figure was always a perfect 10 (her figure had actually been fluctuating as of late due to her recent fascination with nachos and home-made guacamole). The one thing that kept her grounded and reasonably content, as it had been doing since she was only nine years old, the only real constant in her life, was also the one thing she was most embarrassed of: reading teen fiction. When she found herself realizing that the acumen of her happiness was wholly based on stories written for a different demographic entirely than her own, she would feel immensely guilty. So that was the precise reason why she chose just not to acknowledge it. Some things were better left unsaid, right?

Chapter 2

"So what're you doing after work? Want to go shopping?" Sylvia asked her as they power-walked to the elevator down the hall from their respective workstations. "I wouldn't mind picking up some of those tank tops that are on sale at *Unique Chic*".

Darcy opted not to respond right away as she found that the store *Unique Chic* sold clothes that seemed to have been designed by teenagers who made clothes for older women, full of inside jokes and hideous color combinations. She had seen Sylvia with literal combinations of leopard print, velour, and a weird derivative material that looked like a macramé project gone horribly wrong – and that had been all in one outfit.

The remainder of the afternoon had dragged and dragged on, forcing her to momentarily think that someone had intentionally set all the office clocks times back an hour or possibly more to mess with her head and lengthen everyone's work day, but then realized she was thinking crazy thoughts – again. If Sylvia and Darcy didn't get on the elevators right at 4:02, they would have to wait until midnight to get down to the ground level. Being on the 25th floor certainly had its perks (the view, private bathrooms, the coffee cart that came around at 10 am every day) but the whole daily waiting for the elevator event was something that could cause much furor. In fact, the last fire alarm proved that tenfold. Sylvia had almost become a double amputee because of the fervor that had quickly taken over the stairwells.

Sylvia, all boobs and hair as Darcy liked to say, always wanted to shop. She wasn't all that particular about where they shopped – as long as the store in question had shiny, loud, bright colors that were a little too tight and a little too cheap to be considered a sale. Darcy sometimes joined her, often feeling entertained by the woman who fearlessly tried on everything that seemed just a bit inappropriate, but tonight was Friday, and she had bigger and better things planned.

They luckily got on the elevator promptly and began to descend the skyscrapers massive elevator shaft. Sylvia simultaneously played with her frizzy hair and applied some more bright red lipstick. Darcy always marveled by her co-workers ability to multi-task so efficiently with non-work related duties.

The elevator was comprised of a mishmash of corporate executives, administrative staff, and custodians. The smell was a mix of sweat, strawberries and Coco Chanel. She tried not to look directly into the armpit that belonged to a burly gentleman millimeters away from her. She was having a hard time not ogling at the repulsive sight, especially since the pit was not only at her eye level, but also seemed to be beckoning her with its disgusting sweat stain ring and dark plethora of she didn't want to know quite what.

"Can't tonight, Syl," she replied, trying to appear nonchalant as she pretended to look for something in her purse. She found herself having to speak loudly so her friend could hear her on the other end of the elevator, although the actual distance between them couldn't have been more than just a few feet.

Seconds after replying, she felt Sylvia's questioning eyes upon her, and instantly, as they always did, her cheeks began to redden, a characteristic Darcy trademark.

"Oh really? What do you have planned?" Sylvia quickly retorted. "You wouldn't say, um, a certain visit to somewhere where there are both A: No single men, and B: A good chance of being sexually assaulted."

The woman's response caused her to look up quickly from her purse-looking charade. All she really carried in there was Chapstick, her house keys and her cell phone. The odd sanitizer bottle appeared from time to time, however, depending on the season.

"Maybe," she said, trying not to give Sylvia any ammunition to turn her statement into a full-blown tirade, which was a strong likelihood given the sometimes volatile temperament of the older woman. Sylvia could be what you would call a 'loose cannon', an impression not only had by Darcy but shared by the entire office. It could probably take out an army or cause joy in a child's heart – it utterly depended on the type of mood the woman found herself in.

Sylvia's heart *was* in the right place. Being in her mid-forties (or fifties – she was ever so elusive about her actual age) and happily married, Sylvia felt it was her duty to ensure single, lonesome and mildly depressed Darcy met a nice guy, get married, and have lots of babies - precisely in that order. Being promoted at work was also a big wish of Sylvia's for Darcy, but that was definitely lower on the totem pole after the marriage bit - but not by much.

While she certainly appreciated Sylvia's motherly tendencies towards her, and she certainly tolerated it more than she did from her own mother, she found it annoying and relentless nonetheless. She didn't let her own mother dictate her life or tell her what to do, and she didn't know why she let Sylvia, her only real workplace 'friend', talk to her the way she did. She often chalked it up to her inherent Catholic guilt and the instilled rule of respecting your elders.

Both women remained silent as they exited the elevator upon reaching the first floor of the building and were immediately thrust into the throngs of people making their quick attempts to leave their

18

work life and return to their semi-normal, albeit incredibly monotonous, lives in suburbia. Darcy had to struggle to keep up with Sylvia's pace as they quickly morphed into Olympic power walkers making their way towards the invisible goal of home life.

"It's really not that bad," she yelled to Sylvia above the noisy ambient sound of stiletto heels and 10,000 PDA's in the cold city street on that November evening. It was only a little past four pm but it was already dark as midnight. Secretly, amongst most of her other likes, she enjoyed the shorter days and longer nights because it allowed her to not feel as anxious about her non-existent social life, aside from reading her teen books. The usual obligation of having to fill the daylight hours with "fun things" (beers on a patio, hanging out in a hipster-laden park) were gone, which she welcomed as she found herself not particularly liking those things anyway. She sometimes got an immediate feeling of envy when passing a group of friends enjoying a laugh on an outdoor restaurant deck and her walking by all alone, but it soon passed once she was out of eyesight. Hanging out on a patio in the summer never really lived up to its expectations anyway.

Sylvia looked at her over a tiny business man having an intense conversation and laughed as though she had just said told her the world's funniest joke. At first she didn't understand what Sylvia has found so amusing, but then quickly realized that only now was Sylvia continuing the conversation they began moments ago in the crammed elevator.

"Darcy, honey, Ridgewood and Van Sant is on Channel 4 News every night," she replied, her voice not as raucous as Darcy's had been but certainly very audible. "Why just last night I thought I heard a girl around your age was mugged!"

Sylvia was right. Ridgewood and Van Sant was certainly a super sketchy part of town. Located in the eastern part of the city, it was a hotspot for crime, mostly theft and drug related, with a side of the casual random sexual assault. She didn't feel any particularly less

19

safe walking around that neighborhood then where she lived, which was fortunate as because it also happened to be location of her absolute favorite bookstore in the world: Marina's.

***

In the world according to Darcy, Marina's was the one and only literal place in the whole entire world where she felt like she could be herself without being judged or ridiculed. She had been visiting for years, primarily for the bookstore's vast selection of teen fiction books, and had actually only randomly stumbled upon the shop for the first time on a complete whim, which added to its unexplainable magic and allure.

She had just moved to a new neighborhood of Maher Heights five years ago, fresh from having been made redundant at an advertising firm that paid her peanuts but which she loved terribly. After that fateful meeting with her boss about having to let go of some of the staff which she was one of (there was plenty tears shed and snot flowing), she found herself ready to make a big change. She had just binge-watched The Mary Tyler Moore Show, which only further fueled the fire of starting anew in a new city. If possible, she tried to tie in a nice binge TV-watching event with what she may have been experiencing in her personal life at any particular moment. Sometimes she had to reach to find that commonality with the show.

She had been scouting the city on a rather warm April day with her then-boyfriend Chip, who was all teeth and cheeks, but ultimately a really nice guy, if a little dull. They had just moved to their new apartment just a few days before and on that particular day were attempting to find interesting spots and hot pockets to visit, as well as cool, vintage shops to furnish their rather naked apartment. She had dug her heels and vehemently refused to furnish yet another apartment with furniture from IKEA, and so they opted to go the 'antique' (aka 'used') route.

She had come upon Marina's by total accident. Cheeky Chip had wanted to find a coffee shop to rest a bit (they were walking little marathoners), while she had wanted to find a good book to read, not surprising at all to Chip. He knew of her severe love of reading, though she had kept the insatiable love of teen fiction somewhat hidden. Because most of their belongings were still packed in boxes, they were still unpacking to start their life in Maher Heights. Her usual easy access to her expansive teen fiction collection was therefore blocked. She typically wasn't a big proponent of re-reading books, but she couldn't say no to a good Judy Blume re-hash until her next book purchase was made.

Lost, and without a map, and feeling like an addict needing a heroin fix, she noticed that Marina's book store seemed to pop out of nowhere. It was nearly as though it appeared out of the thin, smoggy air. After leaving Chip content at a nearby Starbucks with a latte in his hand and newspaper on the table before him, she opted to see where her fancy took her. She had soon found herself walking down a very quiet and desolated street with the random homeless person curled up on a vent, adding to its urban charm.

"Ooh – what have we here," Darcy said aloud to herself, and began to walk excitedly towards the shop that had the name 'Marina's' blazing on a flashing marquee sign that she had only previously seen in old movies and magazines. It was massive, made of heavy iron and chipped red paint, faded but endearing. The name itself was spelled out in bright mustard yellow, silver stars surrounding the M and A. The window display which sat below the flashing sign was so unbelievably expansive with books of every genre being displayed, from Plato to Kellerman to Koontz. The massive teen fiction section in the store's front window display was what totally caught her eye, and with that view, she flew into the store, not even worrying about leaving Chip on his own at Starbucks. In retrospect, she should have recognized the lack of concern for her

21

then-boyfriend as a sign of their imminent break up, which ironically enough was in a Starbucks.

She soon noticed a more petite sign advertising a small coffee shop within the store and immediately felt a twinge of guilt. Should she run back to Starbucks and ask Chip to join her, or would she have more fun venturing solo? Ultimately, she entered the store alone, which was how she entered it on every other subsequent visit she made.

Even though things didn't work out with Chip, she visited Marina's every single Friday. It was the highlight of her week. She couldn't contain the excitement of being able to find some books that certainly fixed her craving, and over time, she felt less and less embarrassed of making a beehive to the Teen Lit section, which was oddly enough always empty but fully stocked, and color coded.

Over time, she came to know Marina personally, partly because she was in the shop so often (and sometimes, she thought, the only customer) and partly because Marina seemed to be so omnisciently present with every visit she made, which sometimes was more frequent than her usual Friday night drop-in.

Marina was an exotic woman, which did not even do her justice as an adjective. She had the look of a veritable cross between Joan Crawford and Mata Hari, and took an immediately liking to Darcy. Every Friday, she and Darcy caught up on the week's events and Marina would share with her any new deliveries in the teen fiction unit. There was no particular event which precipitated them actually physically meeting each other, but more of a gradual "Can I help you with something" and "Yes, the teen fiction books please" slow-builder of a relationship.

Marina never judged or made Darcy feel strange about her penchant for reading books written for a demographic of 13 year olds. She simply accepted it as a personal preference of Darcy's and for that she was eternally thankful. She was able to shop and peruse the bounty of books that she was often frowned upon for reading without guilt or the necessary need to peak over her shoulder to see what other expressions customers may be throwing her way.

A gigantic bonus for her was that there never, ever any other patrons in the teen section at Marina's book store, thus making her feel even more comfortable in the quaint shop. She had found herself spending countless hours and hours there on those Friday nights, drinking cup after cup of Marina's special tea and throwing herself willingly into the trials and tribulations of self-righteous and confused teenagers who found themselves navigating through high-school and its associated perils. It let her feel both pity for the teens of today and their adult-like problems, but also proud for having survived high school herself the first time around.

***

"Have a great weekend, honey," Sylvia screamed at her as she boarded her packed bus. "And be safe." Sylvia was then immediately swallowed up in the throngs of the hundreds of people who were making their nightly voyage to Suburbia. To be polite, Darcy continued to watch the bus until it departed in the unlikely and rare event that Sylvia got a window seat and began to wave animatedly at her.

As the bus disappeared from her line of sight, she exhaled heavily (out of sheer relief) and quickly turned around to make her ascent to 'Marina's' – her Mecca amongst monotony, and felt a subtle spring in her step as she knew she would be able to get some good reading thrills that evening. She tried to not think too much about how sad this cause of happiness would appear to other people as she walked out of the busy downtown core and into the more solitary, and fairly run down (and her favorite!) part of town.

Chapter 3

Opening the front door of Marina's was always a challenge. It seemed that the hinge was perpetually stuck to the door, forcing her to constantly break a sweat above her brow as she heaved all of her weight against the door to be able to get in the shop. It also certainly didn't help matters that the door seemed to be something built right out of Roman times where the size alone seemed to be at least 2 stories tall and made of 100% cast iron.

"Here, let me help you, Ms. Platt," Griffin said, Marina's right-hand man. He towered over Darcy and smiled gently. Griffin was intrinsically part of the shop and part of the whole 'Marina's' experience. Endlessly in his sixties, with silver hair and dimples on each cheek, Griffin played all kinds of roles in the shop, from cashier to concierge to stock boy. If she was interested in dating older men, she certainly would have gone for the man. She actually secretly harbored a tiny, tiny crush for this man who was always so kind and gentle to her. However, she sort of thought there was something going on between him and Marina, so she let that cat lie.

He opened the door with such ease that she felt embarrassed for not having been able to open it herself. She secretly hid the lack of strength in the arsenal of self-identified faults she kept locked in the back of her mind. She stored it neatly beside her fault of always eating dessert before dinner.

"Thanks, Griffin," she replied, pushing herself over the threshold into the shop with literal giddiness and excitement. Griffin nodded back, returning to his post as cashier/store manager/book expert extraordinaire above the wooden dais that oversaw the entire shop.

His perch on the dais was by far the best vantage point in the entire shop. Without even having to turn his head, he was able to take in the entire view of the store, including both floors that were always so well stocked and organized in its selections. Though the second floor was where Marina's office was situated and off limits to most customers, Darcy sometimes found herself safely hidden in a little crevice up there reading the latest installment of Fear Street or something of the like.

The shop itself was not gigantic by any means but it certainly felt expansive to her. It was not in the same realm of the big box bookstores that often littered big cities, but it was big to her in many definable ways. It could have probably fit into the lighting section at the local Home Depot but she truly adored its coziness and warmth. The wood paneling and wood floors, the beige walls, the accent carpets and framed reproductions of famous literary works – it all gave her the feeling of a big bear hug.

It was also extremely well organized, Marina and Griffin both saw to that, and she felt she could navigate blindfolded in the shop and still be able to find her cherished teen fiction unit. Once, she had even tried to do just that due to the excessive amounts of caffeine she had consumed and a Harry Potter hangover circa The Half Blood Prince era.

On that day she discovered the shop, Chip ensconced comfortably at the Starbucks, was a certainly interesting one for her, even more so in retrospect. She had immediately found herself walking slowly around the never-ending shelves and book displays, feeling completely immersed in the energy and timelessness of the shop. Each section had its own bright sign, a miniature version of the one in the front of the store, highlighting the genre and vast inventory of books. She remembered being impressed at the expansive selection of teen authors that ranged from Francine Pascal to R.L. Stine (yes, for her Mr. Stine was a master of teen storytelling, albeit with murder and gruesomeness). She had been reading the back of a book by Christopher Pike that she had never, ever seen in person (eBay had the random copy here and there but to actually physically touch the book sent sensations down her spine), when she caught the scent of lilacs and Greek olives. Confused by the unique fusion of scents, she turned around to see an older woman, equal parts beautiful and contemplative, staring at her blankly.

Normally, when she caught the random strangers staring at her for whatever reason, she would have her defenses immediately in check, either immediately sporting a heavy frown or returning the stare with a blank-eyed expression - but it was different with this stranger. She felt like she was being studied, and understood, and sort of revered in some strange way. It was a completely strange feeling for her to feel revered because all through her life she struggled simply to be heard.

"You have not come here before, no?" the woman said, her eyes bright green, similar to the Wicked Witch in the Wizard of Oz. She had felt terrible for making that comparison but it was her only real point of reference for that shade of the color green. The stranger had a slight accent, a peculiar blend of Eastern European and Southern Georgian. The woman continued to peer at her, smiling, the red hair atop her head arranged in a tight bun that looked beautifully coiffed.

"No, I haven't," Darcy quietly replied, placing the book back on the shelf, her typical instant reaction when someone spoke to her while she was knee deep in teen fiction. Plead ignorance was her go-to instant-reaction should that situation arise.

"No, I would have noticed if you had been in before," the older woman continued, stepping closer. Her long purple and red dress seemed to float atop the wooden floor, wind blowing it from a thousand invisible fans.

Darcy set the book back firmly amongst its like books, in the right spot she had hoped, and turned towards the woman. She had found the woman's statement somewhat bizarre because she did not consider herself noticeable in any particular way. She had mousy brown hair, never dyed (a fact she was semi-proud of), was 5'5 and slim (ish). Her weight fluctuated alongside her hair length and she thought her blue eyes were just average. She didn't exactly turn heads when she entered a room (she was more of an Anne of Green Gables than Katniss Everdeen), but she was pretty just the same, just more in a subtle way.

"I am Marina. I own this store," the woman continued, her thick eyebrows frowning once she noticed the book she just put back on the shelf.

Great, Darcy thought to herself. *The store owner just saw me reading the jacket for The Graduation, the final book in Christopher Pike's legendary Final Friends series. I'm going to die of mortification.*

"That is a great book. Mr. Pike sure knows how to capture the nuances of teen angst," Marina smiled. The warm expression that spread over the woman's face had the immediate effect of causing her to instantly relax and feel comfortable.

For a split second, she had thought she misheard this Marina person entirely. *Could this woman possibly know the beauty of Pike's prose, let alone compliment a book written for zitty teens?* , she silently monologued.

"Come, I will show you more," Marina went on, gently

27

grabbing onto her raincoat, and proceeded to give Darcy a personal tour of the shop. And just like that, they became bookstore buddies. That first meeting found them chatting for hours about topics ranging from plot points of all of their favorite books to how Marina came to become a store owner. At one point, Griffin brought the two women freshly brewed cups of tea which had the aroma of rose petals and happiness. That first meeting had been like the best date she could have with a new friend.

She had always gotten along well with older adults. There was a compatibility and ease with those interactions that she found difficult to obtain with peers her own age. Her mother had said repeatedly over the years it was because she had an 'old soul' but she surmised that it was because she just didn't like people her own age.

Shaking herself from her flashback and mini-reverie of the first time she had met Marina, she took a glance upwards to the ornate stained glass window that overlooked the shop, which cast red, yellow and blue shadows amongst the book displays and wooden chairs that lined the aisles. Smiling to herself out of literal contentment, she continued her way past Thrillers and Political Novels to her favorite section.

She grabbed a few books from the teen section display and sat in her favorite seat which faced the steep wooden stairwell that lead up to the second floor of the shop where Marina's office and inventory area were. She happily began to skim the new releases that Marina always placed for her on the bottom shelf, after the letter Z, with her name on it. She settled in comfortably, cell phone turned off and her cozy shawl tied around her neck (a gift from Marina), and began to venture into the worlds of teens who were faced with decisions that she felt she could make in her sleep. This assumption made her feel slightly superior to the characters she voraciously read about who were always finding every plot point so overwhelming. Fortunately for them and unlike real life, there was always a happy ending to be had.

28

Chapter 4

For the second time that day she had dozed off because she awoke to the sounds of hurried whispers and slamming doors around her. It caused her immediate alarm as loud sounds were never, ever made inside the safe confines of Marina's, much like noise in a library was prohibited. Normally, these were the types of sounds that she heard on a daily basis (her apartment had a great floor plan but paper thin walls) and did not phase her at all, but within the confines of the Mecca of Marina's, they had the tenacity of police car sirens blaring in the sanctity of a church.

She swiftly stood up, which she later regretted because she had dozed off with her legs crossed and now her right shin felt like an overused dartboard on Friday night at TGI-Fridays. Holding in her yelps of pain, she covertly attempted to discover where the ruckus was coming from without appearing nosy, not that there was anyone else in the shop (there seldom were – she had often questioned how Marina was able to keep the book shop in business).

She glanced over at Griffin's usual perch, where he expectedly stood with his nose buried in a large book that had dust rising from it as he turned the pages slowly. The man seemed entirely unaware of the noises that had awoken her from her apparent reading induced slumber. She slowly sat back down and glanced around the periphery of the store, noticing that the sounds had subsided. She looked at her watch and was shocked that it was close to 10 pm, an hour past the posted closing time hours mounted on the front iron door. She quickly gathered her things, including the four books she intended to buy, and began to walk towards Griffin when she heard the muffled sounds again, this time more discernible in volume.

"… to stay here!" a man's voice said, gruff and stern. The voice was deep and strong, immediately making her ill at ease. She turned around expecting to see some overbearing stranger, but she did not see anyone. She peered upwards to the second floor where Marina's office was located and noticed that Marina's signature office lamp was brightly lit, causing unusual shadows to creep around slowly the inside of the office.

"You must make a choice," the male continued, his voice lower this time. Perhaps he noticed that screaming wasn't acceptable inside a bookstore, not to mention at Marina's.

Suddenly, there was a loud bang of a door slamming closed, followed by a myriad of inaudible whispers and the distinguishable sound of finger nails scratching a blackboard.

"The choice will be made," a woman replied, her voice soft, southern and frightened. There was no mistaking the source of the voice: Darcy knew it was Marina.

"I cannot let her go on without knowing the truth. She will discover it soon," Marina continued, her voice almost pleading in its tone. Darcy had never heard that kind of tone come from Marina before, and it further caused her to feel concerned about what was unfolding.

At that moment, Marina's large, oak office door opened and closed, however, Darcy did not actually see anyone either enter or exit. She felt a sense of panic, not knowing if her eyes were playing tricks on her post-nap or if she were witnessing some paranormal activity. True, she had just finished watching the Paranormal Activity franchise just the night before, but she liked to believe she had a firm grasp on reality, nap hangover and all.

Figuring she had had enough creepiness for one evening, she decided to simply turn around and pay for her books with Griffin at the front counter area. Before she managed to shift her direction towards the man who was still reading his book, she caught Marina staring at her just steps away. The look in the woman's eyes was the exact same one she had had the first day both women had met for the first time all of those years ago. Darcy thought she caught an air of sadness and worry in the woman's eyes, but the muted lighting in the store in itself was not exactly the best. She quickly shook off the thought.

"Hello, Darcy," Marina said, her voice calm. She was wearing her signature red bun and flowing purple dress, and her perfectly applied lipstick.

"Ah!" Darcy screamed at being startled, sending her books flying. She had always been teased for being so easily frightened, and this was no exception to the rule.

"I did not mean to surprise you," Marina continued as she bent down to gather the fallen books.

"No, it's ok. I'm just a jumpy girl," she replied. Once she picked up the books and placed them in a tiny pile, she noticed Marina's grave look.

"Marina, are you ok?" she asked, stepping closer to the store owner. Inexplicably, and all at once, Marina did not seem to have any make up on. Her eyes were red, almost bloodshot. Her impeccable trademark bun then seemed to begin to unravel and become loosened right before Darcy's eyes. The soft red hair fell upon the woman's diminutive little shoulders. She instantly felt like giving the tiny woman a big bear hug, and moved towards her to do

31

just that, but Marina shrunk away.

"Sit down, my girl," Marina said, pointing at the chair that she had hastily stood up from minutes before. Darcy, unsure of Marina's state of mind, did as she was told without hesitation. Marina pulled the chair that sat beside her and sat down. "There is something we need to talk about."

***

"You come here every Friday, looking for books," Marina began, her voice now more typical, a touch more Southern than European tonight. She grabbed a book from Darcy's pile and smiled, and slowly returned it.

"You know I do," Darcy replied, unsure of situation was unfolding before her. Marina was never serious – in fact, she was always infusing joy and laughter into every situation. To see her so morose made Darcy feel extremely uncomfortable.

"You read these books with heroines who worry about finding the right boy or buying the right car," Marina continued. "You want to live in those worlds where things do not matter and everything is resolved by the end. You want to worry about what prom dress to wear and which table to sit at lunch, not paying for rent or preparing lunch to bring to work."

Darcy couldn't help but smile, imagining and sincerely wishing that it could come true. She would love to only worry about things such as trivial as those that Marina had just spoken of. She would wholeheartedly immerse herself into a life where she was taken care of, where no matter what she ate she still looked like a model, and where her boyfriend was better looking than Channing Tatum and Bradley Cooper combined.

"Who wouldn't?" she finally answered, the smile still on her lips. Marina smiled back. "You and I have talked endless times about why I love those books. They make me feel innocent and

32

understood. I feel like I get to live vicariously through these girls. I can be a blonde one weekend, with a rich dad and a bad boyfriend, and the next weekend I can be an identical twin who just woke up from a coma and can't remember a thing about how she got there." If she could live in the Sweet Valley High World, she knew that Jessica Wakefield would be shaking in her boots because Darcy would be the coolest and most beautiful girl in town.

"This is good news," Marina whispered, glancing around to ensure Griffin was not looking. She followed Marina's glance, equally intrigued and concerned as to what the woman was up to.

"Marina, what exactly is going on?" she whispered back, looking deep into Marina's eyes that were now no longer blood shot. In fact, they now seemed to be gleaming.

Marina smiled, her perfect teeth shining bright. She brought her hands swiftly up to her hair and without Darcy even knowing or realizing how, created her signature bun with not one hair out of place.

"Oh Darcy," Marina finally said, inching closer to her. "My dear girl. What if I told you that you could become one of these girls you read about all of the time?"

Darcy laughed loudly, causing Griffin to look at both women and smiling. *She's losing it*, she thought. *The dust from these books has finally gotten to her head.*

***

After noticing Marina did not return her laughter, Darcy stood up from her seat, and adjusted the shawl around her shoulders. She had gotten a chill all of a sudden and was glad she brought the shawl for her reading event that night.

"Marina – things like that don't happen. That is precisely why I read those books – because I can't relive those days. I can't become Bella Swan. I can't put on a pair of magical jeans that fit all of my girlfriends," she said.

It was then she once again gathered her belongings but in her haste left behind the pile of books she was about to buy. For some reason, she was not enjoying the energy that had filled the room. She began to walk towards Griffin when she felt Marina's urgent hold on her shoulder.

"Darcy," Marina said, her voice serious and firm. Darcy stopped dead in her tracks. "If you say yes to me now, I can put you in those books you dream of. Just say yes and that is all."

She would normally think that Marina had completely lost her marbles, but the woman seemed serious. A thousand thoughts flew through her mind: *I'd be stupid to say no. But I'm also incredibly stupid to think that this could actually happen. Should I just entertain the old lady and say sure? Do I say no, which means I would probably be never to come back here? Have I completely gone off the deep end? Have I watched The Neverending Story one too many times?*

Without missing a beat, she swallowed, and turned towards Marina, who now looked as ravishing as she always did: flawless make up, vibrant red hair and a dress of emerald green that had been a pale purple just moments before. And, if she wasn't mistaken, there seemed to be wind ruffling the long skirts of her dress.

"I have to go," she whispered to Marina and made a beeline for the front door of the shop. Her usual reaction to a situation where she felt uncomfortable and unsure how to proceed was to escape. Within seconds, she was crossing the threshold from the shop to the world beyond. Once outside, she took in a fresh gulp of the cool autumn air, her heart feeling like it would pounce of her chest, her cheeks flushing.

She did not know why she was having this kind of reaction to Marina's absurd question. She didn't know if it was because Marina seemed to actually believe that she could do what she was offering her, or because on some weird, secretly hidden level beside her self-assigned faults, she thought the woman possibly COULD do that for her and make all of her dreams and wishes come true.

She shook her head in an attempt to clear it of its crazy thoughts and flagged down a cab to take her home. In her state of mind, riding the subway was out of the question. With the type of night she was having, who knows what would happen to her on the train.

Chapter 5

When she opened her eyes the next morning at a semi-indecent time, she immediately felt the painful nag of a headache. She wasn't one to normally play the headache card, let alone actually get them, but the general pulsating feeling resonated in her temples made her feel both nauseated and annoyed at the same time.

She turned around slowly in her luxurious bed, one of the few truly extravagant things she owned (she had justified the purchase with the fact that she spent so much time in there anyway – reading, of course). The artillery of pillows that flanked both sides of her looked like a little fortress, which sort of added to her intention of wanting to stay segregated from the general public that entire weekend.

Suddenly, as though literally out of nowhere, she was forced to recall and remember what had transpired the night before. It seemed like a dream, all hazy and sepia toned, but she knew it had really happened. Marina had made her a ridiculously unbelievable and impossible offer to enter the fictional world of a teen novel.

She always had the distinct impression that Marina was a unique character with always something a bit off always bubbling beneath her poised and coordinated exterior. It wasn't an ever-constant feeling, just a random impression and feeling she experienced from time to time when in the presence of Marina, usually when she was spending the majority of a random Saturday in the shop she called her second home.

However, the supposed proposition that Marina offered just a few hours ago was certainly something that catapulted the aura and mystery of Marina to a whole other level. She knew the bookshop owner well enough, or so she thought, to know rather firmly that she was not an unrealistic or flighty individual. In fact, Marina always managed to dispense just the right dose of advice at the literal spin of a dime and Darcy always commended her for this. It was no small feat to listen to a sometimes blubbering thirty something year old woman going on and on about something completely meaningless only to interrupt with a one word turn of phrase that not only resolved the issue at hand, but also made the speaker realize that there was never really an issue to begin with.

Getting up out of bed was what she thought would be the best way to deal with the headache, that and popping a few Tylenol that comprised the only real first aid kit she had in her tiny apartment. It was one of those things she always had meant to replenish (What would happen if she cut herself accidentally and didn't have a band-aid on hand? This was a strong possibility as she wasn't exactly known as a coordinated person). Swallowing the tablets with last night's tepid water atop her nightstand, she thought better of starting her day and decided to get right back into the safety and comfort of her bed.

She attempted to close her eyes and fall back asleep but her mind kept racing about last night's reveal. She had so many questions she wanted to ask but could you really ask questions about something that could NEVER HAPPEN? Wouldn't it be like debating the moral compass of a vampire in a Twilight novel when the story itself is entirely fictional and unreal?

Nonetheless, the questions filled her mind something fast and furious. Where was that deep, angry, male voice coming from at Marina's, obviously amidst an argument of some kind with the apparently meek woman? And why was she the only one who seemed to hear the muted whispers and slamming doors, Griffin looking on as though it was just another regular evening at the book store? Why did Marina looked so disheveled post-argument with the imaginary, disembodied voice but seemed to instantly transform into her usual well-put together self during her short but world-changing conversation with Darcy?

The number one question that she felt both simultaneously embarrassed and excited to actually entertain was the possibility of entering the world of one of her revered teen fiction worlds, complete with stereotypical teenaged characters, suburban settings, perfectly temperate weather and neatly wrapped plots that always managed to reach a positive solution by the end. If the rational part of her mind could wrap itself around the possibility of that actually happening, she honestly and truly did not know what her answer would be.

Part of her would happily and blindly enter this fictional realm without any qualms. It was no secret that the reason she exclusively read teen fiction was two-fold: she loved the apparently simplicities of the narratives and worlds created, replete with guaranteed resolution, but it was also because she was not what one would call 'content' in her real life. Sometimes she felt as though she was depressed, crying at the most random of events, but she often attributed this to her hyper-emotional hard-wired settings. But she *was* lonely. Reading the novels she read successfully managed to take her constantly racing and over-analytical mind from her self-titled humdrum existence into a world where there was never indeed a dull moment.

What would she do if she were thrust into the life of suburban America with the sun always shining and friends that were all bronzed and beautiful? What would she do if both the 'bad boy' and the prized school athlete both attempted to vie for her attention? What would she decide if the popular girls tried to peer pressure her into doing something she wasn't comfortable with doing, like trying drugs or getting drunk, or the school nerds tried to recruit her because deep down they knew they weren't really at all different from one another?

It was her dog's notification bark signaling its need to do her business that shook her from the maze of thoughts within her mind. After looking at the large alarm clock on her nightstand, she realized it was already mid-afternoon and she had been entrenched in her mind for the last few hours, which to her, had felt like just a few minutes.

She had always hoped that there would be something, some momentous life-altering event that would happen to her. She would often walk around downtown and secretly imagine that she was going to be 'discovered' as the next greatest and most beautiful 'IT' girl by some visiting photographer for Italian Vogue. Or she sometimes wished that while shopping for chick peas at Whole Foods that she'd be pulled into some sort of covert, undercover international drug ring that would bring her worldwide fame and make her lots of money. Because her two left feet were so firmly entrenched in reality, however, these unbelievable, suspensions of disbelief, Darcy Platt never even afforded herself the minute real possibility that something unworldly could happen to her.

Hoping to help her make up her rather indecisive mind, she decided to just talk a walk in her neighborhood, doing the proverbial 'clear your head bit'. She threw on her cherished navy blue sweat pants with the rather unsightly stain by the left ankle and a pink hoodie and took her little dog outside. Bending down to put the leash on the little lady, she wished she could just escape the business of her head, which was the other thing that she always wished for.

While walking down her street, she felt the brisk, cool fall wind hitting her face, immediately causing her to swear indecipherable words under her breath. The streets seemed to be absolutely deserted. Normally, on her afternoon walks with her dog Lucy, they'd run into some of her little pooches buddies, do the typical small talk thing with the owners, and move on. Today, however, in the overcast sky that towered over her, making her feel itty-bitty, she felt totally and utterly alone. And her little dog did too.

She turned the corner, little Lucy sniffing everything in sight, and briefly contemplated if she should tell her best friend since the proposition she was offered by Marina just the night before. Sonya Maines, the first girl in Darcy's kindergarten class who handed Darcy that tissue to dry her tears once her mother deserted her in that colorful, toy-filled room all those years ago, could still be counted on to give her that tissue that she needed.

Darcy and Sonya had been the best of friends forever, as it seemed, and lived only a matter of blocks away from each other, and literally shared each and every little secret with one another, regardless of how seemingly petty or grandiose they were. Sonya knew all about her prescient predilection for reading teen fiction, in fact she even read a fair bit of it herself. The two girls had talked about the plots of those books incessantly through the seemingly never-ending summers in grade school, and then less and less so as the angst of those high school years came upon them. They didn't exactly talk about it now because Sonya just didn't read that type of book anymore, opting more for Oprah's certified book club selection and the current book du jour, but Darcy still read them with the same amount of excitement and fascination as she had when she was just 12 years old.

Soon enough, she found herself upon Sonya's walk-up apartment and buzzed up. The buzzer had seen better days and sounded like a dilapidated Oldsmobile, always forcing her to cringe upon hearing the high toned audio assault.

Lucy looked up, still after all of these years not used to the high-pitched tone that accompanied the old buzzer. She looked at Darcy with her puppy-dog eyes, as though imploring 'why do you cause me so much pain, mom'.

Sonya didn't reply right away, forcing Darcy to immediately think her friend had either already embarked on a day of shopping or was still sleeping off last night's bar-travaganza. Turning around to resume her walk in the seemingly empty city, she heard Sonya's groggy voice boom over the buzzer.

"What?" Sonya said, her voice scratchy. *Bar-travaganza*, Darcy inwardly confirmed.

"It's me. Can we come up?" she whispered, semi-embarrassed at the sheer volume of the antiquated buzzer system in the relatively newish apartment building. This was when the whole empty street thing came in handy for which she was thankful.

She heard the loud, lengthy beep which signaled her approved clearance into the building and bent down to scoop up her little pooch/best friend. She entered the nouveau 90's era building that her friend had now lived in for several years. The brightly painted purple walls were countered by a deep, plush brown carpet that Lucy just loved (Darcy's own apartment had hardwood floors throughout). The cream colored tiles that adorned the elevator frames shone brightly as though just recently cleaned.

Inside the pristine elevator, she took a quick glance at her appearance in the mirror-paneled that took up the entire back wall and almost lost her breath. She knew she had probably looked unkempt (which she often described as 'lounge-y' though she secretly knew better) when leaving her own apartment just half an hour ago, but her reflection really startled her. Scared her, really. Her hair was in somewhat of a ponytail though most of the mousey-brownness lay on her right shoulder. The stain that she thought was on the bottom of her sweat pants seemed to have now taken over the entire right leg. She didn't know what caused the stain itself but by looking at it, she knew there was no way to ever find out. She made a mental note to throw out the pants as soon as she returned home, or, if Sonya had something to lend her, she would do it as soon as she got upstairs.

Her pink hoodie seemed to have become entirely covered with lint and Lucy hair, which was not a good look, especially together. She must have stepped in some dog poop en route as her running shoes were brown from the laces down. She felt gross and immature, briefly contemplating to just take the elevator back down to the lobby and literally run home, taking Lucy in her arms to save time. But Sonya was her friend and had seen her much worse for wear, and the thought left her mind as the elevator door opened.

***

Her friend was in the hallway throwing garbage down the chute and had her back to Darcy as the elevator doors opened. Lucy ran up to her Sonya and started kissing and panting and doing the usual adorable dog thing she was known to do, and Sonya immediately got down on her knees and gave the dog the attention she so seldom asked for. Making that high-pitched, non-sensical baby-ish talk that people use to communicate to pets of all kinds, Sonya heard herself in the echoes of the hallways and stopped, looking up at Darcy.

"God, Darcy – you went outside looking like that?" Sonya said, the disgust and disapproval literally dropping off of her face. "You look like a homeless person."

"Thanks, Son" Darcy retorted, following her friend into her apartment. "It's my attempt at a new style change. Do you approve?"

Sonya turned back and smiled. "As much as I like your willingness to try new things, I'd have to say this new selection needs to be kaiboshed immediately. Like I'm going to dress you in

42

my own clothes RIGHT NOW."

All three girls walked down the long hallway and then escaped into the apartment, the common hallway just as empty as the streets had been. There really did seem to be something sinister in the air, Darcy thought to herself as she closed Sonya's apartment door shut behind them, happy to be blocking out the outside world.

***

"She offered you what?" Sonya asked incredulously. She and Darcy both found themselves reclining on the large burgundy sofa that they nearly had to nearly take apart in order to fit it up the narrow stairwell of the apartment building when Sonya had first moved in.

They were laying head to toe on the couch so that they were able to see each other when speaking to one another. Lucy had settled onto a cozy little corner on the armchair that sat beside the sofa. The little dog was asleep within seconds of getting to the apartment. The little dog struggled to keep up with Darcy's quick pace on the walk over, and upon being given the chance to be stationary for a quick moment, she immediately seized it to get some much needed shut-eye. Darcy was known to use the same excuse to catch a few zzz's herself.

"I know, I know. It sounds totally crazy and I'm just as crazy for telling you about it," Darcy answered.

She hadn't meant to tell Sonya what Marina had offered her just the night before but it sort of just rolled out of her mouth when the two friends started talking and catching up on the relative non-event events of the week. They had been gabbing about what their Friday nights had been like (Sonya's at a local bar for a work function and Darcy contemplating entering a fantasy world) and out it came.

Sonya's expression had been classic. There was no denying that

Sonya was a ravishing, beautiful woman. Darcy knew this as soon as they met on that first day of school eons ago. When Darcy had come into class that late summer morning, all sweaty and in a brocade patterned dress that did not look good on anyone, she saw Sonya seated, poised, perfectly put together, with a perpetual swimming aura of positivity and confidence. Sonya was still like that to this day, for which she Darcy still in awe over. She didn't know how her friend always seemed to have her life in order, but she always did. Paired with her effervescently positive attitude, she was truly a force to be reckoned with.

Now, atop her sofa, Sonya's beautifully shaped mouth was agape, her tiny forehead wrinkled with shock/surprise/wonder. Even though she had told her Darcy that she had just gotten out of bed, Sonya looked put-together and gorgeous, ready to go out on a date or stroll on a catwalk in Paris.

"I don't even know why I'm thinking about it...I mean, it's totally impossible," Darcy stammered, blushing with embarrassment. It was a knee-jerk reaction. She wasn't shy or embarrassed to tell Sonya anything - they had been friends long enough that awkwardness or dirty little secrets never made an impact because they simply didn't exist.

"It just seemed so genuine, coming from Marina. It's not like she's known to be a crazy person or anything. She's been so nice to me all of these years..."

"Darcy, be reasonable – she offered you a chance to enter the world of a teen novel!" Sonya interrupted, her voice rising. "That is not genuine. It's psychotic."

Darcy sat up quickly, her feelings hurt even though she couldn't really explain why. Her little dog looked up to see her owner, sensing the shift in mood, but then quickly went back to sleep, her fur camouflaged with the rest of the chair.

"I told you I know it sounds crazy, Son. But there's something about the whole thing that seems like it's real, like I could actually

44

do it!" she countered, sitting up and facing her friend. "I know it's bizarre and nuts, but I feel something pulling me towards it."

Sonya followed suit and sat up as well, facing her. She smiled at her friend upon seeing that she was truly being honest, and slowly sat back upon the soft cushions that adorned the sofa.

"Darcy – if there's anyone in the world that knows how much you would give to enter a fictional world where teens prevail and the only worries you have are finding a suitable prom dress or deciding which boy to date, it'd be me," Sonya went on, her voice no longer loud but taking on a rather soft quality. "But you have to admit that what's she's claiming she can offer is pretty effing cray cray. It's actually kind of mean, when you think about it."

"Mean? How is it mean?" Darcy asked. Her voice got a little too high, almost defensive, and she mentally noted to take it down a notch. Or two.

"Well, you've been going to the bookshop for a long time now. You buy all of those novels, read them over and over again, and talk to Magda about them."

"Marina," she cut in. "Her name's Marina."

"Marina, sorry," Sonya continued. "Marina knows that your head is wrapped up in these books and for her to make you a totally unrealistic offer is mean because it's like offering you something you'll never have. It's like offering a heroin addict a football field worth of drugs to go through for a weekend – it just can't happen."

Darcy audibly sighed and lay back on the sofa. She knew Sonya was trying to be supportive, and she knew that what Marina was offering her would never happen, but it was such a fascinating and intriguing concept to think about. It would literally be like a dream come true. She could escape the humdrum existence she lived day in and day out, and be that teen again but in an ideal world and in a perfect body.

"I know, Son – I know. I just wanted to tell you about it, is all," she replied, closing her eyes. "It makes for an exciting story."

45

Sonya got up and disappeared into the kitchen for a few minutes. When she returned, she was holding two cups of Jasmine tea and a tray of cookies. Both girls smiled.

"Now this is reality," Sonya said, and both girls started laughing. There was nothing like spending a cool fall afternoon with a friend eating cookies and being all cozy on a sofa. So why was the only thing she was thinking about was Marina's offer?

***

She hadn't meant to stay longer than an hour but ended up staying until midnight that Saturday night. The reasoning for the lengthy stay was the perfect combination of random instances, mostly governed by the Breaking Bad marathon on AMC (it just repeated so well, Darcy said to herself to validate the 9 hour viewing session) and overactive mind she was experiencing. The latter wasn't exactly a new behavior she had to learn how to deal with. In fact, she had convinced herself that she had a 'restless mind' in the same way some people suffered from 'restless leg' syndrome. She didn't intend for her mind to keep bouncing from idea to idea, from analysis to analysis, just like those poor few who didn't mean to have their legs randomly spasm out and move while trying to fall asleep for the night.

She walked home with from Sonya's and quickly changed back into her pajamas. Fortunately, her pajamas also doubled as 'taking the dog to pee' clothes which saved her the hassle of changing her outfit every time she had to take Lucy out for a bio break.

With her sweats in a mammoth pile on the wooden floor and her goal to throw out her stained sweatpants still intact, she jumped right back into her massive, king-sized bed and reached over to her nightstand to continue reading her 'Bright Nightfall' novel when her cell phone began to vibrate.

She immediately yelped in fright not only from the sudden

sound which soon filled her apartment, but from the shock that someone would be calling her. She used her Smartphone mostly for playing games and listening to music. Receiving calls was the least activity that the phone received.

After seeing the words "Blocked Number" appear on the gadget's display, she surmised that it was probably a telemarketer calling. But would a telemarketer really be calling in the middle of the night? She supposed stranger things did happen.

"Hello?" she responded tentatively, her voice vaguely annoyed and hostile, two things she generally was not. It was just that she hated, hated the concept of telemarketing, let alone bothering some unsuspecting person in their home on a Saturday night. Darcy found it distasteful.

"Hello Darcy," the woman's voice said, small and succinct.

"Marina?" she replied, completely surprised.

"It is I. I am sorry to bother you," Marina continued, her accent barely noticeable. "But I wanted to make sure you were ok after last night. You stormed out of here rather abruptly. Griffin and I were worried sick."

Worried sick? Darcy thought. *Why? Because I left a store hours after it was supposed to close for the day? And how just did Marina get my telephone number?*

"I'm fine," she replied, her voice calmer and strong. "There is nothing to worry about."

"But there is," Marina quickly countered, at once her accent distinct. "I made you an offer and you ran away."

"I wouldn't say it's an offer," she said. "An offer implies a choice to select something that will feasibly occur, often soon."

There was a silence on the other end of the phone that went on for a few uncomfortable seconds before she heard the woman clear her throat.

"I know it is hard to believe but this is a real offer, Darcy. It could happen. You just need to come to me and tell me that you

47

want to do it, to make your fantasies come true."

At that point, she couldn't help but chuckle. Was Marina really that crazy? How could she not have seen it after spending some much time with the older woman? She couldn't shake her gut feeling though that Marina was indeed being genuine, that she was really making her an offer that she would deliver upon.

Sensing her trepidation, Marina continued. "Please think about it some more. Suspend your disbeliefs and tell me your decision. You know where to find me."

And with that the conversation was over. She kept the phone to hear ear until she heard the signal reminding her the call was indeed done. At once, her mind was again a jumble of thoughts. As a defiant act of escapism, she ran into the living room and tried to find something to watch on television that could let her mind be distracted for a bit, and before she knew it, it was 3 am and she found herself pseudo-daydreaming about what it would be like to be a crystal meth maker with a heart of gold, or something like that.

Chapter 6

Sitting at her desk on that agitated Monday morning, she sensed trepidation in the air. There was something intangible lingering there which attributed to the omniscient feeling of dread. She felt a tiny, tiny knot begin to grow in the pit of her stomach at some point between midnight and 4 am the night before. The tiny knot of nerves had seemed to awaken her just as she had fallen asleep from a busy day of housecleaning and reading.

She had finished 'Bright Nightfall' and was going to get started on a new book but found herself rather sleepy after taking her dog out for the night pee. Typically, she would jump right into a new fictional world after having just finished the previous one, but that night she was feeling slightly unusual, askew even. In retrospect, she realized that that was when the tiny seeds of anxiety were starting to grow in the deep recesses of her stomach, nearly reaching the size of a fully grown tree by the time Monday morning rolled around.

That Monday had started like any other (late for the bus, breakfast in the form of a granola bar, a coffee nearly the size of her forearm). Upon arriving at the office, she had thought she was being paranoid about something bad that was going to happen, some impending doom that she often brought upon herself. She was never surprised when nothing came of these feelings of dread.

Sylvia came fluttering into the office in an outfit barely appropriate for work and sat down briefly beside Darcy, her voice high and excited. Darcy felt the seeds rumble in her belly.

"Did you hear? Did you?" Sylvia practically yelled. She tried to remain calm and disinterested even though she knew that on some level that Sylvia had a juicy piece of office gossip that she really wanted to hear.

"Hear what?" Darcy asked nonchalantly, slowly turning on her computer and then taking a sip of her gargantuan coffee.

Sylvia looked like she was going to positively burst out of her shirt, not just because of her barely contained breasts but because there was news she so badly wanted to share and clearly couldn't keep hidden any longer. She estimated that Sylvia probably just found out about 'this news' just minutes before, given the flurry of fresh excitement.

"Oh my god, I can't believe you didn't hear. Absolutely everyone is talking about it in the mail room!" Sylvia replied, her voice high-pitched enough that Darcy thought the windows would come crashing down towards them.

The office mailroom was housed in a long, rectangular room in which all staff had to walk through in order to get to their desks each morning. It was an old building, circa the 60's or 70's if she had to guess, and clearly not designed for an office but rather for a bank. Thus, the walk through the mailroom was strange but expected in a retrofitted location such as the building they found themselves in.

On her own walk through the mailroom earlier that morning, she had sensed an invisible chatter moving around her. Though no one approached her to share any tidbit of news or gossip, there certainly was a perpetual feeling of apprehension and excitement. She instantly credited it to a manifestation of those seeds of worry that had begun to sprout in her stomach just hours before, thus causing her to ignore the notion there actually could be some sort of momentous event or news that was to be shared.

"I didn't hear anything on my walk through this morning," she answered, watching her computer monitor light up and her email box showing 50 emails with the words "Did you hear?" bolded in the subject lines. She turned to face Sylvia, wanting to hear the news in person than through the obvious broken telephone method that populated her in-box.

"Well, you're going to hear all about it now!" Sylvia giggled, moving closer to her. She caught a whiff of Sylvia's trademark overly floral-scented perfume that always itched her nose, forcing her to hold back a sneeze. "Arin is going to make a big announcement this morning at 11 am in the boardroom. Apparently the CEO is here, too. What do you think he's going to tell us?"

She felt her heart sink for no particular reason. She was not worried that she was going to get into trouble for her lack of job performance. Actually, she knew that she was one of the top producers and one of the most accountable in the entire division. But she felt those seeds multiply in her stomach, feeling a forest now beginning to flourish in her inner compartments of flesh and gases.

"I really don't know, Syl. They're always talking about 'restructuring' aren't they? Maybe it's something to do with that?"

Sylvia stayed quiet momentarily as though she hadn't even contemplated that that was the cause of the meeting. She probably thought that they were chosen to participate in some twisted reality show, Darcy thought. *Poor woman.*

"You're always so sensible and always so right," Sylvia replied, sitting up from the desk top and straightening her barely-there skirt. "I guess I'll see you at 11!"

With that, Sylvia moved to a nearby staff at a neighboring cubicle and continued her gossip tirade. Darcy saw in her inbox that there was indeed an email requesting her presence in the boardroom that morning at 11 am, sent from none other than slimy Arin Ray. She felt instantaneously alarmed and annoyed at having to go to such a meeting, partly because she didn't really like to consort with her colleagues if she didn't have to, and partly because of the sense of dread that she begun to feel the night before.

Glancing at her alarm clock that sat atop her desk (a gift from Chip), she felt that the minutes were taking unusually long to pass. She tried to burrow herself into her assigned work, purposely not looking at the time that constantly prevailed on her computer screen or flashing on the alarm clock to her right, but every time she did steal a glance at either of the times, she felt like 11 am couldn't come fast enough.

***

The day had turned somewhat dark, and not just because of the impending doom that she had been sensing. The skies seemed to become full of clouds that blocked any rays of sunshine that could have potentially lifted her moods. In fact, it almost looked like it was just a matter of time before a torrential downpour was set to happen. She even thought she heard thunder, but then later realized it was her stomach growling. The granola bar she had had for breakfast that morning was clearly not cutting it.

If she thought there was a buzz of excitement in the office earlier that morning, then there now was a proverbial symphony made of energy and auras that flooded her fields of vision. It had seemed as though everyone had had just one too many cups of coffee. She tried to appear non-enthused by the general state of insanity in the usual humdrum office.

Once she noticed that 10 am came and went, she forced herself to use the ladies room. She didn't know how long the meeting would go on for, and regrettably she recalled the last meeting the office had held. It was regarding the merger of two law firms, hers being one of them, and it had taken nearly 3 hours to describe the anticipated changes that would impact each and every employee. She had just scarfed down a hot dog and a big gulp (she was post-break up and feeling particularly down on that spring day) and booked it into the meeting.

Halfway through the introductions of the new CEO's and executives, Darcy had felt a gentle tug in her stomach. She thought it was her too-tight pants just once again digging into her tummy area, but soon the tug turned into a loud growl. Her co-workers were polite and didn't look over in her direction, but she knew they heard it. It was impossible not to.

She tried folding her legs to minimize the gurgling sounds that seemed to take over the large, boring, tiled boardroom, echoes bouncing off the walls from time to time. Her face had begun to turn an impossible shade of red, and began to slowly chastise herself for having eaten a meal in under two minutes, and couldn't stand it any longer. She tried to be inconspicuous and walk towards the door of the boardroom where the washroom just lay steps beyond, but to get there, she had to walk by the entire panel of new bosses and their assistants. She opted to just 'hold it in' but soon she became so uncomfortable that she had no choice but to get up abruptly from where she sat beside Sylvia and make a bee-line to the bathroom, en-route knocking over the new CEO's water bottle which she noticed had fallen all over his PowerPoint presentation before she flew into the stall and did her business.

From that point onwards, she had vowed to herself that she would use the washroom before attending anything that had no set end time.

Washing her hands in the bathroom after using the facilities, Darcy noticed two co-workers enter, their voices heightened and their movements hurried, almost as though moving in fast forward.

Darcy didn't know their names but they were Sylvia-esque. Middle aged, slightly frumpy and wearing pastel colors to the max. They continued to speak to one other as though Darcy wasn't in the room.

"…and Mr. Thomas just got up and left," one woman said, applying another layer of red lipstick so dark that her lips almost resembled an open wound.

"Really?!" the other replied, clearly surprised and riveted by her friends reveal. "Didn't he clear out his office or talk to anyone else before leaving the building? That seems a bit of an extreme action, especially coming from him."

Darcy could not have agreed more. Mr. Thomas was their general supervisor and was seen as the unofficial head of the firm, next to his silent partner. It did seem very bizarre for him to take any kind of severe action after having had a meeting of any kind, and to leave the building without even grabbing anything out of his office seemed hard to believe.

"Not a single thing", the other woman said, spritzing herself with perfume whose smell reminded Darcy a bit like a funeral home. "Everyone was looking at him as he ran out and he didn't even look back. So strange."

The two women then descended into other unimportant small talk as Darcy left the room after having taken already too long to dry her hands. She felt the seeds of anxiety flourish in her stomach, reminding her again of her big gulp/hot dog experience, and walked back to her desk, deftly afraid of what the meeting that was only minutes away was going to present to her.

***

The boardroom was average in its decor, which was sort of always a mystery to her seeing as the firm always went on and one about how prestigious it was and how so many famous clients came in and came out of its large oak doors. The doors were indeed impressive and larger than life, but the table that sat in the center of the boardroom seemed to be made out of a poor quality wood. It was indeed enormous, nearly taking up the entire room which was larger than her apartment all together, and could have easily accommodated upwards of 75 people if need be. But today, Darcy noted, the room was only comprised of the staff she saw day in and day out, which couldn't have totaled more than 50.

She opted to venture into the boardroom once she noticed the steady stream of visibly agitated staff members begin to enter its portentous doors. She knew that Sylvia would be angry for not waiting for her make a grand entrance together, but Darcy just wanted to make a clean entrance and quick exit. She wasn't comfortable with large social situations in general.

Venturing to the rear of the room where Artie the mailroom guy and Jocelyn, the overtly sexy administrative assistant to Mr. Thomas (who was notably absent) sat. They were both quiet, which Darcy mentally noted was a rare occurrence unto itself. Artie always had something to say, even if it had to deal with such mundane subjects as the weather or municipal politics that no one really cared about. Jocelyn, who nearly wasn't as chatty as Artie most times because she thought herself superior to most of the staff members, looked like she was battling a very sore stomach. Darcy secretly reveled in the flop sweat that lined the woman's wrinkle-free forehead.

At 11 am, like clockwork, Arin stood up from his perch at the head of the boardroom. He was actually well dressed today, Darcy noted, and his tie matched his suit, which in itself was a rare event. Sometimes she had just wanted to take him to the closest suit shop and pick out all of the possible suit/tie combinations that he could wear so that she would be saved from her internal monologue going on overdrive every morning when she saw his mismatched wardrobe.

"I'd like to thank you all for coming to this morning," Arin began, his voice deep and strong. Darcy began to feel weirded out by this newly confident boss of hers. Normally at their bi-annual staff meetings, Arin was noticeably nervous and even shook at times when he had to address the group as a whole, lip quiver at maximum capacity. There was no lip quiver today, which made Darcy's seeds of anxiety grow into little trees that she thought she felt pushing against the lining of her stomach.

"I realize that you all must be rather apprehensive and curious as to why we decided to schedule a meeting rather on the fly," Arin went on, deliberately trying to make eye contact with the personnel before him. "Normally, we schedule our meetings way in advance but something has happened rather suddenly, I'm afraid."

Sylvia was trying to make eye contact with Darcy, a semi-frown upon her well-donned face full of make-up from the other side of the room, but Darcy ignored her and remained focused on Arin, which was something she always deliberately tried *not* to do.

"Unfortunately, as you can see, Mr. Thomas was unable to make it to today as he had to leave unexpectedly." Darcy thought she heard her stomach growl from the seeds that were growing like they were now on steroids, but she then realized it was only Jocelyn holding back a gagging sound. Darcy didn't know if it was a forced sound or if the woman was actually going to be visibly sick in front of all her colleagues.

"It seems I have some difficult news to share with you all today. Before I tell you, however, I must thank you sincerely for all of your incredible hard work and diligence to make this firm one of the best well know in the New England area. Without you, we would still be a two-partner firm with no famous clients to our name."

It was as though the room, which had moments ago been full of a nervous, semi-excitable energy, had had all of its air completely sucked out of it, leaving everyone open-mouthed and shocked. Bad news was coming, all right, and Darcy braced herself, trees in her stomach and all.

"I'm just going to come out and say it to you all, because you deserve as much," Arin continued, a wry smile on his face. "A new, rather well-known firm will be merging with a new, very well established firm effective tomorrow. Stearns, Miller and Ross will be joining Thomas and Chide."

Darcy was not too well versed in other law firms in her city, but she did know Stearns, Miller and Ross. The firm had a very flamboyant and rather tacky building right on the downtown strip where its partners had pictures the size of billboards lining the front of the building. It was absurdly famous, Darcy remembered, as there was a long list of clients who had won their cases when the entire world was sure of their guilt.

"This is exciting news, yes," Arin hammered on. "But I'm afraid there is bad news that must accompany it. As you very well know, Stearns, Miller and Ross is a very successful firm, and as such, they have a very large staff. Which means, unfortunately, we will have to let some of you go,"

Darcy felt her heart beat quicken, joining Jocelyn with flop sweat appearing on her brow. She was expecting some sort of bad news, there was no denying that, but possibly being laid off was certainly not one of them. She looked over at Sylvia who looked confused and blushing.

"Which ones of us will be let go?" Artie immediately said loudly, startling Darcy and other nearby staff.

"Well, it was certainly a difficult decision," Arin continued. The two foreign faces that sat beside him, one woman who had a striking resemblance to Felicity Huffman while in character in her film Transamerica, and a man who was non-distinguishable in any way, looked at one another as though afraid to face the crowd before them.

"Seeing as everyone here is so hard working, well, for the most part," Arin laughed, causing Darcy to flinch. His comic timing was horrendous and this only confirmed it. "We couldn't lay people off based on job performance. So, collectively, the new firm and I made some executive decisions. Everyone who has less than 10 years seniority will be leaving us effective today. I realize it's very short notice but Gilda here from Human Resources will be able to help you with any questions that you may have. Once you return to your desks after this meeting is completed, you will find a package on your desk for those of you who will be leaving the firm immediately."

Darcy felt her heart fall deeply into her stomach. Actually, she thought it may have fallen into her pelvis and then spill onto her upper thighs. She'd only been with the firm for five years, and despite her stellar work ethic and job performance, she was being let go. The color drained from her face, as did the faces of her colleagues within certain pockets in the room around her. She felt as though she was trapped within a bad dream, a terribly awful one at that, but she knew that wasn't the case. She was being fired and there was absolutely nothing she could do about it.

Chapter 7

If she had to wager money earlier that morning how she was going to spend the rest of her Monday afternoon, she would have been placed in the poor house faster than the rate she was going to it now, post-firing. From the time in which Arin made the announcement that everyone at the firm with less than 10 years of service was being made redundant to her current state (puffy-eyed from crying and cradling a liter of Ben and Jerry's Chocolate Peanut Butter ice cream in her lap like it was a newborn baby) atop her sofa. Even her dog sensed there was some sort of seismic shift happening and she kept her little hiney in the den area that she liked to call her own room.

Darcy felt catatonic, coma-like at best. She found herself wishing with every fiber of her being that sleep would come, but instead her mind continued to play cruel tricks on her and provided seemingly random short memories of the eventful morning at the office. She would nod off at times, either due to the sugar overload or the many tears she had shed, but would always re-awaken instantaneously as though she was being shaken awake by some imaginary force. In those instances, her dog would cock her little head from side to side, long ears standing at full attention. For a brief instant, she thought that perhaps losing her job was indeed just a bad dream that was a result of her over-intake of ice cream, but then she realized that it was no bad dream but a harsh, cold, and entirely unexpected reality.

She sat up on her couch and sighed heavily, hearing the air flow out of her nose. She was a bit congested due to the outpouring of tears, and a pile of used tissues lay beside her on the sofa with a few sprinkled on the cream carpet before her. Before settling into her candy/tear filled catatonia, she did manage to pull her blinds shut to block out any semblance of light that may have entered the small apartment, and ensured that all lights had been turned off to create a cave-like vibe that she felt was the only environment she could tolerate at that particular moment in time.

Looking down at the towering pile of tissues and newborn-sized ice cream container in her lap, she saw a large, brown glob glistening on her blazer. At first she wondered what the stain was and how it got there, but then quickly figured that it was a fallen glob of the ice cream she was manically ingesting. Chastising herself for not changing out of her work clothes (*were they still work clothes if you didn't have a job?* she wondered), she ventured slowly into her bedroom steps away from her living room and changed into a more appropriate sweat suit ensemble.

Leaving her work/unemployed work clothes in a random mound on her hardwood floor, she flopped onto the bed, appreciating its warmth and comfort. She honestly surprised herself with the intense and overwhelming emotions she found herself feeling after being fired. She often guffawed and secretly judged those people who

60

claimed their life was over after being fired from their jobs, for not having a reason to live. You could just get another job, she remembered having thought to herself after many occasions, often saying these words aloud to her television set to an A and E true-life docu-series.

But now that she was experiencing the exact same thing as those untouchable and unreal real people on television. She was inexplicably overcome with disbelief and dismay, and to a certain extent, anger. Darcy Platt was not one to get fired. She had had the same part time job for 8 years, all the way until she finished her undergraduate degree in Sociology. She was the kind of person who left a job willingly, not because she was being forced out. *Darcy Platt*, she thought to herself, *was a walking mess*.

Feeling the stress build in her chest, she picked up the phone and dialed Sonya's work number. She didn't like to bore or bother her friends with her life issues, but she felt that this recent life development warranted a phone call.

Hearing the phone ring, she noticed on her alarm clock that it was nearly 2 pm, and hoped that Sonya wasn't tied up in some crazy deadline or in a marathon meeting.

She felt her hopes dashed when Sonya's voicemail came on, her voice at once chipper and confident.

"Hi, Son – It's me. Bad, bad day. Actually might have been the worst one ever," Darcy said, her voice unrecognizable to herself as it sounded dry and senior-like. "Call me back ASAP. If I don't answer, it's because I have decided to drown myself in the bath-tub in whiskey and rum and whatever else I have left from my New Years Party. Bye."

She waited for a quick call back from Sonya, but nothing came. She added another mental X to the quality of her bad day.

***

It was close to 6 pm when she decided to bite the bullet and take the dog for a walk. The idea of being in sunlight and outdoors, not to mention in the presence of other people, made her feel like she was going to throw up, but she knew she had to take her little lady out. It had been nearly six hours of literal moping around the apartment, in between crying bouts and wall punching. Maybe clearing her head and getting fresh air was not such a bad idea.

They circled the block a few times, each lap picking up more and more momentum. The poor little dog was clearly exhausted, her little legs trying to keep apace with Darcy's long strides. The sidewalks were empty, much to Darcy's contentment, but the sun was so bright she pulled her hoodie over her head to block it out, to no success.

Making the last lap around the block, she saw her apartment building come into view. A UPS truck sat idling out front, its black smoke pluming into the air. She would have glared at the driver had he or she actually been in the truck, but no one was there. She almost contemplated getting in the car and turning the ignition off, throwing the keys into the rear somewhere, but she didn't have the energy to exert anything more than moving her legs.

Once back within the safe confines of her apartment building, she pressed the up button on the elevator, waiting for her ride, when the doors suddenly opened and the UPS delivery man stepped out, startled at someone being so close to the open doors.

"Oh, sorry," the man said, his voice clearly apologetic. "I didn't see you."

He was young, her age probably. She wondered why someone that age would willingly be a delivery person. Did he just work to support his drug habit? He *was* really skinny, she thought. Or was he so loaded that he just needed to do something to earn some cred to his more moderately successful friends? She did notice his stark blue eyes, however. And she felt them staring at her as she didn't make any motion to move away from blocking the elevator doors.

"How could you have seen me? You were on the elevator", she replied rudely, catching herself. He looked visibly hurt.

"Listen, I'm sorry," she apologized. "I just had the more horrible day and you were the first live person that I've run into."

Why am I apologizing, she thought.

"It's ok, I have days like that all the time," he replied, smiling back. His teeth were perfectly straight and white. Non-smoker or coffee drinker there, she thought. "My job isn't exactly blue collar."

"At least you have one," she muttered, stepping onto the elevator. She pressed the button to close the elevator door before seeing him trying to continue the conversation.

Upon getting to her apartment door, she saw a large brown manila envelope taped to her door. Surprised that she actually received a package of some kind, from UPS precisely, she tore the envelope off the door and walked into the apartment.

Kicking off her shoes and throwing her heavily linted blue sweater on the floor, she sat on the small chair by the kitchen table. She examined the envelope, which had her name spelled out in bright, capital letters. In the top corner of the envelope she noticed her Property Management company's addresses imprinted neatly.

Figuring it must be some sort of communication on the importance of diverting her waste or keeping the noises down in the apartment building after 11 pm, she tore open the envelope and scanned over the letter.

The first warning was that the letter was personally addressed to her as the tenant. These letters she received were usually always pretty generic. She felt her back, and guard, rise. She continued to read the letter, her eyes growing larger and larger with every word. It read:

"Dear Darcy Platt.

We regret to inform you that this property has been purchased by Charlemagne Property Co-Operative Services. Thusly, this corporation will be converting this apartment building into condominium units. You will have the opportunity to purchase the apartment at market value. If you are unable to purchase this unit, or are not interested as such, please accept this letter as notification of required removal from the unit effective in 30 days."

Shocked, she dropped the letter to the ground. How could this be? She was being *evicted*? She had lived here for 5 years and not once has the property management company ever let on that the building was for sale. And 'opportunity to purchase the apartment at market value' was not something she could even contemplate purchasing, especially not with her just having lost her job earlier that day.

She felt the blood rise into her face, flop sweat forming on her forehead. She felt both hot and cold, a pulsing headache pounding in her temples. She was in disbelief at the day's events, but she knew that they were indeed factual. Feeling her chest tighten with anxiety, she ran into her hallway and put on her shoes.

She only had one thought on her mind. It was a thought that she did not know why it had presented itself at that particular moment, or why she was acting upon it so willingly. Shutting her door hastily behind her, she entered the apartment hallway with one destination in mind: Marina's Book Shop.

Chapter 8

She burst through the front door of Marina's like a crazy woman running away from an invisible assailant. Her usual sort-of-straight hair was in manic disarray from the sudden wind that had begun to blow fast and furiously at her back as soon as she escaped the subway station. She must have looked like a genuinely eccentric individual, or at least a homeless one, to the casual passengers on the subway that she came across on the short trip from her apartment. Her sweat pants seemed to have gotten more stained from incidents she couldn't even recall, and her sweater was covered completely in dog hair and mammoth lint balls. She hadn't even had time to tie up the laces on her running shoes, and nearly tripped over them several times on her way out of the desolated subway entrance. All in all, she was a Class A mess.

As always seemed to be the case when she visited Marina's,

there were absolutely no other customers browsing the shelves or chatting about recent new releases or rediscovering old favorites. The shop seemed to be as empty as ever. In fact she thought that the store may have been closed to the public, but seeing as it was relatively early in the evening, she nixed the thought as quickly as it entered her head.

Griffin sat at his usual perch at the cashier area and she found herself making a quick beeline towards him. Instantly noticing her intensity and half-crazed look, the older man immediately put down the book he was reading and sat it atop the long, darkly wooden ledge and turned towards her.

"Miss Darcy, are you ok?" he asked, his deep voice full of worry. His wrinkled forehead folded into a thousand little lines of concern and Darcy felt her heart melt a little. If it wasn't for her state of delirium, she thought she would hug the man right then and there – embracing the awkwardness and all. "You look…"

"Insane? I know," she interrupted him. She looked around the shop deliriously, scanning for Marina's whereabouts but also double-checking to confirm that the shop was truly indeed void of customers. She didn't want an audience to witness her current state of apparent mania.

"I need to speak to Marina. Where is she?"

She almost didn't recognize the urgency and ruthlessness in her voice. She sounded demented – the tone totally worrisome to her very own ears. Before her, she took notice of Griffin growing visibly uncomfortable at her shrill tone, despite the obvious fact that he did not bat a single eyelash above his enormously blue eyes.

"Is there something I can help you with? Marina is busy at the moment in her office," he continued. "Maybe a glass of water or a nice cup of tea, perhaps?"

Without even responding to the man's gentle words offering assistance to settle her current agitated state, she instead opted to turn around and head towards Marina's second floor office. Though it seemed longer than that, it was only days ago she had heard the imaginary sounds of the argument between the older woman and the invisible man.

Griffin tried to follow her but she was too fast for him. Before she even noticed how fast she was indeed marching, she had bounded up the shiny oak steps to Marina's office. A light was turned on inside the room but the door was closed, evoking an ambience of eeriness to the already bizarre situation. She felt momentarily guilty for being so curt with Griffin, but she knew that if she didn't do what she planned to do at that exact moment, her unbelievable opportunity would be gone forever.

Without even knocking, she turned the knob that was nearly the size of her waist and used whatever force she could muster to open the door. She felt a slight tug at her shoulder which she hoped would not turn into some sort of pulled muscle situation later that evening. She did not want to risk the chance of knocking on the door only to find Marina not wanting to see her at that moment, and so she threw herself into the office with fervent strength. The pain in her shoulder began to blaze at her most recent exertion.

Marina looked up immediately from the documents she was reviewing at her causal perch behind the oak desk. The desk itself was colossal, almost the size of Darcy's dining table. Bare except for a few sheets of paper, a pen and a lamp, the desk loomed wide before the diminutive woman, making her look even smaller than she already was.

"Hello Darcy," Marina said as Darcy walked hurriedly towards the desk. Darcy noticed that the woman didn't even sound remotely surprised or taken aback from her rude entrance and boisterous attitude. "Please, have a seat."

Pointing to the lone chair that sat before the desk, Darcy sat down quickly.

"You look puzzled. Stressed even," Marina continued. "Not yourself."

"I *am* not myself," she replied, her voice low and oddly serene. She attempted to catch her breath but her rapidly beating heart and sweaty forehead made that impossible to achieve.

"Today has literally been the worst day of my life and I feel like I am falling apart. I don't know what to do."

Tears began to fall upon her reddened cheeks without any kind of warning. She was not normally an emotional person by any means, and she felt embarrassed at the raw admission of emotion before Marina. She prided herself immensely on not showcasing her emotions as easily as her friends and family did. She felt that tears were an incredibly personal event that should only be shown to others at perhaps a funeral - or after the kind of terrible day that she'd found herself just having to endure.

"Losing one's job is not easy," Marina said, staring intently at her.

Darcy was surprised for the umpteenth time that day. How did Marina know she lost her job? Was it that obvious? Was there a nanny cam in her purse, recording and tracking her every move?

"How did..." she began to say but it was now Marina who interrupted her abruptly.

"I know everything and nothing. You are a special person, Darcy. I hope I know the reason why you have come to see me today. As you have said, you have had the 'worst day of your life' and being here before me you would like to change that, yes?"

Darcy couldn't help but nod. She felt exhausted, drained and exhilarated all at the same time. She felt small and miniscule in the chair she sat upon, and also pathetic at her current state. While she did indeed have a completely disastrous day, at that particular moment she felt immature for not being able to handle it like an adult (whatever that had meant exactly she wasn't sure), but she knew it wasn't falling into a puddle of tears, babbling to a middle aged woman who ran the bookshop she loved so much and entertaining the insane notion of entering a fictional world where she

68

would be the perfect teen in a perfect world, leading a perfect teenaged experience.

"The absolute worst. And it's not even as though my life would be less awful tomorrow", she finally said, her voice teeny-tiny. "I feel like I've lost control. And what's funny is that the only thing I could really think of whilst all of these awful things were happening to me was…"

"My offer," Marina answered her. "All you've thought about was the possibility of you becoming the heroine of the books that you've loved so much as a child, and still love so much as an adult."

"Yes," was all she could mutter. After talking with her best friend for most of Saturday, and trying to distract herself with 'life maintenance' as she had called it on Sunday, the idea of Marina's offer always seemed to infiltrate her thoughts. The rational part of her mind, which she noted was all she seemed to act upon in recent times, reminded her of the impossibility of the book shop owner's offer. But the magical part of her, the part that was catered to and made effervescent while reading these teen fiction books, told her to suspend her beliefs and just do it - Nike style.

"I am glad to hear that," Marina stated, getting up from her desk and slowly walked towards her. Looking as well poised and put together as she always did, replete with bun and all, she leaned against her desk and looked deeply at Darcy.

"You are saying that you would like to say yes to what I've offered you? The chance to be the lead character, if you will, in the types of books that you like to read so much?"

"Yes. I would just LOVE to be in these teen books. Any single one – I can't afford to be picky right now. I can't handle this adult stuff. I can't handle the constant difficulties of making decisions that are so important. Of the prospect of finding another job. Or finding another place to live!" she said, noticing her voice rise, but she felt helpless.

"Then close your eyes," Marina replied, her voice low, calm,

69

and strong. "It is time."

"Right now?" Darcy declared, surprised. She didn't know that now was going to be the exact moment that her life would change for the better. She was sort of expecting having to change into some sort of ceremonial cloak and listen to some Enya-inspired music – not sitting in an office chair in dirty sweat clothes.

"Do you know of another good time? Now is when we will make your dream come true," Marina soothed. "Close your eyes."

She did as she was told and closed her eyes, the room suddenly blanketed in darkness. She sensed the lamp in the room being turned off though Marina did not make any movement, no matter how minute.

She felt Marina's soft hands upon her closed eyes. They were cool – and welcoming to the heat that had just been released from her expulsion of tears.

"Just breathe," Marina asked. "Just find your breath and find your way. Just be."

Darcy listened to the instructions and focused on her breathing, relishing in the oxygen entering her lungs and then being dispelled through her nostrils. Her breathing became calm, and instantly her mind began to clear. She had begun to forget about the day's events, and silence and darkness began to blanket her entire body.

She immediately began to feel as though she were floating. It was sort of like when she had had her wisdom teeth removed a few months ago at the Dentist's office. She felt both light and like she was levitating all at once.

Giddy with excitement and her mind, as usual, racing with many, many questions (what would happen to her normal life? Who would take care of the dog? What would she look like as a teen?), she felt herself floating higher and higher, like a rogue balloon flying to the heavens after being let go at a child's birthday party. A cool breeze fell upon her cheek and she felt more alive than she'd ever felt before. A gentle buzz began to sound from within her very core.

It was like she had just ingested about 100 cups of coffee and the caffeine was pulsating in her veins.

She soon realized that Marina was indeed a magical woman. And after watching paranormal movie marathons on television and supposed true accounts of near death experiences, why couldn't this proposition of entering a fake world a-la Neverending Story be true for her? Her life had always been safe, risk-free and semi-boring, making her the perfect candidate to have something unbelievable ludicrous but supposedly feasible happen to. Something otherworldly was indeed happening to her at that moment, and for once in her life, she wasn't worried about what was going to happen.

Chapter 9

"Good Morning, sleepyheads! Today is going to be a balmy high of 84 degrees. Better get your suits on and head on down to Chester Bay before there's no room left on those sandy white beaches!" the radio voice blared, a near perfect blend of Ryan Seacrest and Jay-Z. She tried to reach around to turn the blasted thing off, her hands reaching out and grabbing all around her but touching nothing. The night table that was usually by her bed wasn't. Her hands instead touched something fluffy and soft.

Momentarily confused, she did what she always did when she found herself in such a state and in a bed: she pulled the sheets over her head, deliberately blocking out the outside world for as long as she possibly could. She hadn't noticed any sunlight in her room, which she found odd as she clearly couldn't afford any kind of decent blackout blinds and thus didn't have any, but did not think twice about it. She became aware of the luxurious feeling of the bed sheets (*silk,* she thought, *I can't afford silk sheets*!) underneath her skin. With the sheet firmly draped over her head, she finally mustered up enough courage to open her eyes.

A shred of light tried to infiltrate through the sheet, but like the rest of the room, it was mostly dark under the cover. She had a hard time making out anything in the blanketing darkness, except for her glowing legs, which looked abnormally long and shiny. She ran her hands down them, marveling at how Amazonian and freshly waxed they felt. She couldn't stop touching their softness, until she suddenly remembered what happened (or seemed to) just moments before in Marina's office.

It all came back to her, firing and all, nearly causing her to faint. The strange night at Marina's Book Shop, the weird paranormal activity of the conversation that was had between Marina and the invisible person, the argument that no one heard but her, the doors slamming and loud whispering that didn't even make Griffin look up from his post as Store Master, and the notice that her apartment was going to become a condo. And the conversation between herself and Marina where she agreed to the unbelievable idea of becoming a heroine in a teen fiction novel.

She quickly brought her hand up to her head, rubbing her left temple at the sheer painfulness of remembering the previous day's catastrophes. The short but momentous discussion she had with Marina that seemed to have thrust her into this completely preposterous situation, seemed foggy and untrue. However, upon touching her new legs once more, she knew something fateful had truly indeed happened. But to what extent she wasn't completely sure and was rather reluctant to find out. She blamed this on the non-hangover headache that made her head literally feel like it was going to burst.

"No way!" she screamed out loud, shocked by the sound of her voice. She looked around thinking there was someone else in the bed with her, but as far as she could see, it was still only her and her freakishly long legs. Her voice sounded gravelly and husky, as though talking was some sort of new concept for her.

I sound like Lindsay Lohan, she thought. *It can't be. There's no way Marina could have made this happen. Things like that don't happen. They don't happen to me or to anyone because they're impossible!*

She took in a deep breath. The sudden intake of air caused her to get a cramp in her stomach, but with every succeeding breath, the pain elapsed. She attempted to gain composure and calm herself down but she realized that was not going to happen. Not now, at least. All of her senses felt heightened, new in their tenacity. Her heartbeat was racing a million miles an hour, and she felt hot and sweaty. Given that she was under the cover, she gathered enough strength and threw down the sheet over her body.

You can do this! Darcy continued to think to herself, her thoughts a never-ending monologue. *You're probably just dreaming and will wake up any second. And plus, a really huge, mega plus, you're a 30-something old woman who thinks she sounds like Lindsay Lohan. You're obviously going crazy.*

The darkness she encountered under the sheet was characteristic of the entire room: nary a sliver of light was discernible. After taking a few more short seconds to let her eyes adjust, Darcy began to feel around herself in the permeating darkness, her arms tentative and cautious. She sat up slowly in the bed and slowly stood up. She turned to what she thought was her right (she didn't know – she had absolutely no internal compass) and walked straight into the apparently fluffy nightstand she had groped earlier.

She felt the soft, deep, plush carpeting below her feet, a drastic difference to the usual sale rugs she bought at IKEA. The carpet almost made her feel like she was getting a massage just by walking on it.

She moved her hands quickly now over the low standing fluff ball, aka night stand, trying to find something she could use to get some light into the room. Hoping to find a cell phone or a lamp of some kind, her hands touched what felt like a remote control. Not wanting to turn on a stereo or television or something of the like, but also not wanting to remain in darkness, she hoped for the best and pressed several of the buttons on the tiny remote in her hands.

She instantly heard a gentle buzzing sound that was a cross between a microwave and an electric razor, and suddenly the room began to slowly brighten. The remote control apparently served the purpose of opening the floor-to-ceiling drapes that covered three mammoth windows that took up the entire left side of the room.

This isn't happening, she thought as the room around her became lighter and lighter until the blinds reached flush beside the nearby walls. From where she stood, all she could make out were some treetops and an expansive blue sky. She squinted as she took in the site, and for a moment, her headache disappeared and she felt better.

She slowly took in the room around her, her heart still beating like it was going to erupt of her chest and cause a bloody mess around her. Her forehead broke a sweat, and whatever she was wearing clanged gently to her back.

The room seemed to be about the entire size of her apartment, bearing absolutely no resemblance to her own humble abode. The floor was entirely carpeted in plush cream carpeting, and being the same colors as the painted walls, made the entire room look like one amazing lounge. She sort of half-expected waiters to suddenly appear beside her and ask her what she would like to drink. Instead, the silence of the room was the only kind of volume she thought she could tolerate at that moment.

The king-sized bed where she laid down just moments ago loomed beside her, massive and inviting. What must have been a 50 inch television screen was mounted on a wall directly in front of her, though at least 10 feet away. A desk that had the world's smallest computer on top of it sat just to her right. What Darcy really found herself looking for, however, was a mirror.

I am insane and apparently my state of insanity makes me

believe I'm in a teen girls bedroom, she thought as she looked around the room for a mirror. She saw a door to her left, hoping it opened into a closet or a bathroom, and made a mad dash to see if she was right. En route, she found herself continually pinching her arm over and over again to wake her up from her vivid dream but stopped when her arm began to turn red and feel sore.

She swung open the door and was faced with a closet that while bigger than most closets she had ever seen, still had a charm to it that didn't immediately overwhelm her the way the bedroom reveal had. A full length mirror hung behind the door she had just opened, and she turned around to face herself.

When she saw her reflection, she immediately had to bring her hand to her mouth to stifle the scream that was going to rip out of her. She closed her eyes and then re-opened them, one at a time, to take in the reflection as slowly as possible. She was taller than she'd ever been, venturing to say at least 5'8, her usual mousy brown hair now a glowing strawberry-blonde that fell effortlessly in loose waves over her shoulders. She moved her hands to her waist and marveled at its tiny size. She couldn't remember the last time she was this size – 11th grade maybe?

Her body was thoroughly and completely tanned, something she had never, ever been in all of her life. She noticed that it wasn't an artificial tan that other teenage girls had, but natural. She was secretly thankful for that fact as she thought tanning beds were unnecessary if you lived by the beach. Even though she had just woken up, she looked like she had just come back from a glamorous photo shoot. There almost seemed to be an invisible fan causing her hair to move ever so slowly around her shoulders. She felt like Beyonce.

"Marina! What did you do!" Darcy screamed, this time letting her voice leave her throat. The husky voice that she now came to recognize as her own filled the room, reverberating off the walls. She yelped as she instantly heard a short little knock on a nearby

door, which she quickly deduced was the door to her bedroom. Not saying a word, she waited. She thought if she didn't make a single sound, that her current predicament would disappear.

"Darcy, darling," she heard a female voice say, a tinge of concern present. "Are you ok in there?"

This person must have been standing just outside the bedroom door and she had no idea if the door itself was locked or not, so she decided to just remain quiet.

The doorknob slowly began to turn and the door swung open. She instantly pulled the closet door towards her and shut it so as to not face whomever it was coming into her room, even though locking herself in the closet was probably going to make things ultimately worse. She just needed some time to figure things out. She didn't want to meet the new Darcy's family just yet.

"What are you doing?" the woman continued. She pulled open the closet door and found Darcy, in nothing but tiny underwear and a t-shirt, staring back blankly.

Darcy took in the woman before her. Tall, blonde, tan and beautiful, the woman must have been her mother. Strangely enough, she did not find the appearance of this woman all that shocking as she felt something present that reminded her of her own mother, despite there being no actual physical resemblances. The soft eyes perhaps, or the frown that reminded Darcy how much she was loved, was similar. What was different, however, was everything else. She was much taller than her real mother, that was a given, and she looked like she was either a former model or beauty pageant queen. No wrinkles in sight, this woman looked to have stepped right off of the set of the Real Housewives of Darcy's Insane Dream. Her eyes took in Darcy's scared and frightened expression, and the frown came back.

"Honey, please, it's already past 7:30. You're going to be late for school," her mother said. She reached over and pulled her by the arm and sat her on the bed. "Your father brought in your BMW for servicing so you can borrow your brother's Mercedes since he's not coming back from Prague until, well, apparently next month according to his last email. That brother of yours – going to Europe to 'find himself' in the middle of the fall term in college. When I was that age, your wretched grandmother made me get a job at the Kmart and scout eligible bachelors for her and her Bridge Club members. That evil, rotten, dried-up thing."

Her mother began to tidy up her room, completely absent-mindedly.

My BMW? Darcy thought. *My brother! I don' have a brother! Marina, get me out of here. This is just too unreal.*

"And don't forget to pick up Claire. I promised her mother I'd keep an eye on her while they were closing that deal in Monte Carlo," her mother went on. She took in one last look of Darcy and left the room, closing the door softly behind her.

That was the precise moment that Darcy began to hyperventilate. She looked earnestly for a paper bag to breathe into, knowing full well this new life she was thrust into wouldn't have such a thing, *if this girl even at'*, she thought. She collapsed onto the bed, her pulsating headache back and in full effect. She tried to clear her head, thinking calming thoughts, which temporarily helped in getting her heartbeat to settle down, and to get her breathing back to somewhat normal.

Composed, she got up once more and walked into her closet to behold her reflection. She glanced at her body, starting at the impeccably manicured feet and moving her gaze slowly upwards to her blemish-free face. She had the body of a perfect teenage girl, who lived in an enormous house, and found herself begin to smile.

Hmm, Darcy thought, running her hands through her lustrous hair. *Maybe I can make this work out after all.*

Chapter 10

Mustering up the bravery to finally leave her room some twenty minutes later, there was no denying the fact that she was feeling pretty great. Ethereal, even. Walking on air and the whole bit. Her step was literally lighter because she was *literally* pounds lighter.

She had quickly ransacked her newfound closet to find something suitable to wear for the day, though she did not have any iota or clue of what the day would bring upon her. Ultimately, after a brief heeing-and-hawing session which involved a lot of bottom lip biting and grunt making, she decided upon wearing a pair of skinny jeans that would have normally cut off her circulation, and a t-shirt that clung to her new, young body in all of the right places. With a noticeable spring in her step, similar to the one she typically had when she visited Marina's, she decided to take the plunge and exit her bedroom. If she didn't keep the spring step in check she would propel herself right off the top stair landing.

Exiting her room, she allowed herself a brief moment to take in the beautiful home that surrounded her. The neutrally painted walls, elegant art work (*was that a Dali?* she wondered), and plush carpeting similar to what was in her bedroom, gave the home an elegant and definite high class feeling, a feeling that she was completely unaccustomed to.

She had grown up sensibly with hard-working middle class parents who believed in the value of breaking a sweat and paying your dues to get ahead. Being the youngest child of three girls, Darcy always felt privileged in that unlike her friends, she didn't have to share her toys or clothes and anything, really. Her sisters were all much older. She did envy, however, seeing her friends play with their brothers and glimpsing their special kind of relationship.

However, now knowing that the 'new' her had a brother floating around somewhere out there, in Prague apparently, made her excited and giddy. She would finally have the chance to form a relationship with a brother who would be privy to all of her secrets and emotions because that's what brothers did. There would be a brother related to her by blood whom she could share her feelings with, no matter how inane or trivial.

After reaching the bottom of the stairs, she turned left at the massive staircase with its oak trim and marble handles into the kitchen that was not only blinding white, but completely empty. She hesitantly walked towards the breakfast bar where there lay an assortment of fruit, ranging from what appeared to be freshly cut mangos to what only she thought could have been Star fruit. Whatever it was, it was exotic and excited her, much like how food in any format generally did.

There was a note on the never-ending expansive granite counter top that immediately caught her eye after she wolfed down half of the assortment of fruit. The mango literally melted in her mouth. She had said that phrase in the past many times; however, this was the one time that it was true.

"Darcy, don't forget to pick up Claire. The keys to the car are in the Cat. Love, Mom," the note read in long, cursive writing. The writing itself reminded her of her elementary school teacher Mrs. Lever who said that printing was the lazy man's version of *handwriting.* Oh, that crazy Mrs. Lever. She could still hear her faux British accent that turned into a Brooklyn accent whenever she had gotten flustered or nervous.

The keys are in the cat, she repeated aloud, her voice ricocheting off the pristine cabinets and tiled floor. She glanced around quickly, trying to find something that resembled a cat. She was sincerely hoping that there was not an actual little live pet cat that ate random objects in the house but fortunately she found a massive ceramic cat by the back patio door.

It was the ugliest thing she had ever seen; there was no doubt about it. Standing at about 3 feet high, and entirely white, the cat practically camouflaged into the blinding whiteness of the kitchen cabinets. It stood as though it was crouching and had its mouth over what seemed to look like teeny tiny tea saucer. Lying within the saucer were a set a keys that she immediately grabbed, semi-afraid though the cat was going to scratch or hiss at her. For no particular reason she was afraid of cats, and cats certainly returned the sentiment. She was perfectly ok with that arrangement.

Before she realized it, she was made her way to the front door, as though she had walked down the hallway and around the house a million times before. The doorknob reached her chest, making her feel like a resident of Middle Earth or Alice in Wonderland. She began to slowly turn the knob, but out of nowhere and rather suddenly, she turned back into the house, leaving the door closed behind her.

How will I know my way around, she wondered. Apart from the initial difficulty in finding her closet just half an hour ago, she noticed that she was able to rather easily navigate around the second level of the home. She did not hesitate in taking a shower in the bathroom, or which way to turn when she walked down the stairs just moments ago. The Cat threw her for a loop but she *did* know that the kitchen was to the left of the stairs.

I know this house like the back of my hand, Darcy thought, which was ironic because the back of her hand was entirely new for her (and a bit freckled, she noted as she looked down at the perfectly manicured and young-looking hands before her).

Taking a deep breath, she re-opened the front door, promptly seeing the bright sunshine and cloudless blue sky. She felt her anxiety subside, and purposefully walked towards the gunmetal grey, brightly polished Mercedes that was parked in the eight car driveway. She looked up and noticed two people trimming the rose bushes and willow trees that lay just in front of the house. Both individuals were entirely focused on their tasks, but when they heard the front door slam closed, they looked up towards her, obviously startled by the sudden bang.

"Good Morning, Darcy," a stout, middle-aged woman said, her voice friendly and frail. "It's a beautiful morning."

The woman was tiny but compact, dressed in overalls that were obviously too big for her and wearing a sunhat similar to the one that Darcy, embarrassingly, wore rather religiously throughout her vacation to Mexico a few years ago. Mexico had given her a beautiful, even and golden hue (not the usual red and splotchy look, which always was the case with her) everywhere on her body but her face. Sylvia had had a field day with that one. She had to endure the rather cruel nickname "Splotcha" for weeks.

"Good morning, Glenda," she replied, the name leaving her mouth before she even realized she was saying it. She felt a pleasant and warm sensation for Glenda, like she was a source of support and love for her. Where this was coming from within her, she had absolutely no clue, but she decided to just go with it.

Glenda's dark hair was up in a pony-tail under the hat, she noticed. She was olive-skinned and handsome for an older woman.

The other person who worked alongside Glenda was a young and good-looking man. He, unlike Glenda, quickly returned to trimming the stray branches that grew from the ornate and lush rose bushes that seemingly surrounded the entire front of the home. He was tall, Darcy could tell that much, even though he was about 20 feet away. His hair fell just past his ears, glistening with sweat, his muscular arms moving quickly as he made his way along the bushes. She felt herself blush for no reason, and figured there was something she knew about this guy. She'd have to do some investigating before they struck up a conversation. If she was going to master the life of a teen girl, she was going to start off on the right foot.

Glenda looked at her as she looked at the young man. The woman then looked at the guy and back again at her, but the latter was already walking towards the car. Darcy felt Glenda look between the two of them until she was safely behind the wheel, her heart still beating from seeing the guy who did not even look up while Glenda greeted her so warmly.

Charlie, she said out loud. Just like with knowing Glenda's name without even actualizing it, she knew the young man's name was Charlie. She also knew that she felt something towards him, but what or to what extent she had no idea. All she knew at that moment was that she seemed to be firmly planted in a world that she had only read about for years. A world where she was rich, and beautiful, and had a huge home and housekeepers.

But also a world where your life will be full of problems and chaos, she remembered, turning the key in the ignition. *Which may or may not start with picking up this Claire person*, she thought as she trusted her gut and began driving the beautiful car to pick Claire up. The car handled like she was driving on air and she loved it.

***

"Darcy Platt, you are SO late," Claire screamed from her perch

83

in the driveway as she drove the car in and parked. The massive home was about the same size as Darcy's but couldn't have been more aesthetically different. There were no towering rose bushes flanking the property but she did notice several palm trees that grew very high. There was also a weird and wide assortment of topiary animals that reminded her of The Shining.

She instantly heeded that Claire was absolutely everything that that she had imagined she would during the short 10-minute drive over. All boobs and hair, Sylvia would have said. Sylvia would also have had a few choice words about her other current predicaments, she couldn't help but think to herself silently.

About 5'7 and clearly no stranger to wearing a skimpy bikini to show off her slender frame, Claire was nicely and evenly bronzed as Darcy seemed to be. She smiled as the girl bounced quite literally from the large home behind her, her long, black hair lively right along with everything else.

Claire pulled open the car door and slammed it closed behind her, causing Darcy to slightly wince from the loud sound. Her new friend could have easily been a model, or possibly even was, with her long legs and other ample assets. Even the dark mole above her ruby lips was very model-esque. Wearing a revealing black maxi-dress that just barely covered everything that it needed to, Claire put on her seatbelt and turned to face Darcy.

"What are you so late? You know I have to get to school early to meet Luke," she spat out, hatred and anger in her voice. Darcy was immediately taken aback from the ferocity of the girls words. She couldn't believe such animosity came out of such a perfectly lip-lined mouth, not to mention that the vitriol was directed towards her.

"I'm sorry," was all she could say before re-starting the car. She wasted no time in quickly pulling out of the driveway and turning towards the street, once again silently impressing herself with her built-in knowledge of where she was going. She had absolutely no idea what Claire was talking about or why she was so visibly angry, let alone who Luke even was.

"Yeah, right," her friend laughed, though there was nothing remotely comical in her voice. Darcy maintained her focus on the road before her, growing more and more uncomfortable with the dynamic that was slowly unfolding in the tight confines of the super sleek car. To break the atmosphere's relative discomfort, she decided to lean forward and turn on the radio. This was not the first type of peer-to-peer conversation she was anticipating in her new, idealistic teenage life. In fact, she couldn't remember the last time she had tolerated such an indignant tone.

"You're always sorry," Claire instantly spat back, applying another coat of lip-gloss while looking at herself in the passenger side mirror. "The one time I need you to pick me up early you roll on in 10 minutes late, like you have nothing else better to do or that you're doing me some sort of huge favor. Now Luke's probably going to think I ditched him, or stood him up or whatever, and he's going to ignore me for, like, the whole morning. You're so selfish. And what are you wearing? You look like your mom."

Darcy decided to just let a moment of silence to fill all of the proverbial hot air in the automobile until she could speed her mind up fast enough to think of some sort of retort or response.

"I said I was sorry," she finally replied, honestly apologizing for being late, though in all fairness she didn't know she *was* indeed running late as she had just been thrust into this foreign life. Automatically, she felt like she had the right way to deal with it: *refer to your expert knowledge of teen fiction dialogue*, she thought to herself while Claire seemed to grow more and more noticeably agitated. *How would Jessica Wakefield deal with this?*

"God, Claire, who stuck the gigantic stick up your ass this morning?" she finally countered, wishing with all her might that her selected response would do the trick and take Claire's anxiety and obvious anger down a few thousand notches. "Are you PMS'ing and didn't text me the heads up? You know how I hate to be caught off

85

guard with such pressing matters of our teenage existence."

Claire slowly turned to face her, momentarily shocked at Darcy's witty response, and hastily threw her cherry-red lip gloss into the enormous purse/backpack/duffle bag that sat atop her lap. Darcy momentarily thought she had really blown it but was swiftly relieved when she heard Claire burst out laughing seconds later. The deep gales of laughter seemed to come from the very core of her friend's teeny-tiny body. She felt the breath she was holding leave her body and laughed, too, as Flint Ridge high came into view before them.

The school seemed to be, rather unsurprisingly on second thought, something right out of a book. It sprawled over many acres that were lined with assorted types of trees and wooden fences. Darcy could see actual groundskeepers trimming the hedges in various spots while students looked on, fully entranced by their conversations with their peers. Situated on a hill that had a stellar view of the small town below, the school towered over the two friends. A lump quickly formed in Darcy's throat.

"Sorry, D – I just promised Luke that I'd meet him before homeroom. Let's go!" Claire giggled. The girl practically propelled herself from the car as soon as they slowed down, leaving Darcy behind to gather her own purse and park the gleaming and new-looking luxury car.

Dodged a bullet there, she thought to herself as she cautiously parked the car into a minute spot by a row of oak trees. The trees lined one of the schools many apparent walk ways that led to the school itself. The parking spot also happened to be just far enough from the school's main entrance so she and Claire could make a grand entrance. Hastily exiting the car, she walked quickly to join her friend who was already waiting by one of the enormous trees that flanked the entry to the parking lot.

She instantly felt all eyes fall upon her and Claire as they causally strolled past the tall, looming trees that led to the main entrance of Flint Ridge High. Most students, and a few teachers, seemed to stop and stare at them as they walked by. Some even nodded at them. Darcy soon noticed that Claire had no reaction or response to any of the kind gestures, giving the impression that she didn't even see them.

Following Claire's lead, she kept a blank expression upon her wrinkle-free face as they crossed the threshold of the high school. She barely had time to take in the scene, which seemed right out of West Beverly High, when she saw a woman out of the corner of her eye. A woman wearing a long red dress which was blowing in a non-existent breeze. True to form, there sat a meticulously styled red bun atop the woman's head. The woman stared at her intently, there was no mistaking that, from her position by the fountain that was ensconced in the centre of the busy school hallway which gave the school the appearance of a suburban mall rather than a high school.

Marina, Darcy thought to herself, immediately stopping following her friend before her and instead began to follow the older woman down the heavily populated hallway. Claire appeared in visible shock behind her at Darcy's quick change in direction.

As she had earlier that morning, she began to feel her heart beat speed up, threatening to erupt out of her chest. She followed Marina down another hallway, maze like in its floor plan. None of the other students seemed to find it particularly odd that one of their peers was following a strange looking woman who was completely out of place at the luxurious school.

A few braver students stole a quick glance as she walked by, and this time she smiled back at them. Without Claire in tow, she was slowly beginning to get into the swing of the new her - for however much longer she was the new her, that was.

As Marina opened a heavy aluminum door leading to the stairwell at the back of the school, Darcy found herself wondering, *That's it. It was nice while it lasted. At least I got to feel popular for a few hours. What does Marina want now?*

Holding her breath, she opened the door to join Marina to see what the woman wanted and what her random visit was hoping to accomplish.

Chapter 11

The stairwell smelled faintly of urine, sweat and candy corn. The odd concoction of scents filled Darcy's nostrils as she briskly followed Marina down the many, many steps. At once, she felt she was entering yet another kind of alternate reality as soon as the heavy thud of the door slam shut behind her. The thundering sound caused her to make a slight scream, its echo reverberating in the stairwell.

Just as she was descending the last few steps of the beige, weirdly-scented steps, she noticed her surroundings seem to completely disappear. At first she thought that perhaps maybe the power had simply gone out, but as her eyes adjusted to the overbearing darkness, the stairwell transformed abruptly into a massive, cavernous white room. Feeling like Carissa in her beloved 'Bright Nightfall' series, she slowly took in the new brightly lit environment that surrounded her. She had a rather difficult time differentiating the ceiling from the ground at her feet, which strengthened the palpable energy of the space around her.

As her eyes began to adjust to the white, lavish and seemingly never-ending room that loomed before her, she soon noticed Marina standing just steps away to her right.

The book store owner was in her typical regaled outfit, this one a beautiful, purple gown that just touched the ground, giving the illusion of her floating instead of standing on the indiscernible ground that they both found themselves upon. The woman's trademark fiery-red hair stood perfectly cropped in her trademark bun that was tightly wound atop her head. Marina's complete ensemble stood out in dark contrast to their surroundings, and its blinding whiteness. Darcy found herself instinctively shielding her eyes from the sheer intensity. She had earnestly wished that she had brought her sunglasses with her before leaving the house earlier that morning.

"Marina!" she exclaimed, her voice unintentionally loud. Oddly enough, the high volume of her voice didn't cause an echo in the all-white Mecca she was standing within.

"What are you doing here? What have you done?"

Out of nowhere, and completely inaudibly, a purple chair suddenly appeared before her. It had a very high back, reaching upwards toward the non-distinguishable ceiling. She mentally noted the chair resembled a prop out of Alice in Wonderland and looked very comfortable in all of its elegant plushness.

"Sit," Marina instructed, her voice sharp and pointed. Darcy automatically sat down without hesitation or question.

Finally being able to rest her eyes upon the diminutive woman before her, she noticed that Marina seemed to appear somewhat disparate, but she could not say really how specifically. The woman's appearance was as glamorous and demure as ever, yet something nagged at her that Marina had something noticeably quite offbeat emanating from behind her eyes. She always and only ever noticed warmness and love in the book store owner's expression, but she felt something colder now, almost callous in its nature. The recognition of this coldness caused a shiver to run to from the base of her spine to her exposed shoulder.

"You must have many questions, my dear," Marina began, sitting on a stool that, like the purple chair that appeared before Darcy just moments ago, materialized out of virtual thin air. This stool was red and more regular people sized. She chastised herself subconsciously for thinking such irrelevant thoughts at a time of crisis.

That's an understatement, she thought to herself. For some unexplainable reason, she found it unsettling sitting there before Marina. Spending time with the older woman was invariably always a joyous affair, a time in which she would be free of worry and inhibitions and truly be herself without fear of judgment or repercussions. Now, however, she couldn't help but note that the current situation seemed to be the complete opposite. She not only had the unmistakable feeling as though she was being judged, but she also felt somewhat like a guinea pig in an elaborate and well-coordinated laboratory experiment. She felt as though she was being tested, but for reasons or what end results completely unknown to her.

"In all the years I have known you, Darcy, you have always wanted to live in these worlds of teenagers, yes?" Marina declared, a smile upon her ruby red lips. Her fingers fidgeted. Darcy noticed Marina's nails slowly touching the edges of her stool, making an almost inaudible sound that echoed in the far recesses of the white room.

"Yes. We've gone over this already before you thrust me into small town USA where all of my favorite books are usually set," Darcy snapped back, unsure why she was being so defensive. She just couldn't shake the feeling that she was being interrogated. There was definitely something askew with the whole current environment - time-travel and new life notwithstanding.

"Might I remind you," Marina replied, "That you agreed to this thrusting, as you say."

Maintaining her ever-cool composure, the woman continued. "You said yes when I asked you if you wanted me to make this wish of yours come true. You are not completely innocent in all of this, Darcy."

"I didn't think it would actually happen, Marina," Darcy quickly retorted, her voice subtly quivering.

Are you going to bust out a Delorean now, Is Marty McFly going to take me to the prom?, she thought silently.

"I know this is a lot for you to process," the mysterious woman continued, oblivious to her fairly obvious cynicism. She slowly stood up from her perch atop the red, silk stool and began to slowly stroll towards Darcy, her deliberately exaggerated pace unnerving her more and more.

"But I thought that I should explain a few things to you before you got too immersed in the life of the 17 year old Darcy Platt," Marina went. She seemed to change her mind randomly and decided to sit down once more. She then focused her gaze squarely upon the girl before her.

"Well, don't you think that maybe you should have explained these things to me before I woke up this morning in the body of a teenaged girl!" Darcy yelled, not intending to do so. "I mean, I didn't honestly think that all of this could really happen."

"I understand that you are upset but are you not enjoying yourself?" Marina smiled. At that moment, Darcy caught a glimpse of the Marina she knew so well, the kind Marina, but she just could not shake off the steeliness that glinted within the woman's eye just moments ago.

With all that was going on – the smelly stairwell, her new life, the white room – she hadn't even had a single moment to truly reflect on this question, which self-admittedly was extremely unlike her. The internal monologue that was on an endless loop within her head normally beat everything to death.

She supposed she was enjoying herself in a way, but she was still really confused and shocked that Marina was able to make all of these seemingly actual real-life things occur. Sure, she agreed to enter the world of the books she read so religiously and she couldn't blame anyone else for making that decision for her. But did she think it could actually happen? A big, resounding no was the only word that filled her head.

She felt the teen books she read were always there for her, more than any person in her life ever was. The fictitious pages had acted as a way for her to unwind and put the real world's issues and worries at bay. The characters within these sensationalized, fictional worlds acted like her friends more than her actual human friends did in recent times. But she also rationally knew that these types of life events didn't happen, least of all to the single, thirty something, and lonely Darcy Platt. The girl voted most likely to be average forever. The girl who never dyed her hair. The girl who always pined for something more.

"You have to stop thinking this way," Marina said, interrupting her self-reflective daydream. "You were chosen, Darcy. From the very first day I met you, I knew you were the one," Marina declared, eyes unmoving from her face, confrontationally staring into her soul.

"Were you reading my mind just now?" Darcy asked, her voice small and scared. The words slipped out of her mouth before she even realized it.

"I was reading your heart," Marina retorted, standing up and turning her back to face her.

The words felt like a ton of bricks were thrown upon her chest. At once, she felt speechless but also felt the overbearing yearning to scream out at the top her lungs. While she didn't know why the last words Marina uttered affected her so primal like, she knew that the woman was indeed right.

"The one?" she finally managed to squeak out. She felt her

heartbeat quicken, her throat suddenly dry and parched. She leaned back upon the back of the purple chair, the softness of the upholstery feeling like a giant hug. A glass full of iced water suddenly and inexplicably appeared on a microscopic white marble table beside her. She noticed a large pink straw beckoning to her thirst. She hastily grabbed the glass and drank greedily, as though she were in the Nairobi dessert and hadn't drunk water for days.

"Yes, the one," Marina replied, standing up from her perch once more. Her dress had now turned a vivid emerald green, full of what appeared to be encrusted diamonds that shone brightly. A barrage of invisible fans blew air towards Marina's gown, causing it to flap around every which way. Darcy felt the cool breeze upon her forehead, welcoming its refreshing briskness.

"You have been chosen, Darcy. You are special. You are different from the rest."

Drinking the last few drops of water from the enormous straw, Darcy dabbed the corners of her mouth with her sleeve. "The one? The chosen one to do what?"

"The one who will change things forever. You have been granted the one wish you have always wanted. However, this wish does not come without something you must do for me," Marina whispered. Once again, she sat down atop the stool which changed to a bright, sun-like yellow.

"How will I change things forever? I don't understand," she replied, feeling more confused than ever.

"You have been put into this life of a teenage girl who you will soon find out isn't as innocent as you, or those around her, thinks she is. You will have to make some difficult decisions," Marina instructed.

"I'm sure I can handle it," she responded. She suddenly felt anger build within her chest. "Am I going to go to the prom with the good guy or the bad guy? Am I going to get a makeover or make-under? Am I going to be the mean girl or nerdy girl? I get it, Marina.

94

I've read every book where these decisions are made by a protagonist who has body issues and who may or may not come from a broken home. It's not that really that difficult or complicated."

Marina laughed a loud, shrill laugh. Darcy felt the sound reverberate within her very core, causing her to wince lightly.

"Wake up, Darcy!" Marina screamed. "I have granted your wish. You will live in this world for a time. But only you can decide if you get to stay."

"I don't understand!" Darcy answered, standing up from her chair and accidentally knocking over the glass to the floor in the process of her hasty action. She noticed that it didn't break or make any sound. If she hadn't seen it fall with her very own eyes, she wouldn't have known it wasn't atop the table any longer. Suddenly, the glass disappeared entirely.

"Stop speaking in riddles and clichés, Marina," she continued. "Tell me why I'm here and why you have granted me my wish. What have I been chosen to do? Tell me!"

The small woman took a moment before answering.

"You will live the life of the teenage girl you have always wanted to be. You will get to stay in this world if you get everyone to like you, for you to be able to make them think that you are good, that you are trying. If you do not, then, well, this is where the bad lies…"

"What do you mean? What is 'the bad'?" Darcy replied.

"The bad is my shop. My store will disappear – I will disappear – if you do not accomplish this task. You are special, and I know you saw Clifton that day in my shop", Marina declared.

"Clifton?" Darcy questioned. *Marina's totally losing it*, she thought.

"Yes, that night when I first told you about my offer. I had been arguing with him in my office. He was coming to collect what I owe him. I had told him you were ready to have your wish granted but he thought I was being too hopeful, too expectant of you. Did you not notice that Griffin did not seem to notice the doors slamming? Or our loud screams? Griffin can hear a pin drop on a loud downtown street. Did you not find it odd that he did not even look up?!" Marina yelled.

Darcy shuddered. In retrospect, she did find it extremely bizarre that only she could hear the argument in the shop, but she just thought it was perhaps because Griffin's hearing may have not been what it used to be.

"Coming to collect what?" she then asked, afraid of the answer. "What was Clifton coming to collect?"

Marina's expression quickly changed to one of pain. She looked like she was about to cry, or yell, or scream out in pain. Darcy didn't know which, but she knew it was going to be intense regardless.

"He was coming to collect me. You see, Darcy, you hold all the power. You can live in this world if you choose to, but you will have to make things right," Marina quietly said.

"Make things right? Make what things right?" she quickly replied.

"Only you will be able to know," Marina answered.

"Marina, I don't know if I want all of this responsibility. I don't understand. What will happen if I fail to 'make things right?'

Suddenly, the room that had been a blinding white turned into a composite sea of reds and oranges. The two women were at once on the edge of the horizon at dawn where no one else, no matter how big or small, existed. A giant wind flared up, causing both women to shield away from its strength.

The two women immediately sat up from their chairs, the harsh wind physically moving them. They struggled to stand, to keep their composure, but the wind's absurd strength nearly knocked them down. Darcy noticed however, terrifyingly, was that the wind did not make a sound. No swooshes. No gusts. Nothing. She felt like she was going to faint.

"Marina's will disappear. I will disappear. Griffin will disappear," Marina whispered, tears forming in her eyes. "You are the one, Darcy. You have always been the one. Make things right!"

Without any notice, her entire surroundings turned pitch black. She felt the ground below her give way, causing her to fell through empty space. Her heart fell into the far recesses of her stomach, equal parts nausea and equal parts fear. It was then that she finally did faint.

Chapter 12

"Wake up, Darcy!" Claire screamed, her voice shrill and full of worry. Darcy's new (or was it old?) best friend was hunched awkwardly over her, her lustrous long black hair swinging back and forth as though mimicking the volume of her voice. A few other students had gathered around to see what the big commotion was. Soon silent murmurs and whispers became audible around Darcy's seemingly unconscious body which lay haphazardly atop the linoleum high school hallway. Apparently, it seemed normal to the rest of the kids in school that anywhere Claire and Darcy were, there was sure to be some sort of dramatic developments.

Her eyelids slowly fluttered, the whites of her eyes flashes of light, as she struggled to keep them open fully. Finally, once she opened her eyes completely, she silently took in the scene before her

– Claire's face full of shock, the other students watching and whispering, and other casual passers-by who clearly couldn't care less that there was a student passed out on the floor.

The last thing she had remembered was that Marina was talking to her about "making things right" - whatever that had meant. She had literally no concept of what Marina was alluding to regarding the objective of this whole living in another life scenario which she found herself in, or who or what it was in reference to. She'd have to ponder that later when she wasn't lying on the semi-sticky school hallway floor with her best friend in practical hysterics kneeling beside her.

"I'm ok, Claire," she was finally able to whisper, her voice audibly shaky. Her friend grabbed a bottle of water out of her gigantic pink purse which could have easily fit a small panda bear, and quickly handed it to her. Sitting up, her head still a bit dizzy, she took a sip from the bottle that had a bright ring of red lipstick around the opening. She sincerely hoped Claire wasn't a slut. Getting an STD was the last thing she wanted to experience as a teen. She was proud of herself to make it through her first set of teenage years without getting one and she wasn't intending to get one now.

After swallowing a few more sips of water and regaining some semblance of reasonable composure, she stood up, gathering her fallen things around her. Still feeling a bit vulnerable but on the whole ok, she turned towards Claire who was already chatting with another girl who stood beside them. Judging from the physical closeness between the girls, Darcy noted that this must be a good friend to them both.

"You really scared us, Darcy," the girl said, her emerald green eyes taking in Darcy's slightly disheveled state from head to toe. Darcy instantly felt as though the girl was sizing her up and trying to figure her out. It wasn't an altogether pleasant feeling, but it did sort of fit in with the rollercoaster of emotions she had already experienced that day.

"One second you and Claire were walking into school and the next you're passed out in front of the cafeteria," the girl continued, now looking at Darcy directly instead of the once-over from moments ago. "What gives? Are you feeling ok?"

Darcy managed a weak nod as the three girls slowly began to walk towards their first period English class with Mrs. Chadwick, who according to Claire, was the one teacher in school who thought iPod's were something that people put over their eyes.

En route to the classroom, there were plenty more stares and ogles from the student body around them. Darcy didn't exactly hate the feeling of having all eyes on her, but it was strange for to encounter nonetheless.

"I'm so excited for Chrissy Barr's party tonight!" Claire suddenly shrieked, clearly completely over the drama of Darcy's apparent pass-out spell. Upon entering the nearly full classroom, all three girls seemed to sit completely in sync in their respective desks located at the rear of the room which sat conveniently empty.

"Rena, are you sure you we can still crash at your place after? My mom is being a total bitch these days with me getting in after 11 pm. She thinks that we're still stuck in 1995 or something. She doesn't get that it's only at 11 that the party actually gets started. Ugh."

Rena giggled. Her luminescent red hair framed her angular cheekbones so perfectly that Darcy felt hideous by comparison. The girl could have clearly been a model, much like Claire could have been. They could have very well been models for how much she actually knew about them and their extra-curricular activities.

Rena's green eyes shone brightly, smart and sly, setting Darcy a bit on edge. Sensing her thoughts, Rena turned abruptly towards her.

"Are you sure you're ok, Darcy?" she asked as all three girls noticed Mrs. Chadwick sit up from her desk at the head of the classroom. Darcy followed Claire's lead and grabbed the binder out of her purse/book-bag.

"I think so," she replied, not sure how else to respond. She was feeling confused and unsure but didn't want to make the other girls worry. If she had to 'make things right' as Marina had mentioned, she couldn't let on that she had no idea what that meant or even what this life was going to be like at all.

Mrs. Chadwick coughed loudly, clearly an attempt to get the loud chatter of the classroom to cease. Once quiet, the teacher began to teach, and Darcy felt thankful for having a moment to semi-relax - and to finally have a moment to breathe.

***

She had managed successfully to make it through half of the day's classes without being conspicuously confused, or at least not letting the other students think that she was. She had already begun to feel exhausted of trying to be constantly aware of what her role was and how she was supposed to act, not only around her friends but with the student body as a whole. The only thing that should have been on her mind was what the lunch menu was going to be or what she was going to wear to Chrissy Barr's party, but was she completely preoccupied with her conversation with Marina, which now felt oddly like a distant memory despite occurring just hours before.

English class had been uneventful, if only for the fact that she was able to take a much needed mental break and zone out. She had the nagging suspicion that this new teenaged Darcy wasn't exactly the brightest bulb, or if she was, she was a spectacularly amazing actress.

Mrs. Chadwick essentially ignored her when she asked the class questions about Catcher in the Rye, a book Darcy had read at least 25 times. She had wanted to raise her hand on several instances but ultimately figured it might have been the wrong move. Had she done so, she may have set off some warning bells.

Darcy et al now found themselves within the school cafeteria, which was jam packed upon their deliberately slow-paced entry. The typical group divisions were there – the emo-kids sat moping around in one corner - melancholic, heavily pierced and blue-haired. The kids in the school band sat opposite them, talking about the upcoming Spring Concert. Other splinter groups that she couldn't really figure out also sat in their respective spots of the massive cafeteria, firmly ensconced in high school dialogue that felt urgent and earth-shattering.

She followed the other girls' lead towards the rear of the cafeteria, which was about twice the size and cozier than the Banana Republic at the local mall – and significantly bigger than any other dining area that she had ever seen, least of all within a high school.

When she saw where the girls were heading, it made perfect sense. It was something out of the books she loved to read – the tables they were moving towards were comprised of kids who all looked perfectly tanned, casually dressed, and beautiful. They were all variations of blonde, lean, and attractive. She immediately thought about how she would stick out from the pack before remembering that she was one of them. For now, at least.

Upon sitting at the table at the rear of the room, Darcy saw the few token jock-type boys that the three girls clearly liked to hang around with.

"Hey baby," Luke Masters said, picking up Claire, causing her to squeal loud enough for half of the students in the cafeteria to look their way and smile. His strong arms easily picked the tiny Claire up, his dark hair short, his hands wrapped around the girl's waist. He stole a glance at Darcy before she sat down beside Rena, who was already chatting with some of the other students around them. She caught the glance, unsure of what it meant. Dismissing its importance, she took a sip from the bottle of water she had pulled out of her bag.

"Hey ladies," Luke said after he had put Claire down. "How was

Calculus?"

"Awful," Rena instantly replied. All Darcy could manage to do was to shake her shoulders. The less she said the better, at least until she was able to go home and properly process what was happening. Until then, she going to make every concerted effort keep it together and maintain any false illusions alive and reasonably believable.

"Hey Darcy – let's go pick up those boxes," Luke abruptly said, getting up from his chair beside Claire. He at once stood behind her in a flash as though he had floated all of the way to the end of the long, wooden table that wouldn't have been entirely out of place at Pottery Barn.

"Do you guys have to get them right now?" Claire quickly chimed in, pouting like a child. "We just got here."

Darcy had absolutely no clue what Luke was referring to. She waited for the dialogue between Luke and Claire to pan out before making any decisions.

"It'll be too busy after school," Luke said, pulling on his jacket and tapping Darcy on her shoulder like an eager child. She hadn't realized how tall he was – over six feet, and with teeth that could light up a room.

"Yeah, Luke," she added, trying to sound as casual as possible, taking another sip from her water bottle. "Besides, we just got here. Can't we at least eat first? I'm starved."

Rena quickly stared over at her, obviously annoyed. She mentally filed away that reaction for meting out later.

"Oh come on, Platt. Don't be lazy," Luke chided, taking her gently by the arm. She quickly threw on her jacket and grabbed her purse. "We'll be like two minutes. Let's go!"

Before she knew it, they were outside of the cafeteria, walking down an empty hallway, which had all the classroom doors closed. The multi-colored lockers that lined the long corridor, ranging from blue to yellow to red, housed textbooks and teenaged secrets. Luke walked slightly ahead, not uttering a single word, which she found a

103

tad peculiar. They took a sharp left at the end of the hall and he opened the door to an enormous room that was full of boxes and assorted papers.

She heard the door slam shut behind them while Luke turned on the lights. The room seemed to be a printing room of some kind with many boxes stacked in high piles all around the periphery of the room, as well as in its center area which were sorted into various high columns. She glanced at some of the boxes labels – some said "Freshman," others said "Foxes" and others were labeled "Turtles."

While looking at what seemed to be a gigantic printing press, she felt Luke's hands around her waist, the same hands that had just been around her best friend's shoulders.

"I couldn't wait to see you," he whispered into her ear, pulling her close to him. He breathed gently onto her hair and kissed the top of her head. Shocked, she didn't move, and was unsure of exactly what to do. Luke tilted her face up and looked into her eyes.

"You're so beautiful," he went on, bringing his hand up to her cheek, softly caressing it. She instantly pulled back before things escalated and got out of hand.

"Luke, stop it!" she screamed before realizing that yelling wasn't probably the best thing to do in her current situation. She just needed to get him off of her, and fast at that.

"What's wrong?" he asked sincerely. He looked genuinely hurt, his forehead furrowed, his eyes full of surprise. She felt bad for being so loud and brash with her reaction, but she had been caught off guard and the interaction had felt *so wrong* on *so many* levels. In fact, it made her want to run away from the school and take a long, long hot shower – with bleach and ammonia and other token household cleaning agents.

"We can't do this. Claire is my best friend," she spoke up, quickly walking towards another pile of boxes. It was almost as though they were in some maze-like labyrinth with each column of boxes filling her field of vision. She was trying to put as much distance between her and Luke as possible in the shortest amount of time.

He soon followed her, clearly persistent and focused. She had the distinct impression that his feelings for her were authentic, but there was no disguising the fact that he was her best friend's boyfriend. She would never do something to deliberately hurt a friend.

"Of course we can do this," he laughed, his hands resting on her shoulders from behind. "We've been doing this for almost 6 months."

She slowly turned around to face him and beheld the wide smile on his face.

Six months! she thought. *I've been cheating with my best friend's boyfriend for six months!*

She felt flushed, her face characteristically reddening. Luke leaned in slowly, kissing her tenderly. She didn't pull away, as much as she knew she should have, knowing that what she was doing was wrong and not the type of thing she would ever, ever normally do. His hands slowly raised up her arms, causing chills to move down her spine. She shuddered because his lips felt so good on hers – soft and kind. She touched his arms, feeling the muscles underneath the denim jacket, squeezing them lightly.

She leaned into him and he grabbed her tighter, kissing her harder and harder until she thought she would explode. Finally, she pulled away, the guilt within her taking control of the situation. She knew that it would absolutely devastate Claire to find out what they were doing, least of all just a short distance away from where she sat in the cafeteria. Darcy had absolutely no desire to be that kind of girl who hurt her best friend, no matter how good the hurting may have felt.

Suddenly the door opened and Rena stepped in. Darcy pretended to grab something out of a box, rather unconvincing in her actions. Luke also made a feeble attempt to pretend to find something he was looking for, but they both could not have appeared guiltier.

"Hey guys," Rena said. "I thought you might need some help with those boxes." Darcy turned around, trying to smile. Rena seemed to be oblivious to what had just happened between the two of them.

"The Turtles want their yearbooks," Rena went on. "They want to bring them to their away game at Valley."

The Turtles, along with The Freshman and The Foxes were school teams that comprised Flint Ridge High's sports teams. The school was known for rearing talented athletes that ended up getting scholarships to some of the best schools in the country. It made sense seeing as the school seemed to have an enormous football field located at the rear of the sprawling institution.

"Here they are," Luke said, his voice confident and strong as though nothing had happened. He grabbed three boxes easily and quickly made his way out of the room, leaving Rena and Darcy alone. Darcy grabbed one box and she felt like she was going to fall over because of its weight, but soon regained composure and made her way to the door.

"Let's go, Rena," she said as Rena herself picked up a box without any hesitation. Rena smiled and followed her out of the room, and back down the deserted hallway.

***

The rest of the day passed by at a snail's pace. The sun had continued to shine brightly for the entire afternoon, making it difficult to guess what time it was exactly if you couldn't look at a watch or at a clock. This was certainly the case for Darcy, who for all in her haste that morning, forgot to put on a watch. The school had a rather firm 'no cell' phone rule so she couldn't pull her own mini-computer of a phone out of her bag and lament as to how much longer it would be before she can just go home and lay on her bed and think the hell out of her evening.

She impressed herself at she managed to breeze through the rest of her classes without any major hiccups or disasters – the various events that had happened just earlier that morning were certainly enough. She had even made the feeble but honest attempt to volunteer an answer in her Geography class (if there was one thing she was confident about it was her impressive knowledge of Europe despite never having physically been there). The teacher, Mr. Gordon, seemed to be taken aback at her willingness to learn, as did the rest of the students in the class. Rena, in particular, seemed to find her enthusiasm and newfound knowledge slightly unsettling.

"What are you doing? You positively hate geography," Rena had whispered to her once Mr. Gordon turned his back to write Darcy's response on the chalkboard. All Darcy could do was shake her shoulders. Saying nothing was better than saying the wrong thing. While she felt like telling Rena to cut her some slack with her obvious frequent judgments, she knew she had to rely on her effective body language more than usual until she began to figure things out get more comfortable being a teenager. Again.

In the parking lot after school, the students quickly made their way to their cars and bikes respectively, the joy of having finished another school day palpable in the air. Darcy did not mind school, she never really did, but clearly this was not something her friends thought was acceptable.

"You should have seen Darcy brown nose through Mr. Gordon's class!" Rena giggled, walking alongside Luke and Claire after the 3:30 pm bell signaling the end of the school day reverberated throughout the school's beautifully manicured lawns, hallways and picnic areas. Darcy had purposely chosen to walk behind them, taking in the school's historical architecture, not to mention its incredible view of the town of Martin's Falls below them. She did not exactly feel like chatting it up just then and was

107

comfortable in relying upon her friends to carry any menial conversations.

"Really? Darcy – you hate geography!" Claire laughed, mirroring Rena's statement earlier, high pitched tone and all. Darcy opted to not say a word, welcoming the silence. As the girls chatted in front of her, she took advantage of the time to continue to take in her surroundings. Like her quick glance of the school parking lot earlier that day, she marveled at how beautiful all of the students were. They all seemed to be smiling and happy, and rather unsurprisingly, filthy rich. Their cars were a smorgasbord of money – ranging from BMW's, to Mercedes, to the random Jeeps. Darcy, recognizing her brother's car, made an A-line towards it, forgetting about her friends who were getting comfortable on a picnic bench by the massive trees that were lined up all around them.

She wasted no time in getting into the car and locking the doors. Alone, she exhaled heavily, but jumped when Claire knocked on the driver's side window.

Claire gestured for her to open the window, looking annoyed and bothered. *The typical teenage way*, Darcy thought to herself. She lowered the window, the warm breeze gently caressing her flawless skin.

"Pick me up at 8 for the party?" Claire asked, or rather told her, lowering her head closer to where Darcy sat. She thought she had noticed Luke glaring at her from his perch at the picnic table not far behind from Claire now stood and immediately began to feel uncomfortable. She felt like she was never going to be able to drive away and have some time to herself and her thoughts.

She chose then to just smile and nod, which thankfully seemed to satisfy Claire who straight away turned around and rejoined her crew at the picnic bench. She briskly started the car and amped up the air conditioning. She had suddenly felt very hot and desperately needed to cool off. Without hesitation, or even putting on her seatbelt, she drove out of the lot, leaving her friends confused as to why she was behaving so strangely and out of character. *If they only knew*, Darcy thought to herself as she drove home.

***

As soon as she closed the bedroom door behind her, she dropped her purse on the carpeted floor and kicked off her pink ballet slipper flats. Her hands found the remote control that both raised and lowered the blinds. She happily lowered the enormous slats and welcomed the total darkness that soon enveloped her and her many, many thoughts. Now somewhat knowing how to navigate the room around her, she dramatically threw herself on the bed, welcoming the total silence that pressed in around her, as though almost in a welcoming and warm embrace.

Make things right, she heard Marina's voice say as though the woman was in the room right there with her. *You have always been the one.*

She exhaled heavily, realizing that not one thing had seemed to fit into place or make any sort of sense, the least of which being Marina's prophetic statements made earlier that day. *Maybe this was part of the whole wish experience*, she thought silently. Maybe things weren't supposed to make sense, just like they tended not to do in her real life. But the whole allure for her in reading the teen fiction books that she cherished so much was the clear order of the lives that were depicted and the unclouded choices that had to be made by the novel's end. Her entire day couldn't have been more in contrast to that. Instead of being able to enjoy the life of a girl she had so envied, she was full of questions and worries, visibly made worse by Marina's impromptu and rather dramatic visit.

She was just beginning to nod off when she heard a knock on her bedroom door. She decided not to answer, hoping that whoever it was would just go away and leave her alone. She was in no mood to deal with her hyper-energetic mother at that moment.

109

The knocking continued, forcing her to get up from her comfortable stance on the bed. Grunting, she walked over to the door and pulled it open.

"I'm baaaaaaaack," a young man said, his face a mirror image of her own. He faced her with a wry smile on his lips. "Did you miss me, little sister?"

Chapter 13

"Oh my God – I thought you were going to be away for another month!" Darcy exclaimed, turning on the lights in her bedroom. She reluctantly raised the blinds once more as her brother Mason walked in casually and took a seat on the bed.

Standing 6'2 and looming above her, Mason was clearly the type of guy that girls swooned over. He exuded just the right amount of confidence that she thought she could actually feel. His hair was the same dark shade of blonde as her own. His body was sculpted and perfect, just like Luke's. The orange polo shirt he was wearing made his green eyes bright, almost fluorescent. She couldn't stop staring at him.

They looked alike, that was a fact. Their eyes were large, their cheekbones high and prominent. She felt herself forging an immediate bond with her brother – and her excitement at having a brother made her temporarily forget about the many stresses that were just on her mind a few mere moments ago.

"So did I but Prague wasn't doing it for me," Mason replied, stretching out on the gargantuan bed that took up most of the room. He looked at the frame which housed a seemingly recent picture of Claire and Darcy on her nightstand and frowned.

"How's Claire?" he asked, his voice dropping a few octaves.

"Fine – we're going to Chrissy Barr's party tonight," she exclaimed. "Want to come?"

Mason laughed loudly, momentarily confusing her. His laugh sounded a tad cynical, almost sinister in its timbre. She mentally attributed it to his jet lag.

"You're kidding right?" he said. "You know I wouldn't be able to possibly handle annoying high school kids for an entire evening."

She felt wounded but she also sort of understood. Her brother was a college man; an avid member of a social circle that while reminiscent of high school, was infinitely cooler and more serious. Mason quickly noticed her hurt expression and a smile spread across his face.

"What? You're upset that I said no? Please, Darcy, don't act like we're friends because we're not," he said, quickly getting up from the bed and walking towards the window that overlooked their pool.

Feeling like the wind was knocked out of her, she couldn't help but turn her gaze towards her brother.

Maybe he's being sarcastic, she reasoned to herself. *Maybe he's just cranky. Chalk up another point to the jet lag.*

"Huh?" was all she could muster. She was feeling the exhaustion of the day settling in within her once again. Glancing at the clock on her wall before her, she realized that the party wasn't all that far away and that she'd have to leave fairly soon to pick up Claire. Secretly, all she wanted to do was just hide in her enormous bed and think up a storm, however unglamorous that would have appeared to her new friends.

Mason stared out the window a few moments longer and then

112

turned back around to face her, his smile dissolving into a look of dismay and discontent. She once again felt confused and slightly uncomfortable, not at all like what she had imagined she would feel when looking at her brother.

"Whatever, Darcy, I don't know what you're on but I just came here to ask you for something." He walked back to her bed and sat down. Facing her, she noticed his stern expression.

"What do you want?" she asked, sounding terser than she had intended. She never even used that tone when dealing with rude waiters or telemarketers and she felt quickly embarrassed.

"A-ha," Mason replied, a smiling once again creeping across his face. "That's more like the Darcy I know."

He stood up again, obviously nervous and fidgety. She honestly did not know what to make of this completely bizarre interaction. She decided to just go with it, Adam Sandler style.

"Don't tell mom or dad that I'm back. They'd seriously rip me apart if they knew that I somehow didn't live up to their expectations of having the most perfect European getaway." He looked straight at Darcy. "Promise me you won't tell them."

She felt the urgency in his words. How could she say no?

"Of course. But where are you going to stay?" she couldn't help but ask. Suddenly, they both heard the knock on her bedroom door. Mason put his finger in front of his lips, signaling her to stay quiet. He got up from the bed quietly and tip toed into her closet that was conveniently just steps away. When she saw him close the door behind him, she made her way to the door.

"Coming," she said, trying to sound as non-chalant as possible. When she opened the door, she was surprised to see the gardener from this morning, Charlie. He looked very different from just hours ago. His coal black hair was swept to the side and parted, and he wore a pair of dark denim pants with a tight black t-shirt, showcasing his fit body. She felt a little butterfly or two fly around her stomach.

113

"Hi" he said, looking at her. Not knowing what to do, she just tried to follow Charlie's lead. The feeling she had earlier that morning came back to her in waves; this boy really did have some sort of hold over her. "This came for you in the mail," he said, holding out a brown envelope.

The envelope that he handed her was not much bigger than a post-card. Upon giving her the envelope, their hands touched for a brief second. She felt like electricity was coursing through her body, and thought that her hair was going to stand on end. As soon as she had the envelopes in her grasp, Charlie turned around and walked away without saying a single word. *He's just shy*, she thought to herself.

She turned back around and closed her bedroom door behind her. She placed the envelope on her bed and walked over to her closet door to let her brother know the coast was clear. The door itself was slightly ajar, and when she peaked in, she noticed that Mason was gone.

This is a very strange group of people indeed, she thought to herself, walking over to the envelope on her bed. *I hope Marina didn't inadvertently put me into a vampire themed novel. I think I can handle regular drama, but not vampire-infused drama.*

She tore off the large red ribbon that was tied around the envelope, curious as to what it was, or to who would send her a letter. Seeing no return address listed on the face of the letter, she ripped it open, genuinely excited to see what it was hidden within the tiny folds of paper.

She almost screamed when she saw what she discovered inside. In fact, a high yelp did leave her mouth. Inside of the envelope was a simple note, small and black with white writing. She absently dropped the letter, the soft thump of the paper hitting the floor. She couldn't reason why she was having such an intense reaction to a simple note but underneath the surface she knew there was more to it.

She bent down to look at the note, her curiosity getting the best of her. She grabbed the letter and quickly sat back on her bed, as though if she moved fast enough the ominous note would disappear. With trembling hands, she began to read the simple note:

"I know what you're doing to Claire," the letter read, short, sweet, and terrifying. She dropped the letter once more shock, and ran out of her bedroom, suddenly feeling claustrophobic and short of breath. On her way out, she nearly knocked Mason over but she didn't look back and continued to run downstairs, desperate for some fresh air.

***

After a brief respite from the overwhelming nature of the day, Darcy was able to entrench herself onto a patio chair by the pool and went unnoticed from the flurry of activity that seemed to be unraveling inside the kitchen. Once she couldn't put off getting ready for the party that she no longer was enthused about attending any longer, she slowly retreated to her room to get all gussied up.

It did not go overlooked in the deep confines of her overactive mind that this was the first party, high-school based or not, that she had attended in quite some time. In fact, she'd venture to say that it had been a good few years since she was in a room with strangers and alcohol. She was as comfortable as the next person being thrown into the dynamics of a party, but she knew that what she was to experience that evening was something just a tad different. More than a tad, really. She was temporarily afraid of not being able to continue her charade of being a teen, but she figured that she had nothing to lose.

She didn't see her brother again that evening, which confirmed that he wasn't exactly lying about not telling their parents that he was back from his trip early. She had relaxed a bit after their awkward conversation and his apparently genuine dislike for her.

115

She mentally added it to her list of things to 'make right' as Marina so ambiguously stated was her primary objective to be met.

Lingering over her department store-sized make up collection and closet, she soon realized that she hadn't even looked at the clock once to see what time it was and to ensure she wasn't going to be late to pick up Claire for the party. After noticing on her smart phone that she was indeed running late, she whipped together an outfit and threw on the barest of makeup, hoping that it would be sufficient to continue her disguise.

Literally running out of the house, and ignoring the calls from her parents, she got into the car without looking back once. She pulled out from the driveway and made her way to Claire's house, which would in no doubt, make her disdain for Darcy's apparent new habit of tardiness very well known.

Chapter 14

She ended up being over a half hour late to pick Claire up and she had to hear about it for the entire drive to Chrissy Barr's party. What made being late worse was being late earlier that morning. Claire was apparently used to having a very punctual friend act as her chauffer for events such as this. After her mini-panic attack earlier that afternoon, Darcy hadn't intended at all to take her time in getting ready, it just sort of happened that she lost a total track of time. Perhaps subconsciously she couldn't, or didn't, want to get ready for a party at all. It wasn't that she didn't have the energy or will to get ready and wear some of the amazing outfits that hung in her closet; it was that she was essentially exhausted.

In just 24 hours she had taken on an entirely new identity, learned there was a master plan to her becoming 17 again, was apparently having an affair with her best friends boyfriend, had a brother who practically hated her, and that someone knew that she was cheating with Luke and decided to black mail her or threaten her, whatever the intent of the letter had been. All of these events had made her head spin, which was why she decided to just chill out by the pool, breathing, and subsequently falling asleep - another reason she was late to pick up Claire. While the last event was the least of her worries, Claire was not happy at all about her late arrival.

"…and if you think that this new being late business is ok, you're on another planet! Or really bad drugs. I don't know which yet," Claire yelled, partly out of anger, partly out of trying to be heard over the loud music Darcy had turned up to drown Claire's voice out.

Claire was livid when she arrived late to pick up her up; much like she had been earlier that morning, but this time her ire definitively more serious. Darcy noticed that Claire's long, black hair lay in ringlets around her face, her tiny waist accentuated by a black corset that made her chest look like it was going to cause a minor felony. She had begun to think she may have underdressed in her black mini dress, but she did have enough time to put her hair in a tight bun, an ode to Marina.

"Don't you know that being late to one of Chrissy Barr's parties' means you're going to have to hang out in the kitchen because all of the good looking spots are already taken? God, now we're going to have to hang out with the geeks and talk about Star Trek or whatever nerds talk about", Claire rambled on, taking her voice down a notch. She pulled out her lip-gloss from her purse and added another think and shiny layer though her lips already looked shellacked enough to cause a fire if someone decided to light a match.

"How many times do I need to say I'm sorry? I told you I took a nap, and Mason really upset me," Darcy decided to reply and leaned slightly forward to turn down the volume of the blaring music. The loud, thumping beats were beginning to give her a headache and she knew she didn't need any extra ammunition to have a bad time tonight. Plus, she wanted to have a decent experience at the party and make the best out of her predicament, even if it was only for one single night.

As soon as she mentioned Mason's name, Claire went conspicuously silent. She was now putting bright pink blush on her high cheek bones. Picking up on the sudden silence, Darcy soon found herself intrigued by it. She turned the car into Chrissy Barr's driveway, long and full of shiny vehicles that indicated how rich these kids really were and parked quickly near the end of the driveway. She turned towards Claire who had graduated to dabbing her face with powder.

Soon enough she'll look like a full-fledged drag queen, Darcy thought.

"Let's have a good time tonight," Darcy finally decided to speak up. She really did feel bad for being late to pick up Claire, twice at that. Claire turned to face her, a serious expression on her face, but was quickly replaced by a smile, revealing her perfectly blinding white teeth.

"Is there any other time to have?" Claire replied, a giggle escaping her mouth. Both girls got out of the car, locked arms, and entered the mansion that reminded her a bit of the Taj Mahal in its grandeur and relative tackiness.

***

If the house looked enormous from the outside, inside it resembled a palatial shopping mall. Claire made a bee line the kitchen to presumably grab something for them to drink while Darcy looked around and decided to take in the scene around her. There were at least a hundred high school kids milling about around her, mostly teenagers but some college kids loitered around here and there. There did not seem to be much furniture populating the massive living room, making the entire area appear look like one big dance floor, replete with semi-drunken kids who were also semi-

119

naked. Girls in fluorescent tube tops bounced along to the music while guys in khaki pants and tight t-shirts pounded their fists into the air. She smiled, feeling increasingly comfortable and secure amongst the crowd, and opted to follow Claire into the kitchen, which seemed to be as big as the living room was.

She didn't know why Claire was afraid of hanging out with the 'geeks' because if the people that were in the kitchen were considered 'geeks', then she was positively ok with that. The white, smooth countertops were littered with bottles of alcohol, some larger than she had ever seen before in her life. She also noticed a few kegs of beer near the rear of the room where the bathroom must have been as there was a line-up forming, short in length now but she knew it would be so long soon enough that she'd have to fake a panic attack or minor injury if she wanted to relieve herself.

She caught Claire walking back towards her from the kitchen, carefully balancing the two liter sized glasses that were full of some blue and pink liquid, complete with a pineapple wedge on each brim.

"My own creation! Taste it!" Claire said, bringing the glass to her mouth. She took a sip and immediately felt the sugary rush and energy that alcohol brought on. She automatically took another huge gulp, suddenly super thirsty.

"Whoa, down girl, we just got here. I don't want to hold your head above any toilets tonight!" Claire laughed, pretending to take the glass away. She grabbed for it, laughing as well, and both girls walked back into the living room where a slow song now blared out of the large speakers. The dance floor/living room had thinned out a bit but there were still a few couples swaying slowly to the rhythm.

Claire managed to snag one of the red leather love seats that lined the back wall and sat down. She placed the drinks on the white rectangular table before her and turned to Darcy, her perfectly curled hair bouncing to the music. She was beginning to feel more at ease, the insanity of the day's event slowly leaving her mind.

"So, how's Mason?" Claire quietly asked, trying to sound as

casual as possible, but not relaxed enough for her not to notice the twinge of the urgency in her tone. She immediately remembered Mason pleading with her not to tell anyone that he was back and felt bad for having told Claire on the car ride over without even second guessing it.

"Claire – you cannot tell anyone he's back. He made me promise," she pleaded looking her friend squarely straight in the eyes. She needed to know that Claire was going to keep the fact of Mason's return a secret. She still did not understand why Mason's return was such a vital secret to be kept, but she did know that Mason meant it. Even though he was a complete jerk to her, she knew she had to keep her end of the promise.

"Yeah, whatever. Your parents are going to find out anyway – Mason's not exactly discreet," Claire replied, picking up her glass and taking a few big gulps. "Remember when he lost your dog?"

No, she thought to herself.

"He'll kill me if they find out because of me," she continued. Claire rolled her eyes, trying to appear aloof about the whole thing but she knew there was more going on than she was letting on. Before she could ask Claire more about it, Luke suddenly appeared, his head popping up between both girls from behind the love seat.

Claire squealed, nearly dropping her entire glass of blue/pink insanity. Darcy jumped, catching Luke's coy smile. He walked around the love seat and squeezed his way in between both girls, moving one of his arms around Claire's shoulder, and the other her own, causing her to instinctively to lean forward and drink greedily from her glass.

"The party's pretty awesome, huh?" Luke said, taking a long sip from Claire's glass. His arm found its way around her shoulder again once she leaned back. "Did you see the craziness in the kitchen? It's like a bar in there. Ha-ha, Barr's Bar." She rolled her eyes at Luke's attempt at making a joke.

Claire and Luke started chatting to one another, forcing Darcy to

121

shift her attention to once again taking in the scene before her. She was hell-bent on having a good time, putting her mind on hold. She bopped her head to the music, letting the music take her to another place.

***

Once the living room dance floor filled up once again thanks to one of her favorite songs, she decided to take the plunge to get up and dance. She grabbed her drink, leaving Luke and Claire staring at her in total shock, and walked slowly to the middle of the living room. She began to move around to the beat, letting her worries fall away as she felt herself feeling happier about being part of this world – a world she only read about all of these years.

The other kids around her smiled as she bounced around. She couldn't deny the feeling that she actually liked having all of the attention upon her because she had never experienced anything like it before. It was like she was a true-life Gossip Girl, dressed impeccably in the hottest current designers, her legs long, smooth and shiny.

She then brought her hands to her bun and unclipped it, causing the waves of dark blonde hair to fall upon her exposed shoulders. She saw Luke staring at her hungrily at her while Claire stood up and walked to the kitchen, presumably and probably to get more drinks. He began to walk towards her but she immersed herself into the throngs of dancing teens around her, feeling a random elbow hit her back.

"Oh, I'm sorry", she blurted, composing herself, shaken from her temporarily music-induced reverie. She looked up to see a girl smiling back at her. Her face perfectly round, her eyes bright brown and wide like a baby. She instantly recognized something in the shine that those eyes emanated. Something about her made her feel almost nostalgic, which was absurd given how old she was (or was

122

supposed to be anyway). No, not maternal. It was more of a comfortable feeling. Like she had seen the look I those eyes before...

"It was my fault. I'm notoriously known for having two left feet," the girl replied, laughing. "This party's pretty crazy, huh?"

"Crazy doesn't quite explain it," Darcy replied. She saw Luke approach her but immediately stepped back when he saw whom she was talking to.

"I think you're friend wants to talk to you," the girl said, and then quickly noticing Luke disappear. "Or not."

Both girls laughed as a slow song filled the air. They walked off the dance floor to an empty spot by an enormous window that faced the backyard, which seemed to have as many kids outside as there were inside. Teenagers were swimming in the pool, throwing plastic beach balls and then animatedly diving for them. Glasses were strewn all over the tables that lined the seemingly Olympic sized pool, and speakers blared music that must have been different that what was playing in the living room as the kids outside were dancing manically, not slowly as they were in the living room.

"Chrissy must have some pretty cool parents," the girl went on, looking at the scene outside. Darcy noticed that the girl had no drink in her hand, so she either had just arrived at the party or was driving. Or was a reforming alcoholic.

.She wanted to ask the girl her name, but realized that they may have already indeed known each other, in which case it would seem totally strange if they reintroduced themselves. Thankfully, the girl seemed to be feeling the same way as her. There was a strange confident vibe emanating from the girl and Darcy felt immediately drawn to her.

"Oh, I'm Bennett, she said. "I just moved here." Bennett smiled at her. "You're Darcy Platt, right?"

She was taken aback, but then remembered that she was very popular indeed. "Guilty," she laughed.

Sonya! She felt like screaming to herself. *This girl reminds me of Sonya!* The perpetual confidence, the ease and pleasantness of her aura, all reminded her of her beautiful friendship with Sonya. And at that point she missed her friend terribly.

Suddenly, Claire swiftly seemed to appear out of nowhere, sizing up Bennett from head to toe. Bennett looked down, realizing she was being assessed and judged, her red Chuck Taylor's moving around awkwardly.

"Let's go outside," Claire commanded, taking Darcy by the hand, moving her towards the back patio door which led to the backyard. She pulled her hand away, forcing Claire to glare back at her in anger.

"Wait, Claire – this is Bennett. She's new here," Darcy said. "Bennett, this is Claire Marsh". Bennett reached out her hand towards Claire, but Claire didn't move on iota.

"Outside," Claire repeated. She began walking to the back door. Darcy turned to Bennett.

"Sorry – I guess she really wants to go outside. Want to come with?" she asked. Bennett shook her head.

"No, that's ok. It was nice to meet you. I guess I'll see you around school?"

"Totally. Have fun!" Darcy screamed, and walked towards Claire, who was beginning to seem like a toddler about to have a tantrum of gargantuan proportions.

***

The party was definitely wilder outside. The hot weather forced her to take off the orange cardigan she had been wearing and held it in her hand. The music was also much louder with mini dance floors splintering all over the back yard like a weird web of rampant teenage hormones. To her, everyone that she saw looked so carefree and so happy. She tried to let herself feel it all, welcoming the excitement and feelings of utter freedom, until Claire pulled her off to an empty spot by the side of the house just underneath the kitchen and just beside the shed, which she noted was bigger than her entire first apartment.

"What is going on with you, D?" Claire whispered, taking another sip of her quart sized cup that was nearly now empty of its green and pink concoction which was just near the top of the glass moments ago.

"What do you mean?" Darcy countered; she was honestly unaware of what was now apparently bothering her friend. She was beginning to get the feeling that Claire was not only high maintenance, but also insecure about a lot of things.

"*What do you mean?*" Claire mocked her voice. "What do you think I mean? You were talking to that new weird girl!"

Darcy instantly laughed out loud, although she hadn't meant to, as it only seemed to upset Claire more. Claire's face turned a deep shade of red, causing her to think that she was two steps away from having smoke come out of her ears.

"Why are you laughing? God, Darcy, you are being so bizarre today!" Claire continued.

"What the big deal, anyway?" she replied, not seeing why it was such a huge life-changing event because she was talking to the new, and nice, girl in school.

"The big deal is that we do not make friends with the new kids! They have to work hard to get our attention and then we have to judge to see if they're worthy."

Darcy, who was taking a sip of her drink that was also now empty, nearly choked when she heard Claire's words. With more and more time spent with Claire, she truly began to dislike her.

"I was just being friendly," she replied, looking out at all the kids in the pool, having the time of their lives without a care in the world. She wanted to be with them, splashing water and ruining her perfectly coiffed hair, having her make-up run and laughing, but instead she was off in a corner with a hot-headed teenager who clearly had anger issues. Claire was growing more and more irritating the longer and she silently questioned how this whole friendship was going to pan out.

"Go and be friendly with Rena or Luke. Or, if you're that desperate, even Charlie," Claire retorted, turning her back towards her and stormily walked off in the direction of the kitchen, probably with the intent of filling up her glass and getting more drunk than she already was.

"Just don't mess everything up that we have worked so hard to get. This is high school – one small mistake and we're back to being geeks with no friends."

She watched as Claire disappeared into the kitchen that seemed like it was ready to explode from being too full of too-tanned kids with blonde hair and teeth so white that she felt was beginning to give her a headache. She put her glass down on the concrete ground and sat on a small bench that sat just behind her.

The night breeze moved through her hair, causing a chill to run up her back. She pulled her hair back into a pony tail and put her cardigan back on. The warmth of the sweater made her feel better, but she was still as confused as ever. She had experienced more in one day than she had in the last 5 years of her life.

Staring at the party before her, she smiled. She really was here, she thought. She really was a beautiful teenage girl who had a perfect body and perfect friends, well, near-perfect friends anyway, that any 17-year-old girl would want. She had a glow, there was no denying that, and it was not just from the perpetual tan she seemed to have. It was from somewhere deeper inside – it seemed to originate from somewhere deep within her soul. This life she was thrust into was easy; going to parties on a school night, being able to choose anything out of a closet full of designer labels and not worrying if a dress she bought last summer was still going to fit her this year. She enjoyed the lack of filter she had to use, primarily because her thoughts weren't jaded and caustic, like they were in her modern-day life.

It had always been a flaw of hers, she felt, to over-analyze things until they were void of happiness or joy or elation. She de-compartmentalized things to the point where she had convinced herself that a simple gesture, something as innocent as someone holding the door open for her, was really a commentary on the historic subordination of women as the 'weaker sex'. She wished she could just take things at face value, like things were when she was young, free from the rent she could barely pay, before she worked at a job that she loathed (and was now fired from), which made her feel like she was nothing but a cog that did not quite fit in a wheel that kept spinning whether she wanted it to or not.

As she read the teen books that she relished with every fiber of her feeling, she had wished and wished that she could just leave her humdrum life working for 'the man' and just be that popular girl in high school, that girl who was beautiful and free and the object of adoration of her entire world. And here she was, that protagonist with an uncomplicated perspective on life and the popularity of Mother Teresa, and she was busy spending her time on over analyzing it, a la Darcy specialty.

She knew what was happening defied logic, but there was no mistake that it was INDEED happening. For the entire day, she had wanted to just think and be able to comprehend what indeed was going on, what Marina's cryptic appearance earlier that day really meant. She was forgetting to recognize the magic of what was transpiring – that she had been thrust into this near perfect world which she had fallen asleep to reading every night, hoping to dream about.

She immediately felt bad for being so judgmental of Claire. Claire was just being the typical alpha female character of this genre of books – beautiful, slightly dumb, and completely territorial. She just simply didn't know any better. She lived in a sheltered world where talking to the new girl could spell social suicide. She felt a sort of pity accompany the guilty she feelings she had.

She found herself walking rather absent-mindedly around the mansion that was Chrissy Barr's home, the now steady wind flowing through her hair. She realized she was trying to find a solution to what was happening, a way to deal with it. She was feeling more and more overwhelmed as the hours went by, when she felt it should have been the opposite. She should have been having the time of her life – having an amazing time at the party, having fun with all of her friends, dating boys who were obscenely good-looking, but none of that was happening. Sure, she *was* at a party and seeing friends, but she was always thinking, always overanalyzing each situation to the point that she always had a headache.

She heard her cell phone vibrate, causing her tiny pink purse to shake. She glanced at the name flashing on her screen and let it ring. She could call Claire later. It's not like she didn't know where Claire was.

Then it suddenly hit her. All of this time she had been trying to act like the thirty something year old Darcy and make the choices she would make. She had been trying to make all of the right decisions, to act reserved, to act like an adult. Marina asked her to make things right, but how could she do that by not immersing herself into the life of a girl who obviously had a lot going on around her? She wasn't focusing on getting to know the girl she now was, why she was the way she is, why she had made the choices she did. The only way she was going to make things right was to understand the 17 year old Darcy. The girl with the beautiful eyes and seemingly angry brother. The girl who was apparently screwing around with her best friends boyfriend – the girl who had feelings for the gardeners' son, whether she liked to admit it or not.

It was like a great weight had been lifted from her shoulders. For the first time she was propelled into this new world, she felt like she could breathe. She knew now what she had to do. She now had an idea on how she was going to make things right. And the first thing she was going to do was call Claire back and act like a friend. The only way she was going to figure out how to be the new her was to *BE* her.

Chapter 15

The next few weeks seemed to pass without any major incidents or catastrophes, aside from those that often reared in the life of a typical teenage girl in any teen fiction novel. There were no more random threats via ominous, anonymous messages or unwanted advances from her best friend's boyfriend. This relative lack of excitement was especially welcome in the life of one Darcy Platt, whom had experienced enough trials and tribulations in such a short span of time that she felt that she was going to turn prematurely grey at the ripe old age of 17.

It had taken some time, and some serious effort, for her to fully immerse in her new life and to take it *not* so seriously, with emphasis on the *not*. She made a conscious decision to put her constant judgment on the shelf and to give everyone she came across the true benefit of the doubt. For the most part, her approach was fairly successful. She was definitely having more fun than ever. Claire's strict and hypertensive ways were even growing on her, a concept that she had found completely surprising. She was learning new things about the life of this girl (her!) every single day, though she did find it stressful at times to juggle expectations of who she was and who she is and recognizing the very fine between the two.

Once those first few weeks had passed, she began to slowly settle into the proverbial groove of being 17 again. One of her favorite parts of the new role was being able to eat whatever she wanted without gaining a single ounce of weight, as well as going to the mall and spending all of the never-ending money that her parents gave her. She adored relishing in the popularity that was presented to her every single day. She muddled through the academic side of school, doing the literal bare minimum, and this seemed to be completely kosher in the Platt household, and thus, ok with her.

Flint Ridge High had been completely enthralled in preparation for the upcoming senior prom, though the actual event was still a few months away. And, as a senior, the prom was thus a seriously important event in her (and all of her friends) life. She hadn't thought much about whom she was going to go with, but it was all Claire and Rena could ever talk about.

"How about Carson Kerr?" Rena asked. All three girls were lying on their backs atop her luxurious king-sized bed, nail polish drying on their feet as they waved their feet in the air. Claire immediately made a loud and exaggerated retching sound before falling into deep gales of laughter.

"Ewww, he's like 4 feet tall!" Claire eked out through her intense case of the giggles.

"He is *sort* of cute," Darcy laughed, causing Rena and Claire to momentary stop laughing and contemplate if she was indeed being serious, which she sort of had been.

"Too bad you're not a little person," Claire joked. She swung

131

herself around on the bed and sat up, leaving the other girls on their backs.

"I think you should go with Jason Crone," Claire firmly continued. The other girls sat up, taking Claire's lead.

Jason Crone was the school's second cutest, and single, guy, behind Luke. All of the girls thought he was dreamy and sweet, but the trouble was *ALL* of the girls thought that, including both Claire and Darcy. The two girls also knew that Rena was completely and utterly infatuated with Jason, who in turn barely acknowledged her existence. Darcy found it sort of rude for Claire to even mention his name as a possible date to accompany her to the prom, though she realized she would jump at the chance of going with Jason anywhere, never mind the prom.

Rena tried to act unbothered by Claire's suggestion, but an uncomfortable silence suddenly filled the palatial room. Deciding to break the ice, Darcy got up from the bed to face both girls.

"I don't know. I mean, Jason is clearly gorgeous, but I'm thinking of going solo."

Claire stared at her open mouthed, while she caught Rena's clearly visible look of relief.

"No you're not. I'm going to get Luke to get Jason to ask you," Claire went on, beginning to remove the cotton balls that she had placed between her toes to avoid any nail polish spillage.

What is her problem? Darcy thought to herself. *Claire acted so completely random sometimes.*

When the other girls didn't say anything, Claire decided she wasn't done with commandeering her choice of prom date, or with sparing Rena's feelings.

"Oh come on, girls," she began, beginning to buff her nails. "He's not going to ask you, Rena. He doesn't even know you're alive, sorry to say."

Rena's face immediately turned a deep shade of red and Darcy thought she was going to burst into tears then and there right on her strawberry-colored duvet. Sure, it was true that Jason did not take a second look at Rena or show any remote kind of interest in the girl, it was still an extremely mean thing for Claire to say. Rena got up of the bed and walked into the adjoining bathroom, closing the door quickly behind her.

"What are you doing? You know Rena's in love with Jason!" Darcy whispered to Claire as soon as she heard the bathroom door lock.

"Yes, and I also know that she has no chance. Sorry, Darcy, but she's been moping around after him for, like, 3 months and he hasn't even so much as looked her way. She's got to get over it. Plus, he's super cute and you're super single so I don't see why…"

"That's not the point!" she interrupted. "You hurt her feelings. There's no way I'm going to go with him when I know how Rena feels about him". Both girls heard the toilet flush in the bathroom.

"Darcy – don't be ridiculous. This is the PROM. You cannot go alone. We are all going to get completely and utterly drop dead gorgeous, go with the hottest boys in school and have the time of our lives. Don't get all preacher-lady on me, ok? Rena will find a date. Maybe she'll go with Carson Kerr," Claire giggled.

Rena opened the door and rejoined the girls in the bedroom, her face no longer red but a light shade of pink.

"Come on girls, let's do our French manicures," Rena said, grabbing the kit that sat atop the night table when there was a sudden knock on the door.

She got up and turned down the music they had been listening to as whomever it was at the door knocked again. Her mother had been really annoying lately, popping into her bedroom unannounced fairly often, usually to ask if Mason had called or stopped by.

"Coming!" Darcy screamed and made her way towards the door as the other two girls began to lay out their artillery to do their nails.

She slowly opened the door, fully expected to see her mother's usual appearance of fraught nerves and hyper energy, but it wasn't her mother she saw waiting at the door, arm raised in mid knock. It was Mason.

After their initial confrontation a few weeks ago, she hadn't seen nor heard from her brother. Upon seemingly vanishing into thin air from her closet, he also seemed to vanish completely from her life, which made it relatively easy for her to keep her promise of not telling anyone that he was back early from his trip. As far as she knew, Claire also kept quiet about his whereabouts, though it was easier for her to keep a secret as she didn't live with a mother who was nosier than Clair Huxtable. She still felt a bit bummed about how poorly their conversation had gone, and she really did want to have a relationship with her brother, especially since she had no desire to return to her real life.

"Mason, hey..." she said, closing the door behind her and joining her brother in the plush hallway. She thought she caught his facial expression change when he briefly saw both Rena and Claire on the bed.

"Hey. Girls' night at the Platt house? Talking about boys and doing each other's hair?" Mason mocked, backing up against the railing that reached to his mid back.

"We are 17, after all," she replied, deliberately not matching his rudeness. Mason looked different since she had seen him last. His hair had grown longer, now shaggy enough and past his ears, and auburn-shaded stubble colored his cheeks and chin. He looked thinner, too.

"Mom and Dad think I just got back today so I guess I just wanted to say thanks for being cool with the whole secret thing", he said, shifting his gaze to the carpeted floor.

"It wasn't exactly hard to do, Mason. Where have you been?" she asked, genuinely concerned into the well being of her brother who looked both vulnerable and tired. Behind her, she heard Claire and Rena break into loud laughter. Mason looked towards the door, quickly smiled, and then turned serious once more.

"It doesn't matter. You should go back to your friends," he said, turning around and moving towards the stairs.

"Mason, wait." she said loudly, quickly following her brother. "Do you want to hang out later? The girls aren't going to stay that much longer."

He looked up at her and asked "Why?"

She was surprised at his simple retort because it sounded honest. How *bad of a sister have I been?* she inwardly wondered.

"Because I'd like to hang out with you. Maybe we can catch a movie or something."

Mason continued walking down the stairs, finally reaching the bottom and looking up at her.

"Thanks but no thanks, Darcy," he said. "You're not fooling me with the 'new you'."

She watched as he disappeared into the kitchen, and then out of sight. She questioned why he was being so resistant to spending time with her, and why he was being so secretive. But she was committed to finding out.

Chapter 16

The space around her was beginning to fill up with water. She felt the cold wetness first on her toes, and then began to feel the liquid as it rose so quickly that her ankles were soon completely submerged. Suddenly, the water was lapping at her knees. She tried to move, but found that she couldn't. Her legs felt like they were stuck in cement and were not going anywhere anytime soon.

She began to panic as the water touched her stomach, and then her chest. The long red t-shirt she was wearing billowed in the blue, pristine water, giving the impression of blood entering the sea that surrounded her. Suddenly, the ceiling above her disappeared, revealing a dark, night sky that was full of stars shining so bright that she had to squint her eyes from their overbearing glare.

"Help me!" she screamed, but no words were able to escape her mouth. The cool water soon touched her chin, causing a ripple of coldness to run through her body. She looked around, trying to find something to grasp onto to save her from an obvious imminent drowning, but she seemed to be in the middle of an ocean with no help or safety within sight.

When the water rose so high so that she was completely submerged, she looked straight ahead of her. Expecting to see nothing but an abyss of water, she was surprised to perfectly see that Marina was standing a mere few feet away from her.

The mysterious woman looked as beautiful and well put together, as always. Her red hair was firmly packed in its trademarked tight bun, and her long, ballooning gowns flowed beautifully in the water. She didn't seem to look wet or suffering as Darcy visibly was. Darcy decided to close her eyes for a quick moment to keep the water out of her them, though she realized this was a hopeless cause. She was essentially completely and utterly under water, after all. When she opened her eyes just a brief moment later, she noticed her environment and surroundings had completely changed.

She was now in the white, expansive room she had been in with Marina on her first day as being 17 again. She sat upon the same chair she had sat in once before and was noticeably completely dry. Marina sat directly across from her and stared at her intently. She knew she was dreaming, but everything seemed so vividly real. She couldn't help but be reminded of that day not so long ago when she sat all manically in front of Marina and expressed her desire to take the woman up on her ludicrous offer, which turned out to be not so ludicrous after all.

"Darcy," Marina finally said, her accent thicker than usual. She noticed that Marina's lips weren't moving but she heard the woman's words nonetheless. "You are having a good time, no?"

She looked all around her, completely bathed in the bright whiteness. Like before, she couldn't really discern where the ground began and where the ceiling started, strengthening the dreamlike illusion that the situation was expected to convey.

137

"It's just like I imagined it to be!" she quickly exclaimed. Her voice was so loud that it echoed in the invisible recesses of the enormous space. She hadn't really known why she decided to reply so enthusiastically but perhaps she attributed it to her happiness of not being submerged in an ocean.

"I am happy to hear that," Marina soon replied, her voice lower and deeper than the usual higher pitch that Darcy was accustomed to used to hearing from her. "You remember our deal, yes?"

She frowned, momentarily confused. *How could I forget!* was all she wanted to scream but she opted to take a moment to consider what her response would be.

In all honesty, she hadn't thought all that much about Marina's declaration all those weeks ago. She had been caught up in enjoying the day to day life of being so much like that protagonist in Sweet Valley High that Marina hadn't really crossed her mind since that first day.

"Yes, I do, Marina," she finally replied. She remembered vividly what Marina had told her, but she still had no idea as to how she had to 'make things right', especially since things seemed to be moving along perfectly, aside from the occasional hiccup (i.e. Her brother Mason).

"Time is ticking," Marina went on. "You have to do as you promised, so I may do as I promised."

"But you are doing what you promised," Darcy quickly pointed out. Marina had promised to give her the life of the teenage girl she read so fervently about, and that's what she had exactly done.

"Yes, but it will soon go away if you don't do as you said you would."

"When, exactly, is 'soon'?" she asked, worried and feeling anxiety rise within her.

"Soon is the Prom. You have to make things right by the Prom, or else this will all go away, and I will go away, and my store will go away, and things will go back to just as they were before this

138

happened to you." Marina's voice boomed loudly, reminding her of the Wizard of Oz, minus the large flowing white sheet and the Wiz's signature handlebar mustache.

"What? The prom? That's like in a month and a half!" Darcy yelled, not sure why she was screaming. "I don't even know what it is exactly that you want from me!"

"You will know when the moment comes," Marina ominously replied, looking at her, smiling.

Suddenly, she jerked awake, a stifled scream leaving her lips. She looked around her pitch-black bedroom, her heart ready to beat out of her chest. The enjoyment and adoration she was having in the life of a teenage girl was about to become much less enjoyable and adorable. This she knew with every ounce of her teenage/thirty something year old soul.

Chapter 17

There was a discernible nervous energy in the halls of Flint Ridge High on that warm, sunny May morning. An audible buzz seemed to echo off of the metal, shiny lockers and the freshly waxed linoleum floors. It seemed to radiate off of every single teenager, those in band and the popular kids alike. No one really seemed to be talking, just sort of emanating a high pitched sound full of excitement and apprehension, a bizarre cross between a bumblebee and a nervous dog.

Darcy sat on the shiny white floor in front of her locker, her biology textbook open to the chapter on organisms. The class had been learning about the nature of organisms, including their functions, how species come into existence, and the interactions they have with each other and with the natural environment. They were also listening to the teacher speak about the four unifying principles that form the foundation of modern biology: cell theory, evolution, genetics and homeostasis. She found it particularly relevant to her current situation.

She felt like a brand new organism – a new cell, the basic structure of all living things, ready to grow and form and exist independently. She would have to interact with other cells (people), but she also knew she couldn't fight the natural state of homeostasis. She had no desire to stay the same and be in a steady state. She knew she wanted to experience everything and everything she hadn't done when she herself was 17 the first time around, either because she wouldn't or because she decided she couldn't. She knew, however, very deep down, that she couldn't defy nature.

She slammed the book shut and leaned her head back against the cold metallic surface of her locker. She once again felt the vitality surge through the school hallways. She felt little pinpricks go up and down her arms as though sensing the collective nerves that seemed to be infiltrating the entire school.

Did I forget about something? , she thought to herself as she caught view of kids, her peers essentially, walking to and from their classes, chatting nervously with their friends, fidgeting incessantly.

She grabbed her cell phone but there were no revelatory text messages from Claire, the first person to always warn her about something gossip-related. *Something that Sylvia would have done*, she thought to herself, silently missing the overbearing but ultimately endearing ways of her office colleague

With an audible sigh, she sat up from the floor and began rummaging through her purse for a piece of gum. Her mouth had felt acrid as soon as she had woken up late earlier that morning and didn't have time to brush her teeth. She caught sight of herself in the tiny mirror she had magnetically attached to her locker and noticed that her skin was a bit pale and red in various places.

Her hair looked slightly disheveled and this, too, was because of the whole waking up late factor. She moved her hands through the mess atop her head, attempting to tame the mania. She had managed

141

to make it look halfway decent, when she felt a soft tap on her shoulder.

She quickly turned around, surprised to see the round faced, brightly brown-eyed girl she had met at Chrissy Barr's party a few weeks ago.

"Bennett – hey!" she said, grabbing her purse and slamming her locker door shut behind her. "How're you doing? I haven't seen you since that party."

"Yeah, I've been sort of hanging out solo-style and navigating this teenage experience thing," the other girl replied, her long, dark brown hair tightly braided in a side pony. Bennett had a definite unique sense of style, her Chuck Taylors were two different colors and her vintage Radiohead t-shirt contrasted vastly from the other students' designer duds and dresses.

"Plus, I don't think your friend Claire likes me very much, either," Bennett continued, beginning to walk down the hallway with Darcy by her side. The other kids who saw the two girls walking down the hallways clearly found it strange for them to be together, not to mention actually talking to one another. She had forgotten how shocking it was in high school to see different factions of social circles interact. That was something she definitely did not miss, which was an enormous understatement at that.

"She doesn't like anyone," she quickly replied, suppressing a giggle. Bennett laughed as well, honestly surprised at her lack of filter and willingness to jest her friend.

Both girls soon arrived at the end of the hallway. The large clock that commanded the whole front area of the school, acting as both a teller of time and ominous reminder to her that time was slipping by way too fast, making the Prom come that much sooner.

Sensing the shift in energy in her, Bennett stopped by the clock. "Nervous, huh? The permanence of it will haunt you forever."

For a split second, she thought that Bennett knew exactly what was going on: that she was a farce and that this whole elaborate charade was going to come to a grinding halt in less than a few months.

Sonya? Is that you? she felt like asking Bennett, and she would have asked exactly that if she knew that she wouldn't have come across as a completely psychotic person.

"Huh?" was ultimately all she could muster, looking confusedly at the girl who stood beside her. She couldn't quite put her finger on it or realize why, but she felt like Bennett was someone to be trusted. It was like Bennett understood her, slowing down the urgency of Marina's demands and allowing her to feel like a true teenager, feeling things for the first time. It was like she had known Bennett for eons instead of only actually meeting her the one time at a party thrown by a girl that she had yet to meet.

"I'm exaggerating, Darcy," Bennett replied. "The way everyone's going on about it, you'd think we were all going to be judged by whatever today's brings forever and ever".

Still having no clue what Bennett was talking about, Darcy saw Claire entering the large front doors of the school just down the hallways from where they stood.

"Judged? What do you mean?" she asked, sounding rather dense person. Bennett laughed again, but not in a judgmental way.

"It's Yearbook picture day, remember."

Yearbook picture day! she silently thought. *That explains it.*

As a senior, having an amazing yearbook picture was pivotal to longstanding success as a person, or that's what all of the senior's were thinking about anyway. She wished she could just tell them all that half of them would probably just throw the damn thing out in a few years anyway. She did understand, however, that as a senior, this was one of the last chances to leave a legacy of beauty and popularity, and with her semi-tired face and bad hair, she realized that her legacy was going to be neither beautiful nor remotely popular.

"Uh oh, here comes the party bus," Bennett said, writing

143

something down on a piece of paper she had taken out of her book bag.

"Here – call me. Maybe we can go to the mall or go shoot guns or something?" Bennett handed her the small piece of paper and taking off hurriedly, clearly not willing to take another chance on getting reamed out by Claire who was walking focused towards her. She decided to sit down on the small bench in front of the clock, suddenly feeling tired.

As Claire got nearer and nearer, she knew something was wrong. Claire looked awful, even though her sense of awful was still the goal of beauty other girls aspired to achieve. Her hair was perfectly stick-straight, but her face looked puffy and a subtle light shade of green. Taking a deep breath, she gathered up the little energy she had to deal with the emotional, physical and psychological tsunami that was Claire Marsh, and judging by the looks of her on that bright May morning, it was going to be a real humdinger.

***

After missing the first bell signaling the start of homeroom, both girls finally decided to leave the sparsely populated hallway once hearing the second, and final, sound. If they didn't book it to their class, they knew they would both be getting in major trouble from their English teacher, Ms. Wright, who according to Darcy, was usually anything but right. In fact, Ms. Wright was usually so wrong about things that most of her students fell asleep in class and just read the Coles Notes to the books they had been studying.

While walking to the class, rather slowly at that, she found herself genuinely worried about Claire. Just moments ago, Claire had confided to her that she had been sleeping irregularly, and had been cramping for longer that her usual cycle, hence the light shade of green that dabbed upon her usual perfectly-tanned face. She knew what those symptoms usually meant, but she didn't want to further worry Claire, who seemed just two steps away from a full-blow Mariah Carey style meltdown. It seemed, however, that Claire had been reading her mind.

"No, I'm not pregnant," Claire blurted out, applying lip-gloss absent-mindedly. The red of the gloss made the green in her skin more pronounced. Darcy bit her tongue so she wouldn't say something judgmental. "Well, I shouldn't be anyway. I'm on the strongest pill that the doctor would prescribe. It practically dries your ovaries out completely."

She couldn't help but laugh. She had forgotten how teens candidly thought that birth control pills as the complete and ultimate protective shield from getting pregnant.

"It was just a funny image – ovaries being dried out. Made me think of beef jerky or something," Darcy lied, surprising herself at how easy it came into her head and out of her mouth.

"Yeah, well, I'm glad someone is laughing. I suppose I SHOULD take a test after all," Claire continued. She pulled her tortoise shell compact mirror and looked at herself.

"Oh god, I look positively atrocious!" she screamed upon seeing her reflection before her. She pulled out her make-up bag, which resembled a carry-on piece of luggage, and began to manically apply various creams and powders from tubes that came in literally all shapes and sizes. She watched her friend apply all that make up, like a soldier preparing for war.

"Why did today have to be yearbook picture day? Do you think I can reschedule? Can I call in ugly?"

"Probably not," Darcy had retorted. Claire sure thought highly of herself, she thought. "Besides, your make-up seems to be helping a bit."

"Helping what a bit?" Claire spat back, obviously bating her friend. *Mood swings? Check*, she thought. *This girl might really be preggers.*

Luckily, the first bell rang at that moment, speeding up Claire's application of her ornamental warfare and dropping questioning of her comment. The actual yearbook picture taking wasn't supposed to happen until after English class anyway, so hopefully by then she hoped she would have a chance to put on some make up herself. She needed to look kinda-sorta good.

Now, halfway through English class, the students were listening to Ms. Wright drone on about Death of a Salesman and its protagonist, Willie Loman, who at 63 years old tended to imagine events from the past as if they were real, which she thought was rather fitting as that perfectly summed up Mrs. Wrights teaching style and perspective on life: totally and utterly warped.

She heard her cell phone vibrate, causing her purse to slowly shift around by her feet. Claire, who was sitting next to her, was too on her phone, giving her the impression that it was Claire who was texting her.

While Ms. Wright turned around to write one of her classic manifestos on the blackboard, expecting the class to copy it down word for word, she pulled out her phone and saw there was indeed text message from Claire waiting for her.

"Preg test @ lunch?" it read. Darcy texted back quickly, before getting caught – "Totes there. Make sure u save ur pee" and put the phone back into her purse.

She heard Claire laugh when she read the text. She couldn't help but wonder if Claire was actually pregnant and how that would absolutely change everything. She remembered having been pregnant once in college, and subsequently miscarrying. She could still avidly recall the odd mixture of pain and bizarre elation that came with the whole process. She had been excited on some level to having gotten pregnant, though it was incredibly unplanned, but her rational mind knew that there was no way she would be able to have and support a child. She genuinely did not wish that tumultuous thought process and experience on anyone, especially her new (old) best friend.

She quickly went back to day dreaming about how awful her yearbook picture was definitely going to turn out. She spaced out watching the back of Ms. Wright's bleached blonde, and awfully dry hair as it bobbed while avidly writing on the blackboard in cohesive nonsense about poor Mr. Willy Loman.

Not knowing why, she had a strange inclination to look out the window of the classroom door, upon which she saw Luke waving frantically at her through the glass. No one else in the class around her seemed to notice the most popular boy in school manically throwing his arms about, and she had found it incredibly odd that Claire hadn't noticed as her desk was right beside her own. She inwardly blamed it on all that she had on her mind.

"Ms. Wright, may I have the hall pass, please?" she chimed up, barely a whisper. The teacher turned around quickly as though being tapped on the shoulder, and nodded her head towards the hall pass that lay on the very messy desk. She speedily exited the classroom, anxiety in her tummy over what Luke possibly could want from her now.

***

As soon as she was outside the classroom door, she caught sight of Luke at the end of hallway. He gestured spastically for her to follow him and out the back exit door. Fortunately for her, there was not one single student in the corridor as everyone seemed to be in class. She temporarily debated following him outside, alone, and then realized that she was being overly cautious, as per the usual. She high-tailed it to the back door and went outside to the school field, where Luke sat alone on a poorly maintained bench that was littered with graffiti and carved initials of loves short, fleeting, and insignificant.

UH oh, she thought to herself as she walked slowly to join him.

147

This may not have been such a good idea, she mumbled aloud as she noticed Luke's cheeks were moist with tears.

She decided to take one more full panoramic view of the hallway that surrounded her before joining Luke and the pending uncomfortable confrontation that was sure to unfold. For a brief second, she thought she saw a flash of red hair vanish behind a corner at the end of the hall, but quickly realized it was probably just her paranoia manifesting imaginary images. She was genuinely surprised there weren't more psychoses popping up considering the recent string of events.

***

She couldn't help but look constantly at the watch upon her wrist as Luke continued to blabber on and on somewhat incoherently, alligator tears running endlessly down his finely chiseled cheeks. So far, in what couldn't have been more than five minutes, all she really understood from him were the words "sneak, letter, and weird." She couldn't quite piece his rambling words together into a cohesive whole as he was being pretty dramatic. She had sincerely wanted to grasp what he was going on about in order to help me, but she had to get back to class or else she would be spending her yearbook picture time in detention.

"Luke, listen…" she tried to interrupt, but he was not being responsive to any kind of support or disruption. He had finally stopped crying and sat against the back of the wood bench they were sitting upon, bringing his knees close to his chest. His bottom lip still throbbed and she felt a certain heartfelt pity for him. She also found herself reminded of Arin Ray from her adult job, and with that thought brought all kinds of negative associations.

"I don't know if it's true but I feel like it is, and she's been so weird and distant lately," he droned on. Darcy looked down again at her watch, beginning to freak out when she noticed she had now been gone 10 minutes from class.

"Luke, I have to head back to English class," she said, standing up. He looked up at her, eyes open wide and extremely sad. She felt wanted to be able to spend more time and listen to him but she couldn't afford to get into trouble with the wrath that was known as Ms. Wright.

"Don't go!" Luke said, standing up, moving close to her. Staring at her squarely in the eyes, the blue specks of his irises seemed to lock into the green specks in her own. "You're the only one who understands me, Darcy".

Knowing where this was ultimately going, and there certainly wasn't going to be a happy ending, she attempted to move away. Luke, however, held her by the shoulders and pulled her close to him. His sudden strong grasp surprised her, taking over her instinct to rip herself away.

"Luke – stop. Someone is going to see us," she whispered back to him trying to shake him off, but he would not budge. He was nearly twice her size and was as solid as a tree trunk

"I don't care anymore. I can't stand to be away from you. I gave you the space you needed, didn't I? I've tried to pretend that the last six months didn't happen and that you didn't mean anything to me, but I can't hide it anymore. I love you," he said and pulled her close, kissing her intensely.

She felt his soft lips on hers, gentle but firm. She couldn't help but fall into his arms, letting the tension in her shoulders soften and get wrapped into the kiss that she found herself enjoying. Before getting too involved, she managed to pull herself away, her fear of someone seeing them taking over the craziness of the situation.

"This is so not a good idea," she said, completely separating herself from their illicit embrace. She wasted no time in turning around and running back towards the school door, nearly tripping on a Coke can along the way. She had thought Luke would follow her, preaching his undying love loud enough for everyone to hear, but

149

when she glanced back, he had sat back down on the bench and placed his head into his lap.

Part of her *had* wanted him to chase after her and take him in her arms, telling her again that he loved her, but another part of her knew that nothing could ever come of her and Luke. He was her best friends boyfriend, and even if he loved her (or so he thought), it would have to go unrequited.

Upon opening the red, heavy door that opened up onto the school's main floor, where her English class sat waiting, she was cautious to ensure that no one witnessed the bizarre interaction that had just unfolded beyond them in the school football field. Feeling like Carmen Sandiego, she sped walked to Ms. Wright, albeit begrudgingly.

Chapter 18

The students were lined up in several rows by surname. The energy had started to shift from apprehension to relief as students left the gym where the school photographers had set up camp. Claire, Rena and Darcy all stood beside each other, thankful that their surnames were all within a letter of one another's.

Claire had managed to pull herself together after the marathon bathroom break that followed straight after English class. She had pulled Darcy and Rena into the stall with her and made them praise her for how good she had looked. At first she had thought that Claire was joking, and initially went with it, lavishing her friend with compliment after compliment and taking picture after picture with her phone. Rena was game too. But after a few minutes of this incessant ego boosting silliness, her effort began to wane, and she waited patiently for Rena to also give up and for Claire to join them all in a loud bout of laughter. It didn't happen, and Rena just kept on goading Claire, while Darcy found herself grow quiet.

"You don't think I look good enough for yearbook?" Claire said after it became obvious that she wasn't interested in continuing to lavish inauthentic praise upon her friend.

She almost laughed out loud, sincerely thinking that Claire was also kidding around, having momentarily forgotten that she had just spent the last five minutes telling Claire that she was basically Scarlett Johannsen with a personality. Finally understanding that Claire was in no way joking, she looked at Rena for support but the other girl moved her eyes instantaneously to the cracked tiled linoleum floor.

"You look amazing and never looked better," she finally replied. Claire smiled at her, and then went back to re-applying another layer of cherry red lip-gloss.

"I've looked plenty better, Ms. Pratt, and you know that for a fact," Claire went on, a twinkle in her blue eyes. She looked at her reflection in the mirror one last time and turned around abruptly. "But I do look pretty incredible for only having slept three hours last night and cramping like a bitch."

Rena laughed, her long, red hair bouncing madly upon her shoulders. Darcy watched as Rena also applied more lip gloss, slow and steady-like, almost copying every move Claire had just made. She stared intently at Darcy in the mirror while Claire bent down to tie her pink Keds, a sly smirk across her round face. She didn't know quite how to interpret the odd expression. Was it a knowing a smile? A commiserate smile? She honestly had no idea.

The bell signaling the beginning of the pending picture taking rang loudly. Darcy stole another glance at her own reflection. The makeup that Claire had given her certainly helped her blotchy appearance but she still looked a tad puffy and tired after the terrible nightmare just the night before.

The line-up to take their yearbook pictures moved fairly quickly and the three girls found themselves talking casually about the

152

upcoming weekend and the big senior stay over, an event that she was completely unaware of but both other girls seemed to be elated about.

The Senior Stay Over, she had quickly learned, was the second most important social event in the Flint Ridge High senior's year, next to the prom. The whole senior class would be taking a giant bus over to Beach Bridge, a town four towns away that was known for its rustic cottages and pristine, white beaches. The school had planned special activities to commemorate the student's four past years in high school. She got the impression that it was sort of a summer camp that was only three days long and acted a chance for all of the kids to bond before they went their separate ways at College. Speaking of college, she found it peculiar that her friends never, ever brought up what was looming post-graduation.

Though the idea of a stay over intrigued her, she couldn't quite wrap her mind around the whole concept. In all the books she had read over the years, she had never come across the plot point of a stay over, and she wasn't sure how she would handle such an event. She had just met all of these people after all, and having to spend two nights with them in relative wilderness would be a whole other level of crazy.

"So clearly the three of us will bunk, and Luke, Jason and Kieran will be in the room opposite us, Claire said, once again playing the alpha female of the group.

Kieran, Darcy thought. *That's a new one*. Now she definitely didn't want to go on the stay over, especially with Luke being right across the hall from her. Who knew what late night monologue he would orate to her, especially in the middle of the forest.

"Clearly," Rena replied. She chose to remain quiet and looked around the room surrounding them. The line they were in continued to move rapidly as they inched closer and closer to the gymnasium doors where the photographers were just beyond.

"What IS wrong with you today, Darcy? You're acting all kinds

153

of weird," Claire stated, looking angrily at her. Rena, too, joined in the glare.

"I'm just super tired, C," she replied.

Of you, she wanted to blurt out loud, but bit her tongue. Her exhaustion made her prone to outbursts, but she caught herself before saying something she knew she'd instantly regret.

"Well drink some coffee or red bull or something. You're beginning to get on my nerves," Claire shot back, fire in her words. Rena smiled, seemingly enjoying the argument.

She took a deep breath, trying to maintain her own growing annoyance with Claire and her pedantic ways in check. She felt the glares of both girls upon her, trying to bear into her soul. Feeling a weighty pressure on her shoulders, she sincerely wished that all she could do was get into bed, pull down her black out blinds, and drown out the world around her. She had had no time to ponder her new life. She had been simply plunged into a whole new existence, and she wanted to take some time to properly analyze and make a decent attempt to understand her friends and family. She truthfully did not want to argue with Claire, or anyone at all for that matter, but she found herself reaching the end of her patience. If she couldn't be dramatic as a 17 year old, when could she be?

She heard the photographer's assistant call for students' surnames starting M, and all three girls moved closer, even though they had a few more letters yet.

"Earth to Darcy," Claire went on. "You're holding up the line."

It took every last ounce of will power she had to not lunge over her maybe-pregnant friend and pull her hair, or do whatever it was that girls did when in a physical fight and had to express their anger. Instead, she settled for a deep sigh and walked forward for the big photo op.

***

154

After much finagling with an amateur photographer who had a striking resemblance to Reba McIntire with an advanced eczema problem, she finally settled upon a pose that favored her 'good' side in photographs. Reba wasn't too enthused about letting a teenage girl direct a photo shoot that held no real importance, but she let her move the camera, backlight and even the green screen to capture her best possible angle. She figured that Claire's photograph take-over would probably have made her own appear downright homely.

"I'm ready," she said through gritted teeth, aware of the prescient need to keep her eyes open so as to avoid having a droopy-eyed photo that would haunt her forever.

The photographer took three quick photos in succession and reviewed her work on the expensive-looking digital camera that was set up before her.

"Can I see them?" she immediately asked, walking closer to Reba who instantly pressed the power button to turn off the camera.

"We're not supposed to show you the pictures," Reba promptly replied, hunching awkwardly over the camera as though Darcy would have some sort of x-ray vision to see the photographs through the camera, which was now turned clearly off.

"Why not? It's my photo!" Darcy countered, noting the unpleasant whine in her voice, which made her instantly embarrassed. She did, however, really want to see those pictures.

"Because it will ruin the excitement of wondering if you got a good picture for your yearbook," Reba snidely replied, calling "Next" loudly.

She grabbed her purse and hastily left the makeshift studio set up in the gym. She heard other students trying to take over the photo session to no avail. She couldn't help but think about Claire's photograph session and the poor soul who had to deal with that ticking time bomb.

Chapter 19

Sitting alone in her car, blasting the Fugees and tapping her fingers on the steering wheel to match the rhythm of the catchy song, Darcy looked out ahead at the empty parking lot that stretched out and took up her entire field of vision, desolate and depressing in its lone presence. Even though it wasn't even yet 1 pm, the parking lot looked like it had been evacuated due to some sort of life-altering, catastrophic event. The empty store shops were apparently open and ready for business, but there were no customers to be found. It gave her the creeps. And she wasn't into the creeps.

Claire had made her drive to a remote, practically rural, strip mall where there was a drug store to buy a pregnancy test and mitigating the possibility of having anyone recognize her or question her with accusatory glances. Claire understandably didn't want to have that prickly experience of running into any of their classmates, and Darcy couldn't really blame her. Gossip was certainly something that they did not want to follow them as they gallivanted around school and the mall. At school, however, was a whole other matter.

As a result of the lengthy though picturesque drive, they had both missed Geography class, which was an absence that she knew she'd have to answer to the next day. Their teacher, Mr. Boone, was an avid attendance taker and question asker. A day didn't seem to go by that he didn't ask her for an answer to some sort of geographical related question. Fortunately, she did happen to know most of the answers to the teachers' questions, so in a way she thought perhaps she may have been goading him into asking her all of those times.

With her friend inside the drugstore, which, she noted, looked archaic and so aged that it would not have been out of place in a horror movie, she decided to turn off the music and let the silence envelop her. She had had the air conditioning blasting as it was extremely hot outside, sweat appearing on her brow from just the short walk from the school to the parking lot to where her car was comfortable parked in the shade. She was thankful to be safe in the confines of her car, cool, and alone, with serious emphasis on the alone part.

She looked out before her once more to better scrutinize her surroundings just a little bit more in depth. She momentarily glanced half-heartedly around the empty lot, and then found her focus venturing onto the long row of ash trees that swayed in the hot, humid wind that blew silently through them. Their leaves softly moved to and fro, almost like a lullaby in their gentle motions. She found herself almost beginning to nod off, the sleepless night before her catching up with her rather quickly.

Having been the 'new' Darcy for nearly a month, she quickly realized that she had not once thought about her real adult-Darcy life, though the term real did not really have a conclusive meaning for her these days. She instantly felt guilty for not having thought about it earlier, her heart feeling like it was sinking into the lower depths of her stomach.

She thought of her beautiful little dog, a little Dachshund that was (is?) the light of her life. She thought of the dogs little frantically waving tale whenever she got home late from work, a pizza box in her arms because she was often too lazy to make any sort of reasonably healthy dinner. The dog's long ears were her favorite thing to tickle, and the dog certainly loved all of the lavish attention that was bestowed upon her on a daily basis.

Her thoughts then ventured to that awful day that precipitated her decision to take Marina up on her impossible offer of switching lives. The firing from her job, the notice of her apartment building going co-op – all of those awful events that made up her mind to make this mammoth change which resulted in the predicament she now found herself in. She didn't regret her decision, but she knew she hadn't had the chance to think it through completely.

Claire knocked abruptly on the driver's side window, shaking her from her reverie. She felt like this was what her new life was: a series of interruptions full of dramatic angst that were no way remotely close to the fantastic teenage lives in the books she held so dear to her heart. She felt a pang in her temples – a surefire sign of a pending headache.

She reached over and unlocked the passenger side door and Claire bound in, placing a tiny brown paper bag into her lap. Both girls looked at the bag as though it was going to speak to them or engage them in some sort of conversation. Sensing the gravity of the situation, Claire didn't chime in with one of her signature sarcastic comments, and she found herself thankful for the continued silence in the car as they drove back to school. Both girls refused to speak about the elephant in the car as they made their way back to high school life.

***

With Picture Day now officially over, the girls' return to school after their lunchtime detour was like entering another world entirely. The student body as a whole seemed to exhale a collective breath of air once the last photo was taken, thus restoring some sort of normalcy and balance to their teen-verse. The heated worries about getting a good photo ended and the next, hot topic of discussion was a merger of the Senior Stay over and The Prom.

The week prior, the student council had placed posters throughout the entire school with semi-clever slogans and ads in hopes of recruiting kids to be part of the Prom Committee. The posters were literally everywhere: Darcy couldn't even use the washroom without being 6 inches away from a brightly colored poster showing girls her age dressed in formal gowns, presumably at their prom. The slogan for this years prom was "Don't let high school pass you by... help plan the most important day of your life!" She cringed when she saw it the first time, but with each subsequent bathroom visit (as the posters were literally omnipresent) she began to entertain the idea of joining the committee herself.

When she was in high school the first time, she had tried to join the prom committee since the 10th grade, which was when she would have first been considered eligible. Each and every time the student council thought of reasons why she couldn't join, ranging from "We already have enough girls on the committee" the year that it was all boys who rather infamously planned a Playboy-themed Prom (which got shot down in the final hour), to "Not a chance". All the reasons meant the same thing to Darcy: she wasn't cool enough. Now seemed to be her chance to avenge that lack in her own past high school experience, but when she brought the idea to both Claire and Rena later that afternoon while they packed their purses after their last class, it was as like she said she'd said that she wanted to enlist in the army.

"You'd better be kidding, Darcy," Claire immediately said, her face distorting into a look so disgusted that Darcy almost felt disgusted herself.

"Only the losers and geeks join the prom committee because they know they'd never get asked to go," Rena chimed in, closing her locker not without glancing a look at herself in the mirror, pursing her lips absent-mindedly.

"And not go at all," Claire continued. "Besides, I spoke to Jason today and told him to ask you".

Rena dropped her purse, the contents spilling out all over the white linoleum floor. Darcy bent down instantly to help her re-fill it, though there was no disguising the palpable negative energy that Rena emanated, or the sudden blushing of her cheeks.

"I told you not to, Claire!" Rena screamed, her voice going from 1 to 10 within milliseconds.

"People tell me lots of things. But do I do them? Nope," Claire replied, not even acknowledging Rena's shocked expression. Looking at both girls on their knees, Claire began to scroll through her cell phone.

"Well, what did he say?" Rena finally muttered once her bag was re-filled and both girls were once again on standing upright. They then left the bathroom and began to make their way out of school for another day, long hair waving and with purses almost twice their size.

"He said that he was going to ask Darcy, duh," Claire replied, flipping her hair over her shoulder. She wore it wavy today, the long locks bouncing as she walked.

"You can tell him to not waste his time," Darcy said as they neared her car. She thought she saw a smirk sneak across Rena's face.

"You're not going alone to the prom," Claire firmly replied, leaning against the black BMW. She pulled her sunglasses on, giving her the appearance of a bored celebrity just like the ones that Darcy loved to read about while lying in the tub on a Friday night. It was one of her many guilty pleasures.

160

There was a sense of finality in Claire's voice, her tone implying she was not to be questioned and that the decision has been made and there was no repealing it.

She suddenly felt angry and did not know if she could keep her anger hidden this time. It suddenly dawned on her that since she had her dream come true and she became a character in a teen fiction novel, she had been unable to really enjoy herself and immerse her efforts in being that 17 year old girl that she envied as a 30-something year old woman. She knew there were several reasons adding to the lack of enjoyment: the lack of time to actually get to know herself because of the hectic social calendar she held, having an angry brother whom she was not giving up on, and also having her presumable best friends' boyfriend pursuing her like she was his unrequited love.

But there was one key reason that in all these weeks she didn't realize until that moment that was causing her to always second guess herself and question her ideals, and at that moment it was crystal clear: Claire.

Claire was always proverbially raining on her parade. Every time she attempted to think of something fun to do aside from the usual jaunts to the mall and to the beach, Claire shot her down within seconds and managed to always turn the conversation's focus back to her. Even just moments ago she tried to dismiss her suggestion of joining the prom committee without giving it a second chance. True, this time Claire had Rena's partnership on preparing a united front of the prom committee idea, but most times, it was truly 'The Claire Show'.

She knew very well, not only from being an avid reader of Sweet Valley High but also from her own painful high school memories that she was trying to redeem, why Claire behaved the way she did. Claire was used to being the quintessential 'mean girl' and the object of every lusty teen boy's attention. She was used to calling the shots and deciding what her friends were going to do and be seen with because essentially her friends were an extension of herself. While Rena had no problem with granting Claire the power to be the girl in charge, she herself found it become increasingly different to tolerate Claire's antics, possible pregnancy or not.

Obviously, Claire was not used to being questioned or to have her friends express any kind of independent, rational thinking. And even though she was in this new life only a matter of weeks, her threshold for her friend's questionable behavior had been eradicated and erased completely. She recognized it could have been hormonal (she was having the weirdest mood swings lately), but she also realized that she wasn't shaking her 30 year olds rational self fast enough. At that moment she had had enough, and wasn't afraid of any social impact of what was to come once she honestly expressed herself.

"Oh, not only am I going to the prom alone," she began, opening her own car door which was parked right beside Claire's. "But I'm going to join the prom committee and plan the most craptastic and tacky prom that they'll let me plan."

It was like a bomb had gone off, its pending disastrous impacts littering the world around them. The silence amongst the girls was sudden and severe. Claire and Rena both did not know what to do or say.

She opened the car door and sat inside, the scorching hot leather seat feeling like embers upon her bronzed legs. She turned on the radio and took her time lowering the window as both of her 'friends' were still speechless. Once the window was fully open, she felt some of the cool breeze enter the car, letting the still and stagnant air escape.

She saw both Claire and Rena's eyes widen until she thought it must have been painful for them. Claire's mouth opened slightly in shock, while Rena's stayed closed, red cheeks in full-on flame mode.

"What did you just say?" Claire finally mouthed, her voice low, nearly a whisper by that point. Darcy let the silence linger and purposely did not answer right away, instead opting to turn the car on and letting the air conditioner blast.

"I think you heard me", she replied. She turned the key in the ignition and blasted the air conditioning. "Text tonight?", she said before backing up and driving quickly out of the school parking lot, leaving both girls dumbfounded at her outburst and clear assertion of independence, giving her an undeniable sense of elation as she drove away.

***

At the dinner table later that evening, she noticed that her usual talkative mother was rather silent as she passed around the asparagus. Her dark blonde hair, a few shades darker that her own, hung limply and the usual make up that adorned her youthful-looking face was absent. While her mother was certainly beautiful free of makeup, she found herself growing concerned as to why her mother was acting so unlike her usual hyper-self.

"What's up, Mom?" she said once she got her plate back, full of vegetables and turkey roast. She heard her stomach growl.

Mason shot her a glance as though to warn her to not push the issue but it went right over her head. Even her father, handsome in his yellow polo shirt, looked briefly at her clearly wondering why she would ask such an inane question.

"You know what today is, honey," her mother somberly replied, staring intently at the dinner plate before her. She pushed the food around on her plate, not taking one single bite.

She knew not to ask any more questions. The sullen expression that had soaked up her mother's usual cheery disposition was enough to quell the hunger she had just felt.

She decided to let the conversation move towards her father's rather difficult work day at the law firm and his frustration with his new assistant's virtual incompetence. Remaining quiet throughout her father's tirade, she thought that perhaps subconsciously she held solidarity with her new mom who reminded her so much of her own (old?) mother and let the men govern the conversation.

It was only after dinner did she find out why her mother was so obviously sad, and the news itself was acidly delivered, not unsurprisingly, by Mason who seemed to be brilliant at turning on the wickedness and sweetness within seconds of one another.

She had decided to sit by the pool and stretch out on one of the lawn chairs, rather content in not having to deal with Claire's tirades when she had heard her brother leave the house and close the patio doors behind him, leaving the two of them alone in the yard. It was still warm despite being close to 8 pm, and she was happy she had stayed in her shorts and t-shirt ensemble instead of changing into sweat pants as she usually did when she got home from school.

"I've always wondered, little sister," Mason said as he sat beside her. He rolled up the short sleeves of his t-shirt to cool off. "How do you have such impeccable timing to ruin things?"

She sighed heavily, succumbing to her teenaged tendencies to flare on the dramatic side of things. It was the easier thing to do instead of silently brooding and being over analytical of the interaction unfolding before her with her sibling.

"It's difficult sometimes, I won't lie," she said, her voice calm and uninterested. "It's actually a 7-tiered process that took quite some time to master."

Mason seemed to be surprised by her quick and witty response. Clearly, a quick wit wasn't typical of the old Darcy and she enjoyed this temporarily stumping of her brother's usual vitriol personality.

"Did you learn this process in between shopping at the mall and kissing Claire's ass?" he finally replied, anger obvious in his voice. He looked at her squarely in the eyes, clearly baiting her to engage in some sort of spat. She wasn't feeling like it and so decided to just be honest in her retort.

"Isn't it tiring to be so mopey and angry all of the time, Mason?

In case your Ivy League brain didn't clue in to the little scene earlier at the dinner table, I honestly really don't know why mom is so bummed out. End scene."

Physically exhausted by the entire taxing interaction with her brother, she slowly began to sit up, figuring that her next activity should only include a large tub full of hot water and bubbles. She did have a thing for aromatherapy and the well stocked Bed, Bath and Beyond-ish bathroom that adjoined her bathroom was sure to have something that would lift up her spirits.

"Which is so characteristic Darcy." Mason replied, matching her action and also sitting up in the chair. He looked at her attentively, still avid on having an argument. She decided not to bite and began to walk towards the door entering the kitchen. Mason followed her without hesitation like a little puppy.

"So what's got her so down anyway?" she asked once Mason stayed quiet for a few moments, a rare event unto itself. It was obvious that she should have known the reason, but she figured she may as well continue the 'dumb sister' routine.

"Oh, it's only the anniversary of Grandpa's death, stupid," Mason casually replied as they entered the now empty kitchen. Instantly, and semi-physically, she felt awful about having forgotten such a serious event. The small supper she had eaten just an hour before turned sour and acidic in her stomach and for a moment she felt she was going to throw up right there upon the white marble that seemed to encase every surface in the kitchen.

She chastised herself silently again for not having inferred that it was something serious that she had 'forgotten', but she also managed to quickly reassure herself that there was no possible way to have remembered the sad event that her mother was silently mourning.

"Yes, very stupid," she whispered to herself, loud enough to cause her brother to chuckle. She found his reaction surprising and intriguing, especially seeing as she had not heard her brother heard her brother laugh, let alone seen him smile since the 'switch' began.

"I guess I'd better go make this mess-up right, huh?" she said, grabbing a cold bottle of water out of the mammoth refrigerator. She couldn't help but be awed by the entire section of the fridge seemingly reserved for water bottles, of which she approximated at least 50 all perfectly aligned. Before taking a sip from the bottle, Mason looked up at her, a slight smile still upon his face.

"Yes, I'd say that's a rather good idea," he replied. "Before Mom has a complete nervous breakdown because she thinks her dutiful daughter can't even remember the passing of her grandfather's demise." Darcy thought she heard him stifle a giggle behind his words but wasn't entirely sure.

"Are you ever not sarcastic?" she laughed. She took a sip of water and watched her brother leave the room quietly. *Progress*, she thought to herself. *Baby steps.*

She made her way out of the kitchen and walked to the den where she noticed her mother talking animatedly on the phone. She took a seat beside her mom upon the leather sofa that took up the entire wall of the living room/den and waited to apologize, again, for another flub she didn't intend to make.

***

After a lengthy chat with her mother that resulted in both Platt women shedding tears and laughing loudly intermittently, she made her way back to her bedroom. She figured now was a good a time as any to begin poking around and make a decent effort to try to learn more about her new persona.

She hadn't had much alone time in the past few days, let alone weeks, to fully commit herself to nosing around her own bedroom. The bedroom of the girl that she now was, and still, remained an undiscovered land, albeit one with fluorescent colors and modern technology. And some very slight flourishes of actual style.

166

After spending ample time glancing at the books on the shelf that sat parallel to the bed, she read the spines of the many pieces of writing that faced her. Absent were the books that the modern-day she dearly loved and instead sat books that *she* should have been reading, ranging from To Kill a Mockingbird to The Bell Jar. What caught her eye, however, was the earmarked copy of Death of a Salesman.

She pulled the well-worn book off the shelf and took it with her to the bed. Lying down, she allowed herself to relax. She was surprised to see that the other her had highlighted several passages from the book that seemingly dealt with the obvious themes of superficiality and attractiveness. She found this really surprising, considering all that she had learned thus far about her new personality, superficiality and the adoration of physical beauty was what her life had been built on.

Now it could have been that the former her highlighted these passages because she felt the same way as deluded Willy Loman, but she felt that it was deeper than that. It was almost like the old her was less superficial than the new her, and all those around her thought so fervently.

As she read the various highlighted passages, a sheet of paper fell out of the book and onto the bed. It appeared to be a page that had been torn out of a diary or a journal of some sort, written in the neat writing that she recognized as similar to her own.

She put the book down and lifted the sheet to read it, excited to find out more about the 17 year old her, the enigma.

The mall was the usual routine. I watched Claire try on 5 different black dresses that looked exactly the same. She asked me if she looked fat but I just laughed at that as her body is amazing, which she totally knows. She was buying a black dress for a special date tonight. She said she wanted to look extra hot, which is a huge joke because Claire could wear a garbage bag and look better than most girls at school, including me. My flat chest and big butt would look so ugly in the dress Claire was in. She asked me if I still had her red scarf that I borrowed at thanksgiving, which I thought was weird as I had never borrowed that ugly thing, but in usual Claire fashion, she was convinced I had it.

Flat chest and big butt? she thought to herself. *This girl was deluded.*

She continued reading, completely riveted by the words.

I wonder who she's going out on a date with. It's obviously not with Luke because Luke is meeting me tonight. He keeps asking to come over while C thinks he's at football practice so we could fool around, but I'm not into it anymore. Luke's been totally in love with me since like 9th grade and while I semi-contemplated dating him, Claire totally swooped in and began to date him. I was pissed off at first but I got over it. I mean, I didn't really like the guy after all, but since Claire had become all weird and secretive lately, it was easy to get it on with Luke.

She went on reading, totally enthralled by the journal entry. She found it more interesting to read and savor than the books she had been reading for school, primarily because it was more authentic and real, almost urgent in its cadence. She flipped the page over, interested. What had Claire been hiding?

When I got home after the mall, Charlie was waiting for me in front of my bedroom door. He looked so hot – he was wearing a super tight white t-shirt which showed off all of his muscles, and he had a little bit of stubble on his face which drove me crazy! I had been trying to talk to Charlie for years, pretty much ever since he and his mom Glenda began working for my parents, but he's so shy and quiet. I was really surprised to see him waiting for me. I was so shocked when he asked me to the prom! I told him it was like 5 months away, and he laughed and said that he knew that every other guy in school would ask so he figured he'd get to me first. What a sweetie! I said I'd have to let him know, which made him look super sad, but it's not like I couldn't reply right away.

A girl needs to think about these major decisions in her life. I told him I'd tell him next time I saw him, probably that weekend (which was totally enough time to think!), and he just sort of sulked away as I flew into my bedroom, giddy, suppressing my joy.

I pulled out my cell phone to text Claire, but thought twice about it. She knew that I thought Charlie was super dreamy, but she was always making fun of him, saying how poor she was, and how weird it would look if I dated the housekeepers' son. She was right – it would look weird, but I didn't care. Everyone I hang out with at school, everyone I talked to, are so fake. They only care about looking good and not eating. Sometimes I just wished I could move to like a small town or something and be a normal girl!

She was disappointed to see that she had reached the end of the journal excerpt. It seemed that 17-year-old her wasn't as entirely vapid as she had previously thought, or that Claire wasn't acting more mean than usual. She was intrigued by what Claire had been hiding and who she could have been secretly dating, but had made up her mind that there was no way she would ever find out as Claire wasn't the most divulging sort.

She laid back down on the bed, feeling the softness of the many pillows around her and relished in the silence that the room brought her. After reading the excerpt of the old Darcy's journal, she felt closer to younger version of herself in some way, almost nearer to her, if that could be. Why had that single page in particular had been torn out rather hastily and shoving the fragment inside her apparently favorite book, she wondered to herself. Did that mean that the rest of the journal was around the bedroom somewhere, nestled within another keepsake? As the many thoughts flooded her mind, she drifted off to a sleep that she welcomed with open arms and closed eyes.

Chapter 20

She heard a loud knock on her bedroom window, abruptly waking her up from her deep sleep. It took her a few serious attempts to actually open her eyes, but when she did and she looked around the room, she noticed that it was dark, even with the blinds wide open. Hearing another tap on the window, she quickly switched on her bedside lamp, illuminating the room.

She walked slowly over to the window, mentally noting that it was definitely not a normal teenage event to have someone throw things at her bedroom window, let alone in the middle of the night. Although she couldn't help but think there was something slightly romantic about it. Her clock showed it was close to 2 am. Recognizing that fact, she grew nervous as she slowly continued to make her way to the window.

She snuck up to the side of the massive glass paneling and hid behind the blind, shielding her presence from whatever lunatic was pulling an 80's movie moment and catapulting pebbles upon the glass. She ever so slowly raised the blind, peeking to see who the culprit was.

She saw Luke in mid-throw of another rock and pulled open the window quickly.

"What the hell are you doing?!" she whispered loudly, startling Luke and causing him to drop the rock in his hand. He stumbled back slowly, almost losing his footing.

"Are you drunk?!" she said. Luke looked like he was going to yell something back, but she silenced him. "Don't move – I'll be right down!"

As she hadn't even changed into her pajamas before resting her eyes, she was able to sneak out of her bedroom fully clothed. She quietly opened her bedroom door, ensuring that she wasn't going to intercept her parents or her brother in mid-bathroom walk.

Once she discerned that the way was clear, she made her downstairs and to the backyard to the pool where Luke sat, legs bobbing in the water, completely laid back so that he was facing the sky, which was clear and full of shining stars.

"What are you doing, Luke?" she said, sitting down beside him. He smelled strongly of alcohol and she had to plug her nose just to talk to him. She pulled him towards her so they were at eye level.

"Coming to see my girlfriend," he replied, moving forward to kiss her, but she was too quick for him and pulled away. Luke would have nearly hit the concrete patio if she hadn't pulled him back up.

"Your girlfriend lives about 10 streets away. Why don't you go and throw rocks at *her* window," she spat back. She immediately felt remorseful for her pointed response because Luke looked like he was about to cry, similar to their confrontation in the school yard a few weeks ago. While feeling bad for being so rash, she still was annoyed that his puppy love for her was so hard to shake.

"I can't stand to be away from you, Darcy. You don't

171

understand. I know you don't feel the same way about me the way I feel about you but I can't stand to be apart from you anymore!", he slurred, turning his gaze from her to his feet which looked small in the lit pool.

"Luke – whatever we had…it is over now. You know that," she tried to reason, but he was determined to declare his love for her for the umpteenth time, clearly not afraid to wake up her parents and or anyone else within the immediate vicinity, attributed to the copious amounts of alcohol he had consumed.

"You keep saying that but I know you don't mean it," he went on, tears beginning to well up in his eyes. She felt guilty for treating him like this but he plainly wasn't getting the picture. Judging from the journal entry she had read earlier that night, she had never really liked Luke, and was only toying with his emotions, which certainly was mean-spirited. *Why do I have to clean up this mess*, she thought to herself as Luke abruptly pulled his legs out of the pool, splashing water all over her t-shirt.

"Come on, Luke. You're wasted," she continued. "Let's get you into the pool house."

"Yeah, baby," he replied, thinking they were going to do something completely different than what she had in mind, which was a big cup of coffee and a dry t-shirt for Luke to change into.

Instead of trying to clarify the situation, she put his arm over her shoulder and guided him into the tiny house that was about 10 feet away. Once inside, she turned on the small lamp that sat upon a side table so as to not alert anyone to the fact that she was hanging out in the pool house with a boy in the middle of the night. She grabbed a few towels off of the shelf that faced the tiny sofa that had Luke plopped himself upon.

"I'll be right back. DO NOT MOVE," she said firmly. "I need to change."

"Into something more comfortable?" Luke replied, and then began to launch into a fit of laughter. She quickly shushed him

172

before disappearing into her house once more.

When she returned 10 minutes later in a dry t-shirt and holding a steaming cup of coffee, she found Luke asleep on the sofa. She walked slowly over to him and nudged his shoulder, causing him to wake up right away.

"Oh, hey," he said, rubbing his eyes. He looked around confusedly, surprised to see where he was.

"How'd I get into your pool house?" he asked, looking like a sweet little, innocent kid. She handed him the steaming cup of coffee and he took a big gulp.

"You were declaring your love for me at my bedroom window, Romeo", she laughed, sitting down beside him.

"I'm such a loser," Luke replied, redness blushing his cheeks. "I'm sorry, Darcy."

"You're not a loser, Luke," she replied. He handed her the drained cup of coffee. "You're just a teenage boy in love."

"With a girl who hates me," he countered, sadness in his eyes and redness beginning to color his cheeks.

"I don't hate you, Luke. We just can't do this to Claire. It's wrong and I'm sorry that it ever started. We have to make things right and stop fooling around. It would kill her if she ever found out".

She was surprised to hear Luke begin to laugh.

"You're kidding me, right?" he said, turning around to face her.

"What do you mean?" she asked, genuinely unaware of what Luke was alluding to.

"You're her best friend, Darcy. Don't pretend like you don't know," he went on, incredulous at her obliviousness to his declaration.

"Don't know what? Luke, you're drunk and need to go home and sleep. You can sleep in here if you want until you feel ok enough to drive home," she said, getting up. There was no point in talking to a drunken person.

173

"She's sleeping with someone else," he spat out, forcing her to stop dead in her tracks.

"She has been since we started fooling around. I don't know with whom, but she definitely is. She keeps denying it, but she is. I know it."

"You're being paranoid, Luke. I'll see you at school tomorrow," she replied. She turned around, not interested in pursuing such a delicate conversation with a drunken friend. She soon walked slowly out of the pool house and closed the door softly behind her. She waited by the door until Luke turned off the light and fell back asleep.

She sat herself down on the patio chair by the pool, staring intently at the tiny pool house, which looked like a miniature replica of the mansion she lived in. She marveled at the incredible life she had been immersed into, but also marveled at the endless crises that seemed to infiltrate her new existence that prevented her from achieving true happiness and maintaining a precocious innocence.

So Luke knew that Claire was cheating on him, she thought. She laid back in the patio chair so that it was completely reclined and shifted her gaze to the night sky looming above her. The stars were large and bright, and she felt her eyes grow tired.

But why didn't they just break up? She thought before falling asleep. *And why did do I feel like I know whom Claire was cheating with?*

174

Chapter 21

The rain fell hard the next morning upon every single surface it could get its little wet hands on. The trees swayed back and forth from the strong and gusty winds, making a clear audible whooshing sound that was equal parts scary and soothing. It was not cold outside, but it was not exactly hot either, unlike all of the other days that seemed to fall upon the town. The rain was a welcome respite, and it certainly allowed Darcy the chance to wear something more than a barely-there pair of shorts and a tank top.

"Come and have some cereal, Darcy," Glenda said, her kind eyes and warm smile greeting her as soon as she entered into the kitchen. The housekeeper pulled out a chair from the edge of the table where Mason was already seated. Unsurprisingly, he did not even acknowledge her presence.

She sat down and poured some random sugary cereal from a

fluorescent pink box with an eagle (or was it a pelican?) on the front. Mason looked at her quizzically, but still being semi-asleep, she was without the energy yet to trade barbs with her caustic older brother.

After pouring some milk into her bowl before her, she set the carton back on the table while Glenda handed her some freshly squeezed orange juice. The ease in which Glenda doted on the two Platt children led her to believe that the woman genuinely loved her and her brother. It warmed her heart.

"Hey Glenda, what are you doing after school?" she randomly asked. She surprised herself with the sudden exclamation.

Glenda looked up semi-startled from the behind the counter top where she had been wiping dishes. "Just sorting some things that your mother has collected in the basement," she quickly replied, wiping away.

"Why don't we go to the mall and go shopping or something?" she blurted, surprising Glenda as much as herself with the question. Mason looked at her in shock, his eyebrows furrowed.

Glenda took her time in responding, obviously taken aback by Darcy's offer. As she had previously experienced when she first met Glenda, Darcy felt a certain kinship with the woman, instantly feeling comfortable around her presence.

"Oh, that sounds nice. I do need to buy something for my niece's wedding next month", Glenda replied, her smile wide. "Will you pick me up after school?"

"Of course. I'll be here as soon as class ends. Yay – I'm excited!" she giggled, taking a big spoonful of the cereal, the high sugar content instantly giving her a rush.

She was genuinely excited to spend some time with Glenda, partially because it meant she wouldn't have to hang out with moody Claire or sullen Rena. She also couldn't see a problem with taking a break from being a hyper-attentive teenager. The break itself seemed like well deserved one. She did, after all, always end up hanging out with older, mature people instead of those within her own demographic. She was comforted to know that being 17 didn't change that personal preference.

When Glenda left the kitchen a few moments later, Mason wasted no time in pouncing on his sister.

"Are you being serious? Taking Glenda to the mall?" he said, looking incredulously at his sister.

"Why? What's the big deal? I like Glenda," she replied honestly, taking another bite of the cereal that was beginning to give her more than a sugar high. She felt like her heart had gone from 0 to 60 and would soon erupt out of her chest and right into her cereal bowl.

"Glenda is our housekeeper, Darcy," Mason shot back, his voice raising a few octaves. She found herself having to take a second before replying because she thought Mason may have been joking, but on second thought, she realized he was being completely and utterly serious.

"You are such a snob. Who cares what she is? She takes care of us and takes care of the house. I can spend time with her if I want to."

"Wouldn't you rather spend time with Claire?" he replied, gaining composure. He gingerly took a sip of his coffee, clearly content with himself for causing a rise out of his sister.

"Not that it's any of your business, but no, I don't", she responded angrily, taking one final bite of cereal then proceeded to draining her cup full of orange juice.

"Spat in Sweet Valley High?" Mason joked, but she was just not interested in snide talk with her perpetually angry brother. When she did not reply, he went on.

"Oh come on, Darcy. I'm just teasing you".

"You're always teasing me, Mason. I'm just trying to be nice," she replied. "Don't you have to be in school anyway? Why are you always here?"

"I'm allowed to be here," he quickly responded, seemingly

offended by her statement. "This house is as much mine as it is yours."

"Yeah, but I shouldn't be in a class at a college that's two hours away", Darcy said. She got up from the table and looked for her purse. She thought she had heard her phone chime but couldn't remember where she had last left it.

"Nice, Darcy. For your information, I'm taking some time off of school this semester," he finally replied. Surprised by her brother's information reveal, she decided to sit back down at the table. She didn't want to lose the opportunity of this candid and rare conversation that seemed to be unfolding.

"Why are you taking time off?" she probed gently, trying to ensure that she did not ask too intently or else she knew her brother would clam up.

Mason moved around what was left of the cereal in the bowl before him, his eyes focusing on the mundane task.

"College just wasn't working out," he replied, his voice meek. "It's not like high school, you know. No one wants to be your friend just because they know you live in a big house and drive a really expensive car."

She didn't know if his reply was a dig towards her, but she let him continue.

"You start thinking about who you are as a person, singular, not how you fit into the dynamic of a group. And I guess I wasn't ready for that. I'm only 19, Darcy. I've had everything handed to me. I had forgotten what it was like to make friends. I guess I'd been spoiled in having people practically beg to hang out with me when I was in high school, and when I started college, it was just the total opposite." He suddenly stopped and looked up at his sister. His cheeks reddened and he got up from the table.

"That doesn't mean you should give up on it all together, Mason. You'll make friends. Besides, who wouldn't want to hang out with you?" she said, causing him to look at her, a slight smile creeping onto his face.

"Whatever, it's not important, Darcy," he said, pouring himself some water and drinking it quickly. "Besides, there was something that brought me back to Martin's Falls."

She looked at her brother, her brows knitted. She couldn't hide her obvious curiosity.

"And what was that," she asked, trying to sound non-chalant even though she was totally riveted.

"Wouldn't you just love to know," Mason replied, abruptly leaving his sister alone in the kitchen, who was staring at her brother, or his last spotted area, open-mouthed.

***

She threw her books hastily into her locker, not caring one tiny bit where they fell. She wasted no time in slamming the locker door shut behind her as she quickly headed to the bathroom that was just right of the cafeteria. She had been trying her absolute best to avoid Claire at all costs, given their mini blow up the afternoon before, and was being fairly successful at it until she bumped right into her frenemy as soon instantly upon opening the washroom door.

"Oh, sorry," she apologized, even though there was no physical impact of any kind between the two girls. As always, Rena stood vacant-eyed beside Claire, silently mimicking the more aggressive girl's expression and body language. Claire herself, however, looked both simultaneously livid and sad.

"It's ok," Claire quietly replied, not raising her eyes to meet her own. She found this response strange and unsettling, given that her typical interactions with her friend were intense, to say the very least. She decided to bite the bullet and talk to the girl who seemed so visually in pain, and regardless of how she may have felt about the girl, she couldn't help but try to see if there was something she could do to lighten the mood.

179

"Are you feeling all right?" she posed to Claire, who at that point had walked over to the sink to wash her hands. Instead of running her hands under the tap, Claire just stared silently at her own reflection. The stillness that filled the air was heavy and stifling. She felt like her own throat was beginning to close-up. Rena, recognizing the awkwardness, went to stand beside Claire.

"What is going on?" she inquired, growing more and more uncomfortable by the silence as the time incrementally went on. She knew that Claire would not have taken their argument the previous day that close to heart, but Claire was dramatic, so perhaps she did. Quiet continued to permeate the small bathroom, which had no other visitors save for the three girls.

Claire finally turned on the water to wash her hands, taking her time in lathering up the pink, bitter smelling soap. Rena followed suit, robotic like in her motions. She walked closer to the girls and stood closely beside Claire.

"Claire...what's wro-", she began to say but was abruptly cut off by an angry Claire.

"What's wrong, Darcy?" Claire replied, turning around to face her head on. She instantly noticed the redness in her friends' eyes and the semi-swollen cheeks. She had been crying, and not just for a short while either. "You know what's wrong, and you don't care. You couldn't be bothered calling me back last night after I had called you, like, 50 times".

She suddenly remembered that she had turned off her phone before dinner with her parents and didn't even bother to turn on the phone that morning before heading off to school.

"I'm sorry, my phone was off," she genuinely apologized. "I didn't get your calls."

"Or my texts. Or my emails. God, Darcy, you're so selfish", Claire went on, firmly ensconced in a full-blown tirade. "I really needed you last night and you were MIA. I will never forgive you for this!"

Claire turned around and walked towards the dryer, nearly knocking over Darcy on her way. Rena, as always, followed like an obedient puppy.

"I said I was sorry, Claire! What do you want? My left leg?" she replied, noticing her voice also rise to match Claire's high pitch. She hadn't meant to outburst like that, but it seemed to work. Claire turned around and stared at her shockingly. A few silent moments went on before the confrontation continued.

"Sorry won't cut it. You know what happened yesterday and didn't even bother to get your head out of your own ass to call me to find out!" Claire was breathing heavily now, turning beet-red. She was angry.

"Ohhhhh," was all she could say as she remembered their lunchtime foray to the long-distance pharmacy - to buy the pregnancy test that Claire had to take by herself because Darcy didn't answer her calls and because Claire didn't really trust Rena with any kind of confidential information. She felt her heart fall into her stomach, feeling so incredibly terrible that like Claire had said, she HAD had her head up her own ass and didn't even think about how her friend pregnancy scare.

"Ohhh is right. And obviously I'm so upset because you know what it said". Rena looked at Claire confused, wondering what she was letting on about but she knew better than to ask, especially when Claire was amidst one of her classic dramatic monologues, which she noticed was well warranted at that instance.

"Listen, Claire, let's talk," she said, walking closer to the girl who was now practically shaking with anger.

"I guess we can hang out after school," Claire quickly replied, ostensibly ready to quickly forgive her friend. The abrupt change in demeanor frightened her but she decided to just let it go. While still reflecting at the strangeness in this change in mood, she suddenly remembered her plans with Glenda after school.

"I can't tonight," she blurted out. There was no point in try to ease the sting of the words. And the sting had stung, judging by the slow widening of disbelief in Claire's eyes.

"YOU CAN'T TONIGHT?!" Claire screamed, not caring if any other students were around to hear her shrill words. The students down the hall could hear her clear as day, and Claire knew it. "What do YOU have planned? Pining over the pool boy? Writing in your JOURNAL? You're so pathetic, Darcy. I never want to look at your sad little lame face again".

She was completely and utterly speechless. She did not know how to respond to Claire's outburst that was full of contempt, angry, and clear resentment. Even Rena looked uncomfortable.

"Calm down, Claire. In your state..." she began but Claire walked straight up to her and looked her dead in the eyes.

"My state is something you don't need to worry about. My state is none of your business. Now get out of my way!" She yelled, pushing her to the side, nearly causing her to stumble to the ground.

Claire and Rena left the bathroom, slamming the door closed behind them. She simply stared after them, still clearly in shock from both of Claire's revelations, and leaned back up against the cool wall. Not a good start to her day.

***

When the last bell rang signaling the end of the school day, the usual collective relief shared amongst all the students in school was perpetually felt, and she was no exception.

The rest of the day had been uncomfortable, to say the least. While she had been used to being a literal second half to the high maintenance Claire, she felt a sense of relief and empowerment making her way through her day solo. She had seen Claire out of the corner of her eyes on various occasions throughout the day, but Claire was apparently very good at pretending she didn't exist. She couldn't say that she was particularly bothered by her friends

182

behavior, especially considering the epic fight they had had earlier in the girls bathroom, but it was still unsettling for her nonetheless that Claire was able to so quickly ignore her.

She absent-mindedly filled her purse with the slight homework she had been assigned in Biology class and managed to escape the busy school hallway and make it to the parking lot before the mass of students made it practically impossible for her to get into her car at all. The parking lot, much like the school hall ways, was also quite empty by the time she was behind the wheel and ready to get out.

Thankful for the silence, she started the car quickly. She bent over and raised the volume of the radio as high as it could go when she heard a tap on the window beside her. She turned around quickly to see Jason Crone smiling at her.

His eyes were intense, that was the first thought that entered her head. Her actual interactions with Jason since 'the switch' (What she was now calling the moment when she became the new Darcy) were non-existent, but from what she had inferred from her interactions with Claire et al, Jason was part of the 'cool group', and thus one of her friends. She did see his picture as part of her research in her own bedroom via yearbooks and pictures in some photo albums.

There was no question why Jason Crone was so popular, and being single, so elusive. His green eyes shone bright as though backlit from somewhere deep within his brain, and his teeth shone bright and white from behind his plump red lips. His hair was that perfect mix of messy neatness, and his purple polo shirt showed just enough of the fit body that lay behind it. She couldn't help but feel her heartbeat quicken and feel a little warm. She absent-mindedly turned up the air conditioning while she lowered her window.

"Hey lady," Jason said once the window had been lowered. He stood close to the window and leaned over, so that he was just inches away from her face.

"Hey Jason, what's up?" she asked, trying to sound nonchalant. She knew this interaction was not random – Claire had let on as much. She did not want to go the prom with Jason, and she knew that this was where the conversation was headed.

"Not much, Darcy. I wish I could say the same for you, though," he said, a smiling slowly creeping across his face, showing a tiny dimple on his left cheek. She should have known that Claire would have blabbed to everyone about their fight, Jason not being any exception.

"Yeah, well, the life of a teenager is complicated, to say the least," she replied, trying to sound calm and collected. Though, as she was learning as every day progressed, her new teenage life was increasingly becoming the complete antithesis to complicated. It was becoming painful.

Jason continued to smile, and proceeded to lean over even closer to Darcy's spot in the driver's seat. She thought she smelled cinnamon hearts on his breath but it was just her hunger playing mind games with her. The silence between them was awkward, and Darcy was very aware of that. Jason, however, seemed to be relishing in it.

"So who's the lucky dude?" he finally asked, not taking his eyes away from her face.

"Listen, Jason – I know Claire put you up to this," she countered, trying to sound genuine. "I just think I want to go alone to the prom".

Jason's expression went from humored to confuse within milliseconds. "Huh? I'm not talking about prom, though Claire did ask me to ask you."

Now it was her turn to feel confused. "Oh. Then what are you talking about?"

"Not that I would have asked you to the prom anyway but after what happened, I think going alone to prom is your only option", he replied. The parking lot was beginning to fill up now with more students, which meant that she would most likely see Claire at some point. She quickly decided to steer the awkward conversation.

"I'm not quite sure what you're alluding to, Jason, but I've really got to get going." she said, turning her face towards the front of her car and the steady of stream of students that were leaving the ivy-lined school.

"Don't play dumb, Darcy. I saw you buying the pregnancy kit at the pharmacy in Owens Landing. My brother owns it," he replied quietly.

She felt like a deer caught in the headlights. She turned towards Jason quickly, shocked.

"It's not what you think," she mumbled, not wanting to add fuel to the fire that had been lit. If Jason found out about Claire, then the news would be around school in 2 minutes flat.

"Don't worry, Darcy. Your secret is safe with me. Besides, Claire told me all about it this afternoon, anyway. I just thought you'd want to tell me who the big poppa is so I can give him a pat on the back," Jason laughed. "Drive safely, mama."

With that, he turned around and walked towards a group of students who had gathered around the entrance to the football field.

She immediately raised the window and threw her head on the steering wheel. So Claire told Jason that the kit they bought was for Darcy, and not for herself. She felt hot anger swell within her. Her supposed best friend told one of the most popular boys in school that she was pregnant, knowing full well that it would be a full blown rumor within minutes.

She put the car in reverse and booked it out of the parking lot. On her way out, she nearly ran over a few students, but she didn't care. She sped out of the lot, causing smoke to waft from the pavement where her wheels sped.

Once she was out on the road, she quickly looked for a space where she could pull over to gather her thoughts. She was incredibly angry, and she felt her heartbeat quicken. She pulled over on a quiet street that seemed to be free of students and adults alike, and turned off the car.

185

The longer she was the new Darcy, the more she felt deceived by her entire life. In all of the books she had cherished reading all of those years, the protagonist never had to deal with half of the dramatics that she found herself encountering on a seemingly hourly basis. Claire was an awful person, this much she intuited from their first interaction, but she had been willing to give the girl a chance. She didn't want to jump to any conclusions and alienating any friendships she had. Every chance she had given Claire seemed to blow up in her face.

She had been trying to forge friendship with her brother, and with that, she felt like she was making ever so tiny steps. Her parents weren't exactly interested in learning about what was going on in her life, and she was afraid Luke was going to go completely crazy from his irrational love for her.

She felt overwhelmed and lonely. She wished she could talk to someone about what was happening to her, how she was trying her best to be the protagonist that she loved, and how every day was a challenge in sanity and focus. But she knew that no matter how she would say it, it would come across that she was completely crazy, and going to a psychiatrist or rehab facility would be the least thing she could endure at the moment.

She felt that just didn't know how to move forward. She knew that Marina had told her to make things right, but she didn't know how to do that if everything seemed to be so wrong. She looked at herself in the rear view mirror, and noticed the tears that had fallen down her cheeks. She quickly wiped them away, but more fell right away.

She was embarrassed at what was happening. She felt that this was something she should have under control. As an adult, she dealt with awkward breakups, deaths, her parents' divorce – all of which were much more life-changing than what she had to deal with as a 17 year old girl. But there was no doubt that the pain she felt, the intensity that was part of the discomfort she had to deal with every single day in her seemingly idyllic life, felt like it was tearing the inner core out of her. She knew on some level that it was important to experience all life had to offer, the good and the bad, but she either had forgotten or was unaware that being a teenager was sometimes as hard as being a single thirty-something year old woman.

Pain was pain – regardless of age. Awkwardness never gets easier, and confrontation doesn't get fun. She placed her head on the steering wheel, letting the tears come, and prayed for hope in that things were going to get easier, because it wasn't only her that was on the line if they didn't go right.

Chapter 22

Glenda was waiting on the front porch when Darcy pulled into the driveway later that dreary and drama-laden afternoon. The older, content lady was out of uniform and wearing a simple pair of jeans and a flower print shirt that complemented her tiny frame. Her hair was done up in a small bun, reminding her of Marina, which caused an odd mix both slight anxiety and nostalgia.

Glenda smiled upon seeing the black BMW drive up near her and opened its window. On the quick drive home, she managed to compose herself after her little mini-breakdown that happened just after school. She even went as far to readjusting her make up and fixing her hair to ensure that she looked non-plussed and as calm as she could be.

As Glenda made her way into the car and sat in the passenger side, she stole a quick glance at Darcy, who had already began to pull out of the driveway, making their way in the direction of the local shopping mall.

"Ms. Darcy. How are you feeling?" Glenda softly asked as Darcy kept her eyes on the road before her that would take her to some much needed shopping therapy. She hoped that Glenda was trying to make casual conversation, not addressing her fragile emotional state that was completely out of whack.

She was unsure if she should reply with a false sense of calmness or just empty her multitude of emotions on the older woman. She opted for the former, not sure as to how Glenda would react.

"Great! School was fun and I'm super excited to do some shopping," she said, the words an endless stream of nothingness escaping her lipstick lined mouth. She knew her voice sounded unnaturally superficial. She also knew she wasn't the only one in the car who noticed the faked enthusiasm.

Glenda didn't say a word, opting to let the natural flow of conversation present itself on its own, regardless of how long it may take. Glenda clearly knew that something was bothering her, either through intuition or extended knowledge of the young girls' emotions. Either way, she felt as though the woman was saying something about the situation by choosing to not say anything at all.

"I am worried about you, Darcy," Glenda suddenly said, nearly causing her to abruptly veer off the road and drop both women into a nearby canal. She quickly regained composure (which she seemed to be getting really good at) and tried to pretend there was not a single thing off about the statement that just escaped the older woman's lipstick free lips.

"You haven't been the same for quite some time now," the lady continued, keeping her eyes on the road before her. "You are not the same girl that I have cared for all of your life."

She once again felt like pulling the pricey little car over to the side of the road and confiding every single feeling she felt to the older, warm woman, but she knew she couldn't, or shouldn't do that,

189

no matter how hard she wanted to. She knew she had to maintain the charade of being the new Darcy in order to be able to live the life she had always envied, not to mention save Marina's shop in the process. Though there was nothing more she wanted at that particular time than be selfish and be completely honest with someone for once since becoming a teenager again, she knew she couldn't spill the proverbial beans. At least not yet, anyway.

Plus, she didn't know what would be the consequence of confiding the truth. For all she knew, she could have been thrust back into the life of a semi-depressed thirty something year old women who thought eating in the middle of the night was a proven method to speed up her metabolism, despite the added pounds to her slight frame conveying the total opposite.

After all of that internal monologue which made her feel like she was a character in the epic novel Crime and Punishment (Dostoyevsky would be proud), she chose to stay quiet. She somehow knew that if she decided to say anything at all, it would just be perceived fake, similar to her disingenuous response just moments ago. Glenda, however, had no desire to cease expressing her feelings and motored on, oblivious to both Darcy's apprehensive body language and constant internal monologue.

"I know you know that you could tell me anything," Glenda rambled on, keeping her eyes on the road before her. "But I also know that a 17 year old girl doesn't exactly want to talk about her feelings with an old woman, especially the housekeeper".

Glenda reached into her purse and removed a piece of gum. The cinnamon smell filled the car, making Darcy think about Marina's red hair and seemingly maternal ways. There was something in Glenda that incessantly and constantly reminded her of the old, well-preserved shop keeper who owned the bookstore that had become her second home. It clearly wasn't a similarity in appearance between the two women, in fact they couldn't have been more visually different, but there was some sort of all knowing-ness that

190

both women evoked that she sensed was cut from the same cloth. "But I am here for you in case you ever need to talk. About anything."

A tear escaped her eye before she was even aware of it. It was only when she felt the tiny drop of moisture fall down her cheek that she noticed that she was crying. Glenda handed her a tissue, which she immediately used to wipe away the other drops that had fallen. The women remained in silence for the rest of the ride, and for her, it felt spectacular. It was the best emotional outlet she'd had in a long time, despite its miniscule size.

***

"Try this one, Glenda. You'll knock 'em dead at the wedding," she said, throwing the yellow dress over the change room door where behind it the older woman was trying on everything in the small clothing store. It certainly seemed like everything as she managed to find many nice patterns and dress cuts that complimented the tiny woman's frame.

"Ooh, this is nice," she heard Glenda's muffled voice say as the dress fell on the other side of the tiny change room door. She sat down on the small bench parallel to the change room and waited patiently to see Glenda's reaction.

After the rather intense car ride, both she and Glenda were having a wonderful time at the mall. It was almost like they were the only people in the shopping complex as they were totally enthralled by each other's presence and conversation. They did not seem to see any other shoppers passing them by and browsing sales around them, which, for her, was icing on the cake because she had absolutely no desire to see any of the kids from school, nor the perfect dramatic filled teenage storm that seemed to have been brewing.

Glenda stepped out of the change room in the yellow dress and both women smiled. She looked sensational, there was no denying that. Both women's wide grins expressed the agreement as such.

"You're so buying that!" she exclaimed immediately upon seeing the lady in the dress. Glenda seemed to be radiating contentment. She turned around the mirror like a model, causing both women to break into hysterical bouts of laughing.

"I think I just might buy this," Glenda laughed. "I'm going to turn everyone's head at the wedding!"

She felt her phone vibrate from its place at the bottom of the heap in her purse but chose to ignore it. She didn't want anything to spoil her current good mood.

"Agreed! You look so pretty!" she responded. "Ok, you go change and then we'll go get some yummy ice cream." Glenda stepped back into the change room to change into her regular clothes while she once again found herself settling into a tidal wave of thoughts and voices in her head that entirely wanted to consume her.

She found it just a tad bit bizarre , and also actually pretty hilarious, that she was having more fun shopping with a middle aged women at the local mall then she ever did hanging out with her gargantuan group of same aged friends. It was then crystal clear to her that things were certainly not turning out the way she was expecting them to.

She picked up her purse, which by that time stopped vibrating from the phone buried deep within it. She absent mindedly snaked her hand in and took out her tiny cell phone and stole a glance at the display screen. She had missed 10 text messages from Claire, which she found surprising given their confrontation earlier that day. Even more surprisingly, she noticed a text from Jason, which simply read "Prom?"

She rolled her eyes and quickly deleted the text from Jason, determined to not let her spirit be brought down during this shopping adventure. She skimmed through Claire's messages, which she noticed were all were semi-cryptic but essentially sharing the same essence: call me.

She turned the phone off completely and threw it back into the enormous purse that was nearly half her size.

"Is everything ok, Darcy?" Glenda asked as the door to the change room opened before her. The woman had the yellow dress gently draped over her right arm, concern present in her facial expression that was directed towards her.

"Ok enough," was all she could mutter as both women walked to the front of the store to pay for the dress. She tried to push all other thoughts not related to her impending purchase of ice cream out of her mind.

***

By the time she parked the car back into the driveway of her home, the sun was beginning to set. It caused the world around her to adopt a soft, sepia tinged feel that seemed to make everyone just a bit more relaxed. She hadn't intended to stay out most of the evening with Glenda, but they had such a wonderful time. After getting ice cream, they decided to see the newest Sandra Bullock romantic comedy and then eat some greasy fried food. A perfect evening all in all for both women.

Upon parking the car and taking the key out of the ignition, both women noticed Charlie sitting on the front porch area, head phones over his perfectly coiffed hair. Upon seeing them, he pulled his head phones off, smiled a small smile, and made his way in the direction towards his mother.

"Hi, Mama," he said, leaning down to give his mother a peck on her cheek. The woman glowed at the kind gesture.

"Thank you for tonight, Darcy. I had the most wonderful time. I'm going to go try the dress on again now!" the woman beamed. "Though after what we are that might not be the best idea!" She quickly escaped into the enormous home by a side door she had never seemed to notice before.

Charlie hung around awkwardly as she walked slowly towards him on the porch. There were two rattan chairs that sat empty atop the tiny porch, and she took the opportunity to have a sit down. All that walking in the mall had tired her out, and it didn't exactly help things out by wearing stilettos that were about a size too small. She kicked off the bright pink shoes and sighed audibly as she felt blood once again re-circulate in her feet.

"Did my mom tire you out?" Charlie said, after her s sigh. There was a dimple in his right cheek that was prominent when he smiled. She found herself smiling at him.

"She's got more energy than me. And I can shop like a champion," she replied.

Charlie sat down on the other empty chair, absent-mindedly wiping his bangs away. He seemed to be less shy than the other limited encounters she had had with him, and she felt instantly at ease. Like mother, like son – she thought.

They both sat in silence for a few moments, taking in the sounds of the crickets around them and the warm yellow hues that had begun to fall upon the homes and cars around them. The temperature had cooled significantly since earlier that day, and a cool wind flipped her hair rather abruptly. She quickly tied her hair back into a ponytail so she wouldn't poke anyone's eye out. It seemed she had put in a just a tad too much mousse earlier that morning.

"How come I never see you at school?" she asked suddenly, not sure she was going to say what she said, but was thankful nonetheless as it seemed to be the right question to get Charlie chatting.

"I don't think you really look for me," he replied, his voice low. He moved his gaze towards her, making her blush slightly. His eyes were deep and brown like Glenda's, but the shape was different. His eyes were more almond-shaped then his mothers tiny round circles. Why she was making such observations mystified her.

"School's pretty awful, isn't it?" she said. Charlie laughed.

194

"It's not fun, if that's what you mean. I heard about the fight you and Claire had today," he continued. "The whole school was talking about it."

"Speaking of not fun." she laughed. Gossip in high school traveled faster than the flu in her office in January, she thought. "Claire and I aren't exactly seeing eye to eye these days."

"I don't know how you could see eye to eye with her any day," he said. He seemed to be embarrassed by his quick response. "I'm sorry, that's none of my business."

"No, it's ok," she replied. "Claire is a bit of a beast, and I guess it just took me some time to realize that. Besides, let's not talk about her anymore. She's exhausting."

This caused Charlie to laugh a deep-barreled laugh which in turn made her laugh. It was contagious, and soon she found herself in a bout of hysterics so intense that she forgot about the gravity of her situation.

"I didn't want to be the one to say it," he finally said over gasping for air in between laughs. "But yeah, who needs to go to the gym when you have Claire Marsh around."

"That's why I got abs of steel," she joked, tapping her firm torso. She was surprised to feel the firm muscle below her t-shirt as she was so used to the skin moving around, jiggling ever so slightly.

Silence engulfed them again, but she still felt comfortable through it. She felt a positive tingling energy being around Charlie. He made her heartbeat flutter and brought a slight tinge of red to her cheeks.

"Darcy," he said, standing up from his perch on the chair. He shuffled around awkwardly in front of her.

"Yes, Charlie," she replied, looking up at him. He turned towards her, a slight smile on his lips. She felt her pulse quicken and her breath shorten.

"Um, you probably have a date already but…" he said, quickly breaking his flow of words. "Do you, like, want to go the prom with

195

me? If you don't, I totally understand."

She smiled, taking in the sight of a beautifully shy teenage boy being all beautiful and shy in front of her. She got up off the chair and walked closer to him.

"I would love to go to the prom with you, Charlie," she replied. She thought he was going to have some sort of nervous fit at her response but he slowly regained his composure.

"You would? That's so awesome," Charlie declared. He moved closer to her until they were just inches away. He was only just a few inches taller than her, and she felt his hot breath on the top of her head. The difference in temperature from the cold wind felt good.

She stepped even closer to him. She sensed him stiffening up as she leaned her head against his hard chest. She didn't know what she was doing but she was doing it anyway. She didn't over think her actions, letting the spontaneity take over. She turned up towards Charlie who was looking down at her.

She felt his lips inch closer and closer, almost like they were in slow motion but also feeling like time moving in fast-forward. He leaned in and their lips touched gently until the sound of the front door opening behind them ruined the moment.

Mason stepped out, surprised to see the two of them in such an intimate moment on the porch.

"Ah, Casanova strikes again," Mason acerbically teased. She felt like slapping him squarely on the jaw for ruining the perfect moment and for making Charlie feel so obviously uncomfortable. She did not know, though, who Casanova was in reference to. Was there something he knew about Charlie that she didn't? She then quickly chastised herself for once again over thinking things.

"I'll talk to you later," Charlie quickly mumbled and disappeared quickly into that side door that his mother entered just a little while ago.

Upon hearing the door close, she turned around to her brother who had a wry smile on his lips.

196

"You are such an ass," she whispered. "Why do you always have to be such an ASS."

She bent down to pick up her shoes that were hastily lying on the grey concrete and quickly placed them in her purse. Mason, clearly shocked at his sister's shrewd reaction, and didn't say a word. She slammed the front door shut behind her. She allowed herself to take a split second to look back at her brother who remained open mouthed at her rash response. Well, she thought to herself, he did just manage to ruin one of the sweetest moments she had experienced since becoming 17. Again.

Chapter 23

It was Saturday the next day, and the day off from school added extra icing to her proverbial cake that, at that particular moment, was baked full of the continued sense of drama-free contentment. She made sure to sleep in (by completely turning off her cell phone and lowering her blinds until the room was in complete darkness) and managed to only wake up until her mother rashly knocked on her door, asking if she wanted anything for lunch. She hadn't made an effort to get up from her comfortable position on the bed to answer her mother's hurried knocks. She felt extra thankful when her mother gave up her goal of waking her daughter up on that sunny, and slightly cool, Saturday.

She had had a dreamless sleep, something she knew she totally needed after all of the preceding days. Until today, her nights seemed to be full of disturbing images and freakish situations where she always had to make a choice that always had such negative impacts. Last night was dreamless, and amazing. For the first time in weeks, she actually felt refreshed.

Stealing a glance at her alarm clock that sat on the nightstand beside her, she was surprised to see was nearly 2 pm in the afternoon. Instead of speeding up her actions, she took her time stretching as she slowly got up out of the safe confines of the enormous bed, feeling shockingly guilt free for having nearly slept half the day away. There was no pressing need to run to the grocery store, or to return the movies she had rented, or to travel halfway across town to meet Sonya for coffee or, even more rarely, brunch at a cool new restaurant. She exhaled heavily as she arose out of the bed and began to assemble herself to be semi-presentable.

She took a moment to reflect that the relative guiltlessness and lack of a heavy, persistent conscious was one of the things she liked best about her situation, even if that lack of guilt was due to a certain amount of ignorance to how the world really and truly operated. Tomato, tomat-oh.

She would have loved to continue going about her day aloof and not thinking about the little nugget of information that Jason had dropped on her the day before, or the fluttery feeling she had whenever she saw or spoke to Charlie. What she wished for most, however, was someway for her not to constantly hear Marina's nagging voice in her head, reminding about 'making things right'. If she didn't at least make an effort in trying to complete the old woman's objective, there was no hope in staying in this new life.

After taking a shower and returning to the sanctuary of her larger than life bed, she took out her mobile phone that still lay nestled in her book bag and turned it on reluctantly. While she had reveled in the feeling of being unreachable by her friends, she felt as though she were only postponing the inevitable. She decided to bite the teenaged drama fused bullet and looked at the lit up screen on her little gadget.

Sure enough, she was notified by blinking lights that her

voicemail box was full (20 messages!) and she had nearly 40 text messages that begged to be read. Automatically deleting the one worded text from Jason the previous night (Prom? *Yeah right*, she thought to herself), she began to scan through the many texts from Claire, which all held her typical 'the world is ending' tone of urgency in the shortly worded messages that flooded the phone. She knew that Claire wanted to speak to her about something important, the caps-locked text messages indicated as much. She recognized the urgent tone must have been related to Claire's pregnancy, though her friend did not exactly say she was with child explicitly. Judging from their previous afternoon's interaction, she was positive that there totally was a bun in that uptight oven.

Surprisingly, there was a short text message from Bennett, whom she felt genuinely bad about not speaking to more, regardless of the social stigma that apparently accompanied talking to the new girl in school. She wanted to tell Bennett that she, too, was a new girl, but that would have been rather difficult to explain, to say the least.

Prom Committee meeting next Sunday at 11 am – Excited much? , Bennett's text had read. Momentarily confused, she quickly remembered that just the day before between Biology and English class, she wrote her name on the list that was taped up outside the Student council office canvassing for volunteers to join the prom committee. She was glad to see that Bennett had decided to join the committee as well. She wouldn't now feel so out of place by being on the committee. Even if Claire managed to pull a 180 with her attitude, she found it hard to believe that she would accept her friend being on the planning group of the most important event of the year, voluntarily at that.

Bennett seemed to be a rather normal person, whatever that meant, and made her feel comfortable and at ease. Even though she'd had very limited interactions with the girl in recent weeks, there was something both genuine and interesting with Bennett that

200

she felt refreshing, especially in its vast difference to Claire's insanity.

She happily settled back into a comfortable spot in her bed amidst the many pillows and fluffy duvets surrounding her. She dropped her phone on the nightstand, which also happened to house a framed picture of her and Claire in happier times. She looked at the frame and smiled, seeing that a true friendship was alive in there somewhere, but not feeling one with the girl now, in real like. She raised her drapes a bit to let the sun shine in slightly, causing a shadow effect on the darkened television screen. Her mind began to drift off, random thoughts clouding her mind, non-sensical in nature and fell asleep.

***

It was pitch black all around her. She felt disoriented, unsure of where the ceiling began or where the walls stood before her. By this time, she knew what the lack of spatial awareness meant. Drops of moisture fell onto the back of her hand but she did not where the sources of them were. She tried to discern and make out any familiar sights around her, but it being so black and dark, she only managed to feel enclosed and slightly claustrophobic. She reached upwards instinctively to feel for a ceiling or whatever it was that loomed above her, but her hands touched cold, wet stone.

Am I in a cave?, she thought to herself, a chill running up her spine. Now becoming aware that she was actually standing, she took a deep breath and called up on the courage to begin to move slowly towards the tiny pocket of light she saw that seemed to be just a few feet away from where she now stood.

Suddenly, a slight breeze touched her skin, causing goose pimples to break out across her arms and legs. It must have been only a few degrees in the confined space that surrounded her, she thought. She looked down at her feet and noticed she wasn't wearing shoes, causing the clammy soil and pebbles beneath her naked feet to jab her rather painfully as she ventured towards the light that she hoped would bring some sort of respite to her current uncomfortable situation.

As she made her way towards the tiny spot of the light feet away she mentally noticed how brilliant and nearly blinding yellow hues were. She tentatively took a few more steps forward, dirt cramming between her toes, and seemed to cross some sort of threshold.

The darkness quickly evaporated around her and she was abruptly completely bathed in extreme and total whiteness, forcing her to bring her hands to her eyes to shield them from intensity. At that point, she recognized the familiar setting of total whiteness and the same two chairs that she had seen on her first day of becoming 17 again.

Out of virtual thin air, Marina appeared, perfectly dressed and every single hair in its right place. She noticed that the woman's face looked tired, sad even, but she chose to remain quiet. Seeing the bookshop owner made her comfortable, but the instant tinge of desperation and urgency quickly took over any positive associations with seeing the woman.

Finally deciding to say something and break the silence that enveloped both women, she was genuinely surprised to hear the high-pitched tone of her own voice, making her sound like she had just swallowed a balloons worth full of helium.

"Marina – I am happy to see you!" she exclaimed, momentarily taken aback by the happiness that echoed in the white space that surrounded both women. Marina remained expressionless, her face not quite stoic but not happy either.

Finding the woman's expression unsettling, she continued. "What's wrong, Marina? You don't seem like yourself."

Marina's eyes slowly widened but then returned to their normal size. She didn't know what to make of that subtle change of expression in the shop owner, but the vibes she got was that it wasn't coming from a happy place.

Before responding, Marina slowly made her way to one of the chairs that stood before both women and lowered her tiny frame onto it with an audible sigh. She decided to follow suit and sit across from the older woman on the other lone empty chair, however, no sigh escaped her own lips.

"I am not myself these days, Darcy," Marina finally replied, once again making a heavy sigh as the words left her tiny, dark red lipstick lined lips. "I am worried about your progress in your tasks."

"My tasks?" she muttered, not knowing what else to say.

"You have not committed yourself," Marina mouthed back, her voice soft and gentle. "And for that I am afraid that life, as we both know it, will change forever."

She found the statement a bit dramatic and over the top, but given the complete ludicrousness of her entire current situation, she decided to let it pass. In fact, it seemed to rather fit in well with her current drama infused life.

"I still don't know what has to be done," she countered, her tone meek and less accusatory than their previous meetings. "I'm trying to understand what is going on and what..."

"You are not trying anything!" Marina screamed, cutting her off and startling her in the process. "You are being selfish!"

At once, dark reds and purples colored the vast, expansive space that surrounded both women, almost resembling a lava lamp in appearance. While there was not a single sound being made in the room, She felt a tangible heaviness of bass or some other sound that felt resonating within her very core.

"Being selfish is inherently part of being 17!" she yelled right back, not caring if her raised voice further angered Marina, who began to look like she was going lapse into some sort of psychotic breakdown at any given second.

"Don't be smart with me. You and I both know what is going on. I granted your wish and you are not keeping up your end of the

203

deal. Instead of making things right, like I said, you're making things so much worse."

"How am I doing that, Marina? By speaking up for myself and for defending what is the logical thing to do?" she countered, this time her voice still rising, reverberating in the space around her. "I can't sit back and let other people dictate the decisions that should be made for her, er, me."

"You are her and she is you, this is true," Marina whispered back. "But I can't keep guiding you on what you need to accomplish during this short time. I am putting myself in danger by just appearing to you like this. You yourself said that you wanted to be a teenage girl again, to live a simplistic life, 'to date cute boys'. And that is what you are. But you are still not happy? You are still finding things wrong with everything and ending friendships and breaking hearts and all of the things you precisely should *not* be doing."

"It's not as easy as you think, Marina. Things aren't so black and white." Darcy brought her eyes to the white floor, her eyes beginning to moisten with tears.

"Oh, is that so? Are you saying that being a teenager isn't like the books you've read? That the only things you are thinking about are not who will be taking you to the prom and what dress to wear?"

She felt like she was punched in the stomach at the gravity of Marina's intense questions. The woman was right – being a teenager was absolutely not as easy as the books she read made it out to be. There were things that happened every single day that were not written about, either out of necessity or because it would deter the reader. Had Darcy fallen in love with the idea of a story, or with real life? She was having a hard time differentiating between the two these days more than ever.

"I will try harder, Marina, I promise. It's just a lot to take in. I'm trying to get comfortable in my new skin, but I'm also trying to gain a sense of identity that would make this girl proud. Just don't take me away from this."

"I don't know how much longer I can prolong it," Marina quickly retorted. "I told you that you only have until the prom to do what you need to do. And, as you know, that's only 3 weeks away."

"I know but I feel like I'm on to something, here. Just trust me. I can do this." Darcy said, noticing that she was wearing a pair of hot pink stilettos.

"Ok, Darcy. But remember – things may not be as they seem. There is a lot riding on this, my dear friend. I just hope your efforts will be successful," Marina said, the words, and their heavy connotations, hanging heavily in the air.

Suddenly, she felt like she was being strangled and her hands went instinctively to her throat as the room around her became bathed in darkness once more.

She bolted upright and realized she was back in her bed, safe and sound, pillows all around her. The sun had begun to set, causing tinges of orange and amber to fill the large room. There was still a sliver of light or two that managed to enter large windows, their appearance small and slight, much like Darcy's current emotional and fragile state. She realized she was sticky with sweat, fear still pumping through her veins.

Let the games begin, she thought to herself. *Even though I have no idea what the games are or who's even playing. All I know is what the reward is.*

Chapter 24

It almost appeared as though the weather was starting to get cooler instead of warmer, which was clearly strange and bizarre for the month of May in Martin's Falls. The residents seemed to be confused and bewildered – not knowing if they should be wearing their walking shorts to the grocery store or a pair of jeans. The weather literally changed so quickly that a need for pants would have seemed preposterous on the short drive to the grocery store, but once at the checkout, you silently chastised yourself for not packing a parka.

Darcy was used to rapid changes in temperature (*These people don't know a thing about global warming*, she had already thought to herself at least a half dozen times), having lived in one of the biggest cities in the world that was notorious for rapid changes in temperature, but she found it enjoyable seeing people scramble as to what was up with their tiny town on a tiny part of the gigantic earth.

She knew to pack a cardigan or two before leaving the house that Sunday morning to join Bennett at the Prom Committee that was happening at their local (and only) Starbucks. She and Bennett had become close in the last week that Claire had completely iced her out, and she found herself enjoying every minute of it. Bennett and her seemed to really understand one another and intuit what each other was feeling or thinking. Whereas Claire was an entire question mark, Bennett was more of an ellipsis.

Before rushing out the front door before her parents got all nosy as they did on Sundays, Mason managed to halt Darcy just as she thought she managed to leave the house without interruption.

"Where are you off to this early on a Sunday, sunshine?" Mason asked, his voice high. Clearly he wanted her parents to overhear their daughters' hasty exit, but she wasn't biting.

Instead of replying and getting into a heated confrontation with her brother, as what has come to be the norm in the Platt household, she continued her exit out of the house and shut the door behind her. Mason didn't take that as an end to his inquiry and so he left the house as well, slamming the door intentionally loudly behind him.

She audibly groaned as she bee-lined towards her car which was parked not twenty feet from the front door of the home. Mason was faster than she was and caught up swiftly to her.

"You don't have to be so rude," he said, his voice dripping of judgment and disdain. She had to stop herself from laughing because she thought he was trying to be funny. *Me? Rude?* She thought to herself. *You won't ever meet a more un-rude person.*

She unlocked the car door and quickly threw herself in. Mason, like a dog with a bone, patiently waited until she lowered her power window. He wasted no time in sticking his head inside the car, just inches away from her face. This time, she decided to entertain her brother's decent effort at communication, albeit being done in an obtrusive way.

"I've got a meeting," she replied, starting the car. She

207

intentionally didn't say it was to plan the school Prom because she knew Mason would have a field day with that notion and tease her incessantly, probably right up until the day came where she was in an absurdly expensive dress and walking into the white limo that would be parked in front of her home.

"Oooh, a meeting – how glamorous," Mason replied sarcastically. "Is Ms. Claire going to be accompanying Ms. Platt, the very busy business woman, to this elusive meeting?"

Hmm, she instantly thought to herself. *Why would Mason even care who would be going to a meeting with her, not to mention if Claire would be joining her.* The thought left her mind as soon as her brother kept on talking.

"You seem to be dressed pretty light for a very important meeting," he continued, referring to the pink tank top she was wearing.

"Why are you so concerned about my well being, Mason," she asked, slightly irritated. If her parents heard the front door slam shut (and she was entirely positive that they had and were just biding their time before coming outside to see what the commotion was) it was only going to be a few minutes longer before this conversation would become a Platt Family affair.

"Down girl," Mason replied, leaning closer to his sister. He reached into his pocket and pulled out a scarf and handed it to her.

"Here, in case it gets cold," he said and retreated into the house. She threw the scarf into the backseat and backed out of the driveway before Mason even made it back into the house.

What a weirdo, she thought as she made the short drive to the coffee shop, already 10 minutes late.

***

Seated around a large table at the back of the shop, she recognized some students from her grade, as well as a grade below

208

hers. Bennett sat at the edge of the table, her long red hair tied into a bun that stuck out haphazardly from the every side of her head, reminding her of a half princess Leia.

"Sorry I'm late," she said as she approached the table. Most of the students smiled, except for Chrissy Barr who did not hide the fact that she was on Team Claire and that she wasn't happy about being kept waiting. She caught Chrissy's obvious eye roll before taking the empty seat beside Bennett, who gave her a warm smile once she sat down.

"Well, now that we are ALL here, I guess we can start," Chrissy said, her voice a cross between a child first learning to speak and the Golden Girl's resident slut Blanche Deveraux. "Let's start with the theme. I was thinking we could some something underwater, like the Little Mermaid or something?"

Bennett had a hard time suppressing her giggle at that but thankfully Chrissy didn't notice. She was afraid it would send the little hot head out of control and they would all have had a lethal firebomb to deal with.

"All the girls could get, like, super long wigs or get hair extensions or something," Chrissy went on. The other girls in the group had a glazed expression on their faces which Chrissy did not seem at all to notice. "The guys could get shiny suits that sort of look like fish arms or gills, or whatever they're called."

"And we could get crab purses and maybe have our pictures taken in a real water tank with fish swimming around us!" Bennett spoke up, obviously having reached the maximum of her patience.

"Ooh, that's a great idea!" Chrissy perked up, smiling widely.

"I was kidding, Chrissy!" Bennett soon replied.

"No, I think it's a great idea. Good one, Bennett!"

She looked over at Bennett, who was momentarily confused by Chrissy's inability to really tell that Bennett was being sarcastic, which was clearly her trademark.

Awkwardness and silence filled the air at the coffee shop as

209

Chrissy finally understood that Bennett was teasing her. The girls looked from one to another, edging someone to come up with an idea to have Chrissy shoot down. Finally, she took it upon herself to bring up.

"Well, I was thinking something along the lines of a masquerade ball", Darcy said. She noticed the attention of the group focus on her, surprised that she could command such attention. She was honestly surprised that Chrissy didn't immediately interject.

"We could totally have a classy prom. Imagine how awesome a masquerade theme would be." She was surprised to hear the joy in her voice and took her voice down a notch. She didn't know if she did that out of embarrassment or minding the other patrons of the coffee shop.

"Just think of it… a lavish, fancy ball. We can channel 18th century France with castle decorations, chandeliers, and crazy masks. We could even have a contest to see who comes up with the best, or most creative mask—and make sure there's a great prize!"

"Like an iPad or something?" Chrissy threw in, obviously really into her idea.

"Totally! That way, everyone will want to participate and make it really memorable," Darcy quickly replied. "And it's a theme that everyone could feel good about taking part of. Think of it: the popular kids will wear something nuts and the shy kids will be thankful to be able to hide behind a mask!"

The rest of the girls in the group smiled and nodded, breaking into conversation amongst themselves. Chirssy smiled. Darcy felt that the smile on Chrissy's face would quickly turn into a frown but that didn't happen.

"You know, Darcy, I thought you would want to do something really awful and cheesy, but this is actually a really awesome idea. Props," Chrissy whispered to her, the other girls oblivious to their little exchange.

"Um, thanks, Chrissy," she said, looking over at Bennett who was chatting with another girl, jotting notes down. *I guess a passive aggressive compliment is better than no compliment at all*, she thought to herself as the group began to map out ideas and jot down plans to be made for what they thought would be the biggest event of their lives.

***

"Where'd that come from?" Bennett asked once both girls were on their drive home. They had stayed at the coffee shop for over two hours, clearly enthused and excited about her idea for the prom, which was received with a literal resounding round of applause.

She had felt very happy about having her idea being so well received, especially since she knew how finicky and judgmental Chrissy and most of the other girls were. It had felt good to be able to contribute to the group which made her feel like she was fitting the role of a 'teen' believably and earnestly. At the back of her mind, as it always was, was Marina, and her prolific messaging which made her feel stressed out.

"I don't know," she replied. "It just sort of came out," She was lying, of course. She had had that idea ever since she herself was in high school the first time around. She remembered vividly how if she had been given a chance to join the prom committee the second time around, she would bring up the idea and everyone would rejoice and applause her and thank her for her great idea. Like magic, that's what had completely happened.

Bennett intuited her lie but didn't pry. She, instead, focused her attention on the road before her, both literally and figuratively. All of the prom talk clearly reminded her of the looming deadline to Marina's vague "make things right" requirement if she intended to stay in this life of a new teen. She still had absolutely no idea or inkling what there was to indeed make right or even in what direction to proceed into, but she tried to remain positive.

211

She was undoubtedly ambivalent about the joy factor she was having in her new life. There was no mistaking the fact that the books she read with such earnest in her former life were clearly very fundamentally different than the predicaments she was facing first hand. There was such a strong sense of urgency to every action she had to take, no matter how minor or major. She had forgotten the ferocity of being a teenager, and she wasn't sure how much she liked that, especially experiencing it on a daily basis.

On the other hand, she was enjoying the new (old) life due to the fact of making new friends and not having to work every day at a thankless job where she felt like her sanity was being tested day after day, or the loneliness that sometimes accompanied the weekends she was alone with her dog. And her books. She suddenly then remembered that she didn't actually have a job any longer, but she decided to let that one go.

"Hello, earth to Darcy," she heard Bennett say, as though she was farther away than she was. She looked over at Bennett.

"Oh sorry, I guess I just didn't get enough sleep last night!" she quickly mumbled but she didn't fool Bennett, who strangely knew her well even though they were relatively new friends.

She kept driving, stress on her mind, but a little bit of joy, too. *One moment at a time, Platt*, she thought to herself as both girls made their way down the palm-tree lined street, flanked by enormous homes and almost too-well manicured lawns.

Chapter 25

Rumors were running rampant that following Monday morning about her being possibly pregnant. By the end of the day, it was considered factual that in about nine months time there would be a tiny Platt running around the family palatial home.

She didn't know for certain who had leaked the secret, but if her seldom wrong intuition was right, the gossip monger was equal parts Jason and Claire. The trouble with confronting them was that she wasn't entirely sure. The concrete walls of her high school seemed to have ears of their own, and she wouldn't have really been surprised if it was the caretaker who would spread around such a terrible piece of untrue gossip.

But when there's a juicy bit of gossip, there will always be a lineup of hormonal teenagers biting at the chomp. As soon as she parked her car early that morning before the first bell rang, she felt the heavy and obvious stares from nearly everyone she walked by or was within eye sight of. They weren't even impolite stares, but full on ogles. When she tried to match the stares of a fellow student, the stares remained. She decided to just cope with the uncomfortable abundance of attention and start with the tedium of the school day.

She chose to take the high road and not succumb to her raging teenage hormones. Instead of providing credence to the rumors and adding fuel to the gossip heavy fire, she opted to stay mum on the whole subject and go about her day as normally as possible. In all truth told, it didn't take a lot of effort out of her to just that.

Upon entering the school and fiddling around with her locker, she saw Bennett out of the corner of her eye. Her new friend joined her side and gave her a reassuring pat on the back. She remained quiet and closed her locker door gently and began to walk towards her first period class. Bennett remained right by her side as she began her long walk down the brightly tiled hallway. It was almost as though the student conversations ceased as she walked by, reminding her of a really bad 80's movie. She never thought it would be a true event to occur, but here it was.

"Everyone's saying…" Bennett began to say once they neared the door of English class but she quickly cut her off.

"That I'm knocked up – I know," she said, nearing the nearly full class room that sounded like a cacophony of giggles and murmurs concurrently. "It's not true."

Bennett looked to the ground, redness coloring her full cheeks. Her red hair was styled in two side braids, reminding her of Pippi Longstocking. She was tempted to share her observation but realized that it was likely that Bennett wouldn't have known who Pippi actually was.

"People are saying that Charlie is the one, who, you know…" Bennett stammered on uncomfortably. Both girls halted by the classroom door to finish their conversation. "…and that's the reason why the two of you are going to prom together."

214

She felt her eyes narrow into slits and true anger build up within her tiny frame. In all the years that had elapsed since her first go round in high school, she had thankfully managed to forget how cruel kids were. This cruelty was a plot point that was often omitted (intentionally) in all of the books she loved to read. It sometimes showed up from time to time in the stories she read if it proved to act as a catalyst to some larger event, but it was seemingly a daily event in her actual new lift.

Up until that point, she thought she held some sort of semblance control of any situation that would be thrown at her. How serious could teenage issues be, after all? However, now that someone else was involved, a boy she liked and was innocent nonetheless, the flame of anger within her became a full on flame within milliseconds.

Instead of replying to Bennett, she turned around 180 degrees so that her back was now where her face was moments ago. Feeling the sudden shift in the dynamics, Bennett just stared at Darcy as she turned her glare towards Claire who was sitting by the fountain in the main hallway, steps away from her English class. With Rena in tow, Claire laughed loudly, clearly exaggeratedly as Rena never really had anything funny to say. A few students smiled at Claire's expression of laughter, eager to get in on the joke, but quickly made their way on to their classroom.

Without really realizing she was doing so, she made her way, practically running at that point, towards Claire, Rena, and the pseudo group that had formed around them.

As she drew nearer, the other students noticeably stopped laughing. In fact, they seemed to distance themselves slowly away from Claire and Rena, sensing that an outburst was inevitable. As Darcy approached, she felt Claire stare at her directly. Her flame of anger then instantly became the atom bomb.

"So I'm pregnant, huh?" she practically yelled once she was inches away from Claire's face. Her voice was loud enough for everyone in the hallway to hear her. If the hallway was reasonably quiet before that point, it was now 100% still. Every conversation seemed to stop and all eyes automatically moved towards the group of girls, some non-chalant and some direct.

Claire giggled loudly, as though she had just revealed a hilarious punch-line to a joke. Rena, of course, copied Claire's lead and laughed loudly as well, but she quickly thought she noticed Rena's obvious discomfort at the site that was beginning to play out.

"Are you now?" Claire replied, matching Darcy's volume. "That didn't take long." She giggled again. Claire looked up at the other kids who were still nearby for reactions, but the other students knew better and remained expressionless.

She slowly walked closer to Claire's perch on the concrete bench that stood before the fountain. She lowered herself so that she was at eye level with her frenemy.

"Why would you spread such an awful lie about me?" she said, lowering her voice. Claire didn't flinch. "Is it because I haven't been the doting, brainless friend to you that you clearly desperately need to feel good about yourself?"

Rena leaned closer to hear.

It was clear that Claire hadn't expected her to come back and defend herself so vehemently. Claire's upper lip began to quiver but she kept her voice even and calm.

"I was just spreading news that I thought people should know. That you and Charlie are having a baby," Claire spat back, her voice chock full of venom. "Don't you want me to plan the baby shower?"

They say that everything is 20/20 in retrospect, and for her, that adage could not have been closer to the truth as she revisited that cataclysmic moment many times later. She didn't know what came over her. At that particular point in time, she felt utterly consumed by the anger she had been feeling towards Claire. But there was something else, too. She knew on some level that there was more to her current state of wrath and anger than the recent events.

216

She could literally feel Claire's words like icicles on her spine, drenched and then frozen in blatant lies and bitter sarcasm. She felt the bomb within her awaken something buried very deep, something that was born a long time ago during her original teenaged years. Those years where daily she saw the ways the most popular girls felt it was their right and duty to make the less popular girls feel so inferior, wrecking with their minds well into their adult lives. It was then that she realized that what she had adored and relished in all of the teen fiction books she read was fictional: pure and simple. The real life of a teenager couldn't have been more different than the trials and tribulations of Sweet Valley High or even the Twilight Books. Real life was worse. Far, far worse.

She leaned in closer to Claire, letting the silence in the air hang awkwardly between them. She caught a waft of the strawberry lip gloss that Claire liked to shellac her lips with. Claire looked at her incredulously, obviously riveted by the confrontation. She knew that Claire was secretly enjoying this public event, which added to the ire within her very being.

Before she was even noticed her hand leave the side of her jeans where it has become slightly moist from the discomfort of the situation, she heard the loud smack her palm made as it bounced off of Claire's face. The sound was so loud that kids later said that they heard it in the parking lot.

There was a collective gasp in the hallway as the slap seemed to echo and reverberate amongst the white walls and metal lockers. Bennett stared open mouthed at the scene from her perch beside the classroom door. In fact, it seemed that the rest of the entire student body was agape at the confrontation.

Claire's face immediately reddened. She brought her hand up to where her hand had just temporarily been and rubbed it gently.

She, too, felt her own face redden, embarrassed at her outburst, especially it being so public. She thought Claire would try to slap her back, or engage in some sort of physical fight, but instead she slowly stood up from the bench she sat upon. She gathered her book bag, and with Rena beside her, walked slowly to the bathroom

She soon felt guilty about the slap, but she felt there was no other recourse. Instead of returning to Bennett, she turned around and ran out of the school to the relative safety of her car, unsure of what her next step should be.

***

That evening, and for the rest of the week, she decided to feign illness and skip out on school. Her mother didn't ask her to quantify her sickness, or to venture from her perch in her bed to go visit the doctor, which she was ever so grateful for. In fact, her mother didn't even pester her at all.

She must have spent the first two following days of the outburst with Claire sleeping. She slept true, deep and dreamless sleeps. She was exhausted and couldn't satiate her need for more and more rest. She had turned off her phone that Monday morning, and locked her bedroom door so that there was no surprise Mason visits at inopportune times. She was even sure to lower her blinds and throw the remote to operate them into the deep abyss of her closet.

By Thursday afternoon, she was beginning to go a little stir crazy, but she remained firmly entrenched in her palatial mountain of pillows and blankets. She skimmed through some mindless magazines, and looked with very little effort to find the rest of her journal. She felt as though every time she sat up from her bed, she just wanted to lay back down again. Glenda was kind enough to leave a tray in front of her door at every meal so she was sure to be hydrated and fed, but her virtual non-existent appetite didn't really faze her.

She still felt immense guilt for having slapped Claire, and for doing it so publically. Never having been a support of any kind of physical violence, she was embarrassed at being so out of control

218

and brazen. Her anger had dissipated significantly since then, and she was pretty sure that her confrontation with Claire had essentially squashed the rumors of her pregnancy. But she still felt sorry. She felt sorry for Claire and having to endure being a teenager and pregnant, and she also felt sorry for herself.

She picked up her cell phone which felt like a heavy brick and was momentarily tempted to turn it on, but then thought better of it and let it drop back heavily upon her nightstand. She laid back upon her pillow, feeling the warmness and the sweet escape of sleep beginning to take over, when she heard a quiet knock on her bedroom door.

Her instant reaction was to just not acknowledge the source of the knocks, and that was exactly what she did for a few moments. However, the knocks didn't let up and she decided maybe she should make her way towards the door, which seemed to be feet and feet away.

"Who is it?" she said when she finally reached the door. She glanced at her watch and noticed it was still only 1 pm.

"It's me," Luke said, his voice low. At first, she thought it was Mason's voice but then quickly recognized Luke's tone.

She pulled open the door and saw him. He looked concerned, his brow furrowed as he took in her appearance in. She pulled him into her room and slammed the door shut.

"WHAT are you doing here?" she said. "Shouldn't you be at school?"

She walked back to her bed and sat down. Luke followed behind. *He really is like a little puppy*, she thought.

"Relax, Mom," he quipped. "I was so worried about you. You haven't been at school since Monday and no one has seen you."

"Which isn't that big of a deal, Luke," she retorted. "I can't show my face there. I was such a bitch."

Luke laughed aloud, causing her to look up at him quickly.

"*You're* such a bitch?" he said, in between fits of laughter.

219

"You've got to be kidding me. You couldn't be less of a bitch."

This caused a slight smile to break upon her face.

"In fact, I could say with all truth that you are one of the unbitchiest people I know," Luke went on.

"Ok, ok, I get it. You have to make me feel better," she replied. "And you know what, it's working."

Luke smiled and she thought she saw a slight blush color his cheeks.

"I don't have to make you feel anything," Luke said. "In fact with the way you've been treating me, I should be making you feel worse, not better."

She punched him softly on his shoulder, and he jokingly grimaced in pain.

"How are you?" he then asked, his tone serious once more. She reverted her gaze to the carpeted floor, not sure how to respond. "I mean, seriously. Everyone is talking about how you handed it to Claire, which if you ask me, was a long time coming."

She was surprised that that's how the school was reacting to the drama of a few days before. She had always thought Claire was a force to not be reckoned with, but clearly the other student's allegiance was just not there.

"Yeah, well…its complicated," was all she could say in response. She didn't feel like rehashing everything again, least of all to Luke, who continued to stare at her with his puppy dog eyes.

"It always is," he replied. "You know, Darcy….I have to say, I'm sorry for being such a jerk to you for the last little while. I had a hard time understanding that you just weren't into me anymore but I think I'm over it now."

"Luke, it's not…" she said, but Luke continued.

"I'm not going to harass you into liking me. We had something special but it's obviously over now. You have to give me some time to really move on but I swear I won't be bothering you anymore, and I definitely won't be throwing rocks at your window in the middle of the night after polishing off a bottle of my dad's tequila."

Both friends laughed. She felt comfortable with the moment, and she really was grateful that Luke stopped by.

"And Claire broke up with me," he threw in at the end. She looked at him and tried to assess his reaction to it when he continued. "Which is awesome because I couldn't stand her anyway!"

This caused the both of them to laugh even harder.

"Anyway, I just wanted to see how you're feeling," Luke continued. "You look good, I mean, except for the eye crust and major bed head you're rocking."

She instantly tried to pat down her hair but it felt like hard in her hands. She did manage, though, to remove the eye crust that Luke brought up.

"Thanks, you ass," she laughed. "Hey, thanks for checking in on me. You're a good guy."

They both stood up and walked towards her bedroom door. Before leaving, she went on her tip toes and kissed Luke on his cheek. He quickly reddened before waving at her as he made his way down her stairs.

She closed the door behind her, the pleasantness of the visit warm within her. Getting back into her bed, she felt a burst of energy and a tangible hope that things were going to get better, even if she had to work hard at it.

***

"What're you watching?" Mason asked, plopping himself down loudly on the sofa beside her. She had been in the same position for the entire day (horizontal, twisted at the hip, and head flat against the expensive looking pillow). The large screen TV was keeping her company, and she liked the meaningless chattering of the endless parade of soap operas, mindless game shows and shiny actors-turned-talk show hosts. At this particular moment, however, she was fully invested in a riveting episode of Jeopardy. Alec had just made one of his signature passive-aggressive snarky comments, causing her to quietly snicker to herself.

"Jeopardy, my dear brother," she replied, post-laugh. She was comfortable in her sweatpants and hoodie. She felt a few remnant crumbs of the bag of barbeque chips she polished off between Days of Our Lives and before Ellen under her hand as she adjusted the pillow.

"Could you be any more out of character?" Mason finally said once a commercial break began. "You look like a homeless housewife."

She didn't even take the energy required to come up with a witty retort for her brother and opted to remain quiet.

"Someone is in a mood," Mason goaded, his voice low and patient. She knew he was just waiting for her to bite at his sarcasm, but she had absolutely no intention of engaging in a spat of words. She was too comfortable in her oversized hoodie which felt like heaven upon her shoulders.

"Ok, fine – I get it," Mason went on. He turned his body slowly towards his sister so that the space that lay between them was rather intimate. She squirmed at the intimacy.

Still remaining quiet, she thought she felt Mason's body turning nervous and uncomfortable.

"Maybe you'll be this quiet for the rest of the pregnancy? Silence really suits you."

She sat up at once, the blood quickly going to her head and causing a slight tingling pain at the side of her temple.

"What did you just say?" she whispered, turning her gaze towards him. She saw the tiny smile in his eyes though his lips remained straight. The dimple on his right cheek became prominent.

"You heard me, Mommy and Me. High school gossip tends to spread like wildfire, especially when it's as juicy as the unexpected pregnancy of my kid sister," he replied, his tone even.

"I don't know how you heard the rumors, Mason, but they're just that – rumors," she replied. She felt her cheeks blaze.

"Clearly, I know that. I know you're not a loose girl. But humor me – how'd the rumor start?" he asked, seemingly genuine in his question.

"You don't want to know. It's not a good story," she replied, feeling her heartbeat return to normal. She turned her attention back to Alex Trebeck.

"I'm not expecting to hear a riveting tale," Mason countered, still looking towards his sister. "It just seems like a vicious rumor to start. I thought you were the High school Sweetheart, unlike your other half."

"First of all, it is an extremely vicious rumor to start," she finally said, grabbing the remote on the coffee table in front of her and muting the television. "And secondly, there is no other half. It is all me. A whole. Totally, completely, 100% me."

"I'm sure Claire would disagree."

"Yeah, well, Claire is a major, sniveling and evil bitch," she responded a little too fast, knowing that Mason would immediately be drawn to her outburst. She wasn't wrong.

"Wow – that seems a bit harsh….but wait. Does that mean SHE started the rumor?!"

"Ding ding. You got it, Mr. Mensa. And don't ask me why because I've given up on trying to understand that girl and her convoluted neuroses."

Mason laughed loudly, which then in turn made her start to laugh.

"I wouldn't disagree with you on that one," Mason went on.

"You hardly know her. How could you agree with me?" she replied, a smile still on her lips.

"Yeah, well…" Mason said, nervously sitting up, his back up once more. The change in body language and body tone did not go

223

unnoticed by Darcy who was intrigued at this change in attitude.

"Yeah, well, what, Mason? Do you not like Claire? Has she done something to you?"

Mason took a few seconds to finally reply, which to her, felt like a very, very long few seconds. She thought she noticed his cheeks blush a bit, but it could have been attributed to the setting sun that filled the gigantic windows around her.

"You can say that. Hey, listen, Darcy – I've got to run," he said, getting up abruptly from the leather sofa. He began to walk towards the kitchen but she jumped up from the bed and intercepted him before he disappeared.

"Mason, wait," she said, tapping him on the shoulder. He turned around quickly, the frown on his forehead unmistakable.

"What? I need to go," he replied, whisking her hand away like she had leprosy and continued to make his way into the kitchen.

"What did Claire do to you? I'm not an idiot – I can see you're upset."

Mason laughed before opening the kitchen cupboard to get a glass. "Aren't you observant?"

"I'm many things, Mason. Now tell me! I know that you're hiding something," she countered.

She watched him pour water into his glass and take his time drinking every last drop. She remained firm in her stance and waiting patiently until he drank every last drop.

"There's nothing to say, Darcy. Why don't you go back to your laborious Friday afternoon events atop the couch over there," he said, pointing to the large couch just a few feet away.

"Can't you just be honest with me for once, Mason? I just want to know."

"We all want to know a lot of things, Darcy. Now buzz off and leave me alone." With that, he left the kitchen and walked upstairs, leaving his sister fuming in the kitchen.

Chapter 26

The days now seemed to pass by at a hurried pace. It was as though it was time to go to bed as soon as she woke up in the morning to the sound of her local radio station blaring god-awful dance music. She had settled into a routine where she thought she was being unproductive and rather boring, but the ironic part was that her days were chockfull of events and appointments and meetings that she didn't get to realize she was boring until she let her minds encompass her mind before nodding off to sleep each night.

The teenage existence that had befallen her was not that entirely different from her adult life, a life that she silently found herself missing from time to time. It wasn't that she was unhappy being a teenage per se, in fact, she relished in certain activities that she thought she never would experience after graduating from high school the first time around. She enjoyed being the popular girl, the girl that everyone wanted as their best friend, but she also found it sort of exhausting.

She was unable to walk down the school hallway without some keen freshman trying to engage her in idle dialogue and conversation, and she sometimes felt bad for not being able to converse with them when she was on route from one class to the next. The guilt she felt from not being able to speak to the younger kids more at length came from a place of recognition and awareness. She WAS that kid in high school and she remembered avidly being heavily disappointed when the popular girls wouldn't acknowledge her existence.

She devotedly and passionately threw herself into her new life. She became a rather vocal and leader of the Prom committee which by that point was meeting twice a week after school for at least two hours. She made the effort to tutor kids also twice a week and sparked an unexpected friendship with Glenda. The latter was actually really enjoyable for her as she could just remove the pretense that she often felt when she was in school or hanging out with her co-horts. Glenda was a truly kind woman that she felt instantly at ease with. She found herself pining for Sylvia each day.

At that point, a few weeks had passed since her interaction with Claire and, she thought, that the pregnancy talk had silently abated, especially since the other students didn't see her look any visibly physically different. No fuel was added to the fire of that vicious rumor, and she was thankful, and a bit surprised, that the rumor came and went as fast as it did.

While she still had to interact with Claire in some situations (the group work in her English class had been particularly uncomfortable), she was able to be mature about their fizzled friendship. Claire seemed to be in the same proverbial boat and didn't engage in any catty comments or resurfacings of awkward interactions.

Bennett had been a true friend amidst all of the clear dramatics that had taken over her life. The girl was funny, honest and strangely confident, and a true breath of fresh air to the other acquaintances that she had. She couldn't help but shake the feeling that Bennett knew that she was not all that she had appeared to be, but she never let on nor pried into it. There was no way she could drop that bomb. No one would have believed it anyway.

Now, as she sat alone at a desk in the library which was nearly empty at 5 pm that Thursday afternoon, she felt her thoughts swivel and swoosh about the ever present deadline that Marina had imposed upon her months ago. She couldn't believe that she had been living this life of a teenage girl again for almost 3 months. She felt like she should have experienced some sort of epiphany into the nature of her existence, but instead, it was full of nothing but uncomfortable arguments, partial friendships, and tense familial situations. True, at the beginning of 'the switch', she fully engaged herself in dramatic blow-ups with Claire and her brother Mason, but recently she had begun to wonder how Marina's ominous request of 'making things right' was going to be fulfilled.

She rested her head atop her Biology text book in the small carol, allowing the thoughts to ping around her mind, trying to find some sort of semblance of order or even a slight hint on how she was to fill her end of the deal with Marina. After the first few superficial thoughts left her mind (mostly centering around type of Prom dress that she still had not purchased for the big day), she began to find herself going back to how she had to make things right. She still had absolutely no idea on what it meant, or even if it meant anything at all.

She tried to dissect what 'making things right' meant. Did it mean righting a wrong? If so, what was the wrong? Was it even that simple to identify and recognize? The things that could have been taken as 'wrongs' in her life were things that she knew she could not change, regardless of how much effort she put forth. She couldn't change the fact that the girls in her class were going to have body issues due to the preponderance of unrealistically photo-shopped girls that plastered the magazines they all read and were in the TV shows they all gossiped about in the mornings.

She knew she also couldn't change the dynamics of the teenage existence. She couldn't make freshman students feel more confident in their own skin. She couldn't make her brother treat her better and let go of the clear emotional baggage he carried so heavily with him, day in and day out. She couldn't tell Claire that she didn't have to be so aggressive and mean to give the illusion that she was in control of her life, and in control of who was deemed cool and elite in their school.

As she felt her heartbeat quicken and a slight flop of sweat appear upon her forehead due to her stressful thoughts clouding her mind, she decided to gear her mind towards the things that she could do. Things that she could make a little bit better. Making things right was so objective and ambiguous. Something that may have seemed right to her may appear as wrong to someone else. She decided that she should just put her heart in the right place and act in a kind way. She wasn't going to be a saint, in fact, one of the things she had anticipated mostly in being a teenage girl again was being able to be reckless and carefree. But she figured she could try, regardless of how minute the actions may be, to make someone's existence just a little bit easier, a little big more enjoyable.

She felt her heartbeat slow down a bit with this realization and partial guide on how she was going to move forward. The Prom was only two weeks away and with that, she knew Marina was going to re-appear with her decision made. There were no recent sudden apparitions of the mysterious book owner, which she had taken to be as a good sign and that she was on the good track, whatever that had meant.

She knew that her ability to fulfill her end of the bargain with Marina was the one thing that would either let her stay in the life she was willingly thrust into or thrust right back into her adult life, which she silently remembered had been recently full of events that

228

were stressful, to say the least. She didn't want to let Marina down, and she obviously didn't want Marina to suffer in any way. She didn't want the bookstore that she had called home for all those years to be suddenly gone, and with its disappearance, a piece of her own soul moving away. But no matter how many hours she put into thinking of the clear actions she had to take to make her new life worthy and meet the expectations that Marina so ambiguously laid upon her, she felt resentment grown within her. Had she been set up to fail? How could she live up to and deliver her end of a deal that was so enigmatic that she sometimes had a hard time even remembering what was being asked of her?

Marina had given her a once in a lifetime opportunity, there was no way she could refute that. She was thankful, however, a bit angered that she was expected to deliver something that she had no clue what the tangible result was. Her plan of action was comprised of the one thing she was sure of, and that was trusting her instinct and letting her heart guide her. If she did that, she knew that couldn't be at fault for failing anyone, and least of all, failing herself.

Chapter 27

She did not care much about the apparent abrupt weather changes that comprised her time in Martin's Falls. Often switching to a pair of shorts from jeans midday was becoming a normal practice. It was a major understatement hat she and Claire did not see eye to an eye on a lot of things. In fact, they didn't even seem to have that much in common, other than the school they attended and the friends they had. Otherwise, it was like the two girls couldn't be any more different. She had tried to find some common ground amongst the two girls to grow and nurture their lengthy friendship, but for every effort she made, there just wasn't any grounding there. And there was surely no way that Claire was going to give her anything to work with.

She had chided herself for being overly judgmental and perhaps being too hard on her temperamental and unpleasant friend. She even often found herself trying to mentally make a list of things that she could build upon or flesh out to strengthen the relations between them, but every interaction she had with Claire, regardless of how minor or major, was always unpleasant, to put it mildly. Even post-slap. She couldn't stop thinking about if she had made a mistake in relatively ending that friendship.

With the most recent argument with Claire a few days in the past, she couldn't shake the feeling that this one was going to take more than a casual catch up or text message conversation to soften, if she decided in fact, to resolve their differences. Claire was mad. She knew that she herself was really upset about Claire's recent chain of explosions and outbursts, regardless if she was pregnant or not.

She made every attempt to thrust herself into Prom Committee and growing a friendship with Bennett. Unlike with Claire, her and Bennett had so much in common, from their penchant for early 90's dance music (Bennett had just discovered Technotronic, She had remembered buying the album herself in the local mall), to romantic comedies. She sometimes found herself finding it a bit odd at how much she actually did have in common with her rather new friend, but she went with it anyhow.

On that particular afternoon, she was driving back from the most recent prom committee meeting with Chrissy Barr, Bennett, and the rest of the girls at their local Starbucks. The coffee shop had become their unofficial meeting location for their committee meetings, and the baristas began to get to remember what orders the girls always made, which were often ludicrous concoctions of coffees and creams with levels of sugar that sometimes made her feel like her head was going to pop off at times.

"So, the prom is just a week away, and I'm happy to say I just got off the phone with Lex from Sex Lex Dj's," Chrissy began, taking a quick sip from the plastic cup in front of her that matched the size of her head. "And we booked him!"

The girls around the table began to clap and cheer, and Darcy and Bennett found themselves participating in the teen girl frenzy. Sex Lex was the hottest DJ for miles around, and considering the relative seclusion of Martin's Falls, getting a DJ that was from the capital city was a big deal.

After the squealing had died down, Chrissy continued. "He's charging us exactly what we thought he would, which is both good and bad. I mean, we got LEX, for God's sake, but that also means we have to cut something to make up for the added cost."

How sensible, Darcy thought.

"Any thoughts of what to cut? I was thinking of maybe downsizing the flower arrangements that we were planning on putting on each of the tables?" Chrissy said, looking around at each of the girls, about 10 in all.

Temporary silence surrounded the table. The girls had all had serious difficulty in whittling down the costs that would accompany the prom, and right when they thought they just couldn't cut anything more, they found out the news of Lex Sex's costs.

"I guess we can cut the flower arrangements, but that means the tables are pretty much going to be the plates, some cutlery and the tablecloth", a girl named Mary spoke up. Darcy couldn't remember seeing her before, but was sure she wasn't new.

"Well, then what's your idea?" Chrissy nastily said, starting at Mary, who quietly shrunk against the wall behind her until Darcy thought that the girl was going to disappear.

"I think we might have to make the Prom King and Queen's tiara's a bit lower grade," she spoke up. It was like the wind was knocked out of Chrissy's frame, and for a split second, it looked like she was going to pass out in shock for her even bringing up such a crazy thought.

"You have got to be kidding, Platt," Chrissy finally said, taking a sip from the plastic cup before her and dabbing her forehead with a napkin. She really, really wanted to do a major eye roll but she decided to hold off.

"Nope, I'm totally not," she quickly replied. "There's not really a need to have the Prom Queen and King to get something that is Swarovski encrusted. The tiaras will be just as effective with something cheaper."

"No! No! No!" Christy dramatically yelled. The girls around the table moved their eyes from girl to girl, as though watching a tennis game. "The tiara is, like, super important for the prom queen. It's something she's going to have for the rest of her life and look back on and smile about."

"So you'd rather have everyone sit at tables for a few hours eating dinner without any decorative vases and flowers just so one girl can get something at the end of the night? Seems a bit unfair to me," she replied. Feeling that she made her case and that the other girls would support her, she took a swig of her iced tea.

"Just because you have no chance of becoming Prom Queen doesn't mean the winner should suffer," Chrissy spat back, rather venomously at that. The girls that formed the committee began to look visually uncomfortable, sipping and quietness abound.

"Chrissy, all I'm saying is that Mary's right, the flowers are the only feasible thing that could be cut because of Lex, and we all just talked about it last week."

"Fine, Darcy. Fine. Let's take a vote on it, shall we? Let's see if these other sane girls think that taking away the little token of the celebration of a perfect teenaged existence is the right thing to do," Chrissy replied, her eyes squinting as though having just trapped an animal.

"Ok girls," Chrissy went on. "Hands up if you think making an ugly tiara is the way to go instead of cutting the flowers."

For a split second, there was no activity around the table. She held up her own hand to start, and was relieved to see Bennett raise hers a moment later. Chrissy looked at her meanly as though to say "Hah! Told you so," until all of the other girls began to raise their hands, led by Mary.

233

She thought Chrissy was going to explode upon seeing the raised hands that surrounded the table. Her face turned red and splotchy, and weird red marks began to color her neck. Understanding that she was clearly outnumbered, all she could barely do was make a humph sound and the meeting went on.

About half an hour later, Bennett and Claire were walking in the parking lot to their respective cars which were parking right beside one another. They felt exhausted at the wrath of Chrissy Barr, but they had won. It was clearly the only real option to explore, and in the end, the prom committee agreed.

"I feel like I need a nap," Bennett said as they neared the cars. "Do you think Chrissy is exhausted, like all of the time, because of the way she acts? I mean, it must take a lot of energy to be so high-strung and high pitched all of the time."

Darcy smiled and used her fob to unlock her car. "I think she might just not know how to be otherwise. It's probably normal to her to see things so black and white."

"That's a wise answer, Darcy," Bennett smiled, unlocking her own car. A cold wind suddenly blew at both girls, their hair moving every direction. "What the…"

"I will call you later. I'm too cold!" she laughed and got in the car. She had been wearing just a t-shirt as it had been rather warm when she left the house just a little while earlier, but with the wind that had just blown against her; she wished she had brought a cardigan or sweater with her.

She waved to Bennett as she reversed out of the spot and sped away. The car was also really cold, and she even thought to turn up the heat to high to warm up the small space. However, it felt like it was getting colder instead of warmer.

She groaned out loud and put on her seatbelt and then suddenly remembered that Mason had given her a scarf a little while ago before another one of her Prom Committee meetings. She reached into the back seat for her brother's wise provision and grabbed the heavy scarf that sat in the seat right behind her.

She quickly unfolded it and wrapped it around her shoulders and instantly felt the warmth. The scarf was wool, and she felt the relief instantly. She looked quickly in the rear view mirror to adjust the scarf and began to back out of her spot, when suddenly she nearly crashed into the concrete wall right beside her.

The scarf that was bringing her such warmth was red. Bloody red. So red that she instantly remembered the diary entry she had found written by the old Darcy. Claire had mentioned in that entry that she was missing her red scarf. Surely there were many red scarf's floating around, but why would Mason have a red scarf that was so obviously made for a woman, with its ruffles and label which was from a popular woman's clothing store.

Her heart beat quickened, making the connection. Why did Mason have Claire's scarf? It then abruptly all fell into place. The journal entry. The uncomfortable interactions between Mason and Claire. Mason's always asking about her friend. Mason WAS who Claire was cheating on Luke with. And based on what Luke had confided to her, the fat her of her unborn baby.

She stopped the car because she thought she was going to be sick. And as she suspected, sick was what she became.

Chapter 28

"Well, I never thought she was really into him to begin with," Bennett squealed beside Darcy on the latter's living room sofa. Both girls were knee deep in a bout of giggles after having watched a marathon of one of those Housewives of Wherever shows. This week's cliffhanger included one of the housewives' leaving her plaything after a dramatic confrontation in a castle in Abu Dhabi, colored silk drapes and fabrics blowing around them in the wind.

"His contract must have ended!" Darcy replied, which only made Bennett laugh even more hysterically hard. "At least he can put it on his actor's resume!"

They had just finished the sixth episode of the series and decided to take a breather. It was a cool, May afternoon. Uncharacteristically cool according to most inhabitants of Martin's Falls, though she didn't have anything to compare the temperate weather changes too. She took everyone else's word for it. Both girls, now good friends, decided to blow off their last period history class and catch up on her mom's PVR, which she noted was very similar, if not exactly the same, of her 'adult' life. She attributed this similarity to good taste, though she knew on a deeper level there was a tinge of desperation to it, especially since the characters on the show were very similar to her own teenaged mother.

"I guess. But how could Stefania have take Jina's word over Mikayla's? After all they've been through together?" Bennett asked honestly, looking at her with genuine concern. She stifled back a laugh at her friends' genuine expression of concern.

"These aren't real people, Ben. They're actors, I'm sure of it," Darcy replied, sitting up from the couch and stretching her legs. They had been sitting in various positions atop the sofa for about 4 hours and she was beginning to feel her calf muscles stiffen.

"Yeah, I know, but they should be depicting 'real' relationships and real problems, don't you think? I mean, it is reality TV after all," her friend answered, also getting up from the sofa and stretching out her arms behind her neck. "Like honestly, would you have thought Jina was telling you the truth. Remember – this is the same woman who slipped cocaine in your wine at your father's 80th birthday…and Mika…."

She had to stop Bennett from continuing on her tirade into the credence of reality TV genre and its intent over the today's modern television viewer. She had experienced first hand Bennett getting heated over certain things which always ended in her practically having a panic attack after working herself up into such a frenzy. She blamed it on hormones. And a slight tinge of craziness. Maybe.

"Bennett – it's not real life. Those people are just robots. Come on, let's get something to eat," she interrupted, forcing her friend to immediately stop talking. Both girls laughed again and walked into the kitchen which literally gleamed brightly in the mid afternoon light.

"I know, I know," Bennett continued as she peered into the monstrous fridge that nearly took up an entire wall. "It just makes me mad sometimes. People clearly watch these shows expecting some portrayal of reality but they're so scripted that who knows what's genuinely authentically real and what isn't."

"Very well stated, Madame Bennett," a deep voice countered. Both girls jumped in their spot of looking into the fridge and turned around quickly, both clearly startled.

As both girls turned around, Mason smiled widely at Bennett. She noticed Bennett's cheeks begin to redden and then turn into a deep maroon. It would have been sweet if her brother wasn't such a mega-jerk.

"Oh hi, Mason," Darcy said, her voice monotonous and dry. She wasn't going to let her brother's morose demeanor bring down her pleasant afternoon with her new friend. It was one of the few afternoons that have actually been relatively drama-free since 'the switch' and she was treasuring every single moment of it.

"Don't sound too overjoyed to see me, sister," Mason continued, not taking his eyes, or smile, off of Bennett.

"You now I'm shy about my outward expression of joy and affection towards my loving sibling," she retorted quickly, happy with her quick response. Bennett looked at the both of them awkwardly.

She took out two water bottles and two tubs of Greek yogurt out of the fridge and closed the door quickly behind her. She didn't want to extend the discomfort that was clear amongst the three of them, nor make Bennett feel caught in the middle.

"Thanks, Mason," Bennett replied, surprising her. Bennett typically was mute around Mason, which she thought was because her friend secretly had a crush on him but would never, ever vocalize it. *Give me time and I'll get it out of you*, she thought to herself. She handed Bennett a bottle and her friend slowly opened it and took a sip.

"You're welcome, Bennett. So what piece of seminal episode of the pop culture canon have the two of you been watching anyway?"

238

Mason asked as he helped himself to a bottle of water from the fridge as well. He deliberately took his time walking around Bennett and Darcy noticed a new shade of maroon that she hadn't yet seen shadowed her friends face.

She rolled her eyes and motioned Bennett to walk back to the living room and leave her brother alone. Apparently becoming momentarily mute, Bennett, either intentionally or not, didn't acknowledge the effort she was making. She even resorted to miming rather crudely but Bennett was just not having it. In fact, as she stepped ever so closer to the living room that was adjacent to the kitchen, she noticed Bennett actually step *closer* to her Mason and chat.

Suddenly annoyed and not able to bear the weird comfortable interaction that was unfolding before her, she stormed into the hallway, desperately wanting to step outside and get some air. As she walked towards the front door, she made sure to grab her keys off of the side table that sat beneath the large mirror that sat in the foyer and opened the door quickly.

As she opened the door, she pushed her way determinedly towards outside when she smacked right dab into Charlie.

"Oh, Charlie – I'm so sorry," she whispered, seeing the look of surprise and startle in Charlie's big brown eyes.

"It's ok. You are allowed to leave your house once in a while, you know, he quickly replied, his voice deep and safe-sounding. His yellow t-shirt complimented the olive skin tone that seemed to cover every inch of his body.

"I really should be aware of my surroundings. I'm going to walk right into a moving vehicle one of these days," she replied, blushing and feeling stupid at her silly response. She found it easier to reply the way her 30-year old type would, not the life of an aloof teenager.

"That wouldn't be a good scene. Unless I was there to save you, of course. Being a hero is on my bucket list," Charlie said, a smile creeping up upon his face. The dimple on his right cheek made her heart flutter ever so little.

She smiled back, the redness in her cheeks slowly abating. A cool wind entered the house through the front door, and she felt tresses of her hair bob silently upon her shoulder. She absent-mindedly pulled the orange cardigan she had around her shoulders a bit tighter, and slipped her house keys into her jeans pocket.

"Hey Darcy – do you have a minute? Or were you going somewhere?" Charlie asked.

"I was just going to get some air. It got really stuffy all of a sudden in the kitchen," she replied.

"Oh good. Why don't we take a breather on the porch? It's so nice out," Charlie countered, stepping aside and moving his arm beckoning her to walk outside.

Following his direction, she stepped outside and let the cool afternoon breeze cover her body and let the wind blow her hair in every which way, not really too concerned about how she looked. She felt that same feeling of excitement and bliss at being around Charlie, though she had to admit, she didn't see him nearly as much as she would have liked. She chalked it up to them frequenting different social circles both in and out of school, but she also knew she wasn't exactly making an effort otherwise.

She sat atop one of the high backed wicker chairs that sat on the far right of the large porch which capsulated the whole front side of the home. She watched Charlie walk closely beside her and sit close beside her on the matching chair.

"It's such a beautiful afternoon", she said, not really meaning to. *Ugh, she thought internally. Who says something like that? An old woman*, she silently answered.

"It sure is. Hey, Darcy – I know that you said you would go to the prom with me," Charlie replied, his voice dropping a few octaves. She could hear the apprehension and nerves in his voice. *Poor guy*, she thought. *It probably took him all day to just garner enough bravado to speak to me.*

"I did. And I am," she replied.

"That's awesome!" he said, his voice rising. "I mean, oh, yeah, it's cool."

She giggled, sure not to make him feel uncomfortable or to make Charlie think she was laughing at him instead of laughing with him.

"But I think there's something we should do before going to the prom together," he went on. "Even though the prom itself is like, next week."

"It's totally going to be here before we know it. I don't even have a dress yet. Did you get your costume already? I think the prom committee wants to do an old fashioned masquerade ball theme," she rattled on. "We can coordinate our outfits if you like? Or is that, like, too cheesy?"

Charlie smiled. And she felt her heart flutter again. "Cheesy but good. And yes, we could totally coordinate. Though I have to say I'm not exactly a style maven or anything. I'll perhaps need your guidance on finding the right thing".

"Of course! I would love to help you," she enthusiastically replied.

"As I was saying, and before I lose my guts, but maybe we can go on an actual date before the prom. I mean, I'd like to actually get to know you before having the entire senior class watch us at the prom itself. Maybe we can go to dinner or something? Or maybe drive to the Falls?"

She saw his cheeks blaze up, and she reached forward and touched his hand. She wanted to do something small to make him feel comfortable, at ease even.

"I would love to go on a date with you, Charlie. Anywhere you'd like to go would be cool with me. It would be an honor to get to know you a bit better, too", she replied. She immediately saw the tension in his shoulders evaporate and another huge smile grow across his face.

"Maybe tomorrow? Are you free?" he asked.

"I sure am. Wanna meet me after school?"

"I'll meet you at your car," he replied, his voice high with excitement. At that moment Bennett pulled open the front door.

"Oh, sorry guys," she said. "I didn't mean to interrupt."

"No worries, Bennett. I have to go help my mom anyway," Charlie quickly replied, getting up quickly. She followed suit and watched as Charlie slowly walked down the front steps.

"See you tomorrow, Darcy," he said and smiled, a small wave and then was gone around the side of house. Bennett and Darcy both looked at each other at the exact same time and giggled like a bunch, of well, like a bunch of high school girls.

***

The long-time residents of Martin's Falls have officially declared that that particular May was the coldest ever on record. Not that this information was confirmed or validated against a town almanac of any kind, but it was more of a communal confirmation among the older population, which itself seemed to be quite large in the city.

They said that the uncharacteristically cold spring was not due to an El Nino type of phenomenon, nor the controversial topic of global warming. Rather, it was universally believed amongst the over 60 crowd, that the cold weather was due to a catastrophic event that was going to envelop the entire City and leave no survivors in its wake. The first time Darcy overheard this talk from the misers that frequented Cupps, the morning coffee shop that she went to religiously, she thought it hilarious. Two old men, barely able to hold up their heads or see out of their eyes due to their heavily overgrown eyebrows, had been sitting at a table by the coffee bar where she patiently waited to pick up her coffee.

"It's going to be worse than that Twister in '54," one man said, his voice deep and gravelly. He had the smallest cup of coffee sitting on the table before him that Darcy ever did see. She thought that this was probably because his old, haggard body couldn't take much caffeine. "And we both know what devastation that old bitch made of this town."

This use of profanity got a silent laugh from Darcy as she grabbed her coffee from the friendly barista and poured some cream into the steaming cup. She deliberately took her time sweetening up her coffee just so that she could hear more of this conversation which she found riveting.

"How could we forget that, Bill," the other man said, his voice just as gravelly as Bill's but not nearly as deep. In fact, his voice reminded Darcy of Bea Arthur's. "It took my family's whole farm. It wasn't until 1960 that we finally got back on our feet. Those cows, I swear, were afraid to let us milk them, poor souls."

He took a sip of the coffee cup before him, which was slightly larger than Bill's. He continued: "This cold means one of two things, if you ask me: either another twister is gonna touch down or a flood's a comin'".

"Hah – there won't be a flood, Ernie!" Bill shot back. His voice had risen ever so slightly, but enough to make Ernie be enraptured by what his friend apparently had to believe. "It will be a fire that starts by the Falls and then will take over the whole town!"

Both men remained quiet at Bill's statement as though contemplating the damage and hysteria that was to come. Darcy couldn't believe that small town chatter like that still existed, especially chatter that seemed to be taken to be the truth. She finished adding her sugar and left the coffee shop quickly as both stayed quiet.

It wasn't until she was sitting safely in her car that she thought that perhaps the old men were onto something, or at least what they were saying had some sort of credence to them. There was something strange and bizarre happening in Martin's Falls, Darcy could certainly authenticate that. But it wasn't a major weather-related catastrophe or ravage fire that was going to occur – it had more to do with the presence of the supernatural in a certain high school that sat comfortably in the middle of town.

Could the cold weather be attributed to what's happening to me?, she thought to herself. She almost said the words aloud if the parking lot hadn't become full of kids that went to her school and who were silently staring at her as they walked to and from their nice, fancy cars, massive coffee's in tow.

She shook her head as though to shake the crazy thoughts right out of it but for the rest of the car ride to school, she felt like overhearing the old men's conversation in Cupps was no small accident. IT was more of like a reminder of what was to come.

***

Charlie was already waiting for her at her car when she arrived soon after the last school bell rang. She had mentioned to Bennett that she was going on a kinda-date with Charlie, and that she was super excited, which she undoubtedly was. However, she was also nervous. It wasn't a 'date-nervous' but more of a 'what if I break his heart' nervous.

She could no longer pretend that there were things that she was expected to accomplish during her brief stay in her new life. While she incessantly reflected on Marina's ominous and ambiguous requests, she realized that if she did indeed had to go back to being a semi-depressed thirty year old with cellulite and a penchant for micro waved ice cream, she was bound to leave some destruction in the life she was to leave behind.

It was no small secret that the pre-switch 17 year old Darcy was a pretty bad person. Bad was sometimes an inadequate term to accurately describe the tantrums and difficult situations that the old self her seemed to have gotten into, and she certainly did not heed

244

any consideration to other people's feelings. Was that what she was going to become if she had to move back to her real life? Was the old Darcy going to wreak havoc once more upon the friendships she had tried to mend? On the relationships she was starting?

She wished to the very core of her being that she had an answer. She felt bi-polar at best on most days. She battled acting like a 30 year old in a teenage girls body, which required catching onto lingo and fashion styles instantly without being regarded as crazy or sub-intelligent. Or worse yet, a nerd. When that battle eased, then she would begin the one where her gut was telling her that if she was going to be a teenager, she had to want to act like one, which meant suspending her beliefs and just embracing the moment.

Her head was a constant monologue, and she often fell asleep at night with a pulsing headache. When sleep would finally come, her dreams would be full of what seemed like vignettes where she was being chased by some unidentified monster with red hair on its back. She got the reference for that one right away the following morning.

These are the thoughts that were running through her mind when she saw Charlie at her car, sitting on the hood of her car and looking heart-throbbingly adorable. She found herself really liking this boy, and she thought he felt the same way, but she didn't want to break his heart if she were to disappear abruptly after the prom. She could only imagine the old pre-switch Darcy would inflict upon him if she were to return.

And where is she now? She thought as she got closer to Charlie. He was smiling at her, dimple in full effect. If she was having a hard time acclimating to her new life, she can only imagine what kind of time the other Darcy was having. The thought made her shudder.

"Hey," Charlie said as she quickly sat up from the hood of the car and dusted off his pants. Her car was spotless, but there did seem to be a weird dust that would gather upon any exposed surface these days. *Chalk it up to Armageddon,* she thought. "I hope you don't mind that I was sitting on your car…"

245

"Of course not! I hope you weren't waiting long," she answered, trying to sound all calm and secure. She pressed her fob to unlock the doors and the loud, shrill beep filled the air that meant the locks were being unlocked. *Had it always been so loud?* She thought.

"Just a little bit. I actually have last period as a spare and so I did some reading over here", he pointed to the car's front hood. "It's surprisingly comfortable to read King Lear and having the sun shine on you. Relaxing, almost."

She smiled. "Sounds like it. You look like you could take a nap."

She slid beside him and opened her car door. He walked around to the passenger side and got in. She had to actually turn on the heat slightly in the car as it was so cold outside.

'What is up with this weather? It kind of makes me want to watch 'An Inconvenient Truth' again", she said, turning on the radio. The soft sounds of The Supremes begin to fill the car, making her feel at ease once more. Diana Ross could not not put you in a more serene mood.

"Huh?" Charlie asked after putting on his seatbelt and placing his shoulder bag on the floor of the car before him.

"An Inconvenient Truth?" she stared at him dumbfounded. "You know, the movie about raising awareness about the climate crisis?'

The blank face remained on Charlie's face. "Never heard of it." His cheeks reddened in embarrassment and she decided to change the topic immediately. Although she was sort of disappointed that he didn't know about the film, one of her personal favorites, she remembered he was only 17. He was probably more worried about impressing her than watching movies about the melting of the polar ice caps.

"So where are we going?" she blurted out, sounding a bit manic, so much so that Charlie frowned as thought temporarily confused at the quick change in subject matter.

246

"I was thinking of maybe checking out Bendel's downtown. They have a really good stock of costumes we can rent for the prom. I'm sure everyone has already got their outfits and I'm sort of scared that we're going to have to settle for something ugly."

A first day with a guy and he wants to go shopping? She swooned as she pulled out of the parking lot. She thought she caught a glimpse of Claire at the other end of the parking lot but she didn't think about an awkward confrontation any longer.

"That's a good idea. Where is this place?" she asked, turning right at the end of the school's long driveway and joining the stream of cars that contained her co-students who were wiped after a long school day. And a cold one, at that.

"What? You're kidding me, right?" Charlie laughed, moving his gaze from looking out the front windshield to her.

"Why is that so funny?" she countered, silently racking her brain if she did know where this place was or if there was some sort of reason why she should have remembered it. She couldn't see why a girl whose new age would know the location of a costume rental place downtown, even if the actual downtown of Martin's Falls was a quarter of the city that the older version of herself lived in.

"Um, because you used to work there for like, two summers," he replied and she reddened immediately. She didn't know what she found harder to believe: that she would actually have a job, or that she would work in a costume rental place. She felt like that went against all of the things the former her believed in.

"Oh yeah, it must have slipped my mind or something," she finally piped up after the silence in the car grew semi uncomfortable between the two of them. "You know, all I'm thinking about these days is the prom!"

That, and solving the greatest riddle of my entire existence, she thought silently.

"Besides, why would I want to go there if I don't have to? Working sucks!"

247

She tried to make the statement sound funny and lighthearted but instead it came out like a rich girl who hated working in general. What made this tone even worse was she knew that Charlie had a part time job at the Taco Town at the mall. Not off to a good start, she grimaced.

"You're telling me. Hey - there it is!" he said, pointing to a large, metallic building that was not at all what Darcy was imagining the place to look like. Every place took about 5 minutes to get to in Martin's Falls, and she was surprised that they had gotten there already. She was even more surprised that she knew *how* to get there despite having no recollection of her apparent two summer stint.

"Let's do this!" she said as she parked the car in front of the store. Charlie bounded out and made his way to the entrance. There didn't seem to be many people around the small parking lot that faced the store. She got out of the car and walked towards the large shop that had a giant Marquee sign that reminded her of the one that graced the front of Marina's.

Feeling a strange lump form in her throat and the birth of butterflies in her stomach, she followed Charlie into the shop, equal parts excitement and apprehension.

***

Upon entering the deceptively large shop, the first thought that entered her mind was *"This place looked like Las Vegas threw up in it"*. She could not *not* have thought that as the Bendel's was literally the love child between Liberace and Freddy Krueger.

She was instantly impressed by the sheer size of the shop itself, and slightly bewildered why such a small town would need a costume rental shop that was so massive. As though reading her thoughts, her eyes wandered over to a large poster that sat behind the row of pirate/sluts costumes (she wasn't sure which) that read, in bright red letters, "Even Hollywood rents from Bendel's!" She

248

questioned the validity of such a statement but she, of all people, knew that stranger things have happened.

Just to the right of the large poster, she noticed rows upon rows of costumes of various colors and themes. The place was very well organized not just by color, but by age appropriateness. She was naturally attracted to the 1980's era where fluorescent leg warmers and headbands were displayed prominently on mannequin that could very have been *in* the movie Mannequin, but she decided to follow Charlie as he walked near the rear of the store.

The store was sinisterly quiet, and she heard the sound her sandals made upon the linoleum floor. Even though the parking lot in front of the store was semi-full and trafficky, there didn't seem to be any other customers in the shop itself. All around her the costumes loomed, from sexy nurses to the aforementioned pirates to a whole section devoted to adult baby clothing. Before following Charlie into a tunnel that seemed to lead to another area of the shop, her eyes fell upon what must have been the Fairy Tale section where Easter Bunny, Princess and Prince pieces dominated a wall that rose from floor to ceiling.

"You always did like the Princess stuff," she heard a gravelly, female voice from behind her. She turned around immediately and saw a middle aged woman, glasses resting on her nose, who was smiling at her.

She wasn't sure how to respond so she opted for the trusty 'I'm going to smile my way through this one' technique, but after a moment or two of flashing her pearly whites, she noticed the older woman wasn't buying it. Charlie had by this point disappeared into the back of the shop, clearly not looking back to see if Darcy was behind him, and so she was trapped.

"Cat got your tongue, Darcy?" the woman continued, leaving her perch behind the Superheroes counter where both Superman and Catwoman were posed in a semi-inappropriate poses.

"I've never heard you so quiet before," the woman went on. Her short hair looked blue in the shady lighting of the shop, and the red lipstick that emanated from her lips gave her the look of a woman undergoing a mid life crisis. She had seen that look on Sylvia, and nothing good ever came of it.

She felt as though the smile she had on her face was permanently etched there because she couldn't undo it. She watched the woman approached her, her walk so slow that it became eerie, and noticed the name tag that sat atop her chest.

Of course her name is Candy, she thought to herself, lips wide in her perma-smile. The name tag seemed to shake her somewhat from her self-imposed reverie and she decided at that moment to speak up.

"I'm just stressed out about finding my prom dress, Candy," she replied, trying to keep her voice soft and carefree. She couldn't shake the impression that like many of her friends and family members, Darcy wasn't exactly the easiest person to be around.

Candy walked up so close to her that she thought the woman was going to lean in for a hug. She leaned in too, but when the woman pulled back, she pretended to bend down to re-clasp the strap on her sandal. When she stood back up, Candy was standing so close to her that she smelled the spearmint gum on her breath.

"You haven't come back here in a long time," Candy whispered, her voice quiet and soft. "You look different – more mature, almost."

She smiled. She was expecting colder words to escape the woman's mouth but she was pleasantly surprised at how the interaction was unfolding.

"Thank you," she replied, unsure of what to say to end quantifiable awkwardness of the conversation. "Are all the good masquerade gowns rented already? I shouldn't have left getting the dress to the last minute like this."

Candy suddenly laughed, her child like laughter filling the entire shop. Darcy thought that the laughter would get Charlie's attention and bring him back into the front area of the shop, but when Charlie

250

didn't pop in, she was disappointed.

"That is rather uncharacteristic of you", Candy said through her fit of laughter. "From what I recall, you have always had your clothing options laid out months in advance. You did tell me once that looking good is probably the only thing your good at. I think that you nailed the head on that one."

Because the woman was laughing, it took her a moment or two to realize that what the woman said was mean-spirited, even if she said she was quoting the old Darcy. Becoming increasingly uncomfortable as Candy continued to laugh as though she had just heard the funniest joke in her entire, middle-aged life, she all of a sudden grew annoyed and irritated.

"You have such a good memory for someone that is so close to retirement," she replied, the sharpness in her tone so strong that she thought the woman before her became paralyzed.

The laugh that was coming out of Candy's mouth stopped in mid air. Candy looked at her straight in the eye, her own eyes widening. Redness colored the woman's face, barely visible underneath the mountain of blush that colored the apples of her cheeks. *More like watermelons*, she inwardly thought.

"Well, it was nice to see you," she went on, taking advantage of the momentary silence from the rather mean woman.

"Always a pleasure," Candy finally said. She appeared flustered and surprised at her sarcastic response. She got the distinct impression that being wise with a response wasn't something that people were used to.

She turned around and began to make her way to the rear of the shop where Charlie disappeared into just minutes before, when she heard Candy's shrill voice once again take up the perimeter of the store, just as her laughter did seconds ago.

"Be sure to get that fellow a nice outfit as well. I'm sure he has scraped enough of his allowance together to pay for the rental," the woman said, her voice dripping with snootiness.

251

She stopped dead in her tracks. Beside her on the Star Wars display, Princess Leia gave her a catty look. She slowly turned around to find that Candy had covered the space that she had just walked and was standing once more just steps away from her. *This woman wants a fight*, she thought to herself. *But I'm not going to give it to her, even though I really, really want to.*

Taking a deep breath and gaining her teenaged composure, she decided to choose her words carefully. She did, after all, probably have to re-face this woman again once they had to pay for the actual rentals themselves.

"It's funny you say that," she said, her voice calm. "Charlie was just telling me that he was going to forfeit his college tuition next year to look like the Romeo to my Juliet. And who said romance was dead?"

With that, she left the woman whose mouth had fallen in shock at her eloquent and icy response, drenched with sarcasm. She deliberately walked slowly to the back of the shop, passing traditional Halloween costumes to the right and left of her. She felt Candy's eyes bear into her back but she knew she had won this battle. *Chalk this up to making things right*, she thought to herself.

***

When she finally found Charlie, he was nearly trapped underneath a basket nearly as big as he was full of hats that all had some sort of feather featured prominently near the top.

"Boo," she whispered behind him. He turned around quickly, surprised at the sound. He instantly smiled upon seeing her, and she couldn't help but feel warm and gooey. She stifled an internal eye roll.

"Hey," he said, smiling. "I'm trying to find the perfect hat to complete the Romeo look, even though I haven't even found the costume yet."

252

"Why not start with the hat? Maybe it'll inspire the look we're trying to get. Just remember, we need masks, too. Apparently anyone not wearing a mask will be turned away at the door."

"Duly noted," he laughed, pulling out a hat that looked like a cross between Peter Pan's and Davy Crockett's. "How's this?"

She laughed and pulled it from his hand and threw it back in the pile. "Let's save the rustic Prom look for next year's graduating class".

They both laughed loudly at that one and decided to walk deeper into the rear of the shop.

"Hey, what took you so long at the front? I thought you were right behind me but when I turned around all I saw was Chewbacca staring me down," Charlie said as they stood closely, staring up at a wall that displayed various gowns and suits that seemed to have been inspired from the Renaissance.

"I ran into Candy. We had a little catch up," she replied, taking in the beautiful silks and lavish corsets that comprised many of the dresses before her.

"That's funny. I always thought the two of you never really got along all that well anyway," Charlie said, joining Darcy's attention that was focused upon a golden gown that shone above them.

"You're not far from the truth there, Charlie. Hey – what do you think of that one over there? The one that sort of looks like Belle took Cinderella's gown and Project Runway'd it to create a whole new look?" She pointed up at the gown and Charlie's eyes followed her finger.

"Oh wow, that's really, really beautiful, Darcy," he finally replied. "You would look incredible in that. I mean, you could wear any of these dresses and you'd still be the prettiest girl in Martin's Falls."

She felt her heart beat quicken as she turned around and faced Charlie. He lowered his gaze from the gown that loomed above them and stared at her. The silence was thick and heavy between them and

253

she felt like she was going to explode.

"That's a very nice thing to say", was all she could spit out. It had been a very, very long time before she was given such a compliment that seemed genuine from its origin. Charlie smiled at her, dimple on full display, and a wisp of his hair fell from behind his ear and gently touched his cheek.

Without even realizing it, she reached up and put the lock of hair back behind his ear. She let her hand linger there for a moment and then felt Charlie reach in towards her and gently kiss her lips. She felt like her heart was going to beat out of her chest. All at once, her hands were moist and she felt like her knees were going to buckle underneath her.

So this is what it's supposed to feel like, she silently thought as they kissed, alone and quiet in the back of Bendel's Costumer shop. Sure, it wasn't the most romantic of locations, but it felt like magic for her. Seeing the princess gowns all around them, she silently imagined the room around them full of princes and knights and a castle where music played and joy was had and love was born.

When he pulled away, she smiled so wide that her cheeks hurt for a few hours afterwards. Charlie blushed, took her hand, and walked to another wall of suits for him to possibly rent. She felt giddy, almost as though she was walking on air. Looking back at that perfect moment, the only words she found when trying to describe what had happened were clichés. There's a reason Katy Perry has so many hit singles, she thought as she held Charlie's hand and walked deeper into the shop. It's because all of her songs perfectly capture was a 17 year old girl is feeling.

Chapter 29

When she parked the car in front of her house that evening, the sun had begun to dance colors around the shades of terra cotta that surrounded her neighborhood. She felt both exhilarated and exhausted. They had stayed at the costume shop for nearly 2 hours, trying on various possible rentals of varying themes and color schemes. They also tried on different costumes just for the fun of it and nearly doubled over in laughter as some of the crazy combinations that Charlie decided to wear.

She felt light headed and dizzy, full of adoration and giddiness. Not once did she find herself thinking about Marina's looming deadline, nor the petty arguments had with Claire or with her brother. She had finally had an afternoon that truly and genuinely felt right since the switch occurred. She was able to put her mind on pause and enjoy life in a very simplistic way. That afternoon had been what she had been expecting when thrust into the new Darcy's life. It was like a scene from Sweet Valley High or even from The Vampire Diaries, and she was effervescently grateful that she was able to experience it. She had thought that that kind of carefree moment was so elusive and unattainable, but thankfully she was she proven wrong.

Both she and Charlie got out of the car. Charlie reached into the rear seat and pulled out their costumes, which were firmly secured in large, grey plastic bags that looked more like body bags than actual clothing protectors. They had both finally settled upon the first gown that had so enraptured her attention. When she had tried it on, it magically hugged her body in all of the right places. The length was just perfect upon the ground, and the deep v-neck that took up the top of the dress was tasteful and elegant. She felt like a princess, beautiful and immortal, and was full of gratitude for Marina.

Both she and Charlie had agreed before even trying on the outfits that they wouldn't see one another in costumer until the night of the prom, but they also made sure that their colors coordinated. And so Charlie settled upon a Romeo-inspired costume that was full of deep browns and green that complimented the gold of her dress perfectly. It didn't go unrecognized in her mind that the comment she had made to Candy came true in the end.

When they paid for the rental at the end, she made sure to lengthen the interaction to make Candy as uncomfortable as possible, asking all kinds of irrelevant questions about the history of the store, the cost of purchasing the outfits, and where they could find suitable accessories. Charlie had no clue that she was being deliberately facetious, but it was her way of serving back to the middle aged woman another scoop of cattiness. She knew she had won the battle against Candy, but she really wanted to drive home the fact that Candy's attitude was disgusting and small minded. And she knew she accomplished it, especially when she turned around just as she and Charlie left the shop and saw Candy looking defeated and close to tears. *That's what you get old woman*, Darcy had thought. *Don't be mean to the harmless.*

Now, as Charlie threw the costumes over his arm, they walked slowly to the front door. She took her time in getting her key from her enormous brown bag so that she could spend a few extra precious moments with the boy she felt a strong affinity to and connection with.

"I'm pretty sure my mom will want to press your dress so I'll just take it with me to our place," Charlie said.

"That's fine with me. Just make sure Glenda doesn't let you see it!" she laughed, turning her key in the lock but keeping the door closed. She turned around and smiled at Charlie who, she noticed happily, had been staring at her the entire time.

"Today was really nice, Charlie," she said. "It was the perfect first date."

Charlie's cheeks reddened for the umpteenth time that afternoon as he quickly looked away in embarrassment.

"I had a really good time too, Darcy," he finally said, turning back around and looking at her intently. "I'm really excited to be going to the Prom with you. Honestly, I still can't believe you're going with me."

She giggled. "Why not?"

"Well, because you could have gone with any of the really popular guys. I'm not exactly the elite of MF high", he whispered back. She was going to shush him for making such a silly statement, but she quickly remembered that these were what kids thought about in high school. These were the pressing issues and pressing concerns that would plague their dreams at night and fill their minds when zoning out in English or Biology class.

"I chose to go with you because I like you," she finally replied. She leaned closer to him and gave him a soft kiss upon his lips.

"I like you, too. I guess I'll finally let you go," he said, stepping down backwards from the porch. "Maybe we can do something this weekend? There's a David Lynch retrospective at the Atrium. You

257

had told me once you liked him."

"That sounds awesome!" she enthusiastically replied. She really *did* like David Lynch, and had never had the chance to see one his weird, epic films on the big screen. She knew that there was no way she was going to pass this one up.

"That's great. Ok – I'll text you", he said and was at once gone, rather mysteriously in his prompt disappearance. She smiled and pushed her front door open, letting the lightness of her step guide her up to her bedroom, one small, bouncy step at a time.

Chapter 30

And just like that, she and Charlie became 'a thing'. She couldn't really explain the nature of their newfound and blossoming romance, but she thought the label of 'thing' sort of captured its essence perfectly. When she tried to describe the sort of easiness and fun she had around Charlie to Bennett, words always failed to come to her. That in itself was a rarity as she always had something to say, however irrelevant some of her comments may have been.

"I don't know, Bennett," she had tried to explain for the umpteenth time to Bennett. The girls sat across each other enjoying a pepperoni pizza and drinking diet coke with lots of ice. "He's just really fun to be around. I know that sounds ambiguous but I don't know how else to describe it."

Bennett took a big bite of the pizza before her and chewed quickly, the words burning in her mouth and waiting to escape.

"Which you've said like, a thousand times since the two of you have been dating. But I want to know what his deal is? He's so quiet and broody."

"He's not that quiet", she replied, taking a sip of her gigantic glass before her. "You just have to get to know him."

"That's the thing, Darcy. We've all gone out together but he's so quiet. We need to loosen him up!"

She laughed, but was slightly intrigued by what Bennett had said. While it was true that they did indeed have a few group outings, mainly to the mall and to the movies a few times, Charlie really didn't pipe up. It was mostly her and Bennett trying to keep the conversation a float.

"What did you have in mind?" she asked. She took one more bite of the pizza and realized just how full she was. She threw the rest of the slice on the table like it was on fire. Bennett smiled.

"Maybe we have some drinks at the prom? My mom's liquor cabinet is beyond stocked. I swear she's got some bottles from countries I've never even heard of. She won't even notice if we take one, or two, or ten!"

"Your parents do have quiet the collection," she laughed, remembering the moment when Bennett showed her the extent of the bottle collection that her parents housed in their basement. They had a wine room, but it was really just a glorified location to showcase their hundreds of liquors, spirits, wines and beers.

"But Charlie mentioned to me once that he's not really a drinker," she replied, taking a big swig of her diet coke.

"Oh, come on, Darcy!" Bennett replied, rolling her eyes. "He HAS to drink at the prom. It's like a rite of passage or something. Plus, look at what I got for us!"

Bennett reached behind her into the large backpack that hung off the chair. They were comfortably sitting inside Charlotta's Pizzeria, the local pizza spot. They were surprisingly the only customers in the store. The lack of patrons may have been due to the fact that it was 4 pm, and not really a true meal time. It didn't bother them any – they got to take up one of the large tables that sat near the front of the restaurant and faced Main Street. And there was always something to see on Main Street.

Taking another sip of her Diet Coke, she saw Bennett place two silver flasks on the table. They were a shiny, bright silver color and were so small that the girls could have fit them in their bras without attracting any kind of attention.

"Oh my god, Bennett – these are adorable!" she said, picking up on and looking at it more closely. She noticed the engraving on the backside.

"To all of it" it said in small, cursive writing. It was a typical Bennett phrase. She was always looking forward to the future and all of the amazing things that were going to happen to them. She had always felt like a Debbie Downer when Bennett embarked on one of her pro-future idealist rants because all she wanted to tell Bennett those things weren't that easy as they got older. Quite the opposite, in fact.

"They're perfect!" she continued.

"I know, right?" Bennett agreed, picking up her own and smiling at it. "There's no way Charlie is going to be able to turn down a drink in one of these things!"

"You've got a point there", she laughed. "Wanna fill them up and bring to the prom? I can't believe it's, like, 3 days away".

Bennett grew silent and took another sip of her diet coke. She, too, was very full from the ludicrous amount of Pizza the girls devoured. "Totally. Any special requests? And, no, Peach Shnapps is not an option!"

Both girls fell into a fit of laughter. Peach Schnapps was the one drink that she always drank wherever they went and whatever house party they found themselves at. It was the only drink that didn't give her a headache the next day.

"Fine – you win this one, Bennett," she said, and soon enough they began chatting incessantly about the costumes they rented. Like with Charlie, the girls agreed not to show each other what they had selected for their big night. The excitement was killing them but they held true to their promises.

Chapter 31

All she could think about was how cold it was in that tiny cabin room. There was no way she could have foreseen that it would be nearly freezing in the middle of June, but she should have clued in that being in the north, in the literal middle of nowhere, and in a room made of wood, the cabin was bound to be cold. Even a blanket would have been useful at this point. There was a draft that was hitting the top of her head, even when she pulled it under the thin sheet.

Frustrated, she sat us with an audible sigh and looked at the room around her. The small window that looked outwards toward the lake seemed to have frost on it, and she thought she saw her own breath as she exhaled. In the bunk across from her, the cold didn't seem to be phasing Bennett just one bit. In fact, she thought she almost heard the girl snore ever so slightly. Then again, everything in the cabin seemed to have its sound amplified, as there was no white noise to drown anything out, which was particularly annoying when they had to visit the ladies room, which really was just a pit.

She sat up in the little, uncomfortable single bed and pulled her legs towards her chest, hoping to get rid of the chill within her that she'd been shaking for the last long while. The existence of the chill was not just due to the fairly cold night that surrounded her, but also because of the whole entire combination of the manic and perpetual stress of having to keep up her end of the bargain with Marina and having to skirt around Claire at their Senior Sleep Away that everyone had been so excited about just weeks ago, including herself.

The entire day had been somewhat fun, but there was a constant tinge of discomfort wherever she found herself. The bus ride was surprisingly easy to bear – Bennett and her had figured they would just sit beside each other for the duration of the 4-hour drive. Claire and Rena had opted to drive themselves to the cabins, which was completely frowned upon by the Student Council, as it didn't jive with the whole theme of spending quality time with everyone before they all dispersed for college. She wasn't entirely all that surprised that Claire was defying authority once more in order to serve her own happiness, but on some level, she found it admirable that Claire walked to the beat of her own drum, no matter how odd it may have been at times.

Student Council had planned all sorts of cheesy games for the bus ride, most of which centered around derivatives of 100 Bottles of Beer on the Wall and Broken Telephone. Participation was mandatory, so Darcy and Bennett both made the best of it and threw themselves in the silliness of it all. They avoided purposely confusing the message of Broken Telephone that Chrissy Barr had created, but other kids succeeded in ended up making the message explicit enough that Armie Chive, the kid who was responsible for saying the message aloud, couldn't mouth the words in fear of retribution by the three teachers that traveled on the bus with them.

When they finally got to the Eleanor Ranch some hours later, the energy had dissipated and a comfortable silence had filled the bus, mostly due to the presence of iPod's aplenty with headphones bigger than some students' heads.

The lush greenness that surrounded them from all angles was the first thing that she had noticed, odd as she had seen greenness around her every day near her house and school, but this was remarkably different. The grass was a deeper green, and the trees reached so high into the sky that she couldn't quite make out seeing the tips of them.

Both girls were sure to indulge themselves in taking a short twenty-minute power nap and then subsequently stuffing their faces with energy bars and chocolate. Rested and filled, they put on their swimsuits and decided to join the other students at the lake.

The sand was nearly impossibly white, and luminous large rocks created little enclaves on the beach that were perfect for some partial privacy. She and Bennett created a little cozy area with the lawn chairs and umbrellas they had brought with them, opting to not participate in the group's water sports themed games. Instead, they were perfectly content with watching the ruckus from the safety, and relative dryness, of the shore.

It was all going perfectly well, and the weather seemed to be holding out despite the ever-threatening presence of rain. She felt herself relax and actually begin enjoying this mini-vacation, feeling sure that indeed going to the Senior Stay over was a good idea all in all. That was until she heard Claire and Rena chattering from a distance.

The girls decided set up camp so close to Bennett and her on the tiny beach that she felt as though they were only inches away. Both of the girls clearly didn't mind sitting so close to her and Bennett, but she couldn't help but feel that Claire was either extending an olive branch or making a deliberate game play with their friendship.

265

"It's so hot!" Claire said, much too loud. She casually looked out around her, noticing Darcy and Bennett lain on their lawn chairs just feet away. She lifted her sunglasses, the sunlight catching on the blue eyes that could cause someone to literally freeze in their tracks. "Hey Darcy, How was the bus ride?"

At first, it didn't register with her that Claire had been directing words towards her. They hadn't shared a one single interaction since their mammoth confrontation a few weeks ago, and when they ran into each other in school they literally pretended not to see one another. The school gossip about Darcy's fake pregnancy had ended as soon as it had begun. There were still rumors flying about as to why the two forever friends were still not talking, slap and all, but she had stopped listening to the newest rumors of the day a long time ago.

"Long - and full of cheese," she replied once she realized Claire had indeed been speaking to her. She kept her tone even so as to not sound catty or spur Claire on in any way. She was being overly cautious, this she knew, but she certainly wasn't going to initiate another public argument with her frenemy, nor bite at the chomp of an attempted reconciliation.

Rena glanced at her quickly, also visibly surprised at Claire's attempt at conversation. Bennett chose to stay mum - cautious, and careful. She thought that Bennett had actually maybe fallen asleep. The sunglasses on her face made it difficult to gauge.

"I'm not surprised. Grandma over here was very, very aware of the speed limit on the freeway," Claire responded, cocking her head in reference to Rena. Rena was the world's notoriously slowest driver, but she had the nicest car, so it all sort of worked out in the end.

"I didn't want to get a speeding ticket!" Rena chimed in. "My dad would positively kill me. And he'd totally take the car away."

Both she and Claire laughed at Rena's response because it was totally true. Rena's dad was a local police traffic officer who was known to liberally give out speeding tickets to all of the kids at Flint Ridge High, and the only condition to getting Rena her car was that she wouldn't get a speeding ticket, so they couldn't really fault her for it.

"Oh relax, R. We're just teasing you. Plus, aren't you glad we missed all the lameness of the bus ride?" Claire fanned out an enormous leopard-print beach towel on the sand and plopped herself onto it. She looked over at Darcy with a slight hit of smile before pulling the sunglasses back down over her face.

"Happy Senior Stay Over," she said and laid flat, the short conversation over as soon as it had begun. Darcy, too, lay back down on her lawn chair that she was wise enough to bring from home. The sand looked nice, but lying on top of it for hours on end (which was how long she planned to stay horizontal) was a literal pain in the ass.

As she began to let the sun melt away her worries and letting the warmth seep into her bones, she began to take apart and analyze the interaction that had just unfolded. *What had just happened?*, she questioned. *Did Claire finally realize she was being totally crazy and irrational? Was this part of a master scheme to further humiliate her in some inconceivable way?*

She tried to push the thoughts of her head, hoping for the best of Claire's intentions and the semi-positive short dialogue. It was certainly a small step at reparation between the girls, but it was a step nonetheless. While she had heard from other students in the school that Claire had retracted the rumor about the pregnancy, all was still not forgiven, nor forgotten.

Now, hours later, she quietly got up off the single bed so as to not wake Bennett and walked over to the window. She took in the beautiful view of the lake and the bright moon shining upon it, making her feel serene and calm. The water was still and silent. The moon that night was full, its reflection rippling on the water, reminding Darcy of the still and silent simplicity that nature could provide.

267

It was then that she saw a tiny movement out of the corner of her eye. Was someone walking around out there? Perhaps it was some animal, she rationalized. She glanced at her watch: 3 am. If someone was walking around out there, they were asking to be either eaten by a savage east or was lost, maybe even both.

She pulled on the sweater that lay on the ground by the door and put the hood up. She didn't want to be completely shocked by the cold once she went outside. She wasn't exactly sure why she decided to go outside, and clearly if she were presented with some sort of violent animal attack, she'd have no way to protect herself.

Opening the door was not an easy task. Every little inch she tried to pry it open sounded like a marching band playing in the cabin, but Bennett didn't even stir. In fact, her snoring seemed to have gotten louder. She pulled the door shut softly behind her, semi-resentful that her friend was able to sleep so soundly on the wafer thin mattress and nearly freezing temperatures.

The figure she had glimpsed moments before (she was now sure it was a person) before her wasn't moving now. As she walked towards whoever it was, she questioned whether she should have been doing this at all, in the wilderness of all places, but she kept on walking. It didn't seem to be as cold out here as it was in the cabin. Perhaps it was the adrenaline, or the sweater. There was no wind, no sounds, but definitely eerie.

As she cautiously walked towards the figure, she made sure to look back to ensure that half of the senior class wasn't watching her or that Bennett didn't decide to be the protective friend and follow her out (providing she even woke up from her deep slumber). Once she discerned that she was alone walking towards the figure on the beach, she turned to see the figure sitting on the sand, rather poetically positioned by a jagged rock.

The moonlight was brighter by the water, probably because of its large reflection upon it. Because of the added brightness, she was able to tell right away that it was Claire who was the mysterious shadowy figure. She was not moving now though, opting to sit on the rock and looking out at the water. She didn't even stir, nor glance around, as she silently moved closer.

If Claire was scared, she sure didn't let on. In fact, she didn't even flinch as she climbed the rock and found a spot to sit beside her. Claire was looking out at the water, her hair softly resting on her exposed shoulders. Even in the dark she saw the outlines of sunburn, which perhaps explained why Claire didn't seem cold at all. She thought she also saw the reflective sheen of aloe-Vera, but then attributed it to sweat.

"I'm glad you came out here," Claire finally said, after silence sat between the girls, comfortably. "We have to talk."

Chapter 32

"I didn't realize everyone thought we hated each other," she whispered into the quiet of the surrounding night around the two girls and former best friends. The moon shone brightly above them, its reflection bright and gigantic on the water that faced them. The breeze was still persistent, but soothing, and the cold that had one permeated her down to her core seemed to have abated. Nonetheless, she kept the sweater tightened around her, its softness comforting somehow to her in the wee hours of the night.

"News travels fast, apparently," Claire finally replied, her voice low and vulnerable. Since the switch had happened, she had never heard Claire's voice sound so little and weak, and it really seemed to scare her. Had she been unnecessarily hard on Claire all of this time? Had she forgotten that Claire, like she once was, was just someone trying to keep her head above water in the abyss that was high school?

"I guess we didn't exactly give them any idea to think that we actually *liked* each other," she replied, her voice also small. She felt so defenseless and exposed sitting on the rock by the lake. It was also interestingly rather quite empowering.

"I know I've been a mega bitch, Darcy. I'll be the first to admit it. And I'm sorry, I really am – but it's been tough. Getting pregnant wasn't exactly on my high school 'to do' list, you know?" Claire continued, her voice barely audible. If Darcy hadn't been seated so close to her, she would have had trouble hearing her at all.

"It's no excuse though for the way I've been acting, and I'm totally going to take responsibility for that. I guess I've never really noticed how bossy I could be. Sure, my hormones are semi out of whack, and I couldn't rely on Rena in any way to tell me if I was being hell on wheels, but our fight in the bathroom really bothered me. And then the slap…well, I guess I had it coming".

"It bothered me, too," she finally cut in, feeling sad at hearing Claire fully acknowledge her attitude problem. It certainly wasn't an easy task to fess up to being a monster, this she knew first hand, and to do so at the ripe old age of 17 was a full-blown revelation.

She moved closer to Claire, and before realizing what she was doing, she put her arm around her ex-friends shoulder. She couldn't help but notice at the frail size of her friend and squeezed her close. She felt the words in her throat and she knew if she didn't say them at that time now she never would.

"It also really bothered me that you never told me about you and Mason."

"And to top things off, I've been feeling super gross lately, like, more gross than the blogs say I should be feeling…" Claire continued, not moving away from Darcy's warm embrace and then understanding the magnitude of her words. "What? How?"

Darcy stayed calm. "He gave me your scarf. The one that you lost on your big date that night that you could never find. How could

271

you not have told me?"

It took a moment before Claire responded. "I didn't know how you would react." Behind them, they heard an owl, and they both were startled.

"Clearly better if I had found out then instead of now," Darcy said, the words leaving her mouth before she even realized it. Deciding to drop it, and welcomed the sliver of silence that permeated the dialogue between them.

They heard some odd sounds pierce the night. The noises were being made from wildlife that both girls did not wish to acknowledge as they would have left their cozy spot on the rocks in fear of being mauled by a bear.

"Have you gone to the Doctor to get things checked out to make sure everything is, you know, normal?" Darcy decided to ask. She regretting not being able to phrase her question more eloquently but she blamed it on the intensity of the conversation.

"Nope. I haven't really done anything since the pregnancy test. I mean, there's like no debating the fact that I'm pregnant. I just can't bring myself to see the doctor. I feel like they'll just think I'm another rich kid who's gotten herself in trouble. Do people still say that?" Claire giggled.

"Maybe if it were 1930," Darcy replied, causing the girls to further to fall into another bout of laughter. "How about as soon as this weekend of fun is over we go to the doctor?"

"I just feel like going home, to be honest. I have no interest in lying on the beach and hanging out with people I probably won't even be talking to by Christmas." Claire reached her arms up and stretched, a sigh leaving her lips, sounding extremely loud in the stillness of the night.

"You and me both. But Bennett is super enthused about it all for some reason", Darcy said. "You know, she's actually really nice. You should give her a chance."

Claire smiled. "I know. I will. Attribute the rudeness to my 'condition'. Wow – who knew pregnancy euphemisms could be so fun."

"Hah. It's true. Who knew that you'd be in the 'family way' before Chrissy Barr," she countered, and another bout of hysterics was heard by the two newly reformed best friends by the water.

"We should go to bed. The Breakfast Burrito Bonanza starts in, like, 4 hours," Claire said, getting up from the sand, the sarcasm dripping from her voice. Darcy got up as well, realizing that she was indeed beginning to feel tired as well.

As soon as both girls were standing, Claire let out a loud gasp and doubled over in obvious agony. At first Darcy thought perhaps her friend had gotten a bug bite or something, but when Claire didn't stand upright immediately, she felt her heart fall into the pit of her stomach.

"What's wrong?" Darcy asked, squatting down so she was close to Claire's face.

Claire didn't reply right away, further adding to the heightened drama of the moment. Even in the darkness and the minimal light provided to them by the full moon, she could see that Claire was extremely pale and had a slight sheen of sweat breaking out upon her forehead.

She helped her back onto the ground, slowly easing her on the sand. She leaned her back up against the giant tree beside them, and helped Claire sit against the large bark.

"It hurts. Oh no, Darcy, it really hurts," Claire gasped, obviously in serious pain.

"What is it? What hurts?" Darcy said, trying to help but feeling helpless.

"Ow, everything. My stomach," Claire replied, her voice barely more than whisper. "I feel like someone is punching me in the stomach and stabbing me at the same time. Darcy – this is bad. I think we need to go to the hospital or something".

"How? Do you think Rena would let us borrow her car? You

273

know how she is with it," Darcy replied, her voice rising. She was afraid she was going to alert the kids in the nearby cabins but thankfully no one seemed to notice.

"I don't care! I think we need to go!" Claire screamed.

"Ssssh. You're going to wake everyone up. I'll go get the car. Where does she keep the keys?" Darcy asked, her heart fluttering.

"On the ledge by the cabin door. Go get it! Don't worry – she sleeps like a log, She won't hear you at all", Claire whispered back. "Hurry!"

She walked away quickly, in the direction of the cabin that Claire was sharing with Rena. The adrenaline of the situation made her wide-awake immediately.

***

They wasted no time in driving towards the closest hospital which was apparently about half an hour away, as per Rena's father's immaculately pristine GPS. Half a dozen times she thought she was going to see a police car's lights visible in her rear view mirror or hear a loud, sharp siren, but luckily they seemed to be the only car out on the road.

She figured it wasn't the appropriate time to bring up her story of once placing all of her trust in her GPS only to turn up at the head office for a Sunglass Hut. *Maybe some other time*, she thought to herself, and kept on driving.

Claire, at that point, had begun to literally writhe in pain. She was emitting guttural sounds that made Darcy's skin crawl. Sweat had fully broken out on her brow and her t-shirt had begun to stick to her chest. Even with the air conditioner on full blast, causing their hair to fly every which way, the sweat kept pouring over their foreheads.

Claire turned down the window, at once filling the car with more cool air. She took in gulps of the cold wind, hoping to alleviate some of the pain she was feeling, which she did not know how to read.

"Here, have something to drink," Darcy said after reaching behind the passenger seat to grab a bottle of water. She handed it to Claire who gladly took the bottle and took greedy gulps.

When she saw the well-lit blue H quickly approaching, she felt like she would yell with joy. Claire saw it too and seemed to relax a bit. It seems that they had both been worried about actually reaching the hospital at all. She silently thanked the GPS gods.

Once they turned into the tiny parking lot, she slowed down the car close to the main entrance and immediately helped Claire out of the passenger seat. The two girls walked slowly to the Emergency room where a few nurses chatted animatedly around the nurses' station.

Upon seeing the two girls enter the hospital, they quickly gravitated towards them, one nurse pushing a wheelchair over to them.

"Symptoms, please," one nurse said, her accent a cross between southern and South American. Before Darcy had a chance to reply, they whisked Claire away, leaving her all alone in an empty waiting room in the middle of the night. All she could do at that point was grab an old People magazine from a nearby table and wait to her how her friend was going to be.

Chapter 33

Mason began to pace nervously around the small room, his hands not knowing what to do. He would clench them into fists so tight that his knuckles turned white, and then the next moment he would crack his knuckles, making a sound that could silence a room with fear and trepidation. Clearly, he was uncomfortable and apprehensive, but as with every other emotionally charged moment of his life, he seemed to be unable to deal with the situation.

She felt just as uncomfortable, but she was able to internalize her discomfort much better than Mason could. She had seen her brother react this way many times in the past, this was true, but this time was clearly different.

Still rhythmically pacing, he stole a glance at her, who at that moment was looking at the tiled floor. She noticed every crack and fissure after years of use. She saw the grooves that shoes had made from the exit door to the entrance. The room was a thorough room only, not a space meant for someone to stay within for longer than five minutes at most.

Finally, unable to take the tension any longer, she looked up at Mason who was looking out towards the parking lot that lay beyond the back door. There were no cars, no people, and no hope in that miniscule hospital waiting room that surrounded both Platt siblings. She could feel the sadness permeate the walls. Even the way the moon's rays were causing shadows in the room made her feel like the world was crying.

"Mason, thank you for coming. I just didn't know who else to call," she mumbled, hoping to break the silence with a conversation that they could both have about the situation they found themselves in, but Mason immediately turned towards her when he heard her voice and interrupted.

"I don't want to hear one word out of your pathetic little mouth!" he yelled, spittle gathering on the bottom of his well-defined chin.

"Well, that's too bad because we have to talk about this!" she spat back, trying to match the volume of Mason's voice but fell way short. She wasn't afraid of other people hearing them argue because, quite literally, there was no one else around. The nurses' station was quite a distance away from them.

"You just keep everything in all of the time and don't ever want to talk about what's wrong!"

"You know, Darcy, I've had enough of this transparent act you've been putting on," Mason said, his voice lowering considerably. "Ever since I got back from Prague, you've been putting on this superficial attitude of being so nice and acting like you really care about other people's feelings. You're not fooling me anymore, though. I'm onto you. I've known you too long to know the real Darcy is nothing but a snake and a liar."

It felt like someone punched her in the stomach. She had been trying so hard all of this time to change and to become a better person. To show all of her friends and family that she was actually a good person who genuinely cared about what was going on to those she held dear. To hear Mason say those words hurt her more than she thought they would. She knew she was Darcy Platt, the 17 year old girl who apparently had had a bad attitude for a long time, and was now actively trying to make things right. Only she wasn't fooling anyone, least of all her brother. She was suddenly full of rage and of anger. She was angry at Marina for letting her enter a fantasy world that she thought was going to be so easy and fun and different than her real life as the thirty something year old woman who sometimes ate cake mix with a spoon, alone in an apartment with a widow for a neighbor. She was angry at those around her in this world of 17 year old Darcy for not giving this girl another chance at redeeming herself and proving that not everything was black and white in a teenage girls life. But mostly, she was mad at herself for thinking she could immerse herself in the life of a 17-year-old girl and think that her life would be simple.

She felt the anger boil within her. She felt her face redden and a sweat break on her forehead. She felt her palms moisten and drops of sweat fall down her back. She looked at Mason, who was still staring at her, wide-eyed, hungry for a confrontation, a fight, for blood to be spilled. And Darcy was ready for it.

"The real Darcy? You think you know the 'real Darcy', Mason?" she yelled, her voice rising to pitches she never heard before. She was scared that she would capture the attention of the nurses but in that moment didn't care. "How could you know the real me? Since you've been back from Europe, you've been nothing but rude and snide. You've treated Mom like crap, like it was her fault that you failed at College when all Mom and Dad have done for you is throw their money at you and try to make you happy. I've tried to talk to you, to be your friend, and you've pushed me away at every turn. You really are repulsive. I don't understand…"

"You don't understand a lot of things, Darcy," Mason replied, looking out at the vacant parking lot. "You don't understand what it's like to have to keep the one thing you care most about a secret. You don't understand that having money isn't what life is all about. Mom and Dad just give me money to shut me up, to avoid them having to be involved in my life. You just sit in your bubble, judging from your throne."

"You are ridiculous. You are not even willing to give me a chance to make things right, for me to be your sister. For me to help you!" she continued, her voice stabilizing but still sounding shrill.

"Help me? You want to help me?" Mason laughed. "That's a first. You are only here because your best friend almost died!"

"Take that back," she whispered.

"Not on your life," Mason replied.

She could feel the silence in the room swallow her up. Mason didn't know what he was saying. When she had called him two hours ago, he vowed he would be there as soon as possible. It was like as soon as he heard Claire's name, he didn't want to slow down his being there any longer. He didn't know that what happened to Claire was because of him.

"Take it back," she repeated. Mason started at her, a smirk on his face.

"No," Mason replied.

"You really are clueless, aren't you?" she said, her voice quivering. "You are so blind. She isn't here because of me, Mason."

"Of course she is. You were driving the car," he retorted.

"Of course I was driving because she was having severe stomach pains! She couldn't even speak, let alone drive." Her heart began to beat wildly. She felt the pulse in her ears.

"You're just trying to save your own ass!" Mason yelled back. He began to pace the room like a caged animal, contemplating his escape.

"Mason! Did you really not notice! Claire is pregnant! Stop blaming me and support me. She's my best friend!"

279

***

Mason started at her, his smirk slowly dissolving. It was like he was looking at her but through her. Darcy saw the realization register on her brother's face of the words that come out of her mouth and the fact that they weren't lies. Not even close.

Mason unexpectedly then immediately turned around from his position of standing in front of her and ran quickly out of the room, leaving her alone. She was momentarily shocked, which itself was strange given the last 24 hours she'd experienced, and half expected him to run back into the room. When he didn't, she felt deflated and crumpled up on the purple and ratty chair and began to sob, not caring who heard her. AT that point she realized she was both equally worried about how Claire was doing, but also why Mason reacted the way he did. And why.

Oh God, she thought. *What did I just do?*

Chapter 34

Knowing that the Prom was just about a day away, panic attacks became a new and frequent presence in her teenaged life. She had been racking her brain for the last few hours, trying to determine if there were some clues or ideas that she had been missing in regards to Marina's ominous request of making things right.

She dissected each and every relationship she had either began, ended, or continued since being thrust into her new life. She couldn't believe it had been nearly 3 months since 'the switch' and with that, her feeling like she was not a step closer to discovering and identifying how she was going to keep up her end of the bargain.

She often had Marina on her mind these last few hours. Every red headed person or purple-hued dress reminded her of the gentle woman who gave her a once in a lifetime opportunity that she sincerely wished she wasn't squandering. Unlike her first few weeks in her newly teenaged existence, she felt like she was beginning to make some serious headway with things.

Sure, there were situations that had occurred that still made her heart beat quicken and flop sweat form on her forehead, but she knew that those uncomfortable events HAD to occur. Especially with her defunct friendship with Claire, she understood that the nature of their friendship was built on pretenses that just weren't relevant anymore. Roles has apparently been formed and adhered to between the two friends and Darcy just couldn't in good conscience continue an unhealthy friendship that was heavily reliant upon feeling demeaned and bossed around by an alpha teenage girl who just didn't know any better.

She knew, however, on some deeper, hidden level, that there was some more end to her side of the deal that she had to accomplish by the end of the prom. Did she have to save a life? Solve a crime? Win a contest? She had absolutely no idea.

***

She held her breath tightly before finally working up the courage to seeing her reflection in the mirror. The ornate (and exorbitantly expensive) corset that was enclosed tightly around her tiny frame really wouldn't allow her to take full breaths anyway. Silently chastising herself for renting such a ludicrously snug garment, she quickly turned around to behold the finished product of her marathon make- up and hair styling session.

For the first time since taking on this whirlwind new teenage life of hers, she did not have an endless loop of internal monologue playing in her mind. Instead, there was a genuine and welcome silence as she smiled to herself. The costume had come together perfectly: her hair fell in tight ringlets around her face, her make-up exquisitely applied courtesy of her mother. When she had first approached her mother to apply her make-up, the older woman had looked like she had just seen a ghost. It was apparently a really touching moment.

Taking a sip of water from the glass that sat atop her vanity, she felt the cool water flow down her throat and sit inside her stomach. One of the apparent advantages of wearing something that nearly caused one to faint was a full, visceral experience of ingestion of liquids. She felt as though her heart was going to beat out of her chest. Even though this was a feeling that occurred fairly frequently since 'the switch', she still wasn't all that used to it. She wished she could say that this was a novel feeling for her, this feeling of true excitement and angst, but it was something that happened pretty regularly leading up to the day of the prom. Now that the prom was actually here, she thought she was going to either throw up whatever she had in her tiny stomach, or pass out and wake up in her sad little apartment with Lucy on her lap. The feeling of nausea was heavy and seemed to press tightly upon her, and so drinking tiny sips of tepid water and flat ginger ale seemed to be successful at taking the edge off – for now, at least.

She glanced at her watch quickly and realized it would be just a few more minutes until Bennett arrived in the stretch limo she had rented for both girls to attend the big event. The location where the festivities to occur were just about a 15 minute drive away from where she lived, but both girls had decided that getting a ride from one of their parents or friends just wasn't acceptable to transport them to one of the most memorable nights of their lives. Instead, Bennett had embarked upon a seemingly impossible mission to rent a limo just days before the prom, when most of the long vehicles had already been rented months in advance.

Earlier that afternoon, she had called Darcy and let her know that she had been successful in finding a limo. She added at the end of their conversation that it was 'different', which was code word for something entirely ludicrous and embarrassing. She had felt slightly apprehensive about placing her trust in renting the limo in Bennett's hands, but she resigned as the days went on and she still hadn't gotten a dress to wear.

Turning around from the large mirror that acted as both a vanity and a full length 360 mirror, she looked at the obscenely high stilettos that she had rented alongside the gown. With all the rouching that formed the lower part of her gown, the stiletto's only function would be to add a few extra inches of height to already rather tall frame. No one was going to see them anyway. With this frame of mind, she decided to slip on her favorite pair of green Chuck Taylors. She realized that by wearing them that she seem as though she was trying to be the protagonist in a bad Hilary Duff movie, but she really wanted to be comfortable that night. She wanted to be able to dance around manically and not have blood spurting randomly from her heel or toes as the night wore on.

Closing her bedroom door behind her, she nearly stumbled upon her brother. He backed up quickly from her approach and then steadied himself.

"You look nice," Mason mumbled, an expression of surprise upon his face upon hearing his own voice actually complimenting his sister. She couldn't say anything sarcastic or wry to him because she knew he was making a decent effort in trying to be nicer.

"Thank you. Though, if I have to be honest, breathing is a challenge," she replied.

In the after math of Claire mis-carrying her baby, Darcy and Mason had made slight headways into forming some sort of brother/sister relationship. To some extent, he felt relieved that he didn't have to keep his tryst with Claire under wraps any longer. However, he was clearly very upset when he found out that Claire had indeed been pregnant with his baby.

She began to walk towards the long staircase where her mother and father stood excitedly, cameras in hand. She inwardly groaned and decided to take the plunge down the steps. Mason followed closely behind.

284

"Oh honey, you look just beautiful!" her mother yelled, tears glistening in her eyes. She would have rolled her own eyes but she knew this was a genuinely nice moment for her parents, especially after all she'd put them through lately.

She slowly walked down the steps as her dress was rather difficult to navigate. She knew later in the night she would probably just rip the bottom part of but until then she would try to keep the whole outfit put together, at least until pictures commemorating the event were taken. Upon stepping off the last step, she felt her mother instantly, and rather snugly, hug her, almost completely breaking off the little air flow she could get in due to the corset.

"Thanks, Mom," she whispered back. She was so constricted she could not speak any louder, even if she wanted to. Her dad smiled his silent smile upon her, the emotions that his mother so easily expressed more of a challenge for him. She attributed this to his being a successful lawyer. She'd imagined he'd had to develop those skills being in the courts for all of those years.

As her mother took photo after photo of her striking a myriad of poses, she noticed Mason standing rather forlornly on the steps that rose above her. She felt an instant sadness in her heart at the sadness that seemed to emanate from her brother as he looked upon the scene with puppy dog eyes.

"Come and take a picture with me, Mason," she yelled up at him, over the sound of the flashes of the camera and her mother shouting demands on where and how to pose. Mason looked at her, surprised, and began to walk down to her.

"How can I miss this momentous occasion," he caustically said as they stood closely beside one another as her mother pulled out her hidden paparazzi skills. After feeling like she was going blind in her right eye, she felt Mason slowly pull away.

"Ok, mom – enough with the pictures," she mouthed. "You will see me again, you know."

She realized that that comment wasn't *entirely* true. It was a certain possibility that she wasn't going to come back from that Prom that night at all, well, at least in her old/young Darcy mode. Suddenly, the loud beep of a car outside shook them all from their manic photo taking session, instantly followed by the sound of the doorbell ringing.

She quickly made her way to the door while her parents continued to take pictures of her. She looked back over her shoulder several times to have them get at least one good shot, but her main goal at that moment was to get the hell out of dodge and have some real fun.

She pulled open the door and saw Charlie, resplendent in his brown and black Renaissance-influenced costume. His wavy hair was slicked back neatly behind his ears, but Darcy noticed the few wisps that fell over his eyes, which made him look vulnerable and gorgeous. He wasn't wearing his mask yet so she had a chance to see how his brown eyes looked at her own costume and the mammoth smile that slowly crept upon his lips.

"Wow – Darcy," he finally said, dimples in full effect. He seemed transfixed at the sight of her. His eyes slowly rose from the long, golden gown to the tight bun that rose at the top of her head. "You look perfect."

She smiled warmly, and felt her cheeks redden. Her parents *were* right behind her after all, and Mason could certainly hear without problem any words that were being shared.

"Thank you," was all she could mumble before turning around and waving goodbye, perhaps for the final time, to her new/old family.

Her parents smiled as she walked onto the porch, her arm slowly rising into the nook of Charlie's arm that was raised out to her. She looked back once more and smiled as Charlie guided her down the front steps. She kept her eyes to the ground as she didn't want to fall or make any sort of typical Darcy stumble, so at first she didn't see the car they were slowly walking towards.

286

When she finally raised her eyes to take in the car that Bennett was responsible for renting, she thought she was going to faint right then in there in pure shock. While she had been fully expecting some sort of abomination of a limousine or a weird fusion of a Rolls Royce and an RV, she was pleasantly surprised at the sight before her.

She instantly saw Bennett's mega-watt smile, holding a bouquet of roses, as she stood in the limousine, her head and upper torso hanging out of the car's retractable roof.

"Come one, come all. There's enough room in this thing for almost half of the senior class!" she screamed with sheer delight.

The limousine was at once classy and posh. It was long, not as long as a stretch limousine, but certainly longer than a Town Car. It seemed to vibrantly shine, the hues of the soon-to-be setting sun bouncing off the black chrome, causing Darcy to bring her hand to her eyes and used it as a visor to block out the rays. With the impossible challenge of finding transportation to take them to the Prom in one week in a small town that barely had one decent car rental company, she thought Bennett was going to show up with a jalopy, or even a taxi. She was utterly speechless.

"Get on in here! I know, I know, you were expecting me to show up on my brother's double-rider bike with a wagon hooked onto the back," Bennett said enthusiastically as she tried to get into the limo with as much grace as was possible in a gown that weight about 30 lbs and a corset that made breathing a chore. Charlie helped her in, but for that small spot where no one could help her sit down, she thought she would've busted out of the corset all together.

"You got me," she said, finally being able to sit comfortably. "You scored on this one. Kudos."

The inside of the limo was sleek and smart, just like its exterior. Shiny black leather, which looked like it had just been cleaned, surrounded the three friends. Charlie sat beside her, while Bennett opted to sit across from them along a bench that could have fit about

4 people comfortably. Bennett sure wasn't kidding when she said that they could have fit a good 16 people in that car.

Taking in the sights around her, she felt calm and serene. She also felt really, really happy and content. For the first time since the Switch, she felt like the internal monologue that constantly plagued her thoughts had been turned off and she was able to fully enjoy the excited mood that filled the car.

"Let's get to this prom, people. I want to break it down and see what our beautiful friends and neighbors have decided to adorn us with visually on this night of a thousand nights!" Bennett proclaimed, opting to once again to stick her head out of the retractable roof.

As if that was his cue, the driver started the car and they began to move.

"Is she always like this?" Charlie asked her innocently, a smile upon his lips. His eyes, however, looked semi-frightened.

"Always, Charlie. She's got a lot of energy and a heart of gold," she honestly replied, laughing at Bennett beginning to break down some dance moves, visible only from her torso down.

***

As with every location in Martin's Falls, the ride from her house to the banquet hall where the Prom was being held took under 10 minutes. She had wished it would have taken longer as they were having such a fun time. Bennett had wasted no time in taking out the flasks that she had filled with her parents' alcohol and took a few, big swigs en route. Charlie had even participated, albeit not as aggressively as the girls did, and all three friends were feeling tipsy and giggly as the limo pulled up in front of the hall.

As she stepped out of the car, carefully of course, she instantly had a case of déjà vu. She didn't know if was because of the few shots she had in the car ride just moments ago or just the natural high from being happy and excited for a momentous event in every teenager's life, but she could have sworn the banquet hall itself looked just like the exterior of Marina's Bookstore.

There was a marquee sign that was flashing in red letters proclaiming "Martin's Falls – The Prom". Being part of the Prom Committee, she had known that they had ordered the sign weeks ago and that it was going to be big and bright, but the clear similarities to Marina's flashing sign were nearly eerie. The darkness that seemed to surround the banquet hall itself was also strange – much like that first day that she had stumbled upon the bookstore when she first moved to the big city. It was like the Banquet Hall itself was the only thing that existed for miles around, just like the thought she had had about Marina's bookstore on that secluded street that was not all that far from the urban jungle.

"Are you ok, Darcy?" Charlie asked, noticing her concerned expression while was looking around the sights around her. Bennett was also looking at her warily.

She smiled, taking a small breath. She did not want anything to take away what could have very well been the last few hours of being a teenager again, and at that time, she resolved to just let things be. She had no control anymore of what was to happen. She wasn't even all that sure that if posed with the possibility of going back to her adult life, that she would be heartbroken about it.

"Yes. Let's do this. Masks on, worries off!" she said as all three friends smiled and put on their respective masks, instantly making them mysterious and unidentifiable.

The three of them slowly climbed the few steps that would take them to the event of the evening that they had all been secretly really excited about for weeks on end. They had to take their time as the masks restricted their sight of what lay before them, and Darcy knew she couldn't afford to walk faster than she wanted to at that point as the corset that lay just below the surface of her lustrous golden gown dug into her ribs sharply. She knew that by the end of the night the

289

corset would be off and the dress would have to do the work in giving her a cinched look, but she didn't care, for at that specific moment, she felt beautiful, and she vowed nothing would take that away from her.

***

The interior of the banquet hall where the Prom was being held could not have been better done or adorned, she thought, as she caught sight of the limo pulling out of their final destination. There was a sense of finality in the air that didn't escape her, but she was adamant on enjoying what could be the last few hours she had in this new life.

As the limo drove off, Charlie walked with both ladies deeper into the event location. They teased him for being such a gentlemen as they straightened their gowns and adjusted their masks. That was a strict rule: before entering the prom itself, all attendees had to don their masquerade masks, students and teachers alike.

Her burgundy mask perfectly complimented her golden dress, and both Bennett's and Charlie's masks were similarly green colored. It was pretty crazy at how quickly the masks made their appearance indistinguishable. *Now everyone's wearing a mask*, she immediately thought.

Bennett and Charlie had both gently chastised her in the car (due to the liberal drinking from their now not so full flasks) for being so quiet. She couldn't help it – she felt like she was on the precipice of something that was going to end badly. The non visits from Marina, in addition to her lack of tangible feelings and actions that made 'things better' made her sure that by midnight, she was going to be back in her adult bed, dog in tow, and stressed with the task of having to find a new job.

For this first time in many months, however, she wasn't that entirely turned off by these thoughts. It was no secret that the teenage life she was thrust into couldn't have been more different then the fictional accounts that flooded the books that she loved to read, courtesy of Marina's book shop. She did not have simple conflicts that she was expected to settle, like choosing the typical bad boy or the good boy, or being faced with decisions of taking drugs or having sex when she was not ready. The issues that were plaguing her were more serious and strangely adult, and she wasn't sure, deep inside, if this was something she wanted to explore and experience further. Her first teenaged experience had been bad enough, and having to re-do the whole thing over with larger obstacles to overcome, made her queasy.

"We all look so amazing – just saying," Bennett boasted as all three friends slowly made their way up the bright lights and loud music of the prom that had already begun. Charlie took her hand, and squeezed it gently, a gesture at once both re-assuring and soothing.

They walked into the banquet hall that would not have been out of place at a Renaissance Fair. The entire place was so authentically coordinated and decorated that whoever walked through the entry door felt like they were going back to a time to where there was no electricity, Royalty provided only talks of scandal, and washing clothes in the river was a daily activity and not out of the norm.

"Names please," Chrissy piped up to them as they made their way to the name card table advising them where they were going to be sitting for dinner. At first she thought Chrissy was being difficult in asking for their names but she then realized that the girl probably didn't recognize them – she knew that Chrissy's mask perfectly covered up her expression of usual judgment.

"It's us, Chrissy," Darcy replied. "We're at table 4."

Chrissy momentarily hesitated before grabbing the placard for table 4 and handed it to Charlie.

"Wow – Darcy, you look beautiful," she said. For the first time since knowing the girl, Darcy heard the authenticity in her voice.

291

She felt touched.

"So do you, Chrissy. You've got the prom queen vote in the bag," she replied.

"You're probably right," Chrissy replied back, a smile on the part of her face not hidden by the mask. "Have fun, guys."

They continued to walk deeper into the banquet hall that was cast in shadows and soft lighting. She noticed the ornate set up of the photographer who was taking snaps of students who wanted a photo to commemorate this event, as well as the chocolate fountain that, while not exactly common place for a renaissance themed party, was a hit amongst the kids, judging by the amount of students enjoying the sweet delicacies.

They quickly found table #4 amongst the mania that filled the banquet hall room itself. There were about 20 tables that seemed to be already half full, and the DJ was spinning songs that had a few of the more brave students dancing in the center of the dance floor. The bar was undoubtedly the busiest spot in the place, and while they were promised not to sell any alcohol based drinks, she couldn't help but notice the way the flashing lights of the dance floor seemed to catch upon the flasks that every 3rd person seemed to have in their pockets.

"This really came together awesomely, guys. I'm so impressed," Charlie said as they neared the table. He pulled out the chair for her to sit down on, and once she was seated, did the same thing for Bennett.

"It was a team effort. Chrissy literally ate, drank, and breathed this thing for months," Bennett replied. "But I will take full credit for the tablecloths and napkins combination. My parents supplied them from their shop."

Darcy and Charlie smiled and looked at the seemingly authentically patterned pieces that she just referred to. As the prom committee money dwindled, and the team realizing they didn't even discuss napkins and tablecloths, Bennett was kind enough to get her parents to provide the items in the last minute. They owned an enormous textile company that apparently everyone in Martin's Falls were familiar with.

"Well, kudos to you and your eyes for style," she giggled and all three friends smiled. The flask made one more appearance before she felt the urge to go to the washroom. The corset was not going to let her go that easy. She decided to go to the bathroom and actually loosen the corset a bit, so she asked Bennett to go with her.

Charlie said he was fine staying alone but got up anyway as both girls made their way to the girls' bathroom that was just conveniently located just to the right of their table. She looked back at him and smiled before entering the brightly lit room that had no line up to get in, something that would not be the case later in the evening, she was sure.

"Let's go in here," she said, motioning Bennett into the wheelchair accessible stall that was at the rear of the bathroom. Both girls went in and she immediately sat down, lowered the top part of her dress, and asked Bennett to begin loosening the corset that was making it hard for her to breathe.

"Aren't you going to buy me dinner first?" Bennett laughed and went to work at gently tugging the corset and loosening the ties. She immediately felt the relief and sighed loudly.

"Yeah, you probably don't want to do that in here. We probably will get kicked out before the prom has even started," Bennett said and she laughed. Bennett couldn't have been more right – Ms. Wright, the teacher liaison for the prom, made it abundantly clear that there was to be 'no hanky panky anywhere' and that kids who were caught 'canoodling' were going to be removed from the premises immediately.

Moments later, and lungs gently breathing in full of air, both girls left the stall, giggling, and she nearly fell into Claire and Rena who were applying their make up above the sinks. They had their masks off, as did Bennett and Claire, so they instantly recognized one another. She suspected that she would have recognized Claire anyway. Rena – not so much, considering she sort of disappeared into any background she was in.

"Oh, sorry!" she mouthed, stepping back quickly, nearly causing Bennett to fall back into the stall. "I was having some corset issues. Bennett was helping me out."

Claire lowered the lipstick she was putting on her lips and looked at her from the mirror. The two friends were polite and kind to one another after what had happened at the Senior Stay Over, but their friendships was de facto cancelled. The awkwardness and anger wasn't there anymore, and she didn't know if it was because the prom was happening before them or what, but Claire appeared defeated in some way that she couldn't quite put her finger on.

"I was thinking of wearing one too, but then I remembered that I wanted to be able to breathe and drink on a regular basis tonight," Claire replied, a smile creeping on her lips. Rena, to the surprise of no one, followed suit.

"Well, you were thinking right because I think I broke about two ribs on the way over from my house to get here," Darcy replied, adding to the semi-uncomfortable but all together ok vibe. Rena and Bennett looked at each other as if to acknowledge that they should probably leave and let the two old friends have some time together.

Rena washed her hands quickly and Bennett followed suit.

"See you at the table. Breathe as deeply as you want!" Bennett said, ever the joker, and Rena followed her out the door. There didn't seem to be any other girls in the bathroom.

After a moments silence, which she used to reapply her own make up and wash her hands, she heard the soft music enter the bathroom. It wasn't what she thought the DJ would play, in fact, hearing "There's Always Something to Remind Me", waft through the walls made her instantly nostalgic and sorry. Sorry for the way her and Claire's friendship had pretty much eroded for the last few months, despite being there for each other during some pretty serious

294

drama.

"I thought Chrissy was adamant that there was no retro music to be played tonight", Claire finally said. She turned around and put her lipstick in her makeup case. "She's going to flip when she hears this."

"I think she's too busy sizing up everyone asking for their table cards", she replied. "You look beautiful, Claire. You really do."

Claire, seemingly surprised and taken aback by her genuine compliment, immediately blushed at her former friends comment.

"You look pretty good yourself," she replied, and then suddenly Claire's eyes were moist and a tear fell down her cheek.

She grabbed a tissue and dabbed the tear from the other girls' cheek which threatened to ruin her make-up.

"I'm sorry," Claire replied, waving her hands at her eyes to stop the crying.

"It's ok," she replied, throwing the tissue in the trash can that sat below the sink.

"No, I mean, I'm really sorry," Claire continued, touching her exposed shoulder and pulling her closer. "I'm sorry for being such a mean bitch to you all of these months and for spreading those awful rumors about you. I've been a really, really bad person and I'm truly remorseful for having caused you so much pain and anguish."

She was speechless for a few reasons. She had never heard Claire apologize for anything so honestly and emotionally. She also had never heard Claire used words to describe how she was feeling that didn't include the words 'like, so, and super'.

"We always used to talk about how awesome our prom was going to be," Claire continued. "I remember all of the sleepovers and midnight talks where we would talk about what we would wear, and who we would bring, and what we would do after. And now, here we are, practically acquaintances, and nothing could be more different than what we had talked about for all of those years."

Now she was the one who got emotional and teary eyed. While

she couldn't remember those specific memories for obvious reasons (the switch and all), she knew that Claire was being real and honest. She dabbed her own eye.

"Claire – I think this is part of growing up. We were best friends, the best there could ever really be, but sometimes people drift apart. I don't hate you, I realize now that I don't think I ever could. And while we do things that even puzzle ourselves, it's part of who we are and makes us stronger people. I don't think it matters if you're 13 or 37. Emotions are emotions and people are people. There will always be difficult decisions to be made where someone is bound to get their feelings hurt. And we're always going to find ourselves doing things that seem inexplicable. But we'll get through it, and we'll grow from it, and we'll also learn."

Claire looked at her straight in the eyes as though in surprise and shock. She didn't know where the words that had just left her mouth came from, but they couldn't be truer. At that moment she realized that no matter what happened with Marina and the switch and her friendships and romantic rendezvous in both lives she's lived, she was going to be ok. It wasn't a matter of having a story book life where everything is black and white. Nothing could ever be black and white, she knew that know - fictional or non fictional worlds alike. She felt calm and settled, and warm, as Claire reached forward and gave her a tight hug.

"You always were different, Darcy Platt," she laughed as she pulled herself away. "I just never let you assert it because I was always telling you what to do and what to say. But you're a good person, a true spirit, and I love you."

They hugged once more and Claire made her way out the door, mask on. She looked in the mirror once more and put her own mask on, and decided to go and enjoy the Prom and all that it was bound to offer.

Chapter 35

The meal had been edible, and that was all that the students seemed to care about as they drank freely from their flasks and disappeared into the bathroom frequently to do only God knows what else. Truth be told, the Prom committee itself didn't spend too much time on procuring a caterer that was going to provide a class A meal only because that was not where the emphasis on what would make a classic, memorable evening. In fact, when the caterers had invited the Prom Committee for a tasting of the proposed meal, they hadn't even gone. She had intended to go, but unsurprisingly, she had been completely absorbed by her Claire drama that she had honestly forgotten all about it.

The dinner had ended around 8:30 pm, and with a burst of frenetic energy, the students all decided to immediately descend upon the dance floor as soon as a popular song came on, a song that she had never ever even heard before. It was an interesting site to behold, considering that dancing was difficult pretty much for everyone as all the corsets and gowns that adorned the female segment of the crowds weren't exactly known to be loose fitting.

"Come on, let's dance!" Bennett enthusiastically said as soon as the initial flood of dancers joined the dance floor. Her red hair that had been up in a bun but with some loose tendrils that framed her face bounced along to the music.

"I need to digest a bit before I get a cramp while busting a move", she replied, a smile upon her lips. Charlie looked at her and she thought she saw some minor disappointment come over his usual smiling face.

"Charlie – you should go dance with Bennett. I just need a few minutes to settle. Plus my stomach is pressing so hard against my corset that I don't think I should be getting out of breath just yet," she said.

"Are you sure? I don't mind waiting it out with you, Charlie asked, though there was no mistaking the excitement he was harboring to break it down on the dance floor. And truth be told, she was interested to see how her date moved to the music, unrecognizable as it was.

"Oh, come on, Charlie," Bennett said, sitting up and taking Charlie's hand. "Let the old lady digest while we show her how it's done!"

Bennett pulled on Charlie's arm to join her on her path to the dance floor. He looked back at her to gauge her reaction to his going to dance, but she just smiled and encouraged him. Plus, she reflected to herself, Bennett wasn't that far off from the truth in calling her an old woman.

Once Bennett and Charlie were lost within the swarm of overly energetic, and slightly drunken, teenage dancers, she glanced over at the table beside her where Claire sat with Rena. Luke was nowhere in sight, and since she and Claire weren't exactly friends any longer, she wouldn't have had any way of knowing if she and Luke were truly no longer an item. It did seem strange that there was no pretty boy sitting to Claire's side, but he may have also been dancing or in the bathroom.

Upon glancing over in Claire's direction, she made eye contact with her former friend, who promptly smiled back at her. It was gentle moment between friends that she felt deep within her, almost as though tugging at her proverbial heart strings. Rena looked over and noticed the glance and smiled as well.

Before she even realized it, the loud, ornate looking clock that had been set out at the front of the hall, just ahead of the dance floor, chimed 9 times. Within moments, the dance floor cleared out as quickly as it had filled, and Charlie and Bennett were once more sitting beside her. Charlie took Darcy's hand and squeezed in gently. She heard the DJ begin to play the opening notes of "Don't Dream its Over" by Crowded House and she silently swooned. For a DJ that was apparently known for his preponderance towards top 40 music, he sure was playing the hits that encapsulated the teen flicks that comprised the viewing pleasures of her youth.

They watched as Chrissy climbed slowly atop the makeshift stage at the front of the room that was just beside the large, looming clock. She felt that the clock was teasing her, reminding her that her time was more limited now than ever, and that big changes were coming, whether welcome or not.

Making her way to the microphone that stood nearly as tall as she was, Chrissy adjusted the top of the dress that she wore so as to avoid a major wardrobe malfunction. Much like the corset that enveloped her slight frame, Chrissy's corset was forcing her cleavage to nearly touch her chin, much to the delight of the hormone driven boys that stared at her, open mouthed, spittle almost visible on their chins.

"Hello Flint Ridgers!" she yelled into the microphone, causing some major feedback that forced much of the attendees to immediately shield their ears in defense.

"Oh, sorry – is this better?" she asked as she motioned bitterly to the A/V person who was manically adjusting some controls and pushing buttons at the staging area that held all of the connectors to the speakers and radio and amps for the DJ. Finally, the feedback ended, and she was able to lower her hands from her ears without feeling like they were going to spurt blood all over her dress and on the friends that sat on either side of her.

"Ok, ok – enough of the technical difficulties," Chrissy said, causing herself to laugh. Clearly, much like the rest of the student body, she had enjoying some refreshments that had not been available at the bar at the rear of the room. "Welcome everyone to Flint Ridge's Masquerade Prom! Is everyone having a good time?"

The crowd erupted into a cacophony of loud yells and a smattering of applause. Without really noticing, she caught herself whistling loudly and clapping simultaneously. The overall feeling of the room was excitement and an unbridled freedom that was palpable and felt equally amongst everyone, teachers, students, and chaperones alike.

"Awesome! On behalf of the Prom Committee, we want to say that we are so happy that everyone is having a great time and dancing to our amazing DJ!" Chrissy continued, pointing to the DJ which caused another round of loud applause and cheering.

"So tonight is like the most important night of our teenaged lives, as we all know, and it's so important that we are all here together, especially since after graduation, a lot of us are going our separate ways and everything. So before we get all too emotional in reflecting on the trials and tribulations that we've all gone through these last four years, let's keep it positive and announce what you have all been waiting for!"

She found herself silently impressed at Chrissy's eloquent mini-speech to the enormous crowd before her. All of the students were looking up at Chrissy as she mouthed some silently to another girl that was directly stage left.

300

The DJ seamlessly transitioned from "Don't Dream its Over" to her personal favorite, When in Rome's "The Promise". As soon as she heard the familiar lyrics of "If you need a friend, don't look to a stranger. You know in the end, I'll always be there", she felt tears fill her eyes and she began to cry silently. The tears fell fast and heavy upon her cheeks, the heat of the tears stinging her as they dropped onto her cleavage.

Bennett and Charlie were still focused on Chrissy's pending reveal and didn't notice her sudden release of emotion and tears. She grabbed a tissue atop the table and quickly dabbed her eyes but the tears kept flowing. The song had reminded her more than she wanted to of her own uncomfortable experiences in high school where she found herself questioning her own place in life, and where she fit in within the social strata that was collectively known as the high school existence. She was suddenly again the overweight, acne-ridden girl who found herself escaping into the novels of her youth where high school was depicted as a Mecca in California where love was abound and everyone was picture perfect beautiful. The second hand clothes that she had to wear out of necessity because of the financial situation of her parents and the constant teasing that accompanied the often unkempt appearances that plagued her still pained her, and she didn't know why. It was a long time ago.

She shook herself from her reverie and looked slowly around the room. Shockingly, it seemed like everyone was suddenly frozen in time. Everyone around the room was frozen in mid action, many mouths open in mid-laugh, silent claps in mid air. She shook her head as though to clear her head of the strange vision she was experiencing but the room stayed in the exact same suspended moment in time. She looked at Claire who, too, was frozen in mid stare at Chrissy, the undeniable rim of sadness under her eyes.

The only thing that seemed to keep moving forward in time was the song that blared from the speakers that surrounded the room. The pace of the song did seem to slow down a bit, and she heard the lyrics "I'm just thinking of the right words to say" almost hug her as a bright light suddenly filled the center of the dance floor, almost causing her to scream in fright.

At first she thought that this was part of a surprise plan that Chrissy and the rest of the Prom Committee had thought up, but the inexplicable lack of motion around of the room was still present. The bright light that appeared on the dance floor suddenly began to spark, tiny fragments of lights that illuminated dimness of the room that accompanied Chrissy's announcement.

She stared intently at the light as it began to dim and smoke suddenly appeared. Not the smoke that typically accompanied a fire, but it was more dry ice in its appearance, which actually sort of fit with the environment of the prom. The smoke then began to dissipate as a figure, dressed entirely in purple, sequence shining in the light of the room, appeared.

She gasped as she saw Marina dramatically materialize before her. The woman looked unbelievably beautiful in her elaborate dress which was so purple that it reminded her of twilight. Marina's characteristic bun was piled high upon her head and bright red lipstick adorned her lips. The woman looked incredibly magical. A chill rose up her spine because she knew what this apparition brought with it.

"Hello, Darcy," Marina said as she slowly walked towards her table. The sound of the woman's high heels echoed in the room almost as thought they were in the middle of the Grand Canyon instead of inside a cramped banquet hall full of teenaged kids. The music still played in the background, and she felt her heartbeat quicken.

"The time has come, my dear child," Marina seemed to say though her lips did not move. It was more like she felt the words instead of heard them. Suddenly, she was standing before the woman, not sure of when she got up or walked so that she looked into the kind eyes of the woman who gave her the opportunity that

302

she found herself in.

"You look beautiful, Ms. Darcy. Like an angel who has found her wings," Marina's voice said. Darcy smiled, not sure on how to proceed. The sheer eeriness of the frozen movements around her caused her to feel almost simultaneously apprehensive and strangely comfortable.

"Thank you, Marina," was all she could say as the two women just stared at each other intently. She saw the green specks of Marina's eyes shift subtly.

"You know why I'm here," Marina finally said directly.

She remained silent. She sort of half expected the room to once again be brought back to life and for Chrissy to make her imminent announcement. Marina reached towards her and touched her shoulder gently. She felt as though as electric bolt entered her body and she was suddenly looking at herself on the very first day that she was thrust into the 17 year old life of one Darcy Platt.

It was like watching a montage of your life, but in color and with the soundtrack of The Promise on a slow loop playing in the background. She had imagined it was what people said they saw in their heads when they knew they were going to die and their life proverbially 'flashed before their eyes'.

She saw herself waking up confused in the massive bed in her bedroom, taking in the sights around her. She then quickly saw the run in with Mason and then she was with Claire and Rena at school. She smiled as she saw the body language that was exchanged between the two friends, and felt the warmth that existed there.

Before she could get too wrapped up in that scene before her, she was suddenly with Claire at the pharmacy when her friend was buying the home pregnancy test, which was the beginning of their pending separation. The scenes were quick and effective, as though some master designer decided to linger on certain events just long enough to get the major meaning of what had occurred.

She was then with Charlie renting their prom gowns, and then at

303

the Senior Stay over where her and Claire had talked about what had gone down between them. Then the uncomfortable scene of the hospital was before her, where Claire found out she lost the baby and where Mason learned that if not for the accident, he would have been a father at the young age that he was. At once, the red scarf was around her and she remembered the confusion and weirdness of knowing that Mason and Claire had been an undercover item for quite some time, around the time that her and Luke were together, which was before the switch had even began.

"Was this what you were expecting, my dear Darcy?" Marina said, pulling her from the flashbacks and bringing her back to the relative stillness of the frozen scene around her.

She felt the tears flow down her cheeks. How could she answer Marina truthfully and honestly? There weren't any words she could find, or ever find, that could describe the last few months that she had found herself living. From the inception of being offered to be the teenage girl in the books she read with such fervency, to the current moment where she was made up in a gown fit for a queen on the Italian court - incredulity was all she ever felt. And, as a result, speechlessness was all that came easily to her.

Looking back in hindsight, as things were always clearer in retrospect, she didn't really know what to expect when she made her decision to take Marina up on her offer to be thrust into the life right out of a Sweet Valley High novel. But Marina's requirement of her to 'make things right' wasn't as clear as the older woman seemed to have thought it was, which made things really difficult. She had never really let herself completely immerse herself in her new life because she knew there was some sort of the bargain that she had to keep up and to maintain. All of her experiences were tinged with this expectation, no matter how serious or minor they were. Now here, at the prom and presumably the last moment in time that she would be able to make 'things right', she felt apprehensive and nervous, not really being able to enjoy the scene around her. All that should have been on her mind was how she looked in her dress and how she couldn't wait to dance with Charlie, but like always, she was plagued with worry on what would happen if she wouldn't keep up her end of the offer, as unclear and ambiguous as it was.

She never really allowed herself to think and reflect on her actual enjoyment of the new life she was living. While she knew that what she was experiencing on a daily basis couldn't be more different than the world depicted in the novels she read, often hidden in a corner of Marina's cozy shop, alone and content, there was indeed a certain thrill in it. She loved having a young and agile body again and friend and maybe boyfriend to have fun times with.

What she didn't love, in fact, what she loathed, was the frequent uncomfortable confrontations with a brother who seemed to really enjoy giving her a hard time, and fighting with a former friend who knew her more than she knew herself. Would she be able to repair friendships and better relations if she were to stay as a 17 year old? She didn't know. She also didn't know if she would be willing to if she had been given the opportunity.

"Darcy, I know that when I asked you to make things right, that I was being vague", Marina said. Her voice was soft and calm, immediately having a calming effect on Darcy. "It was no small task for you to have endured what you have endured for the last few months. It is a testament to who you are as a person".

Darcy smiled. Was Marina giving her a compliment or a critique?

"You love Teen books. You love worlds that are written in such a way that paradise is what the teenaged years equate to. But now that you've lived in the life of a teenage girl that seemingly has everything, I am sure you will tell me that things are not as they seem."

She laughed out loud. The laugh surprised her. And surprised her again when it echoed off the walls around her.

"But our arrangement had stakes that affected us both. If you

305

made things right, as I've asked, you can stay in this life and live the life that you've often dreamed about. But, and correct me if I'm wrong, we both know that what you've dreamed and what it actually is couldn't be more different."

"Not even close," she said. "I can't describe it, Marina. I know books are written as an escape for the reader, to put them into a world that they would never, ever get to live and experience firsthand. But I thought that maybe I would get the chance to be that girl that everyone envied, that had easy decisions to make, not fight with friends and faced with angry siblings".

Marina looked at her, a frown appearing on her brow. Even though the older woman didn't say a single word, it was as though she heard so much. It was the acknowledgement of her own feelings that Marina seemed to recognize that made her feel something she hadn't felt in a long, long time – and that was feeling was that she was being heard.

"I am not here to chastise you, my dear Darcy," Marina finally said. "I am here to see if you've kept up your end of the bargain."

She once more looked around her, taking in her surroundings, scene by scene, as though it was her last possible time.

"Making things right is an adage. Things are never really right. What does 'right' even mean?" Marina asked. "What I think is right is not what you may think is right. And this is exactly what I wanted you to learn, Darcy. Perceptions govern our lives. Decisions are different for everyone, and the impacts of those decisions can change our lives in very alternate ways. And it is those decisions you have had in the last little while that may change the entire course of the lives for both the old Darcy and the new Darcy."

She felt confused and looked at Marina, riveted by what the woman was saying. Her heart felt much like the scene around her – suspended in time.

"The life you were thrown into was not an easy one. This Darcy had made some bad decisions, and you were forced to contend with them. You had strained relationships at best with you family, friends, and lovers. But the essence that is you shone through. You made attempts to repair those friendships, and you made concentrated efforts to treat people with respect and dignity. And those actions are what has shown me that, yes, Darcy Platt, you have made things right."

She did not immediately grasp the meaning of the words that had just escape Marina's lips. She looked at the woman with her head cocked to one side, like a dog who heard a sound that its human owner could not.

"What? You mean I did it? I made things right?" she asked, dumbfounded.

"Yes, Darcy, you did. Making things right isn't something that is so black and white, and this is what I wanted you to learn. Life is nothing but an extended sequence of events where we learn things about ourselves, others, and the world around us. What we can do from those experiences is learn and love, or just decide to let anger consume us, which we both know, is not what life is meant to be."

"Oh, Marina," she said. She felt tears once more fill her eyes and down her cheeks. "Thank you. Thank you for this experience. And I'm thankful that you are able to keep your store."

"So am I, my darling," Marina replied, tears glistening in her own eyes. "The store is my life."

She smiled and reached forward to hug the woman. The electric bolt she felt earlier once again enveloped her but thankfully no montage of uncomfortable images of her new life filled her field of vision. However, images did fill her eyes this time. These images, though, were of the old Darcy's life.

She saw herself walking her beautiful dog in the park, smiling at acquaintances and at all of the other dogs that she knew. She was then at work laughing with Sylvia. Lastly, she saw herself deeply riveted by a teen fiction book on top of her own bed, in her own apartment. The sheer happiness emanated from the image, and a chill ran up her spine.

"You have a decision to make, Darcy," Marina finally said, pulling herself away from the tight embrace.

The moment that she was dreading was finally upon her. She felt the heaviness of the imminent decision that she was going to momentarily make press upon her. She at once felt both hot and cold, and goose bumps broke out all over her exposed skin. She was unsure of what she would choose. Did she truly want to be a teenager again? Did she want to experience the heartaches that were sure to come, as well as the highs and lows that would be part of her daily life? It was different when she pulled a book off a shelf at Marina's bookstore and was immediately thrust into a life where very witty teens essentially lived adult lives within the confines of an oppressive institution such as high school.

But was her real life all that much better? She was newly unemployed and soon very possibly have to make some new living arrangements. But as an adult, she was free to make her own decisions and live the life she wanted.

At once, the two women locked eyes once more and it was like all of the air was sucked out of the room. She felt her stomach tighten with the intensity of the moment. She at once knew what she was going to decide.

At that moment things abruptly changed. Marina disappeared at once and Darcy found herself standing alone in the middle of the dance floor. The room came to life immediately around her. Laughs were heard once more, and the sound of claps bounded off of the walls. As soon as they began, they were silenced as the students saw Darcy standing by herself in the middle of the dance floor.

Chrissy, typically not missing a beat took in Darcy before her and continued on her speech.

"Ok, Darcy, let me at least announce the Prom King and Queen before you walk up here. You may not have won it after all," she said, laughter in voice but also with the characteristic Chrissy sharp biting undertone.

She tried to give the illusion that she was joking about it all, and quickly made her way back to the table and sat beside Charlie. Bennett shot her a concerned glance but she nodded and refocused her attention on Chrissy.

"Since Darcy is so eager for me to make the announcement, here we go," Chrissy went on, taking an envelope from a student off to the right of the stage and began to open it.

"So the Prom King is...." she said, purposely building up the suspense that was palpable amongst the crowd. "Luke Silver."

She began to clap and whistle loudly, and then suddenly remembered that she hadn't seen Luke at all that evening. But, without a moment even elapsed by, Luke appeared, dapper and handsome in a tuxedo, clearly not abiding by the dress code rules. He ran to the stage, a huge smile on his lips, and let Chrissy hand him the staff that they got as the award for the winner of Prom King.

"And now for the Prom Queen," Chrissy said, opening another envelope quickly. She was visibly having a hard time opening the envelope.

"I'm so nervous!" she said as she read the name in the envelope. Darcy at first thought she saw a frown slowly appear on Chrissy's face but she shook it off.

"Well, it looks like she wasn't wrong after all," Chrissy giggled. "Our Prom Queen is Darcy Platt."

The room erupted into a chorus of cheers and applause. Charlie was on his feet immediately and gave her a tight, warm hug and a soft kiss on her lips. She was stunned, and stayed stunned as she walked slowly towards the front of the room where the stage loomed.

As she climbed the stage, she looked back and saw Claire clapping and whistling enthusiastically for her. Rena, too, was caught up in the moment and was being more vocal than she had ever heard her be. She bent forward gently a Chrissy placed the

309

golden Tiara on her head. She looked over at Luke who was smiling at her.

"Ladies and Gentlemen: Flint Ridge's Prom King and Queen," Chrissy yelled and once again the room filled with applause and cheers.

She reached over to Luke and took his hand and smiled. She was overcome with the scene before her, and she couldn't help but remember her first attempt to attend the prom the first time around in her yellowed dress and non-date. This was much better.

Before the applause ended, she saw Marina looking up at her from the back of the room. She looked at the woman and smiled. The smile that Marina returned literally lit up the room. She squeezed Luke's hand, and looked happily upon Claire, Bennett and Charlie one final time before slowly walking down the steps off the stage, across the dance floor, and to Marina. She grabbed the woman's hand and looked back one final time at the scene before her.

Much like the montage of images earlier in the evening of the two lives she's led, this time she saw herself on stage, relishing the win of Prom Queen, and listening to the applause that was for her. She smiled as she held Marina's hand and saw the sheer joy and purity of happiness on the old/new her on stage as she followed Marina out of the hall and into the night.

Being a teenager once was more than enough experience and emotions for her. Sure, being an adult had its more than fair share of ups and downs, and the ups were much higher and the downs much deeper. But the choices she made were hers to make. She didn't have to rely on others to make up her mind, and she could do what she wanted when she wanted. She was thankful for this experience of being 17 again, but would she want to relive the peaks and valleys of early adulthood? Of her first true heartbreak? Of the stresses of finding a job? Of finding a lover? Of a parent's death? Of a siblings sadness? She shook her head to her own thoughts as she let Marina guide her out of the school and into the darkness of the night that surrounded her like a warm sweater – gentle and soft. And full of love.

***

Acknowledgements

I could not have written this story without the constant support from MM. Your words of encouragement and ability to make me laugh are the only two reasons I finished this book at all. To the awesome MJM for designing the most amazing, far-out, super cool book cover ever! ST – thanks for always knowing that I could do this. To the wonderful IJ and CU for taking the time to edit Darcy's story and providing me with key insight. For my beautiful LMR – wish you were here to see that I did it. I know that you're beaming at us from above. Much love and thanks to my fam and to LECRM for knowing the exact perfect time when I needed a snuggle.

About the Author

Nick Rossi lives in Toronto, Canada, with his two-legged and four-legged companions.

When he's not writing, Nick loves to dissect pop culture, planning his imminent move to New York City, and not sweating the small stuff. He has one furry daughter who may, or may not, have made a cameo in Page-Turner.